ALSO BY CHRISTINA DODD

One Kiss From You

Scandalous Again

My Favorite Bride

Lost in Your Arms

In My Wildest Dreams

Rules of Attraction

Rules of Engagement

Rules of Surrender

Someday My Prince

Scottish Brides

The Runaway Princess

That Scandalous Evening

A Well Pleasured Lady

A Knight to Remember

Once a Knight

Move Heaven and Earth

The Greatest Lover in All England

Outrageous

Castles in the Air

Priceless

Treasure of the Sun

Candle in the Window

So

Encha

Ever

Some Enchanted Evening

CHRISTINA DODD

Doubleday Large Print Home Library Edition

WILLIAM MORROW
An Imprint of HarperCollins*Publishers*

SOME ENCHANTED EVENING. Copyright © 2004 by Christina Dodd. All rights reserved. Printed in the United States of America. No part of this book may be used or reproduced in any manner whatsoever without written permission except in the case of brief quotations embodied in critical articles and reviews. For information address HarperCollins Publishers Inc., 10 East 53rd Street, New York, NY 10022.

ISBN 0-7394-4496-4

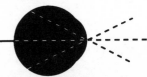

**This Large Print Book carries the
Seal of Approval of N.A.V.H.**

To my daughters,
Shannon and Arwen

Don't frown or your face will freeze that way.
Don't run with scissors.
It hurts to be beautiful.
Always wear clean underwear—it doesn't
matter if you're in an accident,
always wear clean underwear!
Don't pick at that.
If everyone else jumped off a cliff,
would you have to jump off, too?
And I hope you both have a daughter someday
who is just like you.

Make big goals, be happy, be healthy.
I don't want to hear any excuses.
Thank you for your love and support
through all the years.

Love, Mommy

Prologue

Once upon a time, high in the Pyrenees Mountains, there were two tiny kingdoms, happy and properous. In one kingdom, Richarte, a son was born and declared the crown prince.

In the other kingdom, Beaumontagne, three daughters were born amid great rejoicing. Sorcha, Clarice, and Amy were raised in royal splendor by their loving father, the king, and their grandmother, a martinet who demanded they perform their royal duties at all times.

Then revolution swept Europe and swept the two kingdoms into turmoil and anarchy.

In secret, after three years of warfare, the three princesses of Beaumontagne were sent to the safety of England. Their father, the king, was deposed and died. After six years of warfare, their grandmother wrested control back from the revolutionaries. She sent her most trusted emissary for her granddaughters, but Godfrey was not loyal. He had been corrupted and accepted money to kill the heiresses. In the end, he couldn't bear to murder the girls, so he told them to flee, then reported to the old queen that they had disappeared. The old queen sent messengers far and wide, but alas, no one could find a trace of the Lost Princesses.

A cruel usurper, Count Egidio duBelle, threw the prince of Richarte into the deepest, darkest dungeon and there, for eight years, the prince languished. At long last he managed to escape and make his way to Beaumontagne. There he struck a deal with the old queen.

If he had found all three of the Lost Princesses, he could choose one as his bride. When the wedding had been performed, then, and only then, would he be allowed to take the armies of Beaumontagne to overthrow the cruel usurper and assume his own throne once more.

But while the prince searched for the princesses, Count duBelle sent men to hunt the prince, and the princesses themselves, remembering Godfrey's warning, feared to show themselves.

So like many good schemes, the plan to rescue the Lost Princesses went awry. . . .

One

Never call attention to yourself. A princess's reason for existence is to fulfill her duty as a representative of the royal family. Nothing more.
—THE DOWAGER QUEEN OF BEAUMONTAGNE

SCOTLAND, 1808

The valley was his, the village was his, yet the woman rode into the town square of Freya Crags as if she owned it.

Robert MacKenzie, earl of Hepburn, frowned at the stranger who cantered over the stone bridge and into the bustling crowd.

It was market day, and booths of brown canvas were set up along the perimeter of the town square. The place rang with the sound of a hundred voices calling out their wares, but the stranger dominated the crowd, towering above them on a fractious two-year-old colt. The chestnut stepped high, as if proud to carry her, and the quality of the horse alone would have turned heads.

The lady in the saddle attracted even more attention—first fleeting looks, then open stares.

Robert glanced around at the small circle of old men gathered in the sunshine in front of the alehouse. Their wrinkled mouths sagged open as they gawked, the table and checkerboard before them forgotten. Around them the sounds of shoppers and merchants haggling turned into a buzz of speculation as every eye turned to view the stranger.

Her riding costume swathed her from neck to toe with black wool, preserving the illusion of propriety yet outlining every curve of her trim figure. Her black hat was tall, with a broad brim, and black veiling floated behind. The red trim on her sleeves matched the red scarf at her neck, and those small bits of vivid color shocked and pleasured the eye.

Her bosom was generous, her waist narrow, her black boots shiny, and her face . . .

Good God, her face.

Robert couldn't look away. If she'd been born in the Renaissance, painters would have flocked to her door, begging that she pose for them. They would have painted her as an angel, for her wavy, golden hair glowed with a light of its own, giving her a nimbus like a halo. Copper glints in the curls seemed to possess a power to warm the hands, and Robert's fingers itched to sink into the waves and discover the heat and the texture. Her softly rounded cheeks and large amber eyes under darkened brows made a man think of heaven, yet the stubborn set of her chin saved her face from a cloying sweetness. Her nose was slight, her chin too broad to be truly attractive, but her lips were wide, lush, and red. Too red. She rouged them, he was sure of it. She looked like an Englishwoman of good quality—except, of course, no woman of good quality ever rouged her lips, and certainly never traveled alone.

She smiled, giving him a glimpse of straight white teeth—and that mouth he planned to explore.

Robert straightened away from the wall of the alehouse.

Where in blazes had that thought come from?

Hamish MacQueen was boisterous and amusing, his one arm gone in a long-ago accident in His Majesty's Royal Navy. "Who do ye suppose she is?"

A good question, and Robert intended to get an answer.

"I dunna know, but I'd like t' part her beard," said Gilbert Wilson, his sly wit taking a wicked turn.

"I'd like t' give her a live sausage fer supper." Tomas MacTavish slapped his skinny knee and cackled.

Henry MacCulloch joined in the pastime. "I'd like t' play dog in the doublet wi' her."

All the old men cackled, remembering the days when they would have had a chance to woo a beautiful visitor. Now they were content to sit in the sun in front of the alehouse, comment on the doings of the town, and play checkers—or they had been, until *she* rode into town.

Robert's gaze narrowed on the female. He was smart enough, and in his travels had seen enough, to recognize trouble when he saw it. On the surface he appeared to be mildly interested in the doings in the square, but his every sense was alert for a trick. Indeed, he anticipated a trick. After all, the world was not so secure a place as anyone in this small village imagined. The world was full of liars and cheats, murderers, and worse. It was men like him, like Robert, who kept this place safe, and through his vigilance he would continue to do so.

"Ye damned auld fools." The alewife, Hughina Gray, stood with her apron wrapped around her hands and glanced between Robert and the stranger. "Canna ye see she's na guid?"

"I'd wager she's verra guid," said Tomas's brother Benneit, and the old men laughed until they wheezed.

"Ye shouldn't talk so in front o' the laird," Hughina reproved with a sideways peep at Robert. Hughina was Robert's age, attractive, and a widow, and she'd made it clear she had room in her bed for him.

He hadn't accepted the invitation. When the laird slept with the women of his lands, trouble was sure to follow, so when the urge was on him, he traveled over the hills into Trevor and visited with Lady Edmundson. She enjoyed his body and his driving sexuality without caring a crumb whether he loved her, and that made a very satisfactory arrangement for them both.

Lately he hadn't suffered from the urge.

His hand crinkled the much-read letter in his pocket. He'd been too busy making plans, desperate plans, vengeful plans, and now those schemes had been set to naught because one woman failed to fulfill her promise. Damn her. Damn her to hell.

But for the moment he was distracted as the exotic stranger circled the booths, giving everyone a chance to see her, and Robert watched his people watch her. Their expressions were suspicious or inquisitive, but she beamed them a friendly smile as if she had not a speck of intelligence.

Her gaze found and considered the new seamstress.

The seamstress stared back with all the hostility of a plain woman before a beauty.

So for all her timid homeliness, Miss Rosabel had the sense the stranger did not. He glanced back at the still-guffawing old men.

More sense than the men who'd lived here all their lives.

The stranger rode right to the middle of the square, where a statue honored Robert's ancestor, Uilleam Hepburn, who founded the town at the ford on the river. A raised platform surrounded the statue, and there she slid off her horse.

Of course. Already Robert knew she liked to be seen.

She tied her horse to the iron ring and lifted her saddlebags onto the platform that raised her above the multitude. The curious throng gathered. For one moment the female sobered, touched the silver cross around her neck, then took a breath and flung her arms wide. "Good people of Freya Crags, allow me to introduce myself. I am a princess in exile!"

Robert stiffened in outrage and disbelief.

Hughina gasped. "Oh, fer pity's sake!"

The female beside the statue lifted her chin and smiled blindingly. "I am Princess Clarice of the lost kingdom!"

Hamish tucked the end of his shirt over the stump of his arm. The old soldier had his weaknesses, and a pretty woman was the main one. "Eh, a princess! We've got guid taste."

"Aye, and I'll wager she tastes guid," Gilbert said.

All the old men cackled, wild with the joy of having such a colorful distraction in their sedate lives.

Robert glanced at them, distracted by their surging excitement from the pageant in the center of the square.

Then the larcenous wench of a princess made another outrageous claim. "I've come to bring youth, beauty, and joy to your lives!"

His head snapped back toward the royal minx. The words of his aide, Waldemar, came back to him so clearly, Waldemar might almost have been standing beside him, speaking into his ear. *Lor' love ye, Cap'n, there's ne'er a person what falls into yer life without a purpose. Ye just 'ave t' discover wat that is, and use 'em like the instruments they are, and always ye'll get yer way, see if ye don't.*

And with the lightning-quick planning he had developed in the army, Robert realized why this female had arrived in his town, and what purpose she would serve. Yes, he would use her like the instrument she was. She would do as he instructed because she had no choice, and yes, he would get his way.

Fortified with resolve, Robert made his way through the crowd toward the statue, and the princess.

At long last, justice would be served.

Two

*If ye canna see the bright side o' life,
polish the dull side.*
> —THE OLD MEN OF FREYA CRAGS

Princess Clarice Jayne Marie Nicole Lilly took a breath and waited as the curious throng surged forward.

They stared at her, silent and dreary, dressed in brown or black. Here and there she could see a flash of red or blond hair, but the women wore scarves to cover their heads and the men wore hats. The place was clearly prosperous, yet she saw not one smile, not one colorful gown or frivolous hair ribbon. It was as if somehow they'd lost their spirit, as if they couldn't see God's good sunshine or smell the flowers sold in bunches in the stalls.

It was true what they'd said in England. The Scots were dour and drab. These people needed her, needed what she had to offer.

Again she rubbed the silver cross that hung around her neck. The cross was supposed to bring her luck—a luck that had signally failed in the last few months. Perhaps it was because the worry that continually nagged at her had turned to desperation, and the desperation seeped through her usual confident facade to color her voice, her smile, her poise. That was why she had crossed the border into Scotland; her welcome in England had worn thin, and she had to make a living.

She couldn't fail. Too much depended on her.

Everything depended on her.

With the skill of a born mimic, she allowed the slightest Scottish accent to slide into her voice. "Good people of Freya Crags, I can make a plain girl beautiful. I can cure her spots. I can bring a blush to her pale cheeks and make her the object of every man's attentions. Of course, I can do the same for any gentleman who needs a bit of help in the romance department. But, ladies"—she winked broadly—"don't you find that a little soap makes even the ugliest man irresistible?"

A few of the older women grinned and nudged their men. The men grumbled and looked sullen.

She smiled at them. She always smiled at them, no matter what, and usually the men eventually smiled back.

"What're ye sellin', miss?" one plump, bosomy female called.

"Happiness," Clarice replied promptly.

"I can buy that at the pub." The young man was healthy looking, but his dirty, ill-sewn clothing told her only too clearly that he was not married. He jostled his friends and brayed with merriment, then, under her level gaze, his amusement faded and his color rose.

"Can you indeed?" She lowered her voice to reach him and his compatriots. "And when you wake up in the morning and your mouth tastes like cobwebs and your bed is cold and lonely, come and tell me that you're happy so I can laugh too."

His eyes shifted toward a pretty girl with a petulant mouth, who tossed her head and gave Clarice all her attention.

The first of the hecklers subdued, Clarice settled into her pitch. "Who am I, you ask, to claim I can solve all your amorous woes? My name is Princess Clarice."

A gentleman of about thirty years was making his way toward the front, with a slow, disbelieving smile across his lips. At the sight, she forgot what she was doing. She straightened. She stood staring. Up there on the stage she had created, she was aware of only one thing—a man watched her with all his attention.

Clarice was used to attention; indeed, everything she did and said and wore encouraged it.

But this man was different. He wore plain clothes, but of a finer cut than most of the townsfolk. Clarice pegged him as a gentleman farmer, or perhaps a businessman from Edinburgh. He stood taller than the other men by a good three inches, and was completely, blazingly masculine in a way that challenged all that was feminine in her. His hair was black. Not dark brown, black, like black silk that absorbed nothing but the brightest sunlight and transformed it into glints of silver. His face was tanned from the sun, a harsh face that had seen too much of the world and liked little of it. He had a hooked nose and a strong jaw, and his eyes . . . ah, his eyes.

She tried to look away, but she couldn't break the contact.

A woman could write poetry about his eyes. Clear, blazing blue like royal sapphires set in gold, they watched Clarice with the kind of confidence that said he understood what pleasured a woman and would use his knowledge ruthlessly, again and again, until he was exhausted, or she was, or they both combusted with mutual joy.

She didn't want his kind of attention. She didn't need to fight that kind of temptation. She never indulged the flirtations and the frivolities of other young women; she dared not. So she would make sure she stayed far away from him.

Dragging her gaze away from his, she said, "Yes. I'm one of the Lost Princesses. My country's gone, my family scattered, but I can't avoid my destiny—and, good people of Freya Crags, do you know what that destiny is?"

She'd been doing this for almost five

years, and now she saw that she had caught a few of the vulnerable in her net, for scattered throughout the crowd she saw heads shake in response. She told them, "A princess is bred for one purpose and one purpose only—to catch a prince."

Amusement rippled through the crowd. She saw smiles. Ugly, cynical smiles on the older, experienced faces. Bewilderment and a shy interest on the younger faces, and from a few, forlorn curiosity.

"Can I help you catch a prince?" She stepped to the edge of the platform and made a play of lowering her voice. "Well, to tell you the truth, princes are a little thin on the ground these days."

The amusement grew louder and more open.

"But from the time I was a wee child, I had a directive drummed into my head—find a prince and marry him. No other man will do. Since I can't do that, I must turn to my other talent—helping you catch *your* prince. Ladies, these bags"—she pointed at the saddlebags her horse carried—"contain royal secrets from around the world! Of course"—she allowed her mouth to droop—"I have to charge you for them. Exiled princesses have to eat too." Her

voice strengthened. "But you can see by looking at me, I'm not making a fortune, and I
guarantee my work." She'd sold them all.

Well, almost all. A few stood with their
arms crossed over their chests. A handsome
woman back by the alehouse. A short,
middle-aged, mean-eyed man with a chip on
his shoulder the size of an iceberg. A tall,
sad-faced, round-shouldered lady. Those
were the ones Clarice depended on to make
trouble—and to help her clinch the sales.

The fascinating gentleman watched her,
apparently entertained. He was an unknown
entity. Yet he felt far too familiar, as if she
knew him from somewhere—a dream she'd
had, or a wish unfulfilled.

She did not like him.

But she did her best to forget him as she
smiled, inviting the comments she knew
would come.

The alewife shouted, "Ye've got a glib
tongue, I'll say that for ye. Let's see ye do
something."

From the center of the crowd the short man
yelled, "She can't do anything she claims."

The sad-faced lady said nothing, but she
moved back as if distancing herself from
the mob.

"Can I not?" Clarice's gaze landed on the homely seamstress, engrossed and standing close. "What's your name, miss?"

The seamstress glanced around as if hoping Clarice was speaking to someone else. "My . . . my name?"

"Yes, don't be timid," Clarice urged. "Tell us your name."

"I'm . . . um . . . I'm Miss Amy Rosabel."

"Come up here, Miss Rosabel."

Miss Rosabel ducked her head and shook it as if she were shy.

Clarice would have none of that. Appealing to the crowd, she said, "Come, good people! Let's make the young lady welcome."

A few of the younger folk clapped for Miss Rosabel.

Reluctantly she climbed up to stand beside Clarice. She was at least two inches taller than Clarice, but she hunched her shoulders so much, she looked shorter. Her dark hair was pulled tightly back from her face, accentuating the thrust of her narrow nose and her pointed chin. She had dark rings under her eyes, and her complexion was pasty white. Her brown wool gown was appalling.

Clearly to every eye, she needed help.

"Miss Rosabel, I'm going to make you beautiful," Clarice said.

Miss Rosabel pulled her tattered shawl closer around her shoulders. "Nay, miss, but thank ye."

The bandy-legged, mean-eyed, red-cheeked fellow sniggered. "Guid luck with that one. She's fair ugly, and that's na likely to change."

Miss Rosabel drew her shawl over her lips.

The other women winced on her behalf.

Clarice wrapped a supportive arm around her. "Sir, I'll wager you ten pounds I can make her beautiful."

He stepped up to the front. "Done! Let's see ye make her beautiful"—he looked around with a sneer—"right here in the square."

He had said exactly what they all said. Exactly what she wanted them to say. Leaning forward, she asked, "What is your name, sir?"

He folded his arms across his chest. "Billie MacBain, an' what do ye care?"

"I was wondering, Billie, if you'd like me to make you beautiful too." The roar of laughter was gratifying, proof that she'd not lost her timing or her reading of character. Billie's lack of height and his looks had made him hostile and belligerent, and no one in town liked him. She saw his fists bunch, and added, "But no. You're a fighter, you are, and the best in Freya Crags, I'll wager."

His hands loosened. His chin rose. He puffed out his chest, but his squinty eyes didn't waver. "Aye, that I am, and ye'd be wise t' remember it, missy."

She allowed her hand to flutter to her chest. "And a bully to boot, I see." She made him angrier, but the women grinned and nudged each other. She'd made allies of *them,* and they were, after all, her first and best customers.

Billie started toward her, fury in his eyes, pain in his fists.

Her heart leaped to her throat, and for a moment she thought she had gone too far.

Then the fascinating gentleman put a restraining hand on his arm.

In a rage Billie swung around, ready to kill the one who halted him. But when he saw who accosted him, he dropped his fist and glared.

The gentleman shook his head.

Billie backed away.

So. The gentleman must be good with a roundhouse. Handsome, tough, and dynamic.

He commanded respect—and perhaps some fear.

Clarice shivered. Certainly he commanded fear from her. She really, really must stay far away from him.

Her fingers were shaking slightly as she opened her saddlebag and brought forth a soft cloth and a clay jar. Holding up the jar, she announced, "This is a powerful extract of herbs and roots in a gentle cream that refreshes the complexion and brings the first tingle of beauty. Watch as I apply it." Miss Rosabel tilted her chin up as Clarice smoothed the cream on and rubbed it in. "It has the lovely scent of rosemary and mint, and a special secret ingredient known only to the women of my royal family."

"Gold, frankincense, and myrrh," the alewife mocked.

"You're only partly right," Clarice responded, "Of course, my kingdom is far from Bethlehem, but the trade routes were established long ago, back in the mists of time, and my country is known for its mountains, its treasures, and its beautiful women." She laughed at the old men who stood under the eaves of the alehouse, craning their necks to watch her.

Five identical, almost toothless smiles shot back at her, and one ancient fellow collapsed against the wall, his hand on his chest in faked spasms.

The alewife smacked him with her shawl.

Like some peculiar Greek chorus, the other old men chortled in unison, amused by their compatriot and charmed by her.

She loved old men. They said what they thought, they laughed when they wanted, and they always liked her, no matter what. Always.

With the cloth Clarice gently wiped the cream off Miss Rosabel's face. She urged Miss Rosabel to stand straight with her shoulders back, gentled the severe line of hair around her face, and pushed her toward the front of the platform.

The crowd gave a gratifying gasp.

"Yes, imagine that—an improvement in only five minutes!" Clarice pointed as she spoke. "Her dark circles are gone, and her skin is pink and healthy looking." More important, Clarice thought with satisfaction, Miss Rosabel's nose and chin were no longer pointed, and the softened hairstyle gave her a girlish loveliness. "Give me an hour and think what I can do!"

Cautiously Miss Rosabel touched her face. "Am I pretty?"

"Very pretty," Clarice assured her.

"My skin feels so clean and fresh!" For the first time, a smile broke across Miss Rosabel's face, and the men rumbled in admiration. They hadn't noticed her before. Now they did. She wasn't yet beautiful, but she was young and healthy, and she would be swamped with offers to walk in the evenings.

She would have to be careful. Most men treated a single woman with honor, but sometimes they did not, and Clarice anxiously scanned the crowd, looking for potential trouble.

Extracting a swath of soft blue material from her saddlebag, she draped it across Miss Rosabel's bosom. The color made an already attractive face even more attractive, and she said, "So, ladies and gentlemen, is this improvement worth ten pounds from Billie MacBain?"

"Yes!" the crowd roared, and everyone looked around for Billie.

Clarice laughed. Laughed with the pleasure of a win against Billie and a dozen guaranteed sales. "He sneaked away five minutes ago. But I've made my point. You can buy the face cream from me now, and if you'd like to know more royal secrets, I'll be staying at the inn—"

The handsome gentleman reached up and caught her hand. He spoke at last. "It would be best if you stayed up at the manor . . . Princess."

She'd seen MacKenzie Manor as she rode into Freya Crags. Set well off the road on a rise, four stories high and twenty glass windows across, with gargoyles poised on the roof and bronze double doors so big they should have been at home on a cathedral. The gray, forbidding stones weighed down the ground and chilled Clarice's heart. It was as if the house warned her to ride on, and she did, urging Blaize along the road at a brisker pace. Her reaction surprised her, for she prided herself on being practical and not at all skittish.

Perhaps she disliked the place because of her knowledge of its owner. Her spy in the town had written her about Lord Hepburn, a ruthless man who ordered his lands and his family like a despot. Clarice didn't want to stay in the house, and she didn't want to be anywhere near this fellow, who was probably the steward or the butler or . . . or a man too gorgeous for his own good. Or hers.

So with a superior smile that frightened off most men, she tugged to free her hand. "You're very free with your master's invitations."

He didn't release her, and he didn't look frightened.

A rustle of laughter spread through the onlookers.

"No!" Miss Rosabel pinched her elbow hard.

Clarice flinched. She'd made a mistake, although she couldn't imagine what it was.

In a soft voice with a hint of brogue he said, "I'm free with the invitations to MacKenzie Manor for good reason."

No. It couldn't be.

But it was. "I'm Robert MacKenzie, the earl of Hepburn. I'm the laird of Freya Crags—and the master of the manor." He kissed her fingers. His breath warmed her flesh, and for one moment she thought his tongue touched her skin. "I'm not a prince, but still, I insist. Stay at the manor with me."

Three

Clarice wrenched her hand back. *No.* The most handsome man in town couldn't also be the most powerful. He couldn't be.

But as she looked into Lord Hepburn's eyes, she realized—of course he was. He exuded authority. Her luck had indeed taken a turn for the worse—but she had talked her way out of more desperate situations. "I wouldn't dream of imposing on your hospitality."

"To have a lovely woman visit in my lonely home is not an imposition." Lord Hepburn's voice was mild, deep, and implacable, and he looked just like he sounded.

She could only hope she didn't look like she sounded, for her voice sounded dismayed and breathless. "It wouldn't be proper." The place where his tongue had touched was damp, and the breeze cooled her skin. She flexed her fingers to get rid of the sensation.

"I have sisters and a myriad of servants to chaperone us." His blue eyes were framed in lashes as black as his hair, and he scrutinized her inexorably, like a man keeping watch over a treasure.

She didn't want to be his treasure. She could not be any man's treasure. "My business affairs would interrupt the peace of your household."

"I always welcome visitors from the town, especially the ladies, and you—you're special. You're a princess." He cast a smile around at the women who had pressed close to hear their interchange.

Susceptible to his charm, the women tittered like a flock of wrens drunk on berries.

Clarice couldn't detect one smidgeon of sarcasm in him, but she knew that beneath the deep, respectful tone, cynicism was there. He didn't believe she was a princess. But for some dark, inexplicable reason of his own, he invited her into his home. "I—"

Miss Rosabel pinched Clarice's elbow again, hard enough to bruise her.

Clarice recognized a signal when she received one. She had to capitulate. He had won this round, but nothing in her life was ever as difficult as the next two words she spoke. "Thank you." She smiled at him, her best royal, gracious smile. "That is so kind. If you want to ride ahead, I'll conduct my business and follow later."

"I'll wait." He smiled back with lofty civility. "I would hate for you to . . . go astray."

"So kind," she repeated. She hated him for insinuating that she would skip town if she could.

Well, he was right. She would if she could. All her instincts were rumbling. This was the wrong time and the wrong place to sell her wares. But if she didn't succeed in Freya Crags, she faced a bout of hunger and perhaps a stint in the workhouse. No, she didn't dare think of leaving, regardless of what her instincts told her.

She tried to ignore him as she descended

from the platform, but he, damnable man, caught her hand and assisted her down. With gentlemanly grace, he assisted Miss Rosabel too, and then retreated to the back of the crowd.

Miss Rosabel disappeared into the seamstress's shop as Clarice attended to the women who crowded close, their coins clutched in their hands. She sold fourteen jars of face cream to fourteen eager patrons, and tried to speak to each of the other women who lingered close. She recognized their type from other towns, other sales. They were intimidated by her royal status, didn't feel comfortable enough to speak to her directly, and perhaps hadn't the coin to buy her wares. But she worked hard to set them at ease. After all, they couldn't buy if they labored under the fear that they would say the wrong thing. She had to make them comfortable.

The sad-faced lady stood off to the side, watching with wide brown eyes and saying nothing. Clarice noted the quality of the lady's gown; she wasn't one of the townspeople, yet Clarice was sure she could help the lady with her dress, which was drab, and her manner, which was apprehensive. But despite repeated charming smiles, the lady did not move forward.

Nor did she leave.

As the crowd thinned, Lord Hepburn strolled back to Clarice.

The women of the village stepped back, allowing him passage, yet they stayed close enough to inhale the excitement of having royalty in their midst.

He was tall, almost a foot taller than she, and his somber suit emphasized the breadth of his shoulders. She didn't feel threatened. Not with violence. But he overwhelmed her every sense, and he didn't seem to try. He blocked the sky with his height. His scent was clean and fresh, and his touch . . . she'd already suffered his touch, and she didn't relish experiencing it again.

"Are you ready?" he asked.

His voice caused a frisson up her spine. "Not quite." He had forced her hand in the matter of her lodgings, yet she modulated her voice as her grandmother had taught her and made one last attempt to free herself from his dominion. "I always ask the ladies to visit me so I can demonstrate my unguents and creams. You wouldn't like me to do so in your home . . . would you?"

The sad-faced lady stepped forward and slipped her arm through Lord Hepburn's. "I'd be glad to act as your hostess."

Clarice was surprised, but Hepburn looked astonished. "Millicent, would you really? That would be grand." He stared down at the woman with affection, the kind that comes from a long-standing familiarity.

Millicent must be his wife. Well. That made Clarice's stay at MacKenzie Manor more respectable, indeed. She would be glad to stay there knowing that the man with the compelling eyes would be occupied at night with a woman he held in such esteem.

But her informant in the town hadn't mention he was married. With a jolt Clarice realized—no, Millicent wasn't his wife. She was his sister. His older sister—poor thing. On closer inspection Clarice could see the resemblance. Millicent's hair was brown and twisted tightly into a bun, her yellow gown turned her complexion sallow, and the features that sat so aristocratically on Lord Hepburn looked merely too large on her long face.

Not that a new coiffure and a touch of cosmetics couldn't change matters, as well as lessons in how to walk and talk and smile.

With some humor Clarice realized she was already measuring Millicent for a new gown. That, perhaps, was the reason behind Millicent's offer to act as hostess. She was dissatisfied with herself, and wanted to change—and best of all, she had the money to pay handsomely.

Very well. Clarice could help her.

But what was behind Clarice's own inexplicable relief at discovering Lord Hepburn was unattached?

She didn't like this. She didn't like it at all. She was always in control of her emotions, always focused on her goal, and now this man disrupted her concentration by observing her as if he saw through her clothing and her masks right down to her bones. No, worse. Right down to her soul.

He smiled down at Millicent, and in a tone friendlier than he had yet used around Clarice, he said, "This is my sister, Lady Millicent. Lady Millicent, may I present Princess Clarice."

The two women bobbed curtsies.

"It's a privilege, Your Highness." Millicent's voice was pleasant, modulated, and her gaze met Clarice's without artifice.

"Thank you for your generosity, my lady,"

Clarice answered. "The time you'll spend hostessing for me must surely take time away from your other activities."

"It's quiet in the country, and we beg for company." Millicent smiled, and the smile transformed her from a plain woman into one of unusual beauty. "Besides, we're about to be invaded by most of the ton. We're giving a ball, and it is a very special ball. You see—"

Robert made an almost imperceptible gesture.

Millicent continued gracefully. "I am not accomplished at arranging these things."

That hadn't been what she was about to say.

"I suppose, Your Highness, that you are a great planner of balls," Millicent said.

"I . . . yes, I am."

"I imagine all princesses are," Robert injected.

His tone got under her skin. "Precisely. I was in training to care for the palaces I would one day rule, and Grandmamma would not have it bandied about that any of her relations were incompetent."

With a sweetness that seemed a part of her character, Millicent said, "I would so appreciate your assistance. Our younger sister will be making her debut at the ball. She's a little unsure, and she would never forgive me if I allowed you to stay anywhere but at MacKenzie Manor."

As Lord Hepburn grimaced in disgust, he looked almost like a normal brother. "Prudence has gone mad with dresses and hair and hats. I'll be buying royal cream by the gallon."

"The smallest amount works miracles, and for a girl about to make her debut, even that may be too much." Clarice smiled conspiratorially at Millicent. "I find that when I make the young too beautiful, those of us who aren't so young grow irritable."

"Prudence would be the first to tell you she's difficult." Millicent folded her hands and pruned her lips, but her eyes twinkled with humor. "I would be the second."

Startled into a chuckle, Clarice realized she could like the other woman. And liking was always dangerous; in her business, it was best not to become attached to any person for any reason. It made the leaving so much more difficult.

"So it's settled." Lord Hepburn again looked appropriately solemn and not at all like he'd won—again. "Millicent will be the hostess for your gatherings, you'll assist Prudence with her debut, the ladies in the town shall have a jolly time—and you'll come to my ball."

Clarice breathed in a great breath, careful to make no sound, yet needing the fortification. "To the ball? I didn't say I would come to the ball." That would be disaster.

"But you're a princess."

Clarice chewed her lower lip. He was toying with her, she could see that. Sometimes the truth would disarm such a villain. "Pardon me, my lord, but I'm sure you understand that a princess who sells creams brings disgrace on her country." And if *this* princess were seen by the wrong people, it would more than disgrace. It would bring imprisonment, lynching, and death.

Blaize tossed his head and made an impatient sound.

"The horse will stand for only so long," he said. "We'll discuss your attendance on the ride."

Recalled to her obligations, Clarice said, "I'd like to talk to Miss Rosabel in private. Give her some hints on how to improve her hair and dress."

Lord Hepburn's eyebrows rose. "But she hasn't paid you."

"Sometimes a princess has to be kind to those less fortunate." Clarice's voice contained little of the gentle loftiness Grandmother had taught her a royal always used.

"Of course." He gestured Clarice toward the seamstress's shop. "Take your time." With the kind of pleasure only a man who loved horses could show, he said, "I'll walk your colt."

"Do be careful," Clarice said with relish. "He doesn't like men."

Offering his hand to the stallion, Lord Hepburn stood perfectly still as the horse sniffed his fingers, his arm, his shoulder, and then nuzzled his ear. Lord Hepburn caressed the soft nose of her stallion. "I think we'll get along."

Fie on the horse! He gentled only for women—and most women were afraid to go near him. Now this man who reeked of nobility, cynicism, and an indefinable masculinity held Blaize by the reins and petted him as if he were a tame dog, when in fact Blaize was—Clarice ran her finger under the tight collar of her riding costume. Seeing the way Hepburn watched her, she hastily pulled her hand away. She would not behave as if she were guilty. She wasn't guilty of anything. Not here. Not yet. "Thank you, my lord. You're very kind."

Clarice walked toward the seamstress's shop. She turned back before she had gone ten steps. "His name is Blaize. Treat him well." She looked Lord Hepburn in the eye, demanding his consideration. "He has been abused, and he is my friend."

Lord Hepburn bowed before her demand. "Of course." His attention lingered on Clarice's hips as she hurried away. She moved with a lithe grace that held his gaze. He glanced around the square. Held the gaze of every man there. She sold the women face cream. With her bold words and small, curvaceous body, she sold the men something else entirely.

Happiness, she had said.

Perhaps, just perhaps, he was in the market to pay.

Four

Never lower yourself to dishonesty, regardless of the circumstances. Such behavior besmirches the shining white character of royalty and the Fleur family.
—THE DOWAGER QUEEN OF BEAUMONTAGNE

"Yer Highness." Mistress Dubb had lingered close enough to hear the exchange. Hurrying forward, she curtsied. "Yer presence will honor my humble shop." She shot a triumphant glance at the other women.

Clarice gave a silent groan. She knew this woman's type. Mistress Dubb would tell the story of the princess in her shop until the other women were ready to roast the seamstress on a spit. And Clarice needed to speak to Miss Rosabel alone. But there was no helping it; she had to show Mistress Dubb the proper courtesy. To fail would be discourteous . . . and eventually bad for sales. "I thank you for your kindness, to me and to Amy."

Mistress Dubb simpered, curtsied again, and opened the narrow green door. A variety of hats were set in the small window, all as dull and lusterless as everything in this village.

"You're a milliner also!" Clarice exclaimed. "How talented you are."

"I do me best, Yer Highness." She flung the door wide and bobbed up and down as Clarice entered.

In the dim interior of the shop Miss Rosabel stood by the mirror, smoothing the last of the clay off her nose and chin.

Clarice blocked the entrance. "Turquoise is the newest fashion color in London. But you knew that, of course." Clarice lavished a smile on the seamstress as she picked the one color most likely to complement any complexion. "I imagine you're working on hats and gowns of that color right now."

Mistress Dubb took a breath. "Aye. Aye! In the back."

"I'll be doing a private consultation with Miss Rosabel now." Gently she pushed Mistress Dubb away. "Of course, you'll have your turn later. I'm sure you understand." She shut the door on Mistress Dubb's blossoming smile.

"That was skillful." Miss Rosabel stepped out of the shadows. "The old biddy will brag about your kindness for a fortnight."

Her hostility was palpable, her tone scornful, for Miss Rosabel was, in fact, Clarice's younger sister, seventeen years of age. She was Princess Amy of Beaumontagne.

Before she answered, Clarice switched to German. Changing languages as they spoke was something she and Amy did frequently—it kept their linguistic skill thriving and befuddled anyone who might be listening. "I *am* a princess, and I *do* try to be kind."

Amy's exasperated adolescent sigh said too clearly that she found Clarice dim-witted and conventional. "Yes, yes, we're both princesses. Princesses of Beaumontagne." With a jerky motion Amy wiped at the white powder on her face. "Sisters bound by a royal bloodline, trapped together in exile. According to you, that justifies everything."

Bustling forward, Clarice tried to take the towel. "Here. Let me."

Amy jerked away from Clarice, from her touch, and said fiercely, "I can do it. I've done it often enough before."

Clarice's heart sank. The longer they peddled their wares, the more unhappy Amy became.

Clarice wandered about the shop, examining the gowns laid out to be sewn, while Amy completed her transformation from a dull, plain seamstress recently come to town to a girl hovering on the edge of prettiness. After a few more sessions with Clarice, she would be beautiful, a living testimonial to the royal face cream. And when the time came for Clarice to leave, Amy would slip out of town in her wake.

When Amy finished, she leaned her fists on either side of the mirror and closed her eyes. Her voice vibrated with fury as she demanded, "What do you think you're doing?"

Clarice winced but said brightly, "It went well, didn't it?"

"No, it did not!" Freed of the constraints of

the public eye, Amy allowed her ferocity free rein. "When I wrote you, I warned you this was not the place to do our act. But you always think you know best."

Clarice changed to French. "We were out of money and we didn't have time to find another town."

"We could both work as seamstresses." Amy's gaze met Clarice's in the mirror. A silver necklace glinted at her throat. A necklace with a cross that matched Clarice's. "We could settle down somewhere and design clothes. I'm good at it. I wouldn't have to pretend to be ugly. We wouldn't have to keep moving from one place to another."

Slowly Clarice shook her head.

"Oh. I forgot. We're *princesses*." Amy almost spat out the words. "Princesses don't do *menial* work like *sewing*."

"No." Clarice watched her younger sister and wished things could be different. She wanted Amy to be happy, to hold the position of honor she was born to hold. But Amy had been so young when they left Beaumontagne. She'd been only ten. At fourteen Clarice had been the second oldest, and she well remembered the protocol and the luxury, the duties and the joys. She missed it, but more than that, she wanted Amy to know what it really was to be a princess, to enjoy the privileges and treasure the duties.

"Are princesses supposed to sell people products that don't work?" Amy demanded.

Patiently Clarice repeated what she'd said so many times before. "We tried being seamstresses. We could barely make enough money to feed ourselves. We have to locate Sorcha, and together we have to make our way back to Beaumontagne and find Grandmamma."

With a brutality she'd never shown before, Amy said, "She's dead. You know she is. Father and Grandmamma didn't mean for us to be on the streets. Sorcha is lost."

Amy had spoken aloud Clarice's deepest fears, and the pain of those words made Clarice's breath rasp in her throat. "Papa's dead. We know that. Godfrey said so, and so did the papers in London. But the papers said Grandmamma is back in power."

"And Godfrey said that Grandmamma instructed that we should not come back until she sent for us. He said there were bad people hunting us, and that we should hide until she placed an announcement in all the papers that it was safe to return." Amy's quavering voice recalled the fear of that time, when Grandmamma's favorite messenger had arrived at the school and sent Clarice and Amy fleeing while he took Crown Princess Sorcha to a secret sanctuary. "There hasn't been an announcement. We check every paper in every town, and you know Grandmamma. If she said she would put in an announcement, she would."

"I know. I know." If there was one thing both girls comprehended, it was that their grandmother was a force of nature.

"I tell you, everyone's dead, the bad people have won, and we can't go back."

"We don't know that. Sorcha could already be there, waiting for us. I promise you'll love it. The palace is so beautiful, and you'll have the finest gowns and a beautiful pianoforte to play. . . ." Clarice's voice wobbled as she fought back tears.

"Dear Clarice." Amy came to her at once and put her arms around her. "I'm sorry. I didn't mean to hurt you. I only wish we could stop selling ourselves like cheap—"

Clarice put her fingers over Amy's mouth. "We're not selling *ourselves*. We're selling the creams Grandmamma showed me how to make. And the creams really are royal, and they *are* wonderful for the complexion, and—"

"And they really don't make anyone beautiful. If they did, I wouldn't have to go into town a fortnight ahead of you, wearing a fake nose and white powder."

"But for a little while they give the women hope. That's not so bad, is it?" Clarice cajoled.

Glumly Amy replied, "Those people in England who want to hang you from the highest gibbet think so."

"It was that awful man." Clarice set her chin. "That magistrate."

Now Amy's ashen complexion owed nothing to white powder and everything to fear. She lowered her voice as if afraid of being overheard, and in Italian said, "He wanted you."

"I know." Clarice walked a fine line. The wives wanted her creams, but the husbands held the purse strings, so Clarice had to be pleasant and charming to everyone, and at the same time never go over the invisible line that separated the lady from the fallen woman.

Sometimes the men didn't see the line. Frequently they saw only an attractive young female living without the protection of a man.

That made her easy prey—and Magistrate Fairfoot had more than one reason for wanting her dead. She had hurt his pride in every way possible, and even now, in her nightmares, she could see the gray towers of the fortress at Gilmichael clawing the bloodred sky, waiting to swallow her whole and never, ever let her out.

"Now you have another awful man after you," Amy said.

"Is he awful?" Hepburn didn't seem awful. In a way, that was almost worse.

"They're all awful." Amy caught Clarice by the lapels of her jacket and lowered her voice to an intense whisper. "What are you going to do about him?"

"I don't know. I don't know." Clarice whispered too. "I thought from your letter he was older. Much older. He sounded so grim."

"He *is* grim." With a glance at the door Amy said, "They claim Hepburn is a fair man, but he quarreled with his father and the old earl bought him a commission and forced him to go to war. Six years later his father died. Lord Hepburn sold his commission and came back, but the townsfolk whisper that he's changed."

"Changed how?"

"He used to be a young man, devil-may-care, enjoying a fight, drinking the night away, always laughing. Now . . . now he's as you saw. The people in the town admire him—but when they speak of him, there's an edge of fear in their voices."

Yes. It was that Clarice had sensed. He was a man of privilege, and yet he hid secrets in his soul. Secrets that made them alike.

She didn't want to recognize him and his mysteries.

As if she read Clarice's thoughts, Amy said, "Be careful."

Clarice spoke too quickly. "Why?"

"He won't stay in the manor with the family."

"Really?" That floored Clarice. She would have said he made much of his home and his place there. "Where does he stay?"

"In one of the cottages on the estate. He comes in for breakfast and he seems natural, but they say he walks the estate and the district at night like a man haunted, and he disappears for days at a time." Amy lowered her voice as if her own tale made her uneasy. "They say the war turned him a little mad."

"Oh, pshaw. Surely not mad!"

"Yes. Mad. And dangerous. Did you see the way he watched you?" Amy whispered.

With a fair imitation of insouciance, Clarice shrugged. "They all watch me."

"Not like that. He's too . . . he's confident." Amy observed Clarice with a wisdom beyond her years. A wisdom won from hard years on the road and too much innocence betrayed. "He wants—and he gets what he wants."

Clarice knew what Amy meant. After all, hadn't he kissed her hand almost before she knew his name? But just because he had soft lips and a lover's swift tongue was no reason to admit her wariness. Amy had already expressed her uneasiness about the job, and if she knew of Clarice's anxieties, she would push for them to leave. Clarice had lost too much on their last job; having to abandon the town in a hurry had made it impossible to collect the money due them.

At times like this, when disaster loomed on every side, Clarice could scarcely recall when she had lived in a palace, when she had been pampered and cared for, when all she knew of the world was what Grand-mamma told her. Right now, Clarice wished nothing so much as to return to the palace in

Beaumontagne and be that spoiled princess once more.

Foolishness. In the last five years, Clarice had learned well what wishes were worth. So she said, "It's best to be forewarned, so—tell me everything you know about the mad and dangerous Lord Hepburn."

BEAUMONTAGNE
Eleven years before

Dowager Queen Claudia tapped her cane along the gleaming white marble floor in the throne room in the royal palace in Beaumontagne, and like a sleek, old, domineering greyhound, she barked at her granddaughters, "Chin up! Shoulders back!"

Fifteen-year-old Crown Prince Rainger of Richarte stood at attention on the dais, observing as she inspected the three princesses.

He knew his turn would come.

Resentfully, he considered the old lady. She commanded the grand chamber with her presence. Gaunt and mean, she had a whip for a tongue and blue eyes that could see a man's sins before he'd committed them.

Rainger knew, because she was also his godmother, and she exploited that honor and took him to task whenever she thought fit.

She paced back and forth before the princesses who stood stair-stepped on the dais above her. The sunshine shone through the tall windows, brightening the long, elegant, gilded room, and complimenting the three sisters. The girls were dressed alike in white gowns with pink satin bows around their waists and pink bows in their hair. Supposedly they were pretty—for princesses.

Rainger's father, King Platon, said so. Their father, King Raimund, beamed with pride when he saw them. Everyone in both courts whispered at their suitability and their comeliness. Rainger supposed it was true, but he had been coming to Beaumontagne once a year ever since he could remember, and to him the girls were sometimes fun to play with, but usually an annoyance, for they would tease him without any deference for his age or exalted position.

"Today, we're welcoming the ambassador from France. This is an official court function, and all eyes will be fixed on you, the royal princesses of Beaumontagne." Queen Claudia wore her white hair in a chignon, with never a strand out of place and a tiara glittering with diamonds and sapphires. Her cerulean velvet gown perfectly matched her eyes.

Rainger thought she had to be at least one hundred years old, maybe one hundred and fifty, but her skin, while wrinkled, was untouched by blotches or broken veins. Some people whispered she was a witch, and Rainger didn't discount the notion. She certainly sported a long, skinny nose, and everyone knew she brewed secret potions in the palace kitchen. She demanded perfection—from herself, and from everyone around her. She got it too.

He himself had inspected his court dress before leaving his room, making sure his white linens gleamed and his dark suit fit his shoulders flawlessly. He had taken a moment too, to admire his muscled form. Countess duBelle said he was a fine figure of a man. He had to admit the countess was right.

Queen Claudia stopped before her youngest granddaughter. "Amy, let me see your nails."

Reluctantly, Amy extended her hands.

Queen Claudia inspected the princess's

outstretched palms, then examined the fingernails. "Better," she said. "Clean, but a princess does not bite her nails. Remember, your hands and every part of your person are representative of the royal entity of Beaumontagne. Everything you do and say is subject to examination and must be above reproach."

Six-year-old Amy was an imp with hair as black as Rainger's and an honesty Queen Claudia had not yet been able to crush. "But, Grandmamma, I like to bite my nails. I don't want to be a princess if I have to stop."

As Amy's candid response echoed through around the marble columns, Rainger grinned.

Clarice put her hand over her eyes.

Earnestly, Sorcha said, "Grandmamma, Amy doesn't mean what she said. She's only six."

Sorcha was twelve, with red hair the color of new minted copper and a kind and gentle disposition. In Rainger's opinion, Queen Claudia had ground down her spirit with constant lectures about royal duty, and that was too bad, because she and Rainger were betrothed. He imagined he would be bored within a year of marriage.

Queen Claudia fixed her eldest grand-daughter with a freezing look. "I know Amy's age, and such sentiments are unacceptable at any time." She considered Amy until the little girl squirmed. "This honor which you would so freely discard is one given to only a privileged few, and a real princess should be willing to lay down her life for her country and her family. Balanced against such demands, giving up a disgusting habit is easy."

Amy dug her toe into the rich pile of the red carpet leading up to the throne. She muttered, "Then I guess I'm not a real princess."

Clarice released a smothered giggle.

Queen Claudia turned on eleven-year-old Clarice, a blonde with masses of curls springing around her face. Her nostrils flared as she declared, "You will not encourage her in her insolence!"

"No, Grandmamma." But Clarice's eyes still twinkled, and she dug her elbow into Sorcha's side.

Sorcha pinched her back.

Queen Claudia smacked her cane on the floor.

The princesses jumped and straightened.

Since the death of the girls' mother four years before, Queen Claudia had commanded every aspect of their lives, and she was so stern, so humorless, Rainger was convinced she had never been young.

"Amy, I will deliver to your bedchamber an ointment that you'll smear on your fingernails every morning and every night," Queen Claudia said. "That will cure you of your habit, and teach you to mind your manners too."

In a sing-song voice Amy said, "Yes, Grandmamma."

Transferring her attention to Clarice, Queen Claudia said, "Since you believe this is a subject for amusement, you will help me prepare the ointment."

Clarice's face fell. "Yes, Grandmamma."

"Throughout our history every princess of Beaumontagne has been taught the royal beauty secrets. Sorcha knows. It is time that you, Clarice, also—" Queen Claudia leaned toward Clarice and took a deep breath. In tones rife with horror, the dowager asked, "Do I detect the scent of horse?"

Clarice cringed backward. "The French ambassador brought Papa the most beautiful Arabian I've ever seen, and I petted his neck. But only once!"

"Once was evidently enough." Queen Claudia proclaimed, "A princess does not pet horses for pleasure."

Rainger was moved to protest. "Godmother, Clarice loves horses, and she has a way with them which even the hostler admires."

Queen Claudia lifted her cane and poked him in the ribs. "Young Rainger, you're not too old to copy the Book of Kings."

During his annual visits to Beaumontagne, Queen Claudia had often ordered Rainger to write out the Book of Kings from the Bible as punishment for his misbehaviors. Even now, if Queen Claudia told him to do it, he wouldn't have the nerve to refuse.

Yet Sorcha sent him a grateful glance, and he knew she appreciated his effort on her sister's behalf.

In the year since Rainger had last seen her, Sorcha had grown tall, but her feet and hands were still too big, and she moved clumsily, leading Rainger's father to predict she would get taller yet. Clarice had grown a little too, and her figure had filled out. Amy was still a rambunctious child, rebelling at every opportunity at her role as princess.

All the courtiers told Rainger he was lucky that he got to marry one of these princesses.

But he resented having his bride picked out for him. He was mature. He could choose his own bride. He would rather marry Countess duBelle. The only thing stopping him was her age, which was almost twenty-five . . . well, and her husband, who was very much alive. Rainger ignored the niggles of his conscience as he sneaked into her bed, for he loved the beautiful, vivacious, wicked lady.

In that voice that froze the marrow in his bones, Queen Claudia told Clarice, "I can only hope you haven't ruined the reception with your selfishness. As soon as it's over I'll provide you with my special soap and you're to wash to your elbows. Do you understand? To your elbows!"

"Yes, Grandmamma," Clarice said weakly.

"And no more horses." As if sensing another objection from Rainger, she turned on him. "So, Crown Prince Rainger, what will you do at this reception?"

Resentful that she demanded an accounting of his behavior, he bowed, and answered, "Yawn."

In crushing tones she answered, "Being royal means you know how to yawn with your mouth closed."

"Of course." But her quick reply shook

him. He should have remembered. She had a truism for every occasion.

Queen Claudia peered at her oldest grand-daughter. "Is that a spot on your forehead?"

Sorcha touched the swelling. "Just a little one."

"No butter for you. No candy. And you will use my complexion wash to cleanse your face twice a day"—Queen Claudia tilted Sorcha's chin up and examined her criti-cally—"and my color emulsion to cover the mark. A princess must always produce the face of perfection. Remember, not everyone wishes you well."

A door opened behind them on the dais, and a short, stout gentleman stepped in, dressed in a uniform covered with medals and ribbons. King Raimund had a splendid mustache and bushy sideburns, and his blue eyes resembled his mother's, except that they twinkled merrily at the sight of his children. He looked tired, as if the recent troubles in his kingdom had worn him down, but he opened his arms. "Come, my dears, and give your poppa a kiss."

With cries of joy and a total lack of dignity, the princesses broke ranks and ran toward him. They embraced him all at once, bab-

bling in girlish tones about their delight at seeing him.

Rainger was surprised to see the slightest smile tilt Queen Claudia's thin lips. She looked almost . . . fond, and not at all disapproving of the loving display.

Then she clapped her hands, once, sharply.

The children broke away from their father and hurriedly lined up again.

"Mother." King Raimund bowed to Queen Claudia, then came to her and touched his cheek to hers.

Rainger bowed to him. "King Raimund."

"Prince Rainger." With due solemnity, he bowed back.

Rainger suspected his show of dignity amused the king, for at one time, Rainger would have run to him, also. But Rainger was too old for such childishness. He was, after all, a Crown Prince.

Striding to the ancient, dark, carved throne, King Raimund asked, "Is all prepared for the reception?"

"Of course." Queen Claudia looked at the small watch which hung from a gold pin on her bosom. "The footmen will admit the courtiers in five minutes."

King Raimund made a sound, not quite a groan. Seating himself, he donned a simple, gold crown.

"Now." Queen Claudia paced before the girls, and Rainger, once again. "How will you greet the French ambassador?"

With calm assurance Amy announced, "I'll tell him to go back where he came from."

Rainger, Sorcha, and Clarice gasped.

Queen Claudia fumbled for the chain around her neck, and lifted her lorgnette to view her youngest granddaughter in dismay. "What did you say?"

Amy repeated, "I said I will tell him to go away."

"Why would you make such a statement to the man who is the ambassador from France?" Queen Claudia questioned in dire tones.

With impeccable logic Amy said, "Because you said he's not the real ambassador, he's only the ambassador for the upstart French government, and until they return their rightful king to power, we don't like them."

Sorcha and Clarice exchanged startled glances, then dissolved into giggles.

King Raimund laughed. "She has you there, Mother."

Amy had no idea why everyone was so amused, but she grinned cockily, showing the gap where she had lost a tooth.

Sorcha rushed to defend her sister. "Amy is right, Grandmamma. You always say, 'Tell me who you associate with and I'll tell you who you are.'"

In a soft voice Clarice added, "That's true. Should we, the royal princesses of Beaumontagne, associate with a French upstart?"

It was at times like this when Rainger remembered why he liked the princesses. Not even Queen Claudia, with her rules and her sayings, could squelch their spirits.

Queen Claudia fixed them all—Sorcha, Clarice, Amy, Rainger, and even King Raimund—with a grim eye, and made her final pronouncement. "I hope that someday each of you has a child just like you."

Five

Why worry? It'll only give ye wrinkles.
—THE OLD MEN OF FREYA CRAGS

"Where did she acquire you, my lad?" Robert spoke to Blaize, low and soft, while he looked him over. Definitely a two-year-old colt, an Arabian of good lines, and far too strong and wild for a lady. Yet Clarice handled him with astonishing ease. "And where did your lassie learn to control a beast of such strength?"

Glancing at the closed door of the seamstress's shop, Robert said, "I know what she would say. She would say she learned to ride from an expert horseman. Because she was a *princess*."

Blaize snorted in reply and tossed his head.

"Yes. Exactly. Have you ever heard of princesses who are loose in Britain? *No*. Are the newspapers abuzz about lost royalty? *No*." Robert walked Blaize around the square, still speaking to him in that low, gentle voice he used to tame the wild creatures. "God in heaven, I've heard my share of falsehoods in my time. My men told grandiose tales that changed to fit the circumstances."

Blaize had a beautiful gait, and his temperament, while sprightly, was sweet. But wherever Blaize walked, the crowd observed the horse's dancing hooves and moved aside, for the stallion eyed the men warily, as if expecting a blow. Robert wondered what had made the creature so distrustful—and thus a perfect confidant for Robert. "My men were criminals given the choice between the gallows and the army. What excuse does yon lassie have for telling a lie that dwarfs all those other lies?" Robert stroked Blaize's nose and confided, "Although, I have to tell you, that makes her ideal for my plan."

Blaize's brown eyes considered Robert as if the horse were weighing his character. It should, perhaps, have been discomfiting, but in his life Robert had done worse things than blackmailing a princess. Worse things for worse reasons.

As they neared the alehouse, Tomas Mac-Tavish called, "M'lord, bring the beastie over so we can see him."

Robert grimaced. See the horse? Yes, the old men would want that. But more, they wanted to talk about the woman, for as he approached, they were grinning and rocking back and forth in their chairs like a gaggle of matchmaking grandmothers.

"Lovely stallion," Gilbert Wilson said.

"Lovelier wench," Hamish MacQueen quipped. "And 'tis proud o' ye we are, m'lord, fer acquiring her so quickly."

"I didn't acquire her." Not in the way they meant. "I'm taking her where I can watch her." And use her.

"Eh?" Henry MacCulloch cupped his ear and turned to Tomas.

Tomas shouted, "He said he was taking her where he could watch her."

"Aye, watch her, aye." Henry elbowed Hamish in the ribs. "Watch her close, I say. Ye caught yerself a fair one, m'lord."

"I have no interest in—" Robert hesitated.

Benneit MacTavish supplied the words. "Parting her beard?"

The old men's cackling made the horse restive, and Robert walked him across the square, then walked him back. He didn't know why he returned to the old men. Maybe it was because they, unlike any of the other people in this village and in society, had no pretenses. Age, poverty, and loneliness had stripped them of their masks, and they said what they thought and they meant what they said. How refreshing after so many years of lies.

As he drew near, Hughina Gray stepped out of the alehouse, drying her hands on her apron. "Pay them na mind, m'lord. They sit and gossip all day like auld besoms, take up space, and buy scarcely a tankard of ale between them."

Because they had no place else to go except home to relatives too busy to bother with them and no coin to purchase ale to wet their whistle. They looked shamefaced at her accusation, and shuffled their feet and played with their canes. Old farmers, old sailors, old merchants—when they finally died, everyone was relieved. Everyone except Robert, who could come here and listen to them natter about events and times gone by, and never have to talk about himself, or pretend to be whole, or hide the eternal midnight of his soul. "Then serve them up a tankard of ale apiece every day, Hughina, and send the charge to me."

Hughina dropped her apron. "But, m'lord—"

He turned his gaze on her. "I'm good for it."

"Of course ye are, m'lord. I didn't mean t' say . . ." She must have seen something in his face that frightened her, for she paled and stammered, "I—I'll get them now, m'lord."

As she hurried into the alehouse, Henry said, "Thank ye, m'lord. Ye dunna have t'."

Benneit intervened before proud Henry could refuse. "But we're grateful." He stretched out his wrinkled hand to accept a dripping mug from the chastened Hughina. "We'll toast yer health every day."

Robert stroked Blaize's nose. "That's all I ask."

The men lifted the mugs to him, then swallowed the rich, dark brew eagerly.

Hamish sighed with satisfaction. "Mither's milk."

Gilbert cast a dark glance at Hughina. "From a withered tit."

In a flash Hughina recovered her bite. "Ye dunna have t' take it if ye dunna like the source."

Gilbert opened his mouth to retort, saw Robert slowly shaking his head, and swallowed more of the ale instead.

Visibly cheered by the liquid refreshment, Tomas clanked his tankard on the table. "Ach, m'lord, we're all men here. Ye can't expect us t' believe ye have na interest in that fine and royal piece."

Robert sidestepped the question. "She's too young, and I don't tangle with princesses."

"How auld do ye suppose she is?" Benneit wondered.

"Seventeen. Eighteen," Robert said. The same age as his youngest sister, Prudence, and too young to be lying and swindling.

"Two-and-twenty if she's a day," Hughina said. "May I get ye a tankard too, m'lord?"

"I thank you." He didn't want it, but she'd worry if he didn't take it. Worry that he was truly displeased with her when in fact he cared about her not at all. He did care about Clarice's age, and about Hughina's certainty. Was Hughina jealous of the younger woman? Is that why she claimed Clarice was older? Or did she see something he did not?

For if it was true, if Clarice was indeed two-and-twenty . . .

He himself was one-and-thirty, and after the battles and the smells and the death and the hunger, he felt older than dirt. He wouldn't debauch a young girl, but if Clarice were older, with a bit of experience under her belt . . . that changed how he would approach her. There were ways to cajole women that had nothing to do with blackmail.

All the old men's cackling stopped at the same time, and their faded eyes were glued to a spot behind Robert.

The princess must have stepped back into the square.

In a hoarse voice Tomas said, "She's headed right fer us."

"My chimney's smokin'," Benneit whispered.

"Hell, my chimney's afire!" Henry's voice carried halfway to the English border.

While the other old men hushed him, Robert turned to face the square. Yes. Here she came. Clarice looked like an angel and deceived like a demon, and yet when he gazed on her his body stirred. Not because he'd been too long without a woman, but for *her*. Her smile, her walk, her hair, her body . . . that body.

Her blond hair was cradled into a net snood at the nape of her neck, and artfully arranged wisps escaped and fluttered around her face and down her back, catching the heat of the sun and warming the blood of every male in sight. Her dark brows arched over amber-brown eyes that glinted with good humor and a lazy sensuality that each man believed she meant for him.

Hughina made a disgusted sound and with a rustle of skirts disappeared into the alehouse. Sticking her head back out, she snapped, "There's na fool like an auld fool."

As she disappeared again, the men sadly shook their heads.

"That one needs some honey," Gilbert said.

"A honey," Hamish said.

"A husband," Tomas agreed.

Then, in unison, they lost interest in Hughina, for the princess stepped up and cast a merry smile at the old men who were creaking to their feet. "Lord Hepburn, would you introduce me to these handsome gentlemen?"

The old men's papery complexions suffused with color, and Gilbert almost tottered over in an elegant bow as Robert introduced him.

Clarice firmly clasped Gilbert by the arm, and as if she hadn't noticed his unsteadiness said, "Good day, gentlemen. How go the games?"

"Guid." Tomas puffed out his thin chest. "I won."

Benneit retorted, "If ye can call cheating winning."

The princess extended her hand to Tomas. "I've not had a challenging game of checkers for many a long day. Perhaps when Lord Hepburn allows me time free of my duties, I could come and play a game."

"That would be grand, Yer Highness." Tomas cherished her hand between his arthritic fingers.

"I'm na mean cheater meself, Yer Highness," Henry said.

She threw back her head and laughed, a merry laugh without artifice, and the old men's eyes glowed.

Benneit pleaded, "M'lord, ye'll let her come, won't ye?"

Never. Never was Robert letting her out on her own. He would bribe her, of course, and seduce her, and finally blackmail her if it came to that, but she might balk at taking part in his scheme and he couldn't afford to lose another woman. Not so soon before the ball. "I'll bring her myself."

She flashed him a disdainful glance.

"The road between MacKenzie Manor and Freya Crags can be lonely," he explained gently.

Smoothly she removed her hand from Tomas's grasp and came to Robert. Looking up into his eyes, her gaze direct and accusatory, she said, "Perhaps, my lord, you should police the road for the safety of your people as well as for that of your family."

She wasn't afraid of him. She wasn't afraid at all. Robert's blood warmed like brandy over a flame, and he felt the heat of intoxication. He had thought the next few days would be hell. Perhaps so, but he had his own private angel to enter the flames with him.

She reached for Blaize's reins.

Robert let her hands brush his. "Your advice is sound. I shall take it under consideration."

As he stared back down at her and allowed his touch to linger, he saw her swallow. She didn't look away.

Good. Good.

Then Blaize nuzzled her ear as if whispering a secret, and she led the horse a few steps away, leaving a fresh scent behind her.

Like . . . like fresh flowers and homey spices. Robert liked her perfume.

"Ach, Yer Highness, it's na so bad as all that." Henry, a withered, stooped man who had once been the mayor of Freya Crags, leaned on his cane. "A couple of highwaymen are preying on travelers when they're t' be had and crofters when they're na. Bullies, both o' them; they've got a way wi' a cudgel and as long as the odds are in their favor, they're na afraid t' lay aboot them. But Lord Hepburn has put oot a patrol and that's chased them doon the road toward Edinburgh."

Clarice cast a triumphant smile at Robert. "Then I can ride into Freya Crags without worry."

"I fear with the advent of rich coaches on the road to MacKenzie Manor, they'll find the pickings irresistible, and return." Robert did fear that. He also rather hoped they would return, and on one of the many nights when he found sleep elusive. He would like to encounter them and explain, in exquisite, painful detail, why they should find another career. "So you see, Your Highness, why I must accompany you when you come to Freya Crags."

"Young buck," Gilbert grumbled. "Ye're afraid we'll steal her away from ye."

Clarice's smile froze on her face. "I'm not his."

Robert almost—almost!—grinned. *Let Gilbert get himself out of this one!*

"Nay, I didna mean that, Yer Highness, I meant . . ." Gilbert glanced frantically at his cohorts.

Hamish rescued him. "Ye must know fascinating stories, Yer Highness."

She glowered at Robert as if this were his fault.

He raised his eyebrows in studied innocence.

"For instance," Hamish persisted, "how did ye come to own such a magnificent horse?"

"Isn't he beautiful? He's part Arabian, part Beaumontagnian, and one of the finest beasts I've ever been privileged to ride." She petted Blaize as if he were a large dog and not a gigantic horse whose hooves could crush her into the ground. "He was a gift from my father, the king."

The falsehood rolled off her tongue, Robert noted, with the ease of practice. That pleased him, as did the faint, indefinable accent and the husky note he found— indeed, every man must find—so appealing.

She was a liar, an accomplished liar, and he needed her to complete his mission.

Her gaze rested on Henry, who was swaying as if standing for so long had exhausted him. Turning to Robert, she said, "I'm ready, my lord." She was solemn when she spoke to him, a marked difference from the gaiety she shared with the old men. Turning back to her new friends and advocates, she said, "I've ridden far today and have need of rest. So if you would excuse us, gentlemen . . ."

"O' course, o' course." Henry grinned, and like a mad Greek chorus the other men grinned too. "Ye two young folks go on now t' MacKenzie Manor. 'Tis a beautiful place, Yer Highness, and I know m'lord will make ye feel at home there."

The old men nodded encouragingly at Robert, behaving as if Clarice were his last chance of salvation.

When in fact she was his last chance for revenge on the enemy who had stripped him of honor and of friendship.

Sweet, glorious revenge.

Six

The hungry wolf and the wee lamb might lie down together, but the lamb had best sleep with one eye open.
—THE OLD MEN OF FREYA CRAGS

Millicent rode beside Princess Clarice and her brother down the curving, hilly road to MacKenzie Manor and watched with mute contentment as the princess sparred with Robert.

"Lord Hepburn." Princess Clarice held her spirited stallion to a walk without seeming effort, a lively, pretty woman dressed with the kind of dash to which Millicent could never aspire. "I understand you have been home from the Peninsula for but a short time. Tell me, where did your travels take you?"

The day was still and almost warm, the breeze blowing hints of spring into their faces. Dust puffed beneath the horses' hooves. Millicent's hack was perfect for a lady, amiable and spiritless, not at all like the princess's Blaize or Robert's giant golden gelding, Helios. But of course, Millicent was no horsewoman. Not like Princess Clarice.

And, of course, Robert rode Helios like a man born to the saddle. "My regiment was stationed in northern Portugal."

Princess Clarice raised her eyebrows at Millicent as if sharing amusement at his taciturnity. Turning back to him, she asked, "Is that where you spent *all* your time?"

Millicent strained to hear the answer. When Robert had returned from the Peninsula, she almost hadn't recognized him. The charming, debonair young rake had given way to a man with bleak, lifeless eyes who watched the world with weary recognition and never let down his guard. She had tried to talk to him about his years in the army, but he politely changed the subject, asking her about the events in Freya Crags with every semblance of interest, when in fact she feared he cared for nothing.

"I roamed a great deal of the countryside," he said.

Which was no answer at all. Millicent shrank in disappointment.

Princess Clarice didn't appear noticeably discouraged. A small smile played around her lips, the kind of smile pretty women wore because they knew they were irresistible.

Millicent knew she herself was quite resistible. Witness her unhappy debut, as well as the years spent at parties conversing with elderly ladies in need of company. And witness, also, the years of desperate longing for Corey MacGown, the earl of Tardew, a man who barely knew her name.

Yet when Robert looked at Princess Clarice, something stirred in his face. Millicent was only a spinster, but she recognized interest when she saw it, and the beginnings of an unwilling thaw.

Now she watched with fascination as Princess Clarice again prodded at Robert. "My lord, I'm sure your adventures on the Peninsula were always heroic and your travels fascinating."

Millicent thought the princess was flattering him.

Princess Clarice continued. "Perhaps tonight you could regale us with your tales. What you did, who you saw . . . where you went."

With a shrewdness that boded ill for the princess and her queries, Robert said, "Perhaps you're asking because your kingdom is in that part of the world. Are you a princess of Portugal? Or Andalusia? Or Baminia? Or Serephinia? Or—"

With a laugh Princess Clarice held up a protesting hand. "I know and am related to most of the royal families all over Europe. I confess, I did wonder what you could tell me of them."

"You're very discreet about your own background." Robert sounded pleasant, but Millicent heard the steel in his tone.

If Princess Clarice heard the steel, she did a masterful job of ignoring it. "Revolution makes the role of princess not only difficult but dangerous."

"Yet you shout of your royalty in a town square," Robert said.

Princess Clarice smiled with her jaw tight. "I have to sell creams, and women do not try them without due reason. Knowing that they're wearing the same emulsions as the queens of old proves to be the enticement they cannot resist. So I take the chance and proclaim my title, then ride on to foil any abductors—or assassins."

"Convenient," Robert said.

"Necessary," Princess Clarice countered.

Again, that was no answer. This sparring between her brother and the princess fascinated Millicent. Millicent herself would never dare to thwart Robert on any matter. She had so looked forward to Robert's return, but after these few months of speaking to a courteous stranger whose smiles never reached his eyes, she had lost all hope of ever finding her beloved brother again.

Until today.

Princess Clarice had moved Robert out of his self-imposed exile and back toward humanity, so Millicent wanted Princess Clarice close under his nose, where he couldn't ignore her. Where the princess could bring that peculiar expression of pain and amazement to his usually impassive face.

He wore it now as he watched her ride.

In a move that dismissed him and brought Millicent into the conversation, Princess

Clarice turned to her. "Tell me about this ball you're planning."

With a pride Millicent didn't bother to subdue, she told Princess Clarice, "My brother is hosting a ball for Colonel Oscar Ogley."

"The war hero?" Princess Clarice sounded suitably impressed. As well she should be. Colonel Ogley's feats of derring-do had been reported in every newspaper. His name had been on every lip. His height, his handsome demeanor, his nobility, had been reported throughout the land, and it was rumored the Prince of Wales would confer upon him and his family a title commensurate with his valor. Colonel Ogley had even written a book, and Millicent owned it bound in the finest leather. It sat in a place of honor on her shelf. "Colonel Ogley is coming here?"

"He was my commanding officer on the Peninsula," Robert said. "Celebrating his return is the least I can do after his courageous acts."

Princess Clarice sounded impressed as she said, "What a coup for you to have him!"

Robert glanced down, a small smile playing about his mobile mouth.

Millicent knew what he thought. He thought that Colonel Ogley should realize the honor he was paid by the Hepburns. Gently she tried to convey that to the princess. "We're very pleased to have the colonel with us. This is the only ball he has agreed to attend in all of Scotland."

Even before the words were out of Millicent's mouth, Princess Clarice comprehended, and added, "Yes, and what a coup for Colonel Ogley to have the Hepburns honoring his return!"

Which proved Princess Clarice was very gracious and instinctively polite.

Millicent didn't know why Robert had insisted the princess come to stay at MacKenzie Manor, but she had dared to add her own, less imperious invitation to Robert's—and she found herself pleasantly surprised by Princess Clarice's reception. Usually, pretty women intimidated Millicent. Yet for all the princess's beauty, she was approachable and not at all condescending, and when she laughed at Millicent's small joke about Prudence . . . well, Millicent thought they could possibly be friends.

Except that Princess Clarice *was* a princess. Perhaps Millicent was being presumptuous in thinking they could ever have something in common.

Then Princess Clarice said, "Dear Lady Millicent, I would be frazzled at the thought of arranging such a grand ball! Please, you must tell me what I can do for you. I'll be glad to help where I can."

Before Millicent could thank her, Robert said, "Then be present."

Princess Clarice whipped her head around and said swiftly, "Impossible!"

As if she were watching a game of lawn tennis, Millicent looked back and forth between them, amazed at the sudden blaze of antagonism.

"I insist," he said.

"I don't attend balls," Princess Clarice retorted.

"You're a princess," he answered.

"Her Highness, Princess Peddler." Princess Clarice smiled, but with not quite so much amicability as before. "I fear you'll find most of your guests are willing to take my advice but not willing to socialize with me. I promise, my lord, I'm not offended."

Robert didn't give up. "But I will be if you don't attend."

The princess began to lose her composure. "I have no suitable gowns for a ball, and I have no intention—"

"Millicent will get one for you," he said.

"She most certainly will not," Princess Clarice said indignantly.

"She'll be delighted," Robert answered. "Won't you, Millicent?"

Startled to find herself the focus of two sets of eyes, Millicent stammered, "Aye. I can . . . I can easily find one of Prudence's gowns that will suit Princess Clarice. Unworn, I promise, Your Highness. I wouldn't insult you by suggesting you should wear someone's castoffs. Prudence has so many gowns, she'll never miss one."

The princess held out a hand toward Millicent. "You're very kind, and I thank you with all my heart. Please don't misunderstand"— her head whipped back around toward Robert—"but I don't take charity."

At once the sparks sprang to life again. "It won't be charity," he said. "It will be wages earned."

Without finesse Princess Clarice answered, "I'd rather have it in gold guineas."

"I'll pay you whatever you ask." He smiled like a sharp-toothed tiger. "Believe me, you'll earn every pence."

Even to Millicent that sounded like a threat against decency. "Robert!"

The already-high color in Princess Clarice's cheeks blossomed into a vivid pink, and she brought her horse to a halt before the great gates of MacKenzie Manor. "Perhaps I should clarify, my lord. I make people handsome. I'm very good at my trade, but it is my only mission. Regardless of the circumstances, regardless of the requirements, I do nothing that will compromise my reputation or my self-respect."

Robert brought his horse around, using Helios to block Princess Clarice's escape back down the road. "I spoke hastily and in an ill-judged manner. Princess Clarice, I have no designs on your royal self."

Millicent hoped he was lying.

"I'll do nothing to harm your reputation." He sounded and looked sincere.

"Peddlers don't have reputations"— Princess Clarice moved edgily in her saddle—"which is why I have such a care for mine."

Blaize turned restive at being confined, and when Robert shifted back to give the young stallion room, he slipped past Robert's confinement and onto the open road.

It had been, Millicent realized, a trick on Princess Clarice's part to free herself from

Robert's entrapment. The princess was a match for Robert. Now, if only he would rise from the mausoleum where he had entombed himself and seize her.

Certainly it seemed he would as he swiftly placed himself between her and the village. "Princess Clarice, you're unmarried, so I do excuse your wariness, but even if you don't believe me, think on this. With my two sisters in the house and carriage-loads of female relatives arriving, it would be unlikely that I could find the time or the place to seduce a guest, beautiful though she might be. And certainly not as honored a guest as you will be."

"The time? Perhaps not. The place?" Princess Clarice patted Blaize's neck. "The gossip in the village is that you live alone in a cottage."

He gave the princess no more explanation of his peculiar behavior than he had given Millicent and Prudence. "Since my return from the war, I desire privacy."

Oh, dear. If he wished to bring the princess around to his way of thinking, using that clipped tone of voice and that aloof expression was not the way to do it.

But for some reason, Princess Clarice seemed reassured. "Very well, I accept that your intentions are honorable—but I won't be a guest at your ball."

Without taking his gaze from the princess, he said, "Millicent, I wish you would ride ahead and prepare a bedchamber for the princess. The queen's bedchamber would be best. It's close to yours and Prue's, and that most honored showcase will demonstrate to our guests the esteem with which we hold our royal visitor."

He was getting rid of her. Millicent understood that, but she didn't trust him not to frighten Princess Clarice away, and Millicent wanted the princess to visit. She wanted a chance to see if they could be friends. Most of all, she wanted to know if Princess Clarice would continue to burrow under Robert's skin and bring him back to life.

So she sat there a moment too long, and Robert flicked a glance at her. "Millicent. Please."

That still-faced, cold-eyed soldier was back, replacing the man who showed signs of humanity, and she flinched. It hurt to see him so closed off. It hurt to know there was nothing she could do to reach him. It hurt that he reprimanded her in front of a princess, as if she were nothing to him.

Not his beloved sister, but merely a convenient housekeeper for his home. As she had been to her father. As she would be for the rest of her life. Her father had told her no one would ever care about her feelings. Her father was correct.

Hastily, before she dissolved in tears, she said, "Of course, brother. At once." Turning, she hastened toward home. Toward sanctuary.

Seven

A princess always takes care that her words are honeyed, for she may have to eat them.
—THE DOWAGER QUEEN OF BEAUMONTAGNE

Clarice watched Lady Millicent ride away and wished the woman showed a little more gumption—to stand up to her brother, and to stay as protection for Clarice.

Not that Clarice needed protection. She'd found herself in worse circumstances than these—really, what could Lord Hepburn do here on the road?—and gotten herself out.

But it would have been easier to have Millicent as a buffer. "You hurt her feelings."

"What?" Hepburn glanced after his sister. "Don't be ridiculous. Millicent is far too sensible to—"

"Have feelings?" she flashed. "Or too illvalued to dare show them?"

Typical male. He stared at her as if she were speaking a foreign language and said, "I'm sure Millicent knows her value at MacKenzie Manor."

"I'm sure she does too."

Now he stared at her as if he heard the irony, and puzzled over it. No doubt he would dismiss her comment as normal female blather while his sister withered away into the nothingness of cowed spinsterhood.

Clarice would have to do something about that. Millicent needed help, and Clarice needed to stay away from Lord Hepburn.

Because when all was said and done, he made her uncomfortable in a way no man had ever done before, and she suspected he had his ways of enforcing his will that would make her even more uncomfortable.

Yet when she braced herself and faced him, he said only, "Come." Turning, he rode up the shady, hilly tree-lined drive toward the house.

Clarice stared at his disappearing back, then looked around at the empty road. She could ride away right now. Hepburn was a sophisticated man. He wouldn't give chase . . . and even if she had overestimated his decorum, she and Blaize could outride him and that long-legged gelding he called Helios.

Probably.

But . . . she had Amy in Freya Crags, a vast need for cash, and the prospect of a robust salary if she would visit MacKenzie Manor. Hepburn was not a villain; nothing Amy had said gave her any such indication. Even if he gave Clarice a few rough moments, if he followed through on the promise in his blue eyes . . . well, she could handle him. She specialized in taking care of herself.

She turned Blaize's nose toward the drive and stopped.

Yet, obeying him now, following him now, made her feel much like a butterfly willfully fluttering into a very sticky web.

If she proceeded with this project, she would be even more careful than usual. She would be helpful to Millicent and sell her wares to the guests, immediately receiving their payment. If Hepburn stepped one toe out of line, she would tell a fib about assisting Mistress Dubb with her face cream, ride into Freya Crags, pick up Amy, and take flight. That was her plan, and it was a good one.

Tight-lipped and mindful, she started after him.

And as she crossed through the gates, she suffered an almost preternatural jolt, as if she'd traversed a threshold and she could never return to the place where she'd been before.

She almost turned back. She almost did. But the thought of trying to survive the coming winter here in Scotland without enough food or coal, and the magistrate in England who would hang her if he could, drove her on. And always at the back of her mind Beaumontagne shimmered like a silver vision, drawing her forward.

Shaking off her trepidation, she rode into a half-tamed wilderness where giant oaks shivered in the spring breeze, and azaleas bloomed in clumps of blazing pink and virgin white. The scent of pine drifted through the air, and the spicy perfume lifted Clarice's spirits and put heart into her.

She'd done more difficult things. If all went well, if Hepburn kept his promise of payment, she and Amy would be free to take passage back to Beaumontagne, slip into the country and find their grandmother, and help her overthrow the last rebels. Perhaps Grandmamma was growing old and feeble, and that was why she hadn't sent word for them to return. Perhaps she was trying to protect them from harm. She didn't realize the fragile girl-children she had sent away had grown into adults capable of so much more than needlework and dancing. This ordeal with Hepburn was one of the final challenges Clarice would have to overcome, she was sure of it.

When she caught up with him at the top of the rise, she had, once more, become a courageous, rational woman.

His black leather gauntlet pointed the way. "There it is. MacKenzie Manor."

Seen from the main road, the four-story monolith had made her draw back. Seen across a sweep of lawn, through lacy-leafed trees, the gray stone rose abruptly from the soft green grass. Harsh and imposing, it seemed less of a home and more of an edifice designed to awe and humble those who visited the mighty Hepburns. No ivy softened its harsh facade, no flowers grew along its foundation, no portico welcomed visitors. MacKenzie Manor eloquently spoke of wealth and prestige but said nothing of home and the gentle arts.

Once again the sense of being trapped overwhelmed her, and she glanced at the man beside her.

His appearance was as stark as his home. The sunshine dappled his visage, yet the gently moving flickers of light and shadow didn't soften the harsh, jutting contours of bone against skin. His hair had been tossed back from his face by the ride, dipped into a stark widow's peak, and framed his face without alleviating the austerity of his features. The ripple and redness of a burn scarred one side of his forehead, a burn that must have caused much agony.

Yet he seemed not to require compassion for himself, and nothing about him hinted at warmth or pride in MacKenzie Manor. Instead, he watched it with the cool proprietary air of one who possessed without affection.

Then he turned that same assessing gaze on her.

She should have run. She should have escaped down the road and never looked back.

Instead, now she couldn't tear her gaze away from his.

All her life she had watched as other people suffered from unfortunate and precipitous passions and wondered at them, for she was a princess. She practiced control with every motion, every smile, every emotion. Passion was for lesser beings, and she had always believed her breeding and her training provided immunity.

Yet now, as she faced this man, she recognized the stirrings of disorderly infatuation.

His voice was low, reasonable, and civilized. "Please, ma'am, be assured I hold you in the deepest respect. Yet I know that men are drawn to you, and I imagine a good number of them see no reason to restrain their baser desires. Since you're not protected by marriage or family, they believe you are fair game."

She nodded once stiffly. "A refined way of putting it."

"I have a great need for your services to entertain and . . . ah . . . make the ladies handsome, and I suspect you'll find this ball a fertile and profitable endeavor."

Ah, he *did* know what to say to entice her! "Yes, thank you, my lord. I have decided to remain and do as you require—as long as I may sell my creams to your guests." For while he might promise to pay her to stay, she knew better than to trust an aristocrat's generosity.

"Good. Good." He smiled that amused, patronizing smile that revealed he had never doubted she would yield to his will. "You may call me Robert."

Her hackles rose, and she answered without thinking what sort of restitution he would demand. "*You* may call me Your Highness."

"A privilege granted to few, I'm sure." With mocking deliberation he added, "Your Highness."

His tone made her all too aware she had stooped to a condescension as great as his. She, who was usually so glib, had been inept and autocratic.

His fault.

Then she heard her grandmother's voice in her head telling her that a true princess always took responsibility for her actions, and Clarice laid the blame where it belonged. On herself. *I shall have to try harder.* A lump of pride formed in her throat. "Actually, since I'm not in my own country, I encourage people to call me, as you have, *ma'am,* or Princess Clarice, or even *my lady.*" Never had words been harder to force out.

Dreadful! That sounded even worse than before.

But he pretended to be grateful when all the while his eyes glinted in that cynical manner that made her want to give in to yet another ungracious response—and slap him. "Thank you, but if you're to attend my ball as a princess of the realm, whatever realm that is—"

She gritted her teeth.

"—and lend me countenance, I feel I must give you the full weight of respect for your office." Once again he smiled, a smile as sharp as a rapier. "Your Highness."

She had known him only a few hours, but already she had come to hate that smile. "I *cannot* attend your ball."

He ignored her as if she'd never even spoken. "In return for your services, I promise that you'll be protected from those ignominious men, your reputation will be polished to a shine, and when all is said and done, you'll have enough money to immediately return to your 'kingdom,' should you desire, or stay here and live well for the rest of your life."

He must be a devil to correctly read her desires. But she had to object. "To attend the ball given for so great a hero as Colonel Ogley would bring on me an attention that could be dangerous."

"I'll keep you safe."

That voice. Those words. This proved he was a devil, for all these last lonely, difficult years, she'd dreamed of a man saying that to her.

Worse, she must be a fool, for she believed him. "You're promising a great deal."

"I am. I always keep my promises." Leaning far out of the saddle, he took her hand and squeezed it. "But in return you'll do as I require."

"Before I agree to that, you'll tell me everything you wish me to do."

"When the time comes." Lifting her hand to his mouth, he kissed her glove.

That circumspect salute through a covering of leather should have felt less seductive than the kiss he had earlier pressed on her bare hand.

If anything, it was *more* seductive. It brought to mind a whole scope of dissipations involving the slow strip of her leather glove from her fingers. The removal of all her clothes from her body. His lips moving everywhere on pale skin and sensitive nerves.

She yanked her hand back.

She didn't comprehend why he wanted her at his ball, but she did know he desired her body, and demonstrated his need boldly. He watched her with those glorious blue eyes and managed to convey both aggression and passion. And she . . . she wanted both to skitter away and move closer.

The man was a sensual weapon.

"Please tell me what it is you want of me." That was too blunt and sounded vaguely . . . well, it sounded like a question a courtesan would ask.

He knew it too, for he smiled at her. Smiled in a way that had her once again think about the open road and how easy it would be to ride away and never look back.

"It would be easier if you spelled out the duties you want me to assume as your resident beauty maker."

He still smiled and, of course, answered evasively. "For now you have only to be kind to Millicent, be patient with Prudence, and handle my relatives, who are descending on us even as we speak. Keep the girl-cousins entertained. There are scores of them, and when the lasses giggle in that high-pitched tone, they can shatter glass."

"You aren't being completely honest with me."

"When the time comes, I'll let you know what I require of you." He looked deep into her eyes, so deep she wanted to protect the dim, almost forgotten corners of her soul. Softly he repeated, "When the time comes."

Eight

Never smile. It causes smile lines.
—THE DOWAGER QUEEN OF BEAUMONTAGNE

Hepburn hadn't been exaggerating. He did have a lot of girl-cousins. And girlfriends of those cousins, and girlfriends of his sisters, and kin so distantly related, the kinship couldn't be explained with a single breath. All of those girls had mothers, and all of them had arrived that afternoon to prepare for the ball honoring the renowned hero Colonel Ogley—and to prepare for their debuts.

Wisely their fathers and brothers had gone fishing.

Clarice sat a little apart, sipped her tea, and gazed across the huge dressing room filled with ruffles and bows, beads and feathers. She listened to the clink of cups and the sound of female conversation, watched as the girls pounced on the teatime sandwiches and cakes, and found herself relaxing about Hepburn's intentions. Because he really did need her to entertain, assist, and organize.

Hepburn's sister Prudence was useless. A pretty, curvaceous blonde of seventeen, she fit right into the giggling, shrieking crowd of young women.

Nor was Millicent of any aid. Since the girls and their mothers saw no reason to respect a plain, unassuming, and unmarried lady, they ran rampant over Millicent's suggestions and pleas.

Now Clarice watched as Millicent stepped over mounds of shoes, separated two of the girls who were loudly disputing the ownership of a bonnet, and pressed a handkerchief into Miss Symlen's hand so she could wipe her incipient tears. While she paused, Lady Blackston roundly informed her that the menus needed to be planned this minute. This minute!

When at last Millicent arrived at the place

where Clarice sat a little apart from the others, Clarice said in a mock-haughty tone, "You have been remarkably lax about planning this ball. It's a good thing your relatives have descended on you en masse or you would never have it done in time."

Millicent sagged against the wall and laughed hollowly. "But Lady Blackston's right. I should have the dinner planned by now."

"Silly you, not to realize they would arrive four days early." Clarice pressed a cup of tea into Millicent's hands and a plate filled with lemon cakes. "Now sit down and drink your tea."

Millicent dropped into the chair beside her and laughed a little more naturally. "Yes. Silly me."

Clarice scanned the crowd. She'd already memorized most of the names.

There was Lady White, an austere woman whose daughter, the thoughtful Lady Lorraine, watched the proceedings with calm interest.

Mrs. Symlen's gracious smile hid a smug determination to place her sixteen-year-old daughter, Miss Georgia Symlen, into society and marriage long before that immature child was ready to leave the classroom.

Miss Diantha Erembourg, plain and sulky, was there without a parent; her mother was in Italy, touring with her second husband, and her grandmother, old Lady Mercer, chaperoned four granddaughters, including Diantha.

Beautiful Mrs. Trumbull was outshone only by her daughter, Miss Larissa Trumbull, a type of female Clarice recognized and did not like. Larissa was pale and willowy, with shining black hair and large doelike brown eyes that she could widen to attract the gentlemen or narrow to frighten off any competitors. She would be the belle of the ball no matter how many bodies she had to step on on the way, and Machiavelli himself could not outmaneuver her.

And there were more. So many more.

"Are these all of the ladies," Clarice asked, "or will more arrive on the morrow?"

Millicent sipped her tea and ate one of the cakes, then with a little more composure said quietly, "I believe we're missing only Lady Barnelby and her five daughters, but what difference will six more make?"

"What difference, indeed? So I shall entertain them tonight."

Millicent blew her straggling hair out of her

eyes. "That would be wonderful. So I can . . . I can plan that dinner with Cook!"

"If there's one thing I know, it's how to capture the attention of vain young girls." Clarice scanned the matrons who sat, heads together, in the middle of the room. "And their aging mothers."

Millicent glanced at the older ladies too, and lowered her voice yet further. "They haven't spoken to you yet. They're leaving you strictly alone, but they're eyeing you. Will they plague you, do you suppose?"

"No." Clarice sounded, and was, sure of herself. "They haven't made up their minds about me yet."

"I told them you were a princess."

"I know." Clarice had noted the sideways glances, heard the hissed whispers. "The young girls want to believe it. The older ladies doubt my word. Even if I told them the name of my country, they would have reservations. It's not until they speak with me and learn what I can teach them, that they will begin to believe, too."

As if she were ashamed to repeat the accusation, Millicent whispered, "Lady Blackston said she went to a house party and met another woman who claimed to be a princess, and in the morning, the woman had stolen everyone's reticule."

"I have never yet stolen anyone's reticule. When they use my royal creams, they freely open their reticules to me. Don't worry, Lady Millicent, before the evening's out I'll have them feeding from my palms."

Millicent gave a sigh of relief—and admiration. "I wish I could emulate your confidence."

"You can." Clarice patted Millicent's arm. "Before the ball you shall."

"Oh." Shaking her head, Millicent stood up as if putting distance between her and Clarice would help. "No, not me. You must save your magic for the youthful girls who will win every heart."

"But then it's not magic, is it?" Clarice smiled. "You don't want to hurt my feelings by refusing my services."

Millicent gave a nervous snort. "You jest."

"Not at all. I like to help my friends."

"I . . . well, thank you." Millicent looked flustered, pleased, and dismayed. "I had hoped . . . I mean, I thought perhaps we could be—"

"Friends?" Clarice said warmly. "I think we already are."

"Yes. I think we are too." Millicent smiled,

a slow, beautiful smile quite unlike her brother's derisive grimace. "But don't waste your valuable time on me. If you'll entertain these women tonight, that would be kindness aplenty. I don't know what I would do without you." As if she could scarcely wait to escape, she fled the room.

Clarice clapped her hands. No one paid a bit of attention. The girls continued to tumble over each other like anxious puppies, wrapping themselves in shawls and trying ever more ridiculous hairstyles. Their mothers saw no need to award their consideration to a woman who claimed to be a princess from some unknown country, and continued with their conversations.

Lifting her teacup, Clarice tapped it with her spoon until she had captured some of the younger girls' attention. "Ladies, we shall make our way to the conservatory, where I'll show you some activities to make yourself look fresh even after dancing the night away, and tell you about the newest styles from Paris."

The girls stared at Clarice like frogs being lured to a new lily pad.

"Many of you are tanned from your travels." Clarice was careful not to allow her gaze to rest on any face in particular. "I have an unguent that will help remove those stains."

Like offended cats, the mothers sat straighter.

Clarice played her trump card. "But first I'll show you how to clear your complexion and hide the freckles on your noses."

The shriek of rapture that rose from every throat made Clarice flinch and take a step toward the door.

Hepburn was right. Their high-pitched voices and the scent of their perfumes could easily drive a sane man to madness—and uneasily Clarice remembered that Hepburn's sanity had been already been called into question.

But she thought him quite sane. Probably. Only ruthless and . . . dynamic.

And she thought about him far too much for a man she'd met that very day.

Tearing her mind away from contemplation of him, she glanced at the clock on the mantel. In ringing tones she said, "I shall see you in the conservatory at seven o'clock." Slowly and carefully she articulated, "In the conservatory at seven o'clock. Did everyone hear me?"

"In the conservatory at seven o'clock," a few of the younger ladies repeated.

Most of them, Clarice knew, would be late, but they would be there. The sum total of the girls' ambition was to be just like everyone else. Vaguely Clarice remembered a time when she wanted nothing more than the anonymity of being normal too. Now she just wanted to make it through the next week without being hung by her neck until dead— and without spending more time in Hepburn's company.

Slipping from the room, she strolled toward the conservatory and spoke to the first footman she encountered. "Greetings, my good man. May I inquire as to your name?"

"Ma'am? Um, Your Highness? I'm . . . um . . ." The red-cheeked lad couldn't have been more than sixteen, and as his stocking slid down his skinny, hairy leg, he tugged it back up and stuck it beneath his powder-blue breeches. "I'm Norval."

"Norval." She committed his name to memory. Whatever home she visited, she always made sure the servants liked her and wished to do her bidding. One never knew when one might need a fire made up—or to make a fast escape. "I need to have the candles in the conservatory lit, and, Norval, I think you are the man to help me."

"Of course, Your Highness. I am, Your Highness." He beamed so much, she considered using him for illumination.

"Thank you, Norval. I knew I could depend on you." With a smile she walked down the corridor and into the conservatory.

Her casual air comprised part of her confident masquerade, one she always cultivated. She was gracious and made everyone around her feel at ease, and drew the Millicents of the world out of their shells.

Beauty was easy so much of the time. If a woman thought she was beautiful, and smiled and was gracious, she became beautiful. It was all a trick, one that Clarice knew well, one she would impart tonight to those who would listen.

She looked with satisfaction at the conservatory, easily the most welcoming room in MacKenzie Manor. The sun had not yet set, and golden light filled the glass-enclosed chamber. Violets and pinks bloomed together in small pots, while in larger pots pink damask roses grew over short trellises. A dwarf peach tree had been trained flat against the wall, and its espaliered limbs bore small green fruit.

The servants had already placed sofas and chairs in among the flowers, facing the table that Clarice had covered with a lace cloth and with balms and creams, hairpins and swaths of cloth. Now Norval entered with three more footmen, and swiftly they lit the candles set around the room. Before she had finished with the ladies, she would need the light, and the gentle illumination would make her task easier. A woman never looked so fair as by the light of a gently glowing candle.

She thanked each one of the footmen, noting that Norval was easily the youngest footman and therefore the most malleable—important, should she have to leave MacKenzie Manor without Hepburn's sanction.

Humming, she arranged the jars. She had done this presentation at least a hundred times, before ladies and peasants alike, yet whenever she picked a girl out of the crowd and fixed her hair and clothes, made her sit up straight and smile, Clarice saw hope blossom on a young face.

Amy thought they did nothing but bilk their patrons out of their money. Amy pointed to the times they'd had to leave town just ahead of the lynch mob. But Clarice knew that for some of those girls her instruction made them see themselves in a new light, and perhaps changed their lives.

She would do it again this evening. She had already picked out the lucky lass. Miss Diantha Erembourg flounced and sulked, wore the wrong color and the wrong hairstyle. Tonight she would be transformed into a lovely lady—and tomorrow she would buy every ointment Clarice offered her.

Down the corridor Clarice heard the hum of voices and the tap of footsteps. They were coming, filing into the conservatory and jockeying for the best position in the room. She waited until most of them had seated themselves, then used the line that always caught their attention. "I can cure your spots. I can dress your hair. I can tell you about the fashions that are au courant. But why bother with such prosaic transformations, when I can make you beautiful?"

Lady Mercer, outspoken, deaf, and seventy, brayed, "Can you make me beautiful?"

"More beautiful," Clarice corrected her.

Lady Mercer subsided with a "Humph!" and a half-smile.

Clarice loved women like Lady Mercer. She was plump, wrinkled, and soft-looking, an appearance totally at odds with her sharp tongue and razor wit. She was a force to be reckoned with, a woman who wore the newest styles and never tolerated fools. Her observations would keep Clarice on her toes and, more significantly, everyone interested in the presentation. Indicating Lady Mercer, Clarice said, "She knows the most important element of beauty."

The young girls turned to gaze incredulously at the old woman.

"What?" young Lady Robertson inelegantly asked.

"A smile," Clarice told her. "Any man will look twice at a lady who smiles as if she knows the secret of being a real woman."

"I ought to know the secret. I've been married four times," Lady Mercer snapped, but at the same time she blushed so brightly, the rouge on her cheeks disappeared into the influx of color.

The girls leaned their heads together and tittered.

"So first we must practice our smiles." Clarice gestured, bringing their eyes front. "Smile now. Smile as if your dearest love stood before you."

Instead, they froze in place, expressions

of dismay, pleasure, and infatuation on their faces. Then, as one, they smiled, stunning, tempting smiles of melting charm.

Turning, she saw why.

Lord Hepburn stood in the doorway.

Nine

Never frown. It causes frown lines.
—THE DOWAGER QUEEN OF BEAUMONTAGNE

Lord Hepburn wore a gentleman's casual dark blue jacket with a waistcoat and trousers of tan that accentuated his height. His black hair feathered over his forehead and fell around his ears, a shining, barbaric fall. His rough hands flexed at his sides like restless weapons. His face, with its hooked nose, broad chin, and intense eyes, reminded her of a painting she'd once seen of an ancient warrior. A ruthless warrior. A conquering warrior.

Clarice's heart gave a hard thump, then began a rapid race.

Why had she given in to temptation and come to his home? How could she have imagined she could outwit him? All the money in the world couldn't save her from him if he decided to take her.

Her palms grew damp, and she hoped desperately that he didn't plan to stay. Foolish even to think he might, but he made her nervous. She, Princess Clarice, the woman who could speak to any group with confidence.

In her loud tones Lady Mercer said, "Damn, that's one handsome man!"

He seemed not to have heard her. His gaze swept the girls in the rainbow of colorful gowns seated daintily throughout the room. He bowed at them all—and the gust of romantically inspired sighs almost knocked Clarice over.

In an elaborate display of obeisance he then bowed to Clarice. "Your Highness, tonight, when you have a free moment, may I have the pleasure of your company?"

Clarice heard a small hiss; Lady Blackston didn't approve of Lord Hepburn visiting with the princess.

He seemed not to hear but continued. "My

sister and I wish to consult with you on how to make this ball a truly majestic occasion."

From the crowd, Clarice heard an "Aha." So it was all right for her to spend time with Hepburn as long as they discussed the business of the ball—and as long as Millicent chaperoned them.

"Of course, Lord Hepburn." Clarice spoke as formally, as if she were addressing King George himself. "I'm delighted to give you the benefit of my experience."

He inclined his head and bowed again. He must have padded shoulders beneath that jacket. No man could have shoulders that broad. "I thank you."

The older women were eyeing them critically, as if watching for the real truth about Clarice, and Clarice was careful to turn away from him, as if she gave him not a second thought.

Which she didn't. Shouldn't. She should concentrate on selling her creams to the largest, most affluent audience she'd ever faced.

Speaking to Miss Erembourg, Clarice touched the chair she had placed to face the audience. "I shall need a volunteer whom I can make beautiful."

"I have a better idea. Why don't you make him beautiful?" young Larissa called out, and pointed to Lord Hepburn.

Everyone broke into giggles.

Clarice laughed too, relieved to be able to behave naturally. "Lord Hepburn is already beautiful enough."

He solemnly accepted the tribute.

But spoiled, pretty Larissa wasn't about to give up. "His skin is tanned by the sun. You promised you'd show us how to remove the sun's marks."

Prudence clapped her hands. "Yes, yes, make my brother beautiful."

Clarice's hand itched to smack her. The child really did need a restraining hand—or at least the sense God gave a turnip.

"If you made him beautiful, that would be a true testament to your abilities," Lady White intoned.

Lady Mercer sat back with her arms crossed and a smirk on her face. She was enjoying this far too much.

The chortling grew in intensity as Clarice shook her head. "Lord Hepburn would not agree to sit still while I smeared him with cream." She hazarded a glance at him.

His cheek was creased as if he fought a

smile. Lifting the fringe of hair that hung over his forehead, he revealed the burned and reddened pucker that marred his brow. "Can you remove this scar from my face?"

The room grew quiet.

What was he doing? And why was he doing it? He acted as if he were considering this absurdity! "I can't remove it. I can conceal it."

"Very well." He seated himself on the chair she'd placed for Miss Erembourg. "Conceal it. Make me beautiful, and I vow every one of my relatives will indulge in your goods."

Clarice saw mesmerized women nod, and knew it was true. Having the earl of Hepburn seated in her chair, submitting himself to her ministrations, bettered any feat of showmanship she could have dreamed up.

But . . . *but*. She would have to *touch* him. Touch his face. Stroke his skin. Study him intently and then touch him some more.

She didn't want to do it. She could scarcely look at him with equanimity, much less caress him as she would a . . . a loved one.

Yet, as she viewed the anticipatory smiles on every face, she knew when she was trapped. The ladies wanted to see her do this. They wanted to see her fail.

So she would have to succeed. Donning

the smile she always kept ready, she said, "Then, of course, I'll make you beautiful." First she had to push his hair away from his face. An easy task, yet her fingers skimmed his mane, not equal to the task of testing the strands and discovering if they were truly as silky as they looked.

The silence in the room was deafening when she at last sank her fingers into the dark mass. It felt warm, alive with vitality—and contrary as she tried to push it off his forehead and it repeatedly fell back down. Making an exasperated sound, she reached for the yellow ribbon she'd set out on the table.

Miss Symlen broke the silence. "Have you ever worked on a man before?"

"Yes, but I can't tell you who." Clarice walked behind Hepburn, scooped up the length of his hair, and secured it with the ribbon. Then she smiled at the older women, inviting them to share the joke. "Men are as vain as women, but they don't like it known."

The ladies looked between Clarice and Hepburn as if wondering if they dared give way to merriment.

Then Hepburn chuckled deeply, and everyone else laughed too.

Stepping away, Clarice looked at him.

Hepburn should have appeared foolish, sitting in a room full of women with a ribbon tied in his hair.

He did not. Instead, with his hair back, he sported a stark appeal that riveted the ladies.

Didn't the other women see how imposing he was? How dangerous? It was a rare man who would place himself in such a position without having his masculinity threatened, but there was never any question of that. Instead, he imposed the straitening bonds of masculinity on the completely feminine gathering in a way that frightened Clarice—and Clarice didn't frighten easily.

Hurriedly she turned to her table, opened a jar, and dipped in her fingers. Taking a fortifying breath, she returned to Hepburn and dabbed the pale unguent on his cheeks, his chin, his nose, and forehead. Speaking to the audience, she said, "You don't need to apply much of my royal secret complexion cream. It takes only a dab to freshen the complexion in a marvelous way. You'll note the red patch here"—she pointed to his jaw—"where Lord Hepburn's valet scraped the skin while shaving." She dabbed the unguent there. "The cream will take the sting away and heal the injury. In truth, when they shave every day, men need this more than ladies." She pulled a long face. "But I wish you luck in convincing any man to care for his face in such a manner! Any man except Beau Brummell anyway." Making sure everyone in the room could see her motions, she rubbed the unguent in circles all over Hepburn's face.

He sat docile under her ministrations, but irresistibly she was swept back to her childhood when a traveling menagerie had come to the palace. She'd begged to pet the lion, and her father had allowed her. The lion had purred and stretched, but beneath her palms she'd felt the strength of its muscles. She'd seen the length of its claws, and when it had turned its head and stared at her, she had perceived a wildness that no bars could contain.

Grandmamma had discovered her and quickly removed her from the cage, but that wildness had called to her soul.

So it was with Hepburn. He was gloriously perilous and wild, and something about him called to her.

The heat of his skin burned her fingertips, and in his eyes she saw a dark stillness that hid his thoughts. Hid his soul.

"There!" she heard herself say brightly as

she wrenched her gaze away. "That's the first step, and for most men the only step that's needed. But since Lord Hepburn asked that I cover his scar, an infinitesimal mark that only adds to his cachet as a soldier and a hero—"

The ladies gave a murmur of approval and a small round of applause.

"—I'll also need to use a little of the royal secret color emulsion." Clarice moved to her table and selected a smaller jar from among the lineup. "How does that feel, Lord Hepburn?" She didn't look at him as she asked.

"Very refreshing, and I enjoy the scent."

She heard the mockery in his tone; he was playing to the crowd, selling her products, as he had promised.

Miss Larissa Trumbull came gracefully to her feet. "Might I smell the cream?"

"Of course." Clarice extended the jar, but Larissa walked past as if Clarice weren't even there. She strode to Hepburn, leaned close to him, close enough for him to see down her considerable décolletage, and took a long breath. "Ummm." She made a noise that sounded like a moan.

The other girls watched her enviously. Her mother smiled enigmatically, obviously proud that her daughter had taken the lead. Two of the other mothers put their heads together and buzzed like angry bees, but everyone in the room now knew that Larissa had made plans to capture the oh-so-eligible Lord Hepburn.

The *minx.*

The fool. Clarice's gaze swept the chamber. She saw adoring gazes and once again heard infatuated sighs. Most of these young women were on the hunt—for Hepburn. They were all fools!

"So, Miss Trumbull, you concur?" She put the jar down with a snap. "The scent is refreshing."

"Very refreshing." Larissa slowly straightened up, allowing Hepburn another chance to view her figure through the diaphanous folds of her gown.

"Let me smell it too!" Miss Georgia Symlen leaped to her feet.

"And me!" young Lady Tessa Cutteridge followed.

Hepburn held up his hands. "If I might make a suggestion? Princess Clarice will give everyone a private demonstration of her wares later. Isn't that right, Your Highness?"

Clarice smiled tightly. "I will indeed. Later

this evening and tomorrow, and indeed I'll be available at any time in case you have questions."

"Oh, all right." Georgia sulkily subsided.

Larissa tossed her head, then slowly and with a great swaying of hips, she made her way back toward her chair. It was a performance worthy of a stage actress, one intended to crush her rivals and inflame Hepburn.

Clarice decided to not to wait for the grand finale but started speaking again. "As we let the royal secret complexion cream soak into Lord Hepburn's face, I'll explain how to use the royal secret color emulsion." She showed them the contents of the tiny jar. "These emulsions are tinted to match your skin tone and cover any marks that aren't part of your normal, smooth, lovely skin."

"You mean . . . that's an enhancement?" Mrs. Trumbull lifted her plucked eyebrows in horror. "You can't tell these proper young ladies to wear the mask of a slut! Their youth must be their only cosmetic."

Clarice did her imitation of *shocked* very well. "Enhancement? Not at all. I would never suggest that a girl or any lady use anything to alter her natural beauty." Now she slipped into her sincere mask. "But is it fair that a girl go to her first ball and face the scrutiny of every eligible gentleman, and be labeled a wallflower because that day she has a blemish right on the end of her nose?" Clarice wrinkled her own nose, and with a clean handkerchief wiped the extra cream off Hepburn's face.

He watched her knowingly. He knew what she was doing—playing the crowd like an angler with a fish.

Clarice ignored him as well as she could, which wasn't well at all, since she was touching him, looking at him, taking care to leave only the slightest hint of moisture on his face and knowing that that would smooth out the lines sun and weather had driven deep. "I don't know about any of you, but it seems that whenever I'm faced with a most important event, such as a ball, the end of my nose develops a spot."

The young girls laughed nervously, and a few touched the marks on their faces.

Clarice didn't give anyone time to think, she kept talking. "I personally believe a woman should be judged for her beauty and wit, not a momentary blemish—especially since blemishes always seem to arise on the very night of a young lady's debut."

Heads nodded in unison. Almost everyone had faced such a crisis.

But Mrs. Trumbull said, "I cannot agree. If a girl can't control herself enough to maintain a smooth complexion, how will she ever be able to manage a household and keep her husband's interest?"

The heads stopped nodding. No one agreed except the fabulous Larissa, but they didn't dare say so. Mrs. Trumbull was spouting the generally accepted nonsense among the ton—that every young debutante should be made to face the scrutiny of every gentleman without refuge of any kind. It was just that kind of cruelty that drove so many girls into spinsterhood.

Before Clarice could begin her standard reply, Hepburn drawled, "I can't imagine what difference wearing a dab of colored cream could make to a woman's efficiency. I think you'll find, Mrs. Trumbull, that men are not so irrational as to think their wives should be chosen by their control over their complexion."

At the affronted look on Mrs. Trumbull's face, Clarice could scarcely hold back her gurgle of laughter. And from the expressions around the room, she thought others were also struggling, for Mrs. Trumbull didn't dare disagree with the honored Lord Hepburn.

Larissa smiled and turned on Mrs. Trumbull. "Lord Hepburn is so wise, don't you think, Mother?"

Recovering herself, Mrs. Trumbull said, "Why, yes, daughter. He exudes a unique opinion."

A few moist, merry explosions occurred toward the back of the room, and hastily Clarice said, "The royal secret color emulsion is like a bonnet or a gown. Not handsome in itself, but requiring a fresh young lady to give it life." Turning back to the table, she picked up the darkest tint she had, ascertained it matched his skin, then quickly dabbed it on his scar.

Hepburn watched her, his scrutiny so searching, it seemed he wished to strip off not her clothing, but her masks.

Her fingers trembled slightly as she dabbed and smoothed the scarred ripples on his forehead. "Most women close their eyes at this point," she said softly to him.

"Most women aren't interested in the splendor before their faces," he answered.

Sharply she turned away from him toward the crowd, and with her finger indicated the scar area. "See how the redness disappears with just the slightest application?"

"It's very soothing," he said in a tone of wonder. "Not heavy or greasy."

He was a good model. He said the right things, he gave her credibility and respectability—and she couldn't wait to get him away from her. Quickly she finished her application, using all the considerable skill at her disposal, then stepped away and gestured. "There. You see how royal secret creams don't change a face, but merely subtly put the finishing touch on a handsome countenance."

The ladies applauded and murmured politely.

"Thank you, Princess Clarice." Hepburn stood up and bowed to her, then to the crowd. "Now I'll leave you to more feminine demonstrations."

She curtsied in return. "Thank you, Lord Hepburn, for your patience. No other man would have been so kind." It was true—and how she hated it!

Busily, so she didn't have to look at him again, she arranged the jars on her table.

He walked past her toward the door.

She relaxed.

As if pulled up by a thought, he stopped. "Mrs. Trumbull, you're a matron of great expertise in the matter of propriety. May I ask you a question?"

Mrs. Trumbull cast a triumphant glance at the other ladies. "Of course, my lord, I'm glad to help."

"Suppose a guest arrives in your home in time for a ball, and that guest is everything that's noble, gracious, and honored, but has fallen upon ill fortune."

Clarice tensed. *No. He wouldn't dare.*

He concluded, "Should this guest be invited to mingle among the other guests?"

Mrs. Trumbull cleared her throat in pompous keenness. "An Englishman, or in your case, Lord Hepburn, an unusually illustrious Scotsman, must always welcome those of like ilk into their home, especially if they've fallen on bad times. It's the only Christian thing to do."

Hepburn nodded weightily. "So I thought. And it would be churlish of this guest to refuse to participate in such a social event, would it not?"

Clarice clutched a jar to her chest and wished she could throw it at him.

"That would be an indication of false pride.

Understandable, but the good host would find a way to make the guest feel at ease." Mrs. Trumbull's eyes gleamed with the craving for gossip. "My lord, what would be the moniker of this gentleman?"

"Gentleman?" Hepburn blinked in simulated astonishment. "Not a gentleman at all! It is our own Princess Clarice who is so modest she refuses my invitation to the ball."

Thump! Larissa's elbow hit her mother's ribs.

Mrs. Trumbull flinched. She stammered, "But . . . she . . . Princess Clarice . . ."

"I agree," Hepburn said. "Princess Clarice is more noble than anyone who is attending my ball. Her exile is shameful, and her presence is necessary. Yet she's shy and so fears to presume, she has begged to retire rather than attend. But, Mrs. Trumbull, your kind reception to her has undoubtedly changed her mind."

Every eye focused on Clarice.

"Jolly!" Prudence clapped her hands. She elbowed her friends and nodded at the fuming Larissa.

Miss Diantha Erembourg took her cue immediately. "Yes, jolly, indeed, Princess Clarice! We do so want you to come."

One of her cousins, Lady Alice Igglesworth,

followed suit. "It wouldn't be fun without you, Your Highness. Say you'll be there."

"See, Princess Clarice?" Hepburn spread his hands to indicate their audience. "All of your worries were for nothing."

Clarice didn't dare look at him for fear he would be smirking in revolting triumph. With an incline of her head she said, "Thank you for your generous welcome. Of course I'll attend. I'm . . . honored to attend."

Taking her hand, he kissed her fingers. He wasn't smirking. He was serious and intent. In a low tone he said, "Your Highness, remember this. I will have my way."

Ten

The road t' hell is paved with guid inten-
   tions,
so ye might as well supply a few bricks.
                    —THE OLD MEN OF FREYA CRAGS

In the twilight of a Scottish spring Robert stared at the letter in his hand. He had read the flagrantly scrawled script many times, yet still he could scarcely comprehend its message.

I send to you good tidings. I have married. The stain of my disgrace is washed away by Holy Mother Church, and my child now has a father. But My Beloved wishes me to remain at his side here in Spain, and so I cannot travel to your barbaric Scotland and do your bidding. . . .

To have come so close, and to be thwarted now!

Robert struck his fist against the surface of the desk, then cursed the pain he had caused himself. Fury would avail him nothing. This problem required cold, ruthless planning—and his scheme qualified as both.

As the clock struck nine, he heard the patter of feet down the corridor toward Millicent's drawing room. Hastily he folded the letter and tucked it in his jacket.

He heard Millicent speaking, Princess Clarice's faintly accented reply, and . . . oh, no. His younger sister's voice.

Prudence was tagging along.

He had invited Millicent. Millicent was a sensible woman. Her behavior in any situation could be accurately predicted.

He had invited Princess Clarice. He needed Princess Clarice. Needed her for his plan to work. Needed to ascertain her skills and coax her, if possible, or blackmail her, if necessary, to do his bidding.

But Prudence was like a midge, randomly buzzing from place to place, causing such irritation, he wanted to swat her. Yet if he did, he knew very well she would dissolve into such a wailing, he would pay for the next month, and mayhap forever.

Besides, he was not their father, and he would not indulge in the malicious acts and words that had so scarred the family.

He was not his father.

As the ladies stepped in, he stood and bowed with perfect civility to each.

Holding out her hands, Millicent came across and embraced him so gingerly, it was as if she feared he *was* his father. "Robert, this is so good of you to take an interest in our ball."

"The Hero of the Peninsula is gracing our house with his presence even as my dear younger sister"—he leaned down and accepted Prudence's enthusiastic buss on the cheek—"makes her bow in society. I can think of nothing I would rather do more than to assist in every way possible." He glanced up to see if his professions of devotion impressed Princess Clarice.

Apparently not, for she stood with her hands folded demurely before her and a suspicious pucker to her lips. A pucker that smoothed as soon as she realized his gaze was on her.

"Is your scar still hidden?" Prudence lifted his bangs. "It is! Princess Clarice is very clever. She's been selling jars of royal secret creams and royal secret unguents ever since you left!"

"And the royal secret color emulsion too, I'll wager." Again he glanced at Princess Clarice.

Why did she not trust in his professions of affection? His sisters believed him. Had Millicent even realized that the years of war, violence, and betrayal had dragged him into a dark and unbearable pit? No, she didn't. She thought all was well because he took care that it seemed well.

"No, no one has the audacity to buy it from her." Prudence stuck out her bottom lip. "I wanted some to cover my freckles, but when you had left, Mrs. Trumbull started whispering again about strumpets and girls who had spots as divine punishment."

He had loved his sisters once. Distantly he thought that somewhere the emotion still lurked in him. But he couldn't *feel* it, and so love and all the attendant anxieties and joys were dead to him.

Yet he put on a good show. Why didn't Princess Clarice believe the proof before her eyes?

And why was he so sure she didn't believe it?

Prudence continued. "No one dares to thwart that beastly woman."

"It's of no concern. I predict I'll be called to visit almost everyone in the privacy of their bedchambers." Princess Clarice's eyes twinkled. "No one knows what happens within."

She was such an interesting female: wise about human nature and at the same time accepting of their foibles. She saw humor where Robert saw hypocrisy—but of course, she was a hypocrite too. A trickster. A peddler of dreams. "What fascinating creatures women are," he said.

"We are," Prudence proclaimed pretentiously.

"At least we like to think so," Princess Clarice stage-whispered.

Millicent chuckled.

Robert stared at his sister in surprise. The years he'd been gone had placed a dull sheen over Millicent and her personality.

She'd never been a pretty woman, but now she looked tired all the time, as if the perpetuity of dealing with their father had aged her. Robert blamed their father's relentless displeasure. He blamed himself for leaving her alone. Yet what choice had there been?

But under Princess Clarice's care, Millicent seemed happier and more secure.

Or perhaps her transformation was due less to Princess Clarice's company than to Princess Clarice's arts. He examined Millicent's face in the candlelight. She didn't look noticeably different.

Seeing the chance to draw Princess Clarice out, he said, "So, Your Highness, you'll be transforming every lady into a belle."

"Some ladies need more transforming than others." Prudence tittered. "Like Mrs. Trumbull. You couldn't possibly make her appealing to all the men. The gentlemen say she's a wolverine."

"Prudence. That is no sentiment for a lass!" But Millicent's voice was unsteady, as if she wanted to laugh.

Prudence flounced at the reproof. "It's true. You know it is, Millie. You've heard the gentlemen talking. You told me you had."

Millicent pleated her handkerchief. "I didn't mean for you to *inform* anyone."

"This isn't *anyone.* This is Robert and Princess Clarice. They don't mind"—Prudence swung from one to the other—"do you?"

"I find gossip endlessly fascinating and enlightening," Princess Clarice admitted. "However, repeating Lady Millicent's observation could hurt her socially. I don't think you'd like that, Prue."

Not noticeably chastened, Prudence said, "No! I wouldn't, and I won't repeat it again—but it's true. All the men think she's appalling, and none of them like her nose-in-the-air snobbery."

Robert lifted his brows. "So Her Highness can't make Mrs. Trumbull appealing to the gentlemen."

"With enough freely distributed liquor I could," Princess Clarice said crisply.

A gust of amusement caught Robert by surprise—and he laughed. Laughed out loud, a brief bark of irrepressible humor. He hadn't laughed since . . . he didn't remember the last time. Before he left for the Peninsula, he supposed. Before savage deeds and betrayal had stripped him of gaiety. If he had thought about it, he would have said the instinct of mirth had died in him.

But although it pained him, like blood flowing to a frozen limb, Princess Clarice had resurrected the impulse.

Amazing. Impossible.

Terrifying.

His gaze narrowed on her. Damn her. She made his senses stir. All of his senses, and at a time when he required complete control over his mind and his heart.

She was dangerous. That was something to remember.

And she was necessary to his plan. Something else to remember. "But you can't change a woman's appearance to make her unrecognizable." He hoped the challenge would make her rise to the bait. "That's ridiculous."

A smile played around her lips, and she shrugged modestly. "I make a woman—or a man—look better than they have before, but that's nothing more than enhancing their superior traits."

Prudence wasn't interested in Princess Clarice's decorous response. She demanded, "But can you change a person to look like someone else?"

Cautiously Princess Clarice admitted, "Within reason, yes."

That was the answer Robert had hoped to hear.

"That's fascinating!" Prudence bubbled. "Can you make me look like Larissa Trumbull?"

Millicent wrinkled her nose. "Why would you want to?"

"Because she's the belle!" Prudence used an impatient, patronizing adolescent tone of voice that made Robert want to send her to her room.

Princess Clarice said, "Miss Trumbull is the belle only until the gentlemen learn that she's a younger version of her mother. And a younger wolverine is more likely to tear out your throat, Lady Prudence. Remember—a gentleman of sense likes a lady who smiles and puts him at ease, not one who cries at breakfast and demands constant tending."

Like the silly lass she was, Prudence tried to argue. "But—"

"I said a gentleman of *sense*."

Robert wondered if she deemed him a gentleman of sense.

She continued. "And, Lady Prudence, why would you want any other kind of gentleman?" Princess Clarice reconsidered her words. "Well, except to dance with. Men of sense always seem to be able to remember the most difficult intricacies of politics and not the simplest dance steps. But don't worry, Lady Prudence, you'll have all the attention from the gentlemen, sensible or not, that you could desire."

"I don't know," Prudence muttered, "I desire an awful lot."

Millicent chuckled again, a gay, lilting sound that made Robert realize how very solemn his house had been since his return. "I've been telling her so," Millicent confided, "but she doesn't listen to a mere sister."

As if reminded of a grievance, easy tears rose in Prudence's large blue eyes. "Robert, a most dreadful situation has arisen. Millicent won't let me dampen my gown for the ball."

"Oh, no, young lady." Millicent shook her finger at her sister. "You're not dragging Robert into this."

Prudence ignored her and wheedled, "Please, dear brother, you'll give your permission, won't you? All the other girls are doing it."

Millicent took on a combative posture. "All the other girls are most certainly *not* doing it.

Only the girls whose family don't love them enough to put a halt to their flightiness."

Prudence folded her arms across her chest. "That's not true. Bernice is dampening her gown."

"Bernice is a spoiled brat," Millicent said.

"What do you think, Your Highness?" Prudence demanded in a petulant voice. "Shouldn't I be allowed to dampen my gown?"

"It's your debut. Your night," Princess Clarice said warmly. "You should be allowed to do anything you like—"

Millicent's eyes grew big. Her mouth opened.

Robert placed a restraining hand on her shoulder.

"—no matter how damaging to your reputation," Princess Clarice concluded.

"Damaging?" Clearly Prudence had never expected to hear that from the smart, daring princess. "It wouldn't be damaging. It would be fashionable."

Princess Clarice gave the slightest shrug. "You wish to dampen your gown so that the material is transparent, isn't that right?"

"As the French do," Prudence said.

Princess Clarice retorted, "The French also cut off the heads of aristocratic young ladies and eat truffles that are dug up by pigs."

The genuine bitterness of her tone startled Robert, and even Millicent looked taken aback. "You're very harsh."

"Their revolution caught all of Europe on fire, and while they bow to the tyrant Napoleon, the rest of us who were caught up in the flames still live in exile, scrambling to make a living while we wait in vain to be called back to—"As Princess Clarice almost betrayed the name of her country, she caught a distraught breath.

Robert would have sworn she bit her tongue, and he rather admired her acting ability. More and more it appeared he had made an excellent choice.

Certainly Millicent and Prudence were wide-eyed at her virulence.

But when Princess Clarice lifted her gaze once more, her face was smooth and tranquil.

She had hidden depths and secret passions. He would be wise to remember that— he dared not have her lose the game for him in a temper.

She said, "But, Lady Prudence, we were talking about your gown. I have some silver braid in my chamber that is all the rage in

London. If you would like, I can show you how to place it for the best advantage. With your dark hair and your blue gown, it would be most striking."

"All right." Prudence sounded subdued, and she watched Princess Clarice as if troubled by her explosion.

Millicent wrapped her arm through Prudence's, and coaxed, "My silk shawl is just the thing to finish the outfit. Shall we see how it matches?"

"Go on. Her Highness and I will discuss the ball without your able assistance, and let you know what we've decided." No one would ever know he had every intention of using the princess in a nefarious plan. So much depended on its success. If it did not, the man to whom Robert owed his life would suffer and probably hang, and Robert himself would slowly sink into the depths of hell.

But perhaps . . . he was there already.

Coming out from behind his desk, he offered the princess his arm. "We shall walk where we can be seen and thus put an end to all rumors of a romance."

Lightly Princess Clarice placed her hand on his arm.

"I doubt that." Millicent's gaze lingered on

them. "Not when you're the most eligible gentleman here."

"For the moment," he admitted. "The advent of other gentlemen will soon throw me in the shade."

"I doubt that also," Millicent said.

With a saucy grin Prudence declared, "Larissa declares you the Catch of the Season, and she brags she'll trap you."

Princess Clarice smirked.

Millicent yanked Prudence out the door and down the corridor. "Prue, you're such a tattletale!"

He didn't like being the brunt of the princess's amusement, nor did he relish being pursued like a trophy by Miss Larissa Trumbull. "I don't care about her," he said abruptly.

"I didn't imagine you did." For one moment Princess Clarice covered her smiling lips with her fingers. "Neither did I see you look away when she displayed her . . . er . . . wares."

"Her—? Oh." Princess Clarice surprised him by her frankness. Most ladies would never refer to the ample display of bosom Miss Trumbull had exhibited to him. But then, most ladies weren't Princess Clarice. "Miss Trumbull has breasts like a cow."

Princess Clarice took a startled breath.

He had surprised her in return. Good. He wished to keep her off balance. "She made me think of the village." Leading Princess Clarice into the corridor, he went in the opposite direction of Millicent and Prudence. "Freya Crags. Freya is an old Norse name meaning lady. The village was named for the rounded twin hills that tower behind it."

Princess Clarice stopped. Throwing back her head, she laughed. Laughed low and long, taking pleasure in his wit.

Struck dumb by the sound of her mirth, he stopped with her and stared.

She was beautiful. No matter that she was a wench of the road and a thief of uncommon daring. She was truly beautiful. He'd known she was an uncommonly attractive woman the first time he saw her; hell, every man in Freya Crags had known it, and lusted after her. But he hadn't really plumbed the depths of her attractiveness until that moment, when she laughed with uninhibited delight.

Turning his head, he breathed in the scent of flowers and spice that wafted up from her hair. She smelled good, like springtime and, at the same time, like the kitchen on baking day. Just by closing his eyes and inhaling, a man could imagine he had a woman with an arm overflowing with roses and a hand full of cinnamon buns. The perfect woman, indeed.

When her chuckling had died down, she continued on their walk. A dimple creased her cheek as she said, "I should have known you would be thinking only of your people. You're a very responsible man."

"That I am." If she only knew . . . she would understand why he did what he did. But he couldn't enlighten her. Yes, she *was* beautiful; all the more reason not to trust her. "Your foray into sales was successful?"

"Very successful. You were right. I shall make enough in honest sales to finance the return to my country."

"Or you could stay in Scotland." He led her into the older part of MacKenzie Manor, dismal corridors opened only so their still-absent guests would have rooms. Here the carpets were faded, the walls dark and old-fashioned, and the sconces were too far apart for the candles to do more than alleviate the gloom. Its isolation made it the perfect venue for his proposition.

"You mean—because you don't believe I'm really a princess." She still smiled.

He didn't, of course, but of more importance was his developing fascination with her. However, he had no need to discuss that. Not yet. And when the time came . . . not with words. "You don't care a fig if I believe, do you?"

Frankly she replied, "I've faced worse fates than your disbelief, my lord."

Hepburn viewed Clarice as if she amused him. She didn't care about that either. She just wanted him to say what he wished of her and get it over with.

He started with a cool compliment. "You're gifted in the use of cosmetics."

"They're not cosmetics." Clarice had given this speech so many times, she knew it by heart. "Cosmetics conceal a woman's natural beauty. My creams reveal—"

"Please." He held up a hand. "I care not whether a girl wears a mask of rouge or pinches her cheeks to give them color. Women have their tricks to make themselves irresistible and wrap a man in their coils, and that's fair, for men are strong, brutal, and lawless unless the law is on their side."

She raised her eyebrows in surprise. No, more than surprise. In shock. "That's true, but it's a rare man who admits it."

Flatly he said, "I've seen more than most men."

She suspected that was true. Underneath the calm facade he wore experience like a cloak. It was what attracted Larissa Trumbull and made her pronounce him the Catch of the Season. The little wolverine watched him for the same reason all women watched him. Because he was the kind of man a woman could trust to keep her safe from every threat. Every threat—except the one he exuded. The one that warned a woman he could seduce and beguile.

And what woman in her right mind wanted to be safe from *that*?

Oh, dear. She couldn't think of him *that* way. She glanced around. Not when he had led her into a deserted part of the manor. Old-fashioned furniture decorated the wide, endless corridor, and silence echoed like a living thing.

He hadn't denied his intent to use her for some different purpose than to entertain his relatives. He had her trapped . . . now he was ready to talk.

"You'll come to my ball," he said.

"With that scene in the conservatory, you made it impossible for me to refuse."

"Yes." He seemed quite without guilt. "Please make yourself available tomorrow afternoon for the fittings on your dresses."

"My *dresses*? I don't need *dresses*!"

"Wait. Listen." He touched his finger to her lips to indicate quiet. His stroke lingered like lightning. "I want you to come in disguise."

Eleven

Everything goes easier with a wee bit o'
a smile.

—THE OLD MEN OF FREYA CRAGS

Dumbfounded, she asked, "In disguise? What do you mean, in disguise?"

He seemed to think he was making himself perfectly clear. "I have a guest who suddenly can't attend the party, so you'll pretend to be her." He grimaced "She got married."

The sheer, sweeping arrogance—no, stupidity—of his scheme took Clarice's breath away. She hardly knew how to start explaining how impossible it was, but she would try.

"First of all, unless no one knows this person, I can't convince anyone that I'm her, because I'm not. You do comprehend that, don't you?"

Enigmatically he watched her as they paced along. "I comprehend a great deal."

What did he mean by that? Why was he looking at her that way?

Outside, the full moon had risen. Its white light poured through the open curtains. The candles fluttered in the draft. Hepburn moved through moonbeam and then shadow, adjusting to the changing illumination like a man bred to blend into his environs. "I'm giving this ball for a particular purpose—"

"Yes, to honor Colonel Ogley."

"Of course, that too." Hepburn smiled so pleasantly, he frightened her. "But another purpose as well, and my guest was going to help me. Now you'll take her place."

The idea was absurd. Why did he think this would work? "What purpose?"

"I am not going to explain myself."

"You mean—not to me, the woman who pretends to be a princess." When she heard her own animosity, she caught her breath. Why did it matter whether Hepburn believed her? In the larger scheme of her life, he was not important. Or, at least, not important as long as she remained safe while in his custody. "Why must this person be at your ball?"

"Some of the guests know her, hence she must be here."

Again Clarice glanced around at the deserted corridors. If Hepburn were mad, and right now it seemed likely, she could do no more than ease away from him and consider her best escape. Back the way they'd come? He could outdistance her if she ran. Out the window? No, for the servants' quarters and the kitchen was below them, and the twenty-foot drop from the window to the ground would probably result in a broken leg. So she had to stay and try to talk him out of his crazy ruse.

"You're about her height. You have her form." He flicked an analytical glance at her figure, one devoid of masculine interest. "Your tone isn't as deep as hers—she smokes dreadful cigars and they give her voice a huskiness that most women cannot achieve. But you have a similar accent."

In exasperation she said, "Grand! As long as no one sees my face, I'm identical. What about the people who've met *me* already? Don't you think they'll notice the disparity?"

He ignored her as if she hadn't spoken.

"The lady's hair is straight and black, and she wears lace mantillas. I have acquired black wigs and mantillas for you to disguise your curls." He took one strand of her hair between his fingers and rubbed it like a silk merchant assessing the merchandise.

She pushed his hand away. "The scheme is ridiculous."

He paid so little heed, she might never have spoken. "You'll change your voice slightly. I know you can do it. I've heard you don a Scottish accent when you think it profitable."

She bit her lip.

"I have a miniature of her, and I want you to make your face as similar to hers as you and your craft are capable."

"That's not going to work." She might as well have saved her breath.

"You'll be seen from afar. You'll wear her clothes and wave with consummate disdain, like a woman scorned."

Something in his tone gave her pause. "Is she a woman scorned?"

"Used, scorned, and abandoned."

"By whom? You?"

"You've the tongue of a shrew."

She didn't care what names he called her. She had to think of Beaumontagne, of her position . . . and of her sister. Of Amy, alone in Freya Crags, laboring as a seamstress while Clarice entertained the ladies in lavish circumstances.

Yet she couldn't help insisting, "Was it you who used this lady?"

With his distinctive cheekbones and determined jaw, he looked like a creature who prowled the night, at home with darkness and violence and despair. "Not me."

And Clarice was relieved. Relieved that it wasn't this man who could so easily convince her of his integrity. "Who, then?"

"There are things you don't need to know."

"Things you don't want me to know."

"Exactly." It was almost eerie the way he moved, a slow, sinuous stalking that made Clarice glad that it wasn't her he hunted.

For he *was* on the hunt. She had no doubt about that. "So you seek vengeance for the lady?" she insisted.

"*For* her, no—although I have her blessing. No, I seek vengeance for the lies told to me. Lies that made me act to my discredit."

Incredulous, Clarice said, "You would mount this elaborate charade because someone *lied* to you? You're in for a difficult life, my lord, if one simple falsehood shocks you so completely you exact retribution at such cost." And she was in for a difficult time if she couldn't dissuade him from his crusade.

"Sometimes a simple falsehood is more than a lie. Sometimes it's a promise broken and honor betrayed."

"You're being enigmatic, and I promise you, it will get you nowhere with me!"

He spoke at cross purposes, as he seemed wont to do. "Are you an actress, Your Highness?"

"I beg your pardon!" Actresses were courtesans and loose women, and she didn't appreciate his query.

"And I beg yours. I didn't mean to impugn your morals. I was asking simply—can you play a role?" The lids drooped over his eyes and he contemplated her seriously. "Can you look on the embodiment of cruelty and wickedness and pretend to see a champion? Can you pretend equanimity when every fiber of your body screams that you fight the evil before you?"

His words, his tone, made her skin prickle with alarm. With every step she took at his side, she was walking into danger. She sensed it. She smelled it. Yet she didn't know how to avoid it. Painstakingly she said, "I used to think myself a tolerable performer, but not long ago, in England, I discovered that I had my limits." She hadn't been able to hide her aversion to Magistrate Fairfoot. If she had, matters might have concluded without hostility—but probably not. Remembering the vicious twist of Fairfoot's expression, she conceded—definitely not.

"Then you cannot know why I make these demands. But you can trust me and obey."

"Why would I do that?"

Without seeming to move he joined her. His arms slid around her waist. Leaning close to her ear, he murmured, "Because of this."

His breath lifted the soft hair on the base of her neck and spread a chill down her spine—and a bubbling heat throughout her body. Yet she enunciated every word. "Get your hands off me."

His breath touched her just below her ear . . . or was it his mouth that touched, caressed, made her breath catch?

"Stop it." She sounded breathless. "You promised you would look after my reputation."

Lifting his head, he looked down at her and smiled. Not one of his cynical smiles, nor one of his polite, empty smiles, nor one of his dangerous, predatory smiles, but a smile that charmed and beguiled.

Oh, no. It had never occurred to her that he could smile like that. As if the sight of her gave him pleasure. As if he intended to give her the same pleasure.

Oh, no.

For he did give her pleasure. With a mere embrace and a single smile, he made a fool of her.

She gave voice to her dismay. "Oh, no!"

He seemed not at all dissuaded. "Aye." He pulled her close, so close that she experienced the warmth of him from her thighs to her breasts. "It seems impossible, doesn't it?"

"What are you saying?" He couldn't mean what she thought he meant. That would too horrible.

But he read her mind. "That you and I could be so much alike when we scarcely know each other. What do you suppose makes us so much alike?"

"We're not."

He mocked her with his probing gaze and answered his own question. "Similar experiences."

"We share nothing."

"We were both raised in privileged backgrounds and turned out into the cruel world to fend for ourselves without support of any kind."

Oh, no. He was saying the right things. The things she wanted to hear.

And she rejected his empathy. She had to. Truculently she asked, "What are you talking about? Why are you pretending sympathy for me? You don't believe anything about my story is true."

"Convince me." In a sneak attack against which she had no defense, he placed his mouth over hers.

His lips looked like silk.

They felt as cool and smooth as polished marble. They brushed against her mouth in wicked enticement. It was as if her girlhood dreams had come true, as if the statues in her father's palace had come alive.

Her eyes fluttered closed.

Gently Hepburn sucked on her lower lip, mouthing it as if the texture delighted him. Certainly the texture of *his* lips delighted her. And she could almost taste him. Almost . . . and she wanted to taste him. She wanted to devour him, every last delicious drop of his luscious, forbidden body.

Hepburn's hands roamed her back, her

waist, slid down to her bottom and urged her hips into his. The pressure of his groin stirred something wanton in her, something that tightened in her belly and clutched at her throat.

She tried to wedge her hands between them and accomplished nothing but the enchantment of touching him. Through all the layers of his clothing, she felt the heat and the firmness of his chest. Foolishly she pressed her palms to the muscles, exploring the contours with willful gladness.

Her caress changed his careful exploration just as the sun's heat brings the spring. His arms tightened on her. Giving an eager muffled exclamation of excitement, he deepened the kiss. His tongue slid between her lips and caressed the sensitive inner flesh, her teeth, and then her tongue. Her knees weakened under a rush of . . . there was no use pretending she didn't know its name. Under a rush of *desire.*

This was delicious opulence, a feast for her senses. His scent was exhilarating—his lemon soap mixed with masculine pleasure. The aroma went to her head like brandy's intoxicating fumes. His taste strengthened her, created needs she had never imagined.

Each lap of his tongue bound her tighter to him, gave her a greater knowledge of him, created so much intimacy that every breath she took was his breath, every beat of her heart matched his. She had never wanted a man before, but she wanted him.

Running his hands down her arms, he lifted them to his shoulders. She clutched at him and whimpered with delight. She allowed him to probe deep within her mouth, then shyly returned the favor, wanting to take him as he took her. Their tongues sparred, each seeking to win bliss, to give bliss, until the other collapsed in surrender.

Of course, he would win. He had experience on his side, and ruthlessness, and a need that recognized hers.

When she was limp with joy yet clawing him with need, he lifted his mouth from hers. In a husky whisper he said, "Tell me you'll do as I ask."

She lifted lids so heavy she could scarcely raise them. His beautiful damp mouth hovered over hers, offering more of the drug he dispensed with such skill. In a daze she asked, "What?"

Pressing short, sweet kisses on her cheeks,

her nose, her throat, he said, "Tell me you'll perform my masquerade . . . for me."

But although his skill at seduction was undiminished, his eyes were sharp, his chin firm. He weighed her response to him, judging her a slut for desire.

Common sense clouted her between the eyes. Her spine snapped into a straight, rigid line. "You . . . you blackguard!" Without warning she brought her crooked elbow down hard against his sternum.

With a cough of pain he released her and stumbled away.

She backed up and leaned against the wall. Indignation and insult burned in her gut, but she needed the support. "You . . . you did that on purpose. You kissed me on purpose. Did you imagine my character was so weak, I'd give in to your temptation and your extortion?"

A half-smile creased his cheek. He rubbed his aching chest with his palm. "Actually, no. It never crossed my mind that your character was weak, or that you'd do as I wished—but it was an enjoyable attempt."

His admission made her froth with fury.

"Did you think your kisses are so valuable that I would lose my mind and my principles?"

"My kisses *are* valuable. I don't waste them on just anyone."

Not surprisingly his reply heightened her rage. "Did you imagine that I've never been kissed before? I have—and by better men than you!" It seemed very important that she tell him that.

In a deep voice that sent messages she didn't want to hear, he said, "Better men, perhaps . . . but not better lovers."

She froze like a rabbit sighted by a wolf. "How would you know that?"

"I pleased you, and you were surprised." He leaned one hand against the wall beside her, his attitude negligent yet watchful. "Did you think I couldn't tell?"

She swallowed, trying to cure her suddenly dry mouth. She could still taste him on her tongue, smell him on her body, and the heat of him resounded in her mind. Damn him. How could this man, this lord, with his nefarious plans and his overbearing manner, be the one who marked her with his passion? "You promised . . ." What had he promised? "On the road here, you said you recognized the trouble facing me because

I'm unmarried, and you promised you would not damage my reputation."

"True, I promised to have a care for your reputation." A slight difference, but telling. "I didn't promise I wouldn't try to seduce you."

He exasperated her. "Would you please tell me the difference?"

"A reputation is what others think you've been doing. A seduction is what you've really been doing . . . with me . . . if you're lucky."

"Conceited lout."

He glanced out the window. His eyes narrowed. He looked back at her. "I know my worth."

"Conceited, and . . . and . . . I can't let you . . . you seduce me! I'm a princess. I have to take part in a dynastic marriage!"

Again he glanced out the window. "Even a princess should be allowed a little pleasure sometime." His gaze lingered on something, *someone,* outside . . . and he forgot her. As easily as that, all of his concentration switched away from her, and she was glad, for his eyes grew cold. He looked as if . . . as if he could kill now, as if he had killed before, and without a thought to the consequences. Placing his hand on her shoulder, he pressed her against the wall. "Stay here."

She shivered at his abrupt change from lover to executioner, yet she kept her tone cool and composed. "My lord, what is it?"

Ignoring her, he strode to the candelabrum and blew out the flames, leaving the corridor lit only by the moon and by distant candles. He went to the window and vanished behind the drapes.

She caught her breath at his behavior. Was this proof of his madness?

But no, for outside she could see a line of trees on the ridge behind the manor, and there a man sneaked from shadow to shadow, moving toward the well-lit portions of MacKenzie Manor. It might be a footman returning from an assignation with his lass, or one of the laborers walking home . . . yet he moved with skill and stealth, blending into obscurity like a man at home in darkness and isolation.

Then, for one moment, as he ran from one shadow to another, the moon shone full on his face, and she thought she knew him. "Who is that?" she whispered, and started forward.

"I said, stay there!" Hepburn's voice whipped like a lash. Stealthily he slid the window open. "Clarice, go back to the others."

"Should I send someone . . .?"

"No." So suddenly she was breathless, his attention came back to her. In a tone that too clearly told her he hadn't given up, he said, "We'll talk tomorrow. Go." Moving like a serpent, he slipped out of the window and dropped to the ground.

She didn't obey him. Convinced he must have been hurt—not that she cared—she ran to the window and peered out.

She could see nothing, hear nothing in the shadow of the house. Hepburn was gone.

She glanced up toward the other man. Like an apparition, he, too, had disappeared.

Both men were gone, vanished as if they had never been.

The stranger heard the thump as something, or someone, struck the ground. His head swiveled. The sound had come from the old wing of MacKenzie Manor. Slipping behind a tree, he stood still and silent and scrutinized the house he'd been watching the past twelve hours.

There. At the window. A young lady leaned out and looked below her, then inspected the landscape as if seeking . . . him.

His gaze sharpened. *Could she be the one?*

She drew back and hurried away toward the drawing room and the company of other guests.

Then he detected movement in the shadows below the window. Someone had seen him. Someone who moved with the same practiced stealth as he did—hunted him.

He recognized the way the man ran, low and fast, keeping his face down. He recognized it, because since his escape from the dungeon, men had ceaselessly hunted him. They would capture him. They would kill him. If they could find him.

Slowly he slipped backward, following the escape route he had already scouted out. He made no sound. He left no mark.

He was Prince Rainger of Richarte.

He had come to find a princess.

THE ENGLISH COUNTRYSIDE
Five years before

Clarice stood outside the gate of the exclusive girls school that had been her home, and Amy's, for three years. It was an imposing building on large, well-kept grounds. In the summer tall oaks shaded the girls as they took their constitutionals. Now winds stripped the trees of their leaves. The branches scraped the gray sky with bony fingers. Winter was coming.

Here Grandmamma had secretly placed Clarice and Amy when revolution convulsed their country. Here they had been educated, treated like . . . like princesses among the students. The headmistress had not revealed their identities, but Mrs. Kitling had fawned over them and given guests significant hints as to their importance.

Now, clinging to the bars of the fence, Clarice stared across the grounds, trying to understand the events that had led up to this ignominious ejection.

Amy tugged at her arm. "Clarice, are we supposed to go home now? To Beaumontagne? Can we go home?"

"I don't know." Clarice looked at her sister, twelve years old, gawky with adolescence and not comprehending the day's events. How could she comprehend? Clarice herself didn't understand. "I don't know. I couldn't talk to the headmistress. She refused to speak to me." Refused! As if Clarice were an insolent serving girl requesting an interview.

In the last few months Mrs. Kitling's deference had been disintegrating. She had been *making snide comments about taking charity cases, and her expression when she gazed on them had been pinched and sour.*

More important, where were Grandmamma's letters? Every month since she had sent them away, she had written to report on the progress of the revolution, to give them news about Sorcha, to admonish them about the correct behavior for princesses, and to demand letters in return. Four months had gone by with no word.

Clarice pressed her forehead against the cold bars. She hadn't allowed herself to think it, but . . . what if Grandmamma was dead too? What would they do?

Amy persisted. "Where are Joyce and Betty? They're our serving maids. They're supposed to take care of us."

"I don't know. When I asked about them, no one would answer me." Indeed, the three teachers who had escorted them to the gate had avoided her gaze and pretended not to hear her questions. Clarice had never felt so helpless in her life. Not three and a half years ago when the revolutionaries had overthrown the capital. Not three years ago when Grandmamma had sent the princesses away, sepa-

rating Crown Princess Sorcha from her sisters for safety. Not even last year when word had come that their father had been killed in the fighting.

Unaware of Clarice's dark rumination, Amy buzzed and bothered like a midge. "Joyce and Betty are ours. We brought them with us."

Clarice took Amy's mittened hand and patted it. "We don't own them. But I do wish we had spoken to them before we . . . left." She shivered. She and Amy couldn't stand out here like beggars. As the morning progressed it was getting colder. The few of their clothes she'd managed to hurriedly bundle together were stuffed in a pathetic little carpetbag at her feet. Their velvet cloaks and stylish bonnets wouldn't save them from impending rain.

Caution and yearning mingled in Clarice. "I think we have to go home. We have to find Sorcha and go home. We don't have a choice. We have nowhere else to go, and . . . and maybe Grandmamma needs us." She drew Amy along the grassy edge of the lane. "We don't have any money right now"—not a single pence—"but we will beg shelter at the inn in Ware."

"What if they won't give it to us?"

With a confidence she didn't feel, Clarice answered, "They will."

"But what if they don't?" Amy insisted. "Remember that time we saw those children in the workhouse? They were ragged and dirty and skinny, and some of them had sores, and that one boy had a broken arm wrapped in rags. Remember? What if they put us there?"

Of course Clarice remembered. How could she forget?

Then the call of a familiar voice saved Clarice from answering. "Please, Your Highness, wait!"

Clarice turned back to see Betty running across the lawn as fast as her girth would allow. She wore neither cape nor hat, and the carpetbag she clutched bumped against her knees.

"Betty!" Conscious of a great relief, Clarice reached through the bars and grasped her maid's cold hands. "Thank heavens! I was worried about you. Are you ready to go? Are those your things?"

"Ah, nay, Your Highness." Betty glanced over her shoulder as if fearing discovery. "They're yours. Your creams and potions

from Queen Claudia, and more of your clothes and clothes for the little princess."

Amy demanded, "Aren't you going with us?"

"I can't. Mistress won't allow me, nor Joyce, neither. Mistress said . . . she said we could make ourselves useful helping the other girls. To . . . to defray the expenses you two caused when . . . when the money stopped coming." Betty stammered to a halt.

Sharply, Clarice asked, "What do you mean, the money stopped coming?"

Betty lowered her voice. "About six months ago. The servants have been whispering about it."

"Why didn't you tell me?" Perhaps Clarice could have talked to Mrs. Kitling, explained that . . . that . . . she didn't know what she could explain. But she could have tried to work something out.

"You're a princess. I didn't know she would toss you out," Betty said miserably.

"But she can't force you to stay. Neither one of you. Come with us," Clarice urged.

Betty gazed down at the bag in her hand, then started shoving it through the bars. "Your Highness, I haven't . . . I can't." In a low tone she said, "I'm afraid."

Clarice drew back. "Oh." She understood only too well. She was afraid too.

"I . . . I don't want to starve or freeze or"—Betty looked up, misery clear in her eyes—"have to do something for money that moral women shouldn't do."

Amy didn't understand what Betty meant.

Clarice did. Clarice understood only too well, and the thought of her little sister walking the streets in a prostitute's garb produced a pain in her chest that took her breath away. She, Princess Clarice of Beaumontagne, had never had to take responsibility for herself in her life. Now she had to care for Amy. She had to get them home before disaster struck—and disaster had already overwhelmed her country.

Amy shoved her bonnet back. Her black hair flew around her face. "But Betty, we don't know how to travel alone. You have to help us."

"I will." Digging in the voluminous pocket of her apron, Betty brought out a handful of coins. Thrusting it through the bars, she said, "It's all the money we could put together in the kitchen. Me and Joyce gave everything we had. The others put in too. If you're careful it'll keep you through the week."

The week!

With trembling hands Clarice accepted the coins. "Thank you, Betty. You've helped us immensely. If someone comes to the school from Beaumontagne, tell them . . . tell them we're on our way home. Now go back in. It's cold, and you have no cloak."

"Yes, Your Highness." Betty curtsied, then ran toward the house, stopped, and curtsied again. Her simple brow knit at the sight of her princesses. "God speed you on your way."

"No!" Amy lunged after her, her skinny arm reaching through the bars. "You awful, horrible—"

Clamping an arm around Amy, Clarice dragged her down the road.

"What are you doing?" Amy demanded. "Grandmamma told her she was to take care of us, and she's abandoning us. And you're letting her!"

"I'm not letting her. I'm bowing to reality. She's not going to go with us. And if you'll recall, the last thing Grandmamma told us was that a princess is brave no matter what the circumstances, kind to her inferiors, and invariably polite." Clarice gave a quivering sigh. "So I was obeying her directive."

"Grandmamma's directives are dumb. You

know that. Who wants to be a princess anyway?" Amy yanked away from Clarice's grasp. "Especially now when it's all trouble, and no privileges."

"It's who we are. Princesses of Beaumontagne."

Surly, Amy said, "We don't have to be. We're out here by ourselves. We could be anyone we wanted."

As they got to the main road, Clarice answered matter-of-factly, "It's not that easy. We are who we're born to be."

Amy amended, "We are who we make ourselves."

Clarice stood on the grass near a stand of trees. "When we get back to Beaumontagne, you'll feel differently."

"No, I won't."

Clarice looked up and down the thoroughfare. Brittle leaves gathered along the hedgerow and, swept by the wind, skittered down the empty lane. Gray clouds bunched ominously above. And she couldn't remember which way to go to get to the inn. She had never paid attention before. She'd never had to. Someone had always taken her, fetched her, directed her . . . she was seventeen years old, and she didn't have a clue how to find her way in the world. She had to support Amy until they could make their way home, and she didn't even know which way to walk. She wanted to curl up into a little ball and cry.

Then something live, something dark, sprang at her from out of the thicket.

A man, tall, broad, menacing.

Amy shrieked, "Go away!"

He caught Clarice's arm in a crushing grip. He dragged her toward the trees.

She screamed, a single, long, thin scream.

He pulled her behind the trunk of a tree. He released her. Before she could spring away, he said, "Don't be frightened. Your Highness, do you remember me?"

She did. That gravelly voice could belong to one man, and one man only. She put her hand over her racing heart. "Godfrey."

He looked unlike anyone in their country. He was blond, blue-eyed, with arms too long for his tall body. His hulking shoulders and thick waist would have been common on a stevedore, and his nose and lips looked as if they'd been rearranged by too many fights. But he wore fine clothes, he spoke like a courtier, and he had been with Grand-mamma for longer than Clarice had been *alive. He had been Grandmamma's courier, her footman, her loyal emissary. Whatever Queen Claudia needed done, Godfrey did.*

At the sight of him, a weight lifted from Clarice's shoulders. "Thank God you found us."

Amy wrapped her arm around Clarice's waist and glared at the man. "I don't know who you are. Who are you?"

He bowed to them both. "I'm a servant to Dowager Queen Claudia. She trusts me completely."

Amy examined him suspiciously. "Really?"

Hugging Amy, Clarice assured her, "Really. Grandmamma uses Godfrey for her most important messages to faraway lands." Yet why was he here? Now? In agonized suspense she asked, "Is it Grandmamma? Is she—?"

"She's well." His pale, small eyes drilled into Clarice, then Amy. "But the revolutionaries are overrunning the country, and she sent me to urge you to flee."

Clarice's relief mixed with terror. "Flee? Why? Where?"

"Men are hunting you. They want to kill you, to end the royal family of Beaumontagne. You must disappear into the country-

side," he said urgently, "and stay there until Her Majesty commands your return."

Amy still eyed him askance. "If we're hiding, how will she find us?"

"She told me—and only me—that she would place an advertisement in newspapers throughout Britain when it was time for you to return. You should not believe anyone else who finds you and tells you it is no longer dangerous. Without her written word, you may assume they're traitors. In fact"—he dug in the pouch hanging from his belt—"I have her letter here."

Snatching it from his hands, Clarice broke her grandmother's seal and read the brief instructions with a sinking heart. Handing it to Amy, Clarice said, "She's very clear. Run and hide until it's safe." A fragile hope made her voice tremble. "But you'll go with us, won't you, Godfrey?"

He drew himself up. "I can't. I have to go and warn Sorcha."

For the first time in this long, dreadful day, Clarice's heart leaped with joy. "Sorcha! You can take us to Sorcha!"

For a moment he looked disconcerted. "No. No, I can't."

Amy looked up from the letter. "But you

just said you were supposed to find Sorcha too."

"My queen's orders are that the crown princess is to remain separate from both of you." His mouth drooped. "I am sorry, but you'll have to go on your own."

"Grandmamma would never send us anywhere without a chaperon," Amy declared.

Godfrey viewed her with irritation. "Little princess, only in this time of desperation did she consent."

With the insistence of a spoiled child, Amy added, "We want to see Sorcha. She's our sister."

He fearfully glanced around. "Your Highnesses, it's for your protection as well as Sorcha's, for I fear I'm being followed."

Clarice looked around. Before she had worried about the winter and how they would survive. Now she worried if they would survive.

From the pouch, he withdrew a purse heavy with coin. He handed it to Clarice. "This will keep you through the winter. Now you must leave at once. Board the coach in Ware and go as far away as you can. Go. Hurry. Don't look back." He pushed them out of the thicket. "Trust no one."

Twelve

Great minds think alike—especially when they are female.
—THE DOWAGER QUEEN OF BEAUMONTAGNE

Morning sun shone full on Clarice's face as, dressed in her riding costume, she hurried through the meager gardens toward the stables. She had to get away from the giggling girls and their matchmaking mammas, away from the bold—and surreptitious—demands for her services, away from her own thoughts. . . .

Was Hepburn all right? Last night he'd jumped from that window and disappeared.

Just disappeared. She'd gone into the drawing room and watched as the ladies played the piano and sang, but he'd never come in.

This morning she had not heard the servants say he was injured, but she hadn't dared ask about him for fear they would imagine more interest on her part than existed—and she didn't need that kind of gossip to start. Not when . . . not when it was partially true.

The gravel path crunched beneath her boots. A gentle breeze wafted in her face, luring her along. And she was glad to go. She wanted to see Blaize, to pet him, to saddle him, and enjoy the freedom she found only on his back.

Because . . . she shouldn't have let Hepburn kiss her. She didn't even know why she had. Other men had grabbed her, pawed at her, ground their mouths on hers. It was then she showed them how swiftly her knee could make contact with their masculine parts. Never had the touch of their bodies been desirable.

Yet the first time she had seen Hepburn she'd sensed the power and the drive of his sensuality would be irresistible. Her instinct had proved true. He was every bit as skilled a seducer as she feared. And he wanted something from her. He wanted her to do his bidding. He hadn't even cared enough to lie about that. He had swept her away into passion, and all the while been cold-bloodedly plotting to reward her capitulation with *himself*. As if he were a prize to be treasured rather than a despoiler of maidens and a plotter of crazy schemes.

Stopping, she put her hand to her forehead. And what a plan it was! He wanted her to pretend to be someone else. Someone she didn't know. And he gave her only the vaguest reasons, and probably lied about those. She had to assume his plan was dangerous. She had to refuse no matter how much pressure he put upon her. No matter how skillfully he pressed his lips to hers and indulged her in those stupefying and passionate kisses.

She started walking again, weaving slightly, and wondered if he had somehow drugged her. Surely that was the only explanation for her obsessive and wanton behavior. He had somehow taken over her mind.

She couldn't allow that to happen. When she and Amy had been thrown out of that school outside of Ware, Clarice had been a terrified child, suspicious of every stranger. The first winter had been lived between the shadow of two terrors—how would they live when the money ran out? And would they live at all, if assassins found them?

Desperation had given her the idea to sell the royal creams. Experience had taught her how to judge a man's character.

As time had gone on, some newspapers in England reported on the situation in Beaumontagne. Claudia read everything she could find, but details were sketchy and contradictory. Some said Queen Claudia had outmaneuvered the revolutionaries and returned to power. Other newspapers reported that rebels still roamed the countryside.

All Clarice knew was that Grandmamma hadn't yet placed the advertisement for her granddaughters to return.

So although Clarice had relaxed her guard, still she watched, and waited, for their chance to return home. That had been her goal for five years. She would not allow her fascination with the earl of Hepburn to distort her judgment.

As she rounded a corner, she saw the hem of a skirt whisking behind the hedge and resolved to ignore whoever it was. One of the houseguests was probably out here sobbing about some imagined slight.

But she couldn't resist glancing to see who gone to such lengths to escape her.

Down a narrow path stood a small white gazebo, isolated by hedges and overgrown with pink climbing roses. Peeking cautiously from behind the blossoms, looking pinched and anxious, stood Millicent. Clarice would have respected her obvious wish for privacy and waved as she went by, but Millicent's face lit up, and she called, "Your Highness, oh, I wouldn't have wanted it to be anyone else."

And actually Clarice wouldn't have wanted it to be anyone else either. Millicent was nothing like her brother; obviously he'd slurped up all the arrogance and cynicism in the family. Millicent was quiet, genteel, and a pleasure to be around, while her brother was an obnoxious blackguard.

Clarice wouldn't think of him at all today. She certainly wouldn't talk to him today. Not if she saw him first.

Clarice hesitated at the break in the hedge. "Good morning, Lady Millicent. It's a beautiful morning for a ride. Would you like to join me?"

Immediately Millicent's face fell. "I thank you, but I don't ride well and I'd hinder your enjoyment of your beautiful stallion."

Drawing herself up haughtily, Clarice asked, "Am I so shabby that I judge my companions by their riding ability?"

"No! I never thought—" Millicent's face broke into a smile. "You tease me."

Clarice smiled in return. "I do."

"Come and sit for a moment, and we'll discuss the ball. Last night we didn't get a chance."

Discussing the ball was the last thing Clarice wanted to do—well, almost the last thing. She didn't want to talk to Hepburn either.

Although she would like to know if he was hurt. But she thought Millicent already carried too much of the burden of this ball on her narrow shoulders, and if discussing it helped, Clarice would do so.

After she discovered what had happened to Hepburn. Mounting the stairs of the gazebo, she craftily asked, "I trust your sister is well this morning? And your brother?"

Millicent looked mildly surprised. "Indeed, I believe they are."

"Good. Good." Clarice seated herself on a white painted bench. "You've seen them?"

"Seen Prudence? Surely you jest! She can't bring herself to rise before noon." Millicent seated herself also. "I tell the lass she's not royalty, but she doesn't listen to me. Did you sleep until noon every day?"

"Not at all. Grandmamma wouldn't allow it." Clarice wasn't really listening to herself. She was wondering how to press for more information about Hepburn. "We were to rise with the sun and walk vigorously out of doors for an hour, regardless of the weather, then eat a healthy breakfast as approved by Grandmamma, then . . ." She trailed off when she realized Millicent's eyes were rapt. Clarice shouldn't reveal too much about herself. Not that Millicent would knowingly betray her, but Millicent accidentally might say something to the wrong person, and that would be fatal—to Clarice, and to her sister. "That was long ago, and I'm not that princess anymore."

"What princess are you?" Millicent asked pointedly.

"A princess who is a peddler." A princess who would never discover Hepburn's fate.

"I've heard the stories of revolutions and wondered what happened to the people who are displaced." Millicent's gaze was warm and kind. "Now I know. They come to help me."

Clarice stared at the woman before her and wondered how she could have ever thought her plain. Empathy shone from Millicent's face, and her gentle understanding was balm to Clarice's battered soul. Impulsively she asked, "How have the men in Scotland been such fools as to let you remain unmarried?"

Millicent drew back as if she'd been slapped. "Not such fools, in fact." But color rose in her cheeks.

Aha. Millicent was not so unruffled. "Tell me true—has no man ever made your heart beat quickly?" Clarice asked.

Shrugging with elaborate indifference, Millicent said, "Even when I was young, I never harbored great hopes."

"About who?" Clarice asked craftily.

"About . . . no one."

A clumsy evasion.

Millicent carefully avoided Clarice's gaze. "What man would be interested in me? I'm plain and dull."

"Not plain, but unadorned. And as for dull, I find your conversation charming and your kindness unique, and you deserve more than to serve your family for the rest of your days."

Primly Millicent folded her hands in her lap. "Other women do so and find satisfaction."

Clarice snorted, a rude noise of disbelief

she made no effort to soften. "No, they don't! You don't believe that any more than I do. You've seen those women, the maiden aunts, the unmarried daughters, who act as unpaid companions and governesses, fading into nothingness because they're not even human beings in the view of society. Pshaw, in the view of their family!"

At Clarice's plain speaking, Millicent's eyes rounded. "Well . . . but . . . the Bible says resignation to fate—"

"The Bible is full of stories about people who take their lives in their own hands and make it what they wish." Clarice clenched her fists in illustration. "Look at Ruth, and Esther! They were strong women who took charge and created a new world. Why shouldn't you?"

Millicent looked alarmed. "I don't want to create a new world. My dreams aren't so grand as that."

Aha! Now we're getting somewhere. "What are your dreams?"

"Oh . . . they're not important. Just what you might imagine . . . for an old maid."

Clarice smiled encouragingly and nodded.

Millicent confessed in a rush, "Nothing more than my own home with a man who loves me."

"And why shouldn't you have that?" Clarice asked warmly. "That's easily done."

"He's never even looked at me. I mean—"

"He?"

"He . . . you don't know him."

I will. "Will he be at the ball?"

"He's a friend of Robert's, so I suppose he might be."

Clarice bent a stern gaze at Millicent.

"He will," Millicent admitted, and surrendered with a sigh. "He's the earl of Tardew. Corey MacGown, the finest man ever to grace the shores of Scotland."

The lyricism of her reply told Clarice everything she needed to know. "He's handsome."

"With hair the color of sunshine and eyes as blue as turquoise stone. He rides and he hunts and he gambles and he dances"—Millicent's eyes grew wistful—"like a dream."

"You've danced with him, then?"

"Once. When I was seventeen. I stepped on his feet." Millicent ducked her head and mumbled, "I deserve no better for aspiring to such heights."

Clarice's temper rose. "Who told you that?"

"My father."

Clarice swallowed the hot words that rushed to her lips. She couldn't malign Millicent's father. At least, not to Millicent's face. So gently Clarice said, "Sometimes the people who love us most are blind to our attributes."

"Papa wasn't blind. He was righteous and upright."

"Perhaps so, but he didn't know anything about beauty." Clarice didn't give Millicent a chance to argue. "I'm going to help you with your hair and your gown, and you'll walk like a queen and smile like a siren, and Lord Tardew will be stricken with love."

Millicent laughed.

Clarice didn't. "I'm serious." Standing, she patted Millicent's shoulder. "Start thinking about it." Turning, she walked away.

She heard Millicent's feet strike the boards of the gazebo as she stood. "Princess Clarice, no!" The tone of her voice was easily as imperious as Clarice's own. When Clarice faced her, Millicent said, "I'm in earnest. Concentrate on Prudence. Help me with the ball. Above all, please be my friend. But don't try to fix my life. I'm content as I am."

Thirteen

A princess will catch more flies with honey than with vinegar.
—THE DOWAGER QUEEN OF BEAUMONTAGNE

The stables drowsed peacefully in the sunlight. The hostlers and stable boys moved about their business. Clarice hurried down the line of stalls, eager to see Blaize and pet his velvet nose once more. He demanded nothing from her except a firm hand on the reins and a loving rubdown after a good ride. He never pushed her away out of fear or brought her close to hurt her. Nothing made sense at this place, but Blaize would. Unlike the other male in this household, Blaize was a sensible beast.

But when she arrived at Blaize's stall, it was empty.

Panic leaped into her throat. Frantically she looked around for him, but the other horses didn't have his brilliant chestnut color or his noble lines.

Where was he?

Blaize hated men. If one of the hostlers tried to exercise Blaize, the horse would savage him. But underneath her reasonable worry was a stronger, less-logical fear—had *they* come to take him away from her?

She strode toward the paddocks, glancing from side to side, seeking explanation, seeking Blaize. Stepping outside, she blinked in the brightness of the sunshine—and saw the stallion, saddled and ready for her.

Hepburn, damn Hepburn, was holding the fractious horse and petting his nose.

Relief found its expression in fury. Obviously Hepburn wasn't hurt. Obviously Blaize was still safe. And obviously the two of them were getting along wonderfully well. She wished she had never wasted her time worrying about either of those stubborn males. Snatching the reins from Hepburn's hands, she said, "What do you think you're doing?"

"Waiting for you." He wore the same impassive face he always did, as if last night with its stolen kisses had never happened.

All right. She could be as offhand as he was. After all, what happened last night wasn't important. Illicit passion was just that—illicit, and not to be repeated. Most definitely not to be repeated.

"You're late," he said.

As if they'd made an assignation to ride together! Narrowing her eyes at him, she asked, "How did you know I would be at the stables?"

"Intuition."

Intuition? No, this man had not a scrap of intuition in his soul. *He'd had her watched.* "I don't like your kind of intuition," she said. "Don't use your intuition on me again."

He bowed his head in seeming obedience. "As you wish."

But his cool capitulation heightened her unease. A man like Hepburn did not *obey*—unless he had a reason. And she feared to know that reason.

Glancing around at the riding yard, she

saw that Hepburn's horse, Helios, stood waiting at a mounting block.

"I am not late." She batted Hepburn away when he tried to help her into her saddle. "I am precisely on time for my *private* ride on my own horse."

Shrugging as if bewildered by her ill humor, he turned away and swung easily into the saddle. "You don't like the morning. I would have never suspected."

She mounted her horse with just as much ease and skill. "What are you talking about?"

"Simply that you seemed the kind of woman to rise early and cheerfully. I see that's not true."

"I am perfectly cheerful!" She was perfectly ridiculous, and she knew it. But he irritated her like a burr under the saddle.

He considered her with false concern. "Did you omit breakfast? It's not healthy to ride on an empty stomach."

His concern had to be false. She deemed matters worse if it was real.

Forcing each word between her teeth, she said, "I did not skip breakfast."

"Then you have no excuse. Come along. Let's ride." He went off at a canter away from the stables and toward the wildness of his estate, where crags and valleys rose and fell in patches of rock and grass.

As it had the previous day, the road beckoned. She could ride into Freya Crags, gather up Amy, and ride away. She had collected a great deal of gold for her creams. They could go to Edinburgh and survive another winter.

Another winter without going home to Beaumontagne. And now . . . a winter spent looking over her shoulder, fearing Magistrate Fairfoot from England. Fearing Lord Hepburn, who would want his revenge on her for fleeing before his demands.

Was she a coward?

She didn't used to think so. Amy had called her foolhardy. But Hepburn frightened her, and in more ways than one. He frightened her, for he really didn't seem to see the folly of his plan. And he frightened her because he embraced her as if he poured his heart and soul into the pleasure of their kiss. And because it seemed when he kissed her, she would give him her heart and soul in exchange.

She told herself it was curiosity that drew her after him. Certainly not fear. Certainly not anticipation. Most definitely not desire for a man who was perhaps crazed and certainly far too arrogant to bear.

Catching up with him, she asked, "What happened to that man?"

"What man?"

"The one you went chasing last night."

He slowed. "He got away."

"How that must irk you, to have someone escape your net."

Slowly Hepburn turned his head. Deeply he looked into her eyes. "Yes. It does."

Her hands must have tightened on the reins, for Blaize skittered sideways. Quickly she righted him.

Had Hepburn just threatened her? She swallowed. Yes, of course he had. Last night he'd tried seduction. Today he would try intimidation.

Regrettably for him, she was not easily intimidated. He was only an earl. She was a princess, and she would be wise to remember that and act accordingly.

Grandmamma had warned that familiarity bred contempt. Here was the proof. But in every aspect of her life, Grandmamma had demonstrated how to halt such presumption.

With a toss of her jaunty hat, Clarice moved ahead of Hepburn, trusting to her posture, her riding, and her air to put him in his place, and all the while suspecting that the boundless arrogance of the man could not be undermined.

As they rode, they left the stables far behind, lost sight of the house, saw no one and nothing except the wild birds. Out there, the blue sky stretched from hill to peak, the grass waved in ripples on the breeze, and the wild roses bloomed in clusters of pink and white. This land was so different from her home in the Pyrenees—tamer, less mountainous—yet the rocks and wind sang with a ferocity that spoke to her soul.

A ferocity she saw echoed in Hepburn.

Beastly Hepburn, who couldn't leave her to enjoy the morning. As the path had widened and faded into nothingness, he caught up with her. "What a haughty expression, Your Highness. Have I somehow offended you?"

He offended her by breathing. "Last night you made demands I cannot fulfill. Demands that are inappropriate and impossible." Then, to make sure he understood she spoke of his ridiculous scheme and not of his polished kisses, she added, "I hope you understand that I can't pretend to be someone I've never met, especially not for reasons I don't comprehend."

Smoothly he asked, "So you *have* thought about my proposition?"

She pulled Blaize up. She turned to face Hepburn. In a slow, regal voice, she said, "I'm a princess." She raised her hand to stop any comment. "I know you don't believe me, but it is the truth, and I know my duty. I have an obligation to my station, and that obligation does not include disguising myself for the purpose of deceit and trickery."

His voice changed, became the lash of a whip. "It does if you have no choice."

He was driving her into a corner she couldn't escape, and she didn't want that. She had to talk her way out. Somehow, there must be a way. "If I did this thing, I'd be in disguise and couldn't come to the ball as myself. What lie would you tell your guests when I, the princess you've introduced to one and all, the princess you've virtually blackmailed into attending your ball, doesn't?"

"You'll attend." Helios moved forward a step. "As the princess."

In exasperation she said, "I thought you wanted me to wear a wig and a disguise."

"Both are easily discarded." Hepburn's

gaze never wavered from her. "Nothing will be allowed to cast doubt on Senora Menendez's presence."

"Why does it matter so much that she be here? Is it so important that you impress people with her presence?"

"Of course." He spoke slowly, with impassive earnestness. "This is the first social function I've hosted since my return from the wars. The status of my family depends heavily on the success of this party."

She didn't believe him. "Liar."

He surveyed her and judged her. "You're intelligent."

She basked in his admiration—and that was unwise. She couldn't soften toward him and perform in his farce. *She couldn't.* If anyone recognized her, she would be lost.

Amy would be lost.

But Clarice knew how to play her refusal: with good humor, not defying him, not allowing him to see the depths of her desperation. And of course, if she could distract him with a little light flirtation, that was a good idea too. Not too much, of course—last night he'd kissed her with no provocation. She didn't want a repeat of that . . . wonderful passion. She recognized a precipice when she stood on one, and this was a precipice most high.

Moving close to him, she smiled, using her dimples to good advantage. In a soft, engaging tone, she said, "My lord, what you ask is impossible. If I were caught, I'd be ruined."

She saw no sign of softening. If anything, his jaw grew harder, his eyes colder. "You won't be caught. I won't allow it."

He was unyielding.

She was rational. "In schemes such as this, there's always a chance of a misstep."

Impatience rolled off his still figure. "No."

Her heart beat faster. Beneath her black gloves her palms grew sweaty. He was dangerous. Dangerous and implacable. And mad? Still, she had to refuse. She *had* to. "My lord, I cannot do this thing."

He looked down as if masking his thoughts, then up again to search her face. She thought he was looking for something. "That's your final word?"

The uneasiness that had plagued her since the first moment of their meeting doubled, and doubled again. "It must be."

In a gentle tone at odds with his menace, Hepburn said, "It was only a month ago when I heard of a horse, a most amazing two-year-old stallion in Gilmichael. He was the magistrate's horse, half Arabian and half Beaumontagnian, a rare beast of unusual color and spirit."

Clarice felt the blood drain from her face. Her hands tightened on the reins. Blaize moved restively, and she fought the desire to pet the stallion reassuringly. "What are you saying?"

"You stole your horse." Hepburn smiled with chilly satisfaction. "You stole Blaize."

Fourteen

Ye canna be angry and think clearly at the same time.
—THE OLD MEN OF FREYA CRAGS

You stole your horse. Hepburn knew the particulars. He knew the truth.

And he did not cavil at blackmail.

The urge to run away grew in Clarice, to flee from her life with its different towns and its indifferent people. To urge Blaize to gallop and gallop, to have the wind in her face, to abandon her duties—even Amy!—and never look back. "No. No, my father the king—"

"He's gone." Hepburn slashed the air with

his hand. "And if he were alive, he didn't give you that horse. Blaize is a two-year-old. By your own account, you've been in England for more years than that."

Trapped. Trapped by her own thoughtless lies. By this man with a beautiful, soft, passionate mouth and flint in his soul. What to do? First she should try to appeal to Hepburn's love of animals. "All right, it's true. Magistrate Fairfoot fancied himself a trainer. He tried to break Blaize, and when he couldn't . . . he was going to kill this gorgeous—" Humiliated, she faltered. "Blaize doesn't deserve to be destroyed because a ham-handed English magistrate has to break every creature of beauty and spirit he comes in contact with."

Nothing softened in Hepburn's face, and his voice was flat. "Did he try to break you?"

Better yield to me, girlie, or I'll slap you and that sister of yours into the dungeon and you'll never see the light of day again. Embarrassment at the memory of that dreadful scene roiled in her. The torn bodice. The bruises on her wrists. The lucky chance that brought Amy to her aid.

Color swept Clarice's cheeks. She knew from experience she couldn't ride fast enough or far enough to get away from the memory. But she wanted to. Dear Lord, how she wanted to!

She sidestepped Hepburn's question. "His wife walks and talks, but she's broken. Dead inside. Please, my lord, don't send Blaize back to him. Blaize will never be broken. He can only be led. Magistrate Fairfoot will kill him, and it will be an agonizing, grisly end."

"I won't send Blaize back to him." Hepburn extended his gloved hand, demanding she put her hand there as a token of her agreement. "As long as you do my bidding."

She stared at the hand. She looked up at him. At the man who cared for nothing but that his stupid ruse succeed.

It wasn't fair that she, a princess bred to be spoiled and pampered, had had to grow up so early, to take responsibility for herself and her sister's welfare. And be left worrying about their other sister. It wasn't fair that she was forced to face this man who held the trump and rush into danger at his bidding.

Giving in to the frustration, the anger, the anguish, she incited Blaize to flight. The lively stallion leaped forward, eager to run as he had been bred to, his long legs stretching out as they sped across the meadow.

She heard Hepburn's startled call, then the thunder of his horse's hooves behind her.

She didn't care if he chased her. He didn't matter. Nothing mattered but the exultation of this flight, the illusion of escaping, the blessed sense of intemperance.

She and Blaize raced across the meadow and straight up the hill at the far end, then sped down the other side. They approached a wooden fence; beneath her, Blaize gathered himself and vaulted it in smooth, glorious flight. A long valley lay before them. Blaize stretched out his neck, tasted the bit, sensed her expert grip on the reins, and allowed himself to run, and run, and run.

Tears ran down Clarice's cheeks from the cool wind on her face. Or perhaps it was resentment and rage at the noose that held her by the throat. At Hepburn, galloping behind her, always right on her heels, ruthless and coldhearted. There was no escaping him. He was faster, stronger, bigger than her. Wilier, more ruthless . . . damn him!

He held the other end of the noose, and there was no eluding him.

As she acknowledged that, her brief rebellion failed. Good sense reasserted itself, and as the land rose again, she pulled her steed to a halt.

As Hepburn rode around to block her, he caught Blaize's reins in his grip. Hepburn's lips were drawn back to show his white teeth. His nostrils were flared, and white, furious lines bracketed his mouth. His blue eyes were molten fury, and he shouted, "What did that prove?"

She didn't care what he thought of her anymore. No smile, no compliment, no touch on the hand, would dent that pitiless determination. So she shouted back, "I didn't do it to prove anything. I did it because I wanted to."

"You can't outride me. There's nowhere you can run where I can't find you, and breaking your neck won't accomplish anything."

"I won't break my neck. I can ride as well as any man—and Blaize is mine." She threw the challenge at him.

"I'll make sure he's yours when you've done as I've told you." He flung the bribe at her and extended his hand again.

So she had run away, raced across meadow and over jumps, and she was right back where she'd been ten minutes earlier, with Lord Hepburn demanding that she put her hand in his to seal the bargain.

She hated Lord Hepburn. She hated him, and feared him . . . and lusted after him. If she only she could understand why. Why she wanted him when he infuriated and frightened her.

"Why are you doing this?" she demanded. "Why must I perform such an absurd charade?"

"I seek justice, and freedom, for a friend." Hepburn spoke steadily, without fanfare, as if justice and freedom and friendship were worth any effort.

She didn't care. "Friendship?" She wanted to spit into that extended palm, but her breakdown in civility couldn't extend that far. "What does a man like you know of friendship? You don't know how to be a friend." She tried to stop talking. She really did. She even rode away. Then she thought of Millicent, of his poor sister, and she rode back. "You don't even know how to be a brother."

Her accusation took him aback, for his hand dropped to his side and his voice was truly puzzled. "What do you mean?"

"Look at you!" She gestured at him. "You come back from the war, all unhappy and brooding, and you pay no attention to the needs of your sister."

Sarcasm coated his voice. "I have two sisters."

Clarice pretended surprise. "You noticed! Yes, and Prudence is a lovely young girl who thinks everything is fine because you say it is. She sees life as a jolly adventure— because Millicent took care that she should. But Millicent . . . have you even noticed her concern for you?"

"Of course."

"So you just don't care?" Her tone whipped at him.

"There's nothing to be concerned about." He sat so still in the saddle, he seemed to be a statue. "She should believe me."

"Maybe if you ever sat down and talked to her, she would. But you avoid her, and she worries." Clarice's voice was again rising uncontrollably. "Where did you learn such shabby behavior?"

He flinched as if she had struck a sore spot.

She was glad. She hoped he suffered pain from some memory, and she prodded at him in hopes of hurting him once more. "After your father died, she cared for your estate and your home. And I'll bet she raised Prudence. Didn't she?"

"Yes."

"Yes," Clarice mimicked. "And you've never given her a word of encouragement or thanks. Have you?"

"No."

"Lady Millicent is a sweet, charming, attractive woman who's been buried in the depths of the country, doing her duty, and no one cares or notices. Not even the brother she adores."

He didn't look guilty.

Of course not. If blackmailing a princess didn't make him feel guilty, why should his cavalier treatment of his older sister? "You tell her you want to have a ball, and immediately she leaps to work. You don't give her enough time to plan it, you allow the ladies to come early so that she has twice as much labor as she should—"

He lifted an unemotional eyebrow. "I thought they would help her."

"If helping includes sitting on their padded bottoms and criticizing her, then yes, they're doing a wonderful piece of work. That gaggle of ladies needs to be organized, they need constant entertainment, and someone always, always needs a shoulder to cry on.

Since they've arrived, Millicent has never been without a soggy shoulder."

"She shouldn't be so sympathetic. They'll stop coming to her to cry if she—"

"—rejects them? As your father rejected her? As you've rejected her? I think not, my lord. Millicent well understands the pain that accompanies such a rebuff." Was Clarice even getting through to him? "She should be dancing at your ball, not agonizing over it."

And because he was a stupid, insensitive male, he answered, "She doesn't like to dance."

"You mean no one asks her to dance. Do you know why they don't ask her to dance?"

"You're going to tell me."

"Someone has to!" Clarice took a long breath and tried to get her temper under control. But she lost it so seldom, and there was no retrieving it now. "She doesn't get asked because she thinks she's unattractive and she has convinced everyone else she is too." Clarice pointed her thumb at her chest. "But I can fix matters. I can arrange her hair and her clothes, I can improve her complexion, and most important, I can teach her how to walk and talk and smile. And you know what? She won't let me. Do you know why?"

"You'll tell me that too."

"Any man would be lucky to win her as his wife, and she won't let me show her anything because she doesn't think she's worth it. Whose fault is that, my lord? Whose fault is that?"

He watched Clarice with deepening interest, as if her indignant compassion were an oddity he scarcely understood. "I'm sure you would tell me it's mine."

"Perhaps," she said with stinging scorn, "you should pretend she's your friend instead of your sister and do what you can to help her."

But she had lost his attention. The uncaring bastard looked up the hill as if startled.

Then she heard it. Carried on the wind. Faint screams. The thunder of horses' hooves. And a gunshot, sharp and final.

"The MacGees!" Hepburn wheeled Helios around and galloped up the steep rise.

Clarice followed, and as she topped the hill, she saw a scene that had played in her nightmares. Nightmares formed of war and revolution in her homeland. Nightmares brought to garish life before her very eyes in a peaceful valley in Scotland.

Below them, two apple trees grew on either side of a tiny crofter's hut. A garden grew in a sunny spot on the south slope, and chickens pecked in the bright green grass.

The hut's door hung open on its hinges. A woman lay lifeless, sprawled in the garden, bright red oozing from beneath her prone body. Two lathered horses were tethered to a tree. One of the owners of those horses placed relentless punches on a kilted man held erect by the other highwayman.

A low snarl rumbled up from deep in Hepburn's chest. "Cockscum."

Clarice tore her gaze away and turned to stare at him. As she watched, his countenance changed. His lips curled back to reveal his strong white teeth. His nostrils flared, his eyes narrowed on the two marauders.

The sound of fists striking the poor man's abdomen, his face, the crunch of his bones, his thin, pathetic cries, sent Blaize rearing.

Clarice fought for control of the frightened horse. Fought, too, her own desire to flee.

Those men were pitiless murderers, laughing as they killed a man blow by blow.

She subdued Blaize, then because she knew her duty, she said, "My lord, there are two of them. I can help. Tell me what to do."

He shot her a look that made her draw back, more afraid of him than of the killers below. Letting out a war cry that made her gasp and Blaize rear again, he dug his heels into his horse's flanks. Like the warhorse it was, it leaped into action, racing down the rocky slope toward the hut with as much assurance as it might onto a flat battlefield.

At the bloodcurdling shriek, the thieves lifted their heads in surprise, but when they realized only one man raced toward them, their alarm turned to bellows of laughter. Almost casually one of them lifted his pistol and pointed it at Hepburn.

Fear blossomed, clouding Clarice's vision with red anger. Screaming Hepburn's name, she urged Blaize into motion. She galloped down the slope, Blaize's hooves striking the ground like flint against tinder.

But Hepburn's horse gathered itself and made a smooth, long leap right at the gap-toothed reaver.

As the horse's hooves flew at his head, the thief screamed. He rolled. The pistol discharged, and when he staggered to his feet, Clarice expected to see blood. On him, on Hepburn.

But the shot had gone astray. Clarice pulled Blaize up, trying to decide what she should do to help Hepburn. Rush in and distract the thieves? Or stay out of the way?

Giving a roar of rage, the reaver threw his smoking, useless pistol aside.

His friend, broad-shouldered and big-bellied, abandoned the savaged crofter. Grabbing a stout staff from the woodpile, he made it whistle as he spun it over his bald head. He raced toward his horse.

But Hepburn wheeled around and cut him off. In a feat of riding that left Clarice breathless, he cantered between the villains' horses and the tree, freeing their reins as he went. He let loose another one of those shrieking, terror-inspiring war cries, and the villains' horses panicked, galloping away in a frenzy.

The thieves shrieked their fury—and their panic. Hepburn was mounted. They were not. He would ride them down. . . .

But he didn't.

He galloped in a circle around the bald man with the staff, making him twist and turn, then, while he was off balance, Hepburn charged him and snatched the staff from his hand.

The bald man slipped onto one knee. His curses rang through the valley.

Halfway down the slope, Clarice held Blaze still. Hepburn knew what he was doing. She didn't, and she didn't want to get in Hepburn's way.

She was *afraid* to get in Hepburn's way.

He hurled the staff like a spear at the first man, rode past the bald robber, and while the horse was in full canter threw himself from the saddle onto Baldy. They went tumbling, fists flying in a brutal physical battle that raised goose bumps on her flesh. She'd never seen, never heard, such a fight.

Hepburn was on the bottom, taking, giving, blow after blow.

Toothless drew a knife from his belt and charged toward the fray.

She shrieked, "Robert! A knife!" and started Blaize galloping once more.

At the sound of her voice, Hepburn lifted Baldy with his feet and fists and threw him at Toothless. The two villains sprawled in the grass.

Hepburn stood, pointed his finger at Clarice, and shouted, "Stay!"

As if she were a dog. As if she were his serf!

And, hands trembling, heart pounding, she obeyed him like a dog or a serf. She didn't dare not. She didn't recognize this man, this Hepburn. He was a savage, and she was more afraid of him than of the louts he fought.

The louts had grown afraid too. She could see it in the way they stood, slowly rising to their feet and mumbling to each other, trying to come up with a strategy to defeat the lunatic who stalked them with feral intent.

They let him come, then circled, one on each side of him.

Hepburn grinned. Clarice could see his glee. He gestured them in, closer and closer, and when Toothless charged him with the knife, Hepburn stepped aside, caught his wrist, and twisted.

When she heard the bones snap, Clarice's stomach turned.

Toothless went down screaming, writhing in agony.

Above the noise Clarice heard Hepburn saying, "You were on my estate last night, weren't you?"

No. Clarice had seen the man on the estate. It wasn't one of these men.

"I dunna even know who ye are." Baldy backed away as Hepburn stalked forward.

"Liar." Hepburn flexed his fists. "You dared to spy on my home."

"I'm from Edinburgh. I dunna know who ye are, and I'm na' a spy. I'm an honest thief, I am." Hepburn's blow caught Baldy's ear so hard, his head snapped sideways.

Like a prizefighter, Baldy slipped under Hepburn's guard and landed him a blow on the chin.

Before Clarice could do more than choke off a gasp, Hepburn dodged the next hit, avoiding Baldy's hamlike hands, and placed two punches to Baldy's nose. Blood spurted, and Hepburn said steadily, "Blackguard. You were watching my house."

Baldy tried to smash him to the ground.

Hepburn weaved away and clipped Baldy's eye. "Who paid you to watch the house?"

Baldy staggered back. "Ye're a crazy whoreson, ye know that?"

"I know." Hepburn hit him again. "Who?"

"I ne'er been t' yer house." Wheeling, Baldy tried to run.

Hepburn's foot shot out. He tripped him. Waited until Baldy lurched to his feet. Tripped him again. Standing over him, Hepburn asked, "Were you going to rob me?"

Baldy's arm swept under Hepburn's knees.

Hepburn did a somersault and came back

to his feet. Reaching down, he grabbed Baldy and dragged him up to stand on his feet. "What were you going to steal?" He clipped Baldy on the chin.

"Nothing. I vow. Nothing." Baldy was weaving, punching, trying to strike Hepburn.

Hepburn punched him in the chest, boxed his ear, smashed his nose.

Blinded by his own blood, Baldy fell to the ground and gasped. "Don't know ye."

Hepburn stood staring at the men on the ground, chest heaving, his expression demonic. To the writhing Baldy he said, "I'm the earl of Hepburn. These are my people that you killed, that you robbed."

Blubbering, Baldy promised, "Ne'er again."

"That's right. Never again." Leaning down, Hepburn pulled him up by his shirt and punched him again.

Clarice couldn't watch anymore. She rode to his side. "Lord Hepburn!" She slid from the saddle. "Lord Hepburn!" She caught his arm as he prepared to hit the now-unconscious man. "Lord Hepburn, stop. You have to stop!" The sour taste of bile coated her throat, and her voice quivered abominably.

Lifting his head, Hepburn stared at her as if he'd never seen her before. His hair stood on end. His sleeve had been slashed by the knife. Blood sheeted his arm. He looked as if the devil himself had taken possession of his soul, and she feared he would hit her too.

Then his chest rose in a long, slow breath. His face cleared. He dropped his arm. He dropped the body. In a voice that sounded frighteningly calm and normal, he instructed, "Your Highness, ride back to MacKenzie Manor and send someone for MacGee. I'll tend to him until they get back."

"But"—she indicated his wound—"my lord, you're hurt."

Glancing at his arm indifferently, he said, "I've had worse. MacGee hasn't, poor bastard." He whistled for Blaize and the stallion trotted over.

Hepburn lifted her into the saddle, and the touch made her shiver in terror. But not revulsion, God help her. Never revulsion.

"If we don't get MacGee help, he's going to die." Hepburn slapped Blaize's rump to start him off. "Hurry."

Fifteen

A princess performs needlework to create an object of beauty, and to display her beautiful hands and graceful gestures.
—THE DOWAGER QUEEN OF BEAUMONTAGNE

From the window of Hepburn's study, Clarice watched Robert ride in, bloody, bruised, and apparently unfazed. She marked his progress through the corridors by the female shrieks of horror and his low, reassuring murmur. She stood in the twilight shadows as he entered the room, and she heard him say, "I'm fine, Millicent. I don't need a surgeon to stitch up such a small scratch. I must look at the mail that arrived this afternoon, then I promise I'll rest. Go back to your guests. God knows they need you more than I." He shut and locked the door in his sister's anxious face and made his way toward his desk, where the mail was stacked on a silver salver.

Clarice took the moment to study him. He sported a slight puffiness around his eyes, a little bruising at his jaw, but all in all, for a man who had been in a vicious fight only a few hours before, he looked very good. Except for that slash on his arm—it needed tending.

Without lifting his head, he said, "Don't hover there, Your Highness, come out and care for me. That is what you intended, isn't it?"

He hadn't appeared to, but he had noticed the table she'd set up with her scissors, her sewing kit, and the basin of warm water. He had noticed her too, and as she stepped into the light, he looked directly at her.

His eyes were red-rimmed.

He was still in a rage.

Her heart speeded up. She wanted to run. She wanted to stay. She wanted to make sure he was all right. She didn't care. She had seen him at his worst, in an uncontrollable rage, a rage so deep and murderous he would have gladly killed. And she'd seen him at his best, for he'd been fighting for his people.

But the composure and compassion Grandmamma had taught her was deeply ingrained, and he . . .

With great deliberation he looked away, putting a distance between them that had nothing to do with proximity and everything to do with rebuff.

So she managed to speak with serenity. "How is MacGee?"

"His wife's dead, but he'll live." With a sneer at the pile of mail, Hepburn moved toward her. "He's with the surgeon in town."

With much satisfaction she noted Hepburn wasn't going to deny his injuries to her.

"You've got blood on your hands from handling MacGee." She dipped Hepburn's hand into the basin of water. Red oozed off his knuckles—and oozed, and oozed. It was his blood, she realized, Hepburn's blood.

Of course. The way he'd battered those men had been fierce and brutal. How could he not have hurt his hands?

She said, "I'll wrap your fingers as soon as

I stitch the slash on your arm. Remove your shirt."

He didn't move. He stood there as if he hadn't heard her, or as if she were speaking a foreign language.

She reached for his wrecked cravat, intending to help him, but so swiftly she never saw him move, he knocked her hands away. With his right hand he grabbed the gaping slash in his left sleeve, ripped the material off, and tossed it away. "There."

Modesty? From the man who only last night urged her toward his bed? She picked up soft strips of cotton, dampened them, and gently wiped off the dried blood from his wound. *She didn't believe it.*

"Where did a princess learn to stitch a knife wound?" He stood with his head hanging. His chest rose and fell in hard breaths, and his voice was guttural. Yet the question was reasonable.

"Grandmamma isn't a woman who suffers fools lightly." Carefully Clarice touched the edges of the wound, trying to see how deep the knife had gashed. The muscle was mostly intact, but the skin curled back and would take more stitches than she'd realized, which made his indifference all the more incredible. He had to be in intense pain. Absentmindedly she continued. "Grandmamma taught all of us girls to sew, and when the revolution started, she told us that we might have to work among the wounded. She said it was our duty to our loyal soldiers. She said we would be the symbols that they were fighting for."

"And did you work among your loyal subjects?"

"No. Grandmamma said we should stay and die for our country. My father thought not. He sent us to England. Sometimes I wish we hadn't gone . . . but that's foolishness, I suppose. I suppose, if we had stayed, we would be dead too. As long as we're alive, there's hope that—" She caught herself. She didn't like to talk about hope. She didn't like to feel hope. It made an otherwise perilous life almost unbearable.

She especially didn't want Hepburn to know that in the deepest, darkest corner of her heart, a tiny flame of optimism never died, for she feared that somehow he would use that flame against her, just as he had used her affection for Blaize to ensnare her into the madness of his charade.

She urged him toward a chair beside the

table. "Won't you sit while I place the stitches?"

"No." The muscle in his jaw flexed as he stared straight ahead. "I'll stand."

"As you wish." Ah, love was a burden almost past bearing, yet when Clarice looked at him standing there, wounded in body and soul, she experienced longings that stirred her heart more powerfully than any other emotion in her life.

Not that her feelings were love. She wasn't fool enough to think that. But she craved and hated him. When she was gone from this place, she would dream of him still, for he had invaded her soul with his touch and his kisses and his jewel-bright eyes.

Now she had to touch him. Heal him. And do it without alerting him to her affection, for he showed no such fondness to her. Indeed, he stood completely still, ignoring her as if she were a piece of the furniture. Threading her needle with the catgut, she tried a jest. "Shall I use a fancy cross-stitch?"

"Just sew it up." He watched his own fingers as he flexed them. "How many sisters do you have?"

Shock rippled through her. "Sisters?"

"You said you had sisters."

"No, I didn't." *She didn't. She hadn't.*

"You said, *All of us girls.*" He took his hand out of the water and dabbed it dry with a towel. "You're from Beaumontagne."

Fear lit a swift flame in her gut. "You don't know that!"

"I do now."

He had tricked her. He'd tricked her. Now he knew the name of her country and he could sell her to the villains who wished her dead. He'd discovered another threat he could hold over her head.

She didn't hesitate when she jabbed the first hole in his skin.

He barely flinched. "So I'm right. The first day I saw you . . . I wondered. The English don't know much about your little country, but when I was on the Peninsula, we soldiers noted that there was a look about women from Beaumontagne, a freshness about them."

She could scarcely speak for fear. "Due to my creams."

"And you, of course, are a princess of Beaumontagne." His tone mocked her. "With sisters who live . . . where?"

He didn't know about Amy. Clarice took a strong breath. Amy was safe. "My sisters are none of your concern."

She risked another glance at Hepburn. And this man wouldn't betray her. Not by accident anyway, and if she did as he told her, she hoped to come out relatively unscathed.

Of course, as far as she was concerned, he could travel the road to Hades and beyond. He was a rude, crude, beastly male who deserved nothing from her.

Yet he'd saved MacGee's life. Clarice knew he wouldn't get help if she didn't give it to him, so she would render him aid whether he wished it or not.

Stretching the edges of his skin together, she pulled them tight with the thread. As she tied off each stitch, she demanded, "How did you know I was from Beaumontagne?"

"You said Blaize was half Arabian and half Beaumontagne. Not very many people know there's a tiny country called Beaumontagne, much less that they breed horses there."

"How do *you* know about Beaumontagne? And the horses?" Her fingers trembled. "How do you *know* these things?"

Prudently he caught her hand and held it. "I went to war on the Peninsula. I traveled all over Spain and Portugal. I went into the Pyrenees and, among other places, I visited Andorra and I visited Beaumontagne."

She dug her fingernails into his flesh. "Then you know about the revolution."

A pang of homesickness struck at the heart of her. The newspapers report so little. "Tell me—is the country still in turmoil? Or is Queen Claudia firmly in control?"

"I don't know."

She wanted to shake him until he gave her information. "What do you mean, you don't know? You were *there.*"

"Riding in, riding out, in the dark of night." He eased his hand from hers. "Drinking in inns, listening for news of Napoleon's army."

She had waited for years to be called back to Beaumontagne. She had listened for tidbits of news. She had longed to go to the embassy in London and ask questions, but she didn't dare. Godfrey had said neither Clarice nor Amy was safe from assassins, and while she was willing to take a chance with her own life, she dared not expose Amy to imprisonment and possible death. Now disappointment tasted bitter on her tongue, and she lashed at Hepburn with the most ridiculous accusation she could imagine. "What were you, some kind of spy?"

"No."

No. Of course not. English noblemen were

not spies. They considered such secretive work beneath them. They would rather dress in fancy uniforms, ride fine horses, and slash helpless foot soldiers with their swords.

Then, in a flat tone Hepburn confessed, "I was shoddier than a spy. I was lower than a spy. The conscripts in the army performed more respectable missions than I did."

She stared at him in astonishment. Heat rolled off him in waves. His tousled hair stood up in clumps. And while she didn't doubt him, she didn't understand. "You're a man of consequence. How is such a thing possible?"

He laughed, a dry, coughing laugh. "Someone had to do the dirty work, and I got very good at it."

"What kind of dirty work?"

"The kind that stains a man's soul." He indicated the half-stitched wound on his arm. "You should have been a surgeon in the army. I've never had such neat sewing done on me before."

"How many wounds have you had?"

"A few."

A few. Of course. When a man fought with the kind of disregard to pain Hepburn showed, he would be injured.

She resumed her work and reflected on

him. How swiftly he put conclusions together. How cleverly he had first tried to seduce her into doing his will, then, when that didn't work, to blackmail her. Now he manipulated her into confessing her background. She wanted to stab the needle in him just for fun—except she suspected he wouldn't feel the pain. But she knew her duty—she had to treat his wounds. Her dedication wasn't personal. She would do as much for a dog who'd been hit by a wagon.

She finished the stitching. Opening one of her jars, she dabbed her prized salve on him.

He watched, his eyes shadowed by his lashes. "What's that?"

She didn't like the way he asked, as if he suspected her of poisoning him, and she snapped, "A healing unguent. It'll keep away the infection."

"Why don't you sell that in your demonstration?"

"It's impossible to get here." She finished and wrapped his arm in a long strip of cotton. "This is my last jar." With precious little left.

"You shouldn't be wasting it on me," he rumbled.

"But Grandmamma instructed us to place others' welfare before our own, and I can't discard her teachings—no matter how much I'd like to." And while it was true, Clarice would have liked to do no more for Hepburn than necessary, she couldn't bear to imagine him developing a fever and falling into unconsciousness. She shuddered to imagine this man who fought like a berserker, and lived on the thin edge of desperation, still and cold in death. And if that death occurred because she had failed to do all in her power to heal him. . . .

"Mustn't disobey Grandmamma," he jibed.

Ingrate. Cad. His mockery incensed her.

Taking his other hand from the water, she examined the bruised knuckles. Pressing the joints one by one, she watched to see if he winced. But he remained blank-faced. So be it. If he'd broken a bone, he'd have to suffer. After smearing her salve on the scrapes, she wrapped the worst of the sores in soft white cotton. "There. I leave you to go to your bed."

"Not yet."

That deep, brooding tone cut no mustard with her, and she asked briskly, "Are you hurt somewhere I can't see? No? Then my work is done."

He extended his large hand to her. "Earlier

today . . . we made a deal. Your cooperation for Blaize. We never shook hands."

She stared at that hand, bloody and bandaged, steady as a rock, and belated caution curled in her gut. Did he never forget anything? Did he always insist that his partners, willing or not, seal their agreement with the ancient contract? Did he imagine she had some outdated sense of honor that would hold her to his demands as long as she shook his hand? "You hold Blaize in your stables. You already have my cooperation."

"Nevertheless, I'll have your hand on the deal."

Maybe that dark, brooding tone did work for her, for she fought the sudden rising of two different desires—one to flee, one to fight. She took deep breaths, still staring at the hand, then at him. He stared at his hand too, waiting, waiting. . . .

And, blast him, he was right. She did suffer with an outdated sense of honor. His blackmail would hold her only as long as he held Blaize. But the handshake would detain her until the charade was finished to his satisfaction.

To his satisfaction . . .

Slowly she reached out her hand and put it in his. The shock of the contact ran up her arm, lifted the hair on her head, slithered down her spine.

His fingers curled around hers. For the first time since she'd begun her work, his gaze rose and met hers—and singed her with its heat.

She recognized this man. This was Hepburn without any of his masks. This was the warrior who had today fought for a dead woman and her wounded husband.

Now the battle still raged in him. And not only today's battle. The rage, the tumult of the war, still burned in his soul. Today's fight had stripped away the camouflage of tranquillity. He lived with pain, a pain that transformed itself into a fury of passion.

He wanted her.

Sixteen

Don't just aim high, reach oot and grab some happiness along the way.
—THE OLD MEN OF FREYA CRAGS

Fear leaped in Clarice, the fear of a female who faces a strong, ruthless man. A man who people whispered was mad. A man whose eyes kindled and burned.

And with the fear came a rush of excitement. Hepburn wanted her beyond reason, beyond etiquette, beyond willpower. Her blood leaped to meet his desire. When he wrapped his arm around her waist and pulled her close, her breath caught. Her breasts pressed against his chest, her loins against his loins. He stared down at her face, his lips slightly open, his white teeth gleaming, and all the long-forgotten fairy tales her nursemaid had told her about hungry wolves came back in a wild rush.

Her heart thundered. She pushed against his shoulders.

He was going to devour her.

His lips took hers in a savage kiss. His tongue thrust inside her mouth and tussled with hers, subduing her rebellion, wresting unwilling excitement from her.

He was mad. And the madness was contagious, for she ached with need. Her skin grew taut, her breasts tender. Her knees shook, and the place between her legs swelled with passion.

He took her breath as if it were his right and gave her his like a conqueror laying claim to a country—and she was that country.

Pleasure rushed through her veins, moving as swiftly as an obsession. She moaned into his mouth. He tore his lips from hers and kissed her cheeks, ran his teeth along her jaw, sucked at her neck and along her collarbone. It was as if he wanted to taste every inch of her, and every inch of her wanted him to seize the privilege.

He bent her over his arm, and in one smooth move slid her bodice down and freed one of her breasts from its confinement. Briefly she surfaced from this flood of ardor to realize that he was too knowledgeable, too experienced. He'd practiced his moves many times before, and that made her want to hit him.

Then he growled low in his throat, and she hoped no other woman had ever viewed that expression on his face. He was hungry. He was ravenous, and she stiffened with alarm.

He was going to hurt her.

But his mouth, when it wrapped around her nipple, was warm and soft as velvet. The friction of his textured tongue made her moan again, sharper, higher, and her fingers clutched in his hair. Gripping the dark strands, she held him in place as he sucked on her, and fireworks burst beneath her closed eyelids. She'd never felt like this in her life, never imagined a battle of sweet and violent emotion could rage in her veins.

Yet at the same time . . . she comprehended again why she shied away from Lord

Hepburn. She had always suspected he could infect her with his madness—and she would be powerless to resist.

All these years . . . all her discipline . . . washed away in a flood of foolishness.

Yet, as he worshipped her with his mouth, it felt right. For the first time since she'd arrived on Britain's shores, she felt at home.

When she was gasping for air, when the cruel world had vanished and only this man remained, he lifted his head.

The cool air against her damp nipple made it tighten unbearably. Dizzy and breathless, she sucked in air, looked up at him.

And he was smiling. Watching her, smiling, his teeth white in his swarthy face. His eyes . . . oh, God, they still had that crazed cast about them. Her hands trembled as she clutched at him, trying to balance herself on a wildly tilting earth.

Fruitless endeavor. His hands slid down to cup her bottom. He lifted her onto her toes, thrust his leg high between her legs. His thigh pressed against her feminine parts, pressed firmly, and he forced her to move, back and forth, back and forth.

Good sense pierced the heady fog of passion. "No!" She shoved at him as hard as she could, for if he didn't stop . . .

"No!" If he didn't stop, she would . . .

"No!" She didn't know what she would do, but she did know she would be out of control. That would be unacceptable. Embarrassing. Unbearable. "Stop!"

But he didn't listen. He didn't stop. He didn't even seem to hear her.

And the ache within her grew.

Her strength crumpled beneath the onslaught. Her knees sagged. The pressure intensified. Dark passion clawed at her, stripping away her pride, her very identity. Her fingernails dug into his shoulders, into the heated skin hidden beneath the thin layer of his shirt.

Putting his lips close to her ear, he whispered, "You're mine. To do with as I wish."

"No." But while her lips formed the word, she had no breath to speak it, and still his thigh relentlessly moved between her legs.

"Tonight you're mine. Give yourself to me." And he bit her earlobe hard enough to bring her arching toward him.

Hard enough that shock drove her over the edge into the dark abyss of climax. Her body spasmed against his, helpless against the wave after wave of sensation so strong she couldn't speak, she couldn't breathe, she could only feel.

And the feeling was like nothing she'd ever experienced before. She moved, moaned, *was,* without conscious thought.

He lifted her before she had finished and lay her on the rug at their feet. The floor was hard against her back. His hands were rough as they caught her skirt and lifted it to her waist, but his expression was intent, triumphant, almost . . . worshipful.

She should be embarrassed to have her legs bared, to suffer the wash of air over her private parts, but somehow this man, with his experienced fingers and inciting lips, transmitted his sense of triumph, and she opened her arms to him.

He dropped to his knees between her legs, stripped his pants down and lay on top of her. The shock of his bare skin against hers blocked the breath in her lungs. He radiated heat, branding her flesh. Bracing his elbows on either side of her head, he dipped down to taste her lips, then delved deep with his tongue. The slow, steady motion of his probing, the gentle caress of his fingers on her chin, made her tremble in eagerness . . . and trepidation. His scent filled her nostrils, and the overwhelming intimacy of mouth and body broke through all the barriers she'd erected to protect her heart.

Sliding her hands up into his hair, she clutched it and held him, taking the thrusts of his tongue and returning them in bashful increments. He groaned as if her enthusiasm gave him pain, and the vibration of his lips against hers carried her to a higher level of excitement. In a rush of daring she rubbed her leg along his hip, and as if that deliberate contact broke his precarious hold on restraint, he reared back. She caught a brief glimpse of eyes heated to the temperature of blue coals.

Then he thrust his hips against her. His manhood probed for entrance. She stiffened in shock, but nothing could stop him now. He found her feminine opening, pressed hard . . . and for the first time she felt the presence of a man pushing within her.

He hurt her. He burned her with his passion. His hands rested beside her head. His elbows were locked, supporting his chest. He dominated her with his position and his power.

Tears ran from her eyes, but she didn't stop him. How could she, when his arched neck, flared nostrils, and agonized expression told her only too clearly of his own hurt? Inch by inch he fought his way inside, breaking down her maidenhead, taking her, claiming her. And while he did, she absorbed his agony, soothing him, exchanging his pain for hers.

Then he was all the way inside, pausing, adjusting . . . waiting for something. For what?

Her gaze flew to meet his.

His hips pressed hers to the floor. Intently he observed her, his eyes wide and wild. Sweat beaded his forehead. He strained to hold himself still.

She could see it. He was a man on the brink of folly—and she refused to descend into folly alone. She wrapped her arms around his back, wrapped her legs around his hips, sliding into a position that accepted him—his domination and his manhood—more fully.

And as if her acquiescence destroyed the last remnants of his sanity, he descended on top of her. Drawing back his hips, he plunged inside. Over and over he took her, blind and thoughtless with exhilaration.

Yet she found herself rising to meet him, matching passion for passion. She had no idea where anguish left off and pleasure began. It didn't even matter. All that mattered was this primal mating, this meeting of their two bodies, the way they merged to become one. The act was imprudent and unbidden and glorious beyond measure. Never in her life had she done something for the pure joy of the act, but now, exuberantly and without thought, she mated with him.

As his body moved on her, within her, he drew her with him down the path to breathless release. Her blood roared in her ears, her heart labored in her chest. She whimpered and clutched at him, her palms damp with desire. Deep in her womb, her muscles seized at his manhood, trying to hold him inside.

Yet always he slipped away. The motion and the struggle between them grew more ferocious. She wanted him as she had never wanted anything in her life before, and when he slid his hands beneath her bottom and lifted her to take his concentrated thrusts, he propelled her into fulfillment.

Furious, demanding, aggressive fulfillment.

The reckless violence of orgasm caught her, lifted her in ferocious spasms to a place where pleasure banished thought. Obeying some deep, ancient instinct, she writhed beneath him, a creature at one with him—with his rage, with his anguish, with his glory.

His pace increased, drew her further into the dark splendor of gratification. He groaned aloud, a deep animal sound that came from the depths of his tormented soul, and as if that were the sign of his breaking, he arched in the throes of irresistible, unstoppable bliss. He braced himself, every muscle taut, his body hammering against hers, and his abandon pulled her under again.

She went without complaint, too new to realize that what he did to her was almost impossible—to carry a virgin to the heights not once, but twice. The force of pleasure made her gasp for air. Her body was no longer her own, but a thing for Hepburn to have and use . . . and cherish. For one moment, when her pleasure was at its pinnacle, she thought she was dying.

But no. As his motion ceased, as he sank down atop her, she became aware that she was very much alive. Every inch of her skin blushed. Her heart sang. Her womb quivered with the last fading shocks of satisfaction. Beneath her the floor was hard, the rug was rough, the strands of her hair caught in its coarse weave. Her eyes, lids heavy, opened to gaze on him, and never had she seen anything as beautiful as his sweat-dampened face.

In utter silence they stared at each other. He had fulfilled all the promises he'd made with his crystal eyes, his confident walk, his steady grip. He'd given her joy beyond anything she had ever dared imagine.

As if disoriented, he shook his head. His voice rasped as if the question had been dragged from a cavern deep within him. "Why did you let me . . . take you?"

She should box his ears for his insolent assumption of authority over her, but somehow, with the weight of him on her and that bewilderment on his face, she hadn't the spirit. Gently she told him, "You didn't take me." The place between her legs ached, but she had to tell him the truth. "I gave myself to you."

Slowly he withdrew from her body, leaving her lonely. Already lonely.

"Why?" he asked.

The answer. It was so simple. How could he not know? "Because you needed me."

Seventeen

Be careful what ye wish fer. Ye might get it.
—THE OLD MEN OF FREYA CRAGS

Because you needed me.

What the hell did that mean?

As ferocious as a wounded tiger, Robert limped away from his cottage and toward the manor. Morning had passed; he had awoken to the noonday sun, to the scent of Clarice's perfume on his body, and the stupefied realization that he'd slept deeply for the first time since his return from the war.

Never mind that he'd found in Clarice the

kind of joy he'd thought had disappeared from his life forever. Never mind that he'd taken her maidenhead . . .

Bloody damned hell. She'd been a virgin.

At the thought that haunted him, he pressed his palms to his forehead and stumbled a little from the weakness in his leg. He had a huge bruise on his hip from one of yesterday's blows, although he didn't remember one. His arm ached where Princess Clarice had placed the stitches. His eye and jaw were swollen and—he flexed his fingers— his knuckles were stiff beneath the scabs. Nothing worth being concerned about. In the past he'd had much worse.

No, it wasn't his war trophies that bothered him. It was the truth he came back to again and again. Clarice had been a virgin. He wasn't worried that she was really a princess, or that she'd destroyed her chance at a dynastic marriage. Those tales were simple bumblebroth on her part.

But she was an unmarried woman, and he'd ruined her. When he'd planned her seduction, he'd believed her to be experienced. She had misled him with her air of confidence and her worldly travels. He'd been wrong, and he had ruined her.

Worse, no matter how he lectured himself, he couldn't feel sorrow. He liked knowing he was her first. He wanted to be her last. But he had ruined her, and she . . . she had said . . .

Because you needed me.

He didn't need her. He didn't need anyone.

Clarice was convenient. A woman in the right place at the right time. He needed to make that clear to her.

But the gentlemen would be arriving soon, smeared with dirt from their hunting, needing baths and wanting food. When could he find the time or the opportunity to speak to Clarice alone?

He entered the house through the side door and looked around in irritation.

And where was everyone? Why hadn't any of the men turned up yet? Were the ladies primping in their rooms?

For the first time since he'd come home, he wanted company. He wanted to speak with people, he wanted to hear voices . . . because he didn't want to think about Clarice's words.

You needed me.

Blast her.

He wanted to speak to Clarice and tell her—

No. He *needed* to see Clarice. Not in the way she meant he needed her, but because Colonel Ogley was on his way. If Hepburn's information was correct, and it was, Ogley would be here before tea.

Hepburn took a long, slow breath of anticipation. Time was running out. He needed to prepare Clarice for the task ahead.

He stalked the corridors, listening and looking. She was nowhere to be found.

Gesturing to a young, gangly footman, Hepburn asked, "Where is the princess?"

The footman jumped and blushed bright red. "M'lord, Her Highness is in the conservatory."

"Again?" Hepburn snapped.

The footman's eyes bugged in alarm. "M'lord?"

"Never mind." Hepburn started down the corridor. "I'll find out soon enough." She wasn't doing another demonstration, was she? Damned if he'd let her decorate him again. He didn't know if he could bear to have her touch him, because the mere thought of her made his blood heat as well as other, less biddable parts.

As he approached the conservatory, he first caught her scent. Like nutmeg and flowers and warm, rich wine. The aroma drew him back into the memory of last night, when he lay on top of her and thrust inside her. He didn't want to think about that, to remember how she'd felt as she moved beneath him, giving herself with unceasing generosity. Yet he breathed deeply, and his heartbeat speeded up.

Then he heard her voice.

You needed me.

But no. She didn't say that. She was saying, "You need this to affect a smooth line of the brow. See how it shapes and defines?"

She was talking about cosmetics again, unceasingly selling her salves and her unguents. She was as driven as he was, but for different reasons. She wanted money. To go back to Beaumontagne and take her place in the royal family, she would say. He would say . . . well, he didn't know what drove her. He didn't understand anything about her. And he wished he didn't care.

Keeping to the shadows, he glanced inside at the gaggle of ladies staring raptly toward the front. Millicent sat beside a small table, a cup of tea at her elbow, her cheek cradled in her hand. She looked plain and, well, lonely, just as Clarice had shouted at him just yesterday. Millicent *was* unvalued by his father, by Prudence, and by him. But he didn't feel guilty. Guilt was useless. Instead, he pondered how to correct the situation. He made decisions, and before the ball was over, Millicent would have what she wanted, whatever that might be. He would do what it took to make her happy.

Miss Larissa Trumbull and her mother sat there too, scornful moues distorting their mouths.

Hastily he stepped out of their view. The last thing he needed was to hear Larissa Trumbull's calculatingly sultry voice and be subjected to another extravagant display of her overlavish breasts.

He angled so that he could view Clarice.

She truly did have a regal air about her. She was petite, yet she stood like a tall woman, with her shoulders back and her arms curved gracefully at her sides. She was unerringly kind to those less fortunate, yet like someone who feared intimacy and its ultimate betrayal, she held a bit of herself apart. That detachment challenged him.

Was she the princess of some faraway

country, or a fraud of unimaginable skill? He didn't know. He knew only that he had had her but still hadn't won her.

Her beauty took his breath away. Her hair . . . some said a woman's hair was her crowning glory, but with Clarice, it was true. Her curls were truly golden, catching the light in their soft, reflective curves. She had it pulled back and pinned it so some strands were held and others escaped in a careless array and draped onto the column of her neck. He longed to push those curls aside, to brush the nape of her neck with his fingers, with his lips. He wanted to kiss the soft arc of her cheek, the bow of her rosy mouth. His gaze lingered on her shapely bosom, so sadly neglected last night in his frenzy to mate, and resolved to make up for his negligence with long minutes . . . no, *hours* of attention.

Catching her scent, hearing her voice, seeing her, created such a mixture of craving—*not need*—in him that he feared to have anyone see him in this state. His cock was as erect as ever it had been during his adolescence, and he had as little control over himself as a lad in his first fever of wanting. His hands shook with the desire to go in there, to pick her up and carry her away. Away from the persuasive words, the simpering ladies, the trappings of civilization, and into a place of his making where nothing existed but him and her and their nude bodies tangled together until he enjoyed her in every way a woman could be possessed.

Clarice had a girl in the chair—what was her name?—Miss Rosabel, that seamstress from the village. The ladies watched—Millicent and Prudence, Lady Mercer and Lady Lorraine, Lady Blackston and Miss Diantha Erembourg—as Clarice pointed at Amy's chin, her cheeks, her nose. Taking the girl's hair in her hand, Clarice pulled it back from Amy's face, then tilted her head so Robert had a clear view of her profile.

She was a pretty girl, he thought idly. A lucky girl to have Clarice showing her how to create allure, for he recalled how Miss Rosabel looked when first she'd come to Freya Crags. She hadn't warranted a second glance.

As Clarice talked, the girl grimaced and shot a resentful sidelong glance at her.

How odd. Why would she be resentful?

And he'd seen that expression before on someone else. Something familiar about the girl's expression haunted him. He narrowed his gaze on her.

Then Clarice grimaced too, and he knew. Without fanfare he realized—they were sisters. Clarice and Amy were sisters.

They didn't look alike, but their gestures, their expressions, the way they walked, were identical.

He stepped back.

For with that realization came another one. The new seamstress wasn't a chance wanderer who had come to Freya Crags for a job. Their plan was deliberate. A few weeks before Clarice rode into town, this seemingly homely female arrived and waited to be transformed, in public, into a lovely young lady.

He didn't know whether to applaud their ingenuity or to curse the knowledge that Clarice was a charlatan of unusual proportions.

Both. Neither.

For to know that Clarice had to support her younger sister put a new cast on their charade. The role of beauty maker set easily on Clarice's shoulders. But the role of rascal seemed unlikely. Had the weight of a sister's security driven Clarice to deception?

More important, he had surmised she

had sisters, but she had never admitted to their existence. Were there more sisters lurking about, or was it only Miss Rosabel she protected?

No matter. Nothing had changed. He still required Clarice to perform her duties at the ball. He still needed her as much as ever.

Going back to the footman, he said, "When Her Highness is finished, please direct her to my study." No, not his study. Memories haunted the study. "Rather, direct her to the library. I'll wait for her in the library."

Clarice walked arm in arm with Amy toward the servants' entrance. "You came at just the right time." Based on the clarity and fine texture of Amy's skin, Clarice had sold another dozen jars of her most expensive unguent, the royal secret luminous eye cream. "You are the ideal model."

"That must have been why I walked all the way out here." Amy's lower lip stuck out precipitously. "So I could be a model for your demonstration."

Guilt ripped through Clarice. Amy lived the life of a seamstress, sewing until her eyes ached, living in Mistress Dubb's minuscule bedchamber under the eaves, walking instead of riding the road to MacKenzie Manor. No wonder Amy resented Clarice.

Guiding Amy into the solitude of the small sitting room, Clarice said, "I realize you came for a reason of your own, and I want to hear about it without delay. It was just that you arrived right after I started the demonstration and I dared not tell them I had to stop and speak to you—"

Amy stared at her, hostility radiating from every pore.

"—my sister?" Clarice finished on a questioning note, trying to explain what didn't need to be explained.

"No, you couldn't tell them that. That would ruin everything. The whole ridiculous royal secret charade." Amy whirled away from Clarice's touch. "Look, Clarice, I'm tired of being a demonstration"—she took a deep breath and shouted—"and I'm tired of being a princess."

Hastily Clarice shut the door and for good measure switched to Italian. "What do you mean? You are a princess. You can't change that."

"Don't be ridiculous." Amy paced across the room. "We're not princesses. We don't have a country."

"We do have a country!" Clarice had explained this to Amy before. "We're in temporary exile."

"Temporary exile for the rest of our lives." Amy wrung her fingers until the knuckles turned white. "I'm not doing this anymore. I'm not riding into town ahead of you. I'm not fooling people into thinking you've transformed me from a witch to a beauty. It's over."

"That's fine." Clarice tried to take Amy's hands, to comfort her, but Amy would have none of her reassurance. "This time I'm going to make enough money to carry us back to Beaumontagne."

Amy mocked her. "I thought we weren't supposed to go back until we get the word."

"I've started to wonder if someone is sabotaging Grandmamma's attempts to reach us. That would make such a difference." Clarice tapped her fingers together. "I'm tempted to write Grandmamma."

"If it weren't for me, you would have already gone back to Beaumontagne. Isn't that right?"

Amy's astuteness made Clarice falter. "Why do you say that?"

"I know you. You're as brave as a lion. If you weren't worried about my safety, you'd have made the trip already and discovered the truth of what's happening there." Amy watched her far too closely. "Wouldn't you have?"

"You were only twelve when we left the school, and I deemed it unwise to go back so soon." Which wasn't an answer, but it would have to do.

Yet Amy wouldn't give up. "But later. You've been thinking about going back for a long time, I could tell. If you weren't responsible for me, you would have returned no matter how many difficulties you faced."

"I hardly dare cross Grandmamma's will." That wasn't an answer either, and Amy knew it. Clarice could tell by the derisive twist of her sister's mouth. "I have now resolved to write to Grandmamma, and when I do—"

"You don't understand." Throwing up her hands in extreme exasperation, Amy paced away. "It doesn't matter. I don't care. I don't want to go back to Beaumontagne."

Patiently Clarice followed her. "You don't mean that."

Amy whirled on her, eyes flashing. "Yes, I do. You've worked so we could go back to Beaumontagne, but you've never asked me what I wanted."

Bewildered, Clarice asked, "What *do* you want?"

"I don't care about some faraway country that I scarcely remember!" Amy took Clarice by the shoulders and looked into her eyes. "I want to find someplace in England or in Scotland where we can settle down and do real work—designing clothes or anything that makes the magistrate ignore us."

"Amy." *Amy didn't know what she was saying.* "I'm sorry you don't remember Beaumontagne as I do, and I blame myself for not keeping it in the forefront of your mind—"

Amy blew out an exaggerated, exasperated breath. "I remember it! I was nine when I left, not two. But what good are memories? You're so busy remembering Beaumontagne, you can't look at the landscape around us. You're so busy remembering our lost family that you don't notice the people we talk to every day. You can't live today because you're so eager to live when you get back to Beaumontagne. You're as above the day-to-day occurrences as if you were still living in that castle in Beaumontagne."

Dumbly Clarice stared at her sister. If only it were true. If only she lived merely for tomorrow.

Last night she'd lived for the moment. Robert MacKenzie had dragged her from her preoccupation with what was right and proper for a princess and into his life with its rage and its pain. She'd felt those emotions with him, had given herself to help him, and nothing would ever be the same again.

As the words boiled from her, Amy didn't notice Clarice's anguish. She kept talking faster and faster, as if she had dammed her sentiments for too long. "Me—I'm tired of waiting for tomorrow to live. I want to live here, now, before I'm so old there are no tomorrows left."

"We can't be like normal people. We're not normal people. We're princesses, and all that that entails applies to us." Clarice was surprised to realize how rational she sounded, not at all like a woman who last night had betrayed her heritage in the worst manner possible. "We must remain above the common walk of life—"

Amy talked right over the top of her. "I've heard it all before. I don't care." Taking Clarice's cheeks in her hands, Amy looked into her face. "I refuse to be a princess any longer."

Clarice smiled, although her lips trembled. "Dear sister, I know how frustrated you must be, but I promise if you'll be patient for a few more days, I'll have enough money for us to travel cautiously and wisely back to Beaumontagne."

Amy looked down at the carpet. Traced its design with the toe of her sturdy boot. Looked up and smiled—and the sadness in her smile shook Clarice. "You haven't heard a word I've said, have you?"

In frustration Clarice said, "Yes, I've heard you, but I don't know what you want."

"You've heard me, but you haven't listened." When Clarice would have argued, Amy waved her to silence. "Don't worry, I really do understand. I only wish . . . well, if wishes were horses, the beggar would ride. Isn't that correct? I'll see you when the time is right. Remember, I'm older than you were when you had to begin caring for me."

"When I think how green I was—"

"I'm not green. I'm much more experienced than you were. Now, you must take care of yourself as well as you've tended to me. This is a volatile situation and I worry about you." Amy kissed Clarice's forehead, then stepped away.

"I'll be fine." Although Amy was right. The

situation was volatile and would be more so when next Clarice saw Lord Hepburn. "I have everything under control."

"Of course you do. You can always take care of yourself." Amy smiled with what looked like admiration. "Just remember, I learned to care for myself watching you, and you're the best sister anyone ever had." She moved toward the door.

Amy's assurances alarmed Clarice as nothing else could, and she followed her sister. "Wait, Amy."

But as Amy reached for the knob, a knock sounded. She swung the door open wide to reveal a tall, young footman.

It was Norval, looking more nervous, if possible, than ever. "Yes?" Clarice questioned gently.

He bowed, his long legs awkward. "Yer Highness, His Lordship wishes t' meet wi' ye in the library. He asks that ye go t' him immediately."

Nothing else could have diverted her from Amy's purpose as did that message.

Hepburn wanted to see her again.

Of course, she knew rationally that they would have to see each other again, but to have the moment defined shook her, made her want to run and hide . . . and at the same time, she wanted to rush to him.

Who was she? The princess she knew herself to be? Or simply a woman so foolish as to desire a man beyond sense and propriety?

Amy slipped around the footman and took a few steps down the corridor. "God bless you, Clarice."

Distracted, Clarice answered, "I'll come into the village as soon as the ball is over and we'll talk."

Amy nodded, smiled, waved. "Farewell."

Eighteen

The most interesting people are the people interested in you. A wise princess can use this knowledge to rule her world.
—THE DOWAGER QUEEN OF BEAUMONTAGNE

Clarice started down the corridor toward the library, Norval forgotten, Amy forgotten, the demands of the ladies and their complexions forgotten. Nothing mattered except the clench of her gut and the rising anticipation she experienced at seeing Hepburn again.

Then she noticed the footman's frightened

eyes staring at her anxiously. She didn't care; she just didn't care what his problem was.

But the sight of his hangdog expression clung in her mind. Before she turned the corner, she found herself stopping. "Is there a problem, Norval?"

He shuffled his feet. "Yer Highness, the master told me t' immediately direct ye t' the library when ye had finished wi' the ladies, and . . . and I was working elsewhere." He flushed miserably under her inquiring gaze and corrected himself. "That is, I was speaking t' one o' the maids, and I missed telling ye straightaway, like the master instructed."

"Then we won't tell him." She tried to leave, to go see him.

"The master sees everything, and he has a fearsome temper." Norval lowered his voice. "I hear that yesterday he killed ten rogues wi' his bare fists."

"Two men, and he merely beat them." She couldn't believe she was comforting Norval about an event that had awed and frightened her.

"They say in the kitchen that the master's mad," Norval whispered.

"He is most certainly not mad," she said

with irritation, "and so you may tell them in the kitchen."

Norval bowed as she moved off at a brisk pace.

How ridiculous to think Hepburn was mad because he'd beaten those men! Yes, at one time she might have thought so, but last night had changed that. Last night . . .

She tucked a wisp of hair back with trembling fingers.

Last night she had hated him and loved him and feared him . . . and she had lain with him.

Oh, God. All the previous days of her sojourn in MacKenzie Manor she had feared his madness. Now she wondered at her own. She was going to see him again, and she didn't know what to say. Grandmamma had taught her how to act in every eventuality— except this one.

The bright sunlight coming through the windows should have given her courage; instead, she feared it would expose her thoughts for everyone to see.

An internal voice mocked, *Everyone?*

No one lingered in the corridors. She fooled only herself. The one from whom she wanted to shield her thoughts was Hepburn, because last night had been wonderful and awkward and too much to comprehend.

The door to the library loomed before her. Standing still, she stared as if it were a portal to another world. *He* was on the other side. Last night, when she'd made her way to her bedchamber, she had slept only with difficulty. Her mind had been a tangle of new revelations and old dreams, her emotions swinging from exhilaration to despair. Now she had to face him again, and she wasn't prepared.

She would never be prepared.

The rustle of silk and the patter of feet brought her head around. Larissa hurried toward her, her gimlet gaze fixed on Clarice with all the charity of an eagle spotting its prey. "Princess Clarice!" Her demanding voice was nothing like the sultry tone she affected before Lord Hepburn. "I require your attendance in my bedchamber at once."

How interesting. Larissa and her mother had made their opinions of her ministrations clear. "May I know the reason?"

A slow wave of crimson climbed from Larissa's low bodice to the top of her forehead. "Because I said so."

But Clarice could now see the reason. In public Larissa might say she wouldn't deign to wear Clarice's concealing creams, but a red spot glowed between her eyebrows.

"Just collect your royal secrets and meet me in my bedchamber!" Larissa snapped.

"I'm sorry, Miss Trumbull, but that's not possible. I have another appointment." Clarice remained civil, her voice steady. "Perhaps later?"

If anything, the color deepened on Larissa's face and the spot between her brows turned purple. "Princess Clarice"—she rolled the *r* in *princess*—"you do not know to whom you speak. I am the only child of Reginald Buford Trumbull of Trumbull Hall and of Ann Joann Stark-Nash of Castle Grahame, and we do not put up with insolence from mere peddlers." She smiled with tight haughtiness. "Not even peddlers claiming to be the dispossessed royalty of some mysterious unmentioned country, existing, no doubt, in the fevers of your brain."

Clarice had been insulted before, and by better people, but something about Larissa's snotty assurance got under her skin. Clarice's smile could be called only majestic, and her voice had a bite she normally reserved for yapping dogs and men who dared more than they should. "My dear Miss Trumbull, I am sure your antecedents are all that you claim. However, whether or not you believe me to be royal is a matter of indifference to me. What does matter is that I've given my word to go assist someone else, and I always keep my word." Her tone contained a whiplash of scorn. "I'm sure someone of your consequence realizes the value of keeping one's word."

Rage swept Larissa's face clear of any semblance of civilized behavior. Stepping close, she lifted her arm to land a full-handed slap to Clarice's face.

And from the library Hepburn said, "Your Highness, I thank you for taking the time out of your demanding schedule to speak with me."

Larissa's hand trembled, then dropped to her side.

"Oh, Miss Trumbull!" He sounded startled as he propped himself against the door frame, but his languid posture mocked Larissa, telling her only too clearly that he had seen and heard everything. "I didn't notice you. I hope, Your Highness, that I'm not interrupting your chat with Miss Trumbull."

Larissa's bosom heaved as she fought to get breath and make her excuses, but she could say no more than "I . . . I didn't hear you."

"No." His gaze surveyed her from top to toe, and he made it clear he found the view in poor taste. "I know that you didn't."

Larissa realized what she'd done—showed only too clearly her cruelty and pettiness to the man she had declared she would win. Being Larissa, she tried to pass the blame. "Princess Clarice was insolent to me."

Gradually Hepburn straightened away from the door frame, dominating the scene more and more as he abandoned his indolent pretence. "Miss Trumbull, among the things I detest is the obvious display of feminine charms better hinted at than revealed. But above that, I find rampant jealousy vulgar to the extreme. You are guilty of both, and until you learn a more appropriate behavior, I would suggest you return to the schoolroom."

As Larissa stared at Hepburn, the blood drained from her face. She took a breath to respond, but nothing came out. Finally she turned and, with a pathetic attempt at dignity, tottered away.

Clarice stared after her, uncomfortably aware she'd allowed her temper full rein and had hurt someone in the process. "That was badly done by both of us."

"What do you mean?" Hepburn took her

arm and led her into the library. "Miss Trumbull's an overgrown, insolent lass and she deserved to be slapped down."

"Yes, but forever after she's going to be embarrassed to look you in the eye."

"I would hope so."

He didn't understand, and he didn't care, so she said the thing he would understand. "Overgrown, insolent lasses like her have a tendency to make trouble for humble peddlers like me. I should have played the toady."

It appeared Clarice had forgotten what passed between them last night. Robert didn't like that. "Perhaps you think I should have been less dismissive?"

"Yes!"

What a little goose Clarice was, to worry about Larissa, when he *stood only two paces away.* In a sensual growl he said, "But I do as I like."

Her head snapped around, and she stared at him with her full, pretty mouth hanging ever so slightly open.

He almost laughed as sexual awareness flooded her face. Now she remembered. Her gaze dropped. She blushed and took a step back.

He followed, impatient to move the conversation to a topic of interest to him. A topic like whether she had regretted giving herself to him. Or did she long to try him again? "Forget Larissa. She's not important to us."

"Yes. I mean no." Clarice edged past the bookshelves, a vision in a simple pink gown that gave a glow to her cheeks. "I mean, she might not be important to you, but I've suffered the kind of humiliation she just suffered, and it's painful."

"She'll recover. That kind always does." He wondered how many buttons he would have to undo before the gown slipped off her shoulders and pooled on the floor around her feet. He would enjoy undressing her, making sure he didn't frighten her with the flash of his passion. He did know how to take his time . . . last night had been aberration, a rash and unique desire. Next time would be different.

And now . . . he would court her. Show her he wasn't always a savage who lost himself in a fight, then found himself in a woman's arms.

Stopping at the cabinet, he poured two glasses of pale golden wine and extended one to Clarice. "Tell me about yourself. What have you done that was so bad, it brought you humiliation?"

She stared at the glass as if it were bait in a snare. Which it was. The kind of bait that brought her back in contact with him and at the same time loosened the restrictive corset of her caution. He didn't smile when she snatched the wine from his fingers and sprang back, but he wanted to, and that in itself was interesting. It had been a very, very long time since he'd been so amused so often.

"Humiliation occurs. One does everything one can to forget the circumstances, and that doesn't include relating them to a gentleman who . . ." Her voice trailed off in a satisfying confusion, and she took a hasty sip of the wine. Her startlingly dark brows winged upward. "A good wine! From Germany, I think?"

"Yes, very good." She knew her wines. Taking her arm, he led her into the part of the library with oversize, comfortable chairs, large windows, and carvings set artfully on shelves and tables. "Please, won't you take a seat? It would be most advantageous for us to discuss the evenings ahead." He was surprised to see a smile on her lips. What about the evenings ahead diverted her so?

Then he followed her gaze, and saw her examining the replica of a small marble statue of Hermes about to spring into the air. "What?"

She sank into the chair he'd indicated. "I was remembering one of the occasions of my humiliation."

Ah, a confidence, freely given. Matters were proceeding very well. Taking the bottle, he stepped close to her chair. "You're not distressed by that memory?"

"No. No, it was more hilarious than distressing." Shaking her head, she passed her fingers in front of her eyes and smiled as if she could see the scene before her. "When I was nine, Grandmamma decided that all the statues in the palace—fine art, mind you, collected by my ancestors from the time of the Renaissance—were obscene." Clarice gave a gurgle of laughter, her piquant face alight with remembered glee. "She ordered them draped in togas to protect our delicate, princessly constitutions."

Her sisters. She was speaking of her sisters. He topped off her glass. "Did your constitutions feel protected?"

"Until then we hadn't even noticed the statues. They were nothing more than part of the palace. But once she made a fuss about them, we spent a great deal of time twitching the togas aside to examine the . . . er . . . evidence."

"But of course." He leaned against the wing of her chair. "Forbidden fruit is always the tastiest."

She looked up at him. She stared for a moment too long, and her smile faded. Forcibly she brought her smile back. "My older sister, Sorcha, was to be made crown princess and at the same time become betrothed to Prince Rainger of Richarte." Clarice made a face. "An obnoxious boy. I felt very sorry for her. So she and I and my younger sister rigged it so that when Papa made the announcement, we pulled a rope and all the togas fell off." Clarice started to laugh, a merry laugh of pleasured memory.

Robert watched her in silence, his groin tightening under the renewed pressure of desire. She wasn't the most beautiful woman he'd ever seen. She was too short, too winsome . . . too guarded. She was also silky-smooth, golden-tanned, and excessively softhearted. He'd had her, and he wanted to have her again. And again. And again, until all the world had disappeared and only Clarice, with her soft arms and soft heart, was left.

Not suspecting his thoughts, Clarice continued. "Some of the togas got caught on certain body parts, if you know what I mean—"

He did know what she meant, and he couldn't help it. He grinned.

"—and that made it so much worse," she went on. "The ambassadors were dreadfully offended, and Grandmamma was shaking with fury."

She reminded him of a time when he was young, confident in the ultimate goodness of mankind, secure in his superiority and his position. He had believed in family, in love, and that the good were rewarded and the bad were punished.

Now he didn't believe in anything. Nor did he fear anything. Not even death.

Clarice burbled on, unaware of his melancholy reflection. "But Papa . . . I would swear he was laughing too." She took a sip of wine. "We went to bed that night without supper, even the newly betrothed crown princess."

On a swift silent breath Robert realized he believed her. He believed Clarice was a princess. The memories were too ingenuous, the mixture of her sadness and her amusement too real. She tried to hide the glitter of her tears as she spoke of her lost family, and she smiled, but her lips trembled.

She was a princess, a princess in exile, and he would use her as he wished, and take her as often as he could. Because, in the end, no matter what else was between them, the passion could not be denied. He had been with a lot of women, some beautiful, some mysterious, some earthy, some experienced, but none had tugged at his senses as Clarice did. Something existed between the two of them, something so rare as to be a treasure, and he would capture it if he could.

She said, "Of course, you think I'm a liar, but nevertheless, my memories are gold."

"No." *He shouldn't confess this.* "I do believe you."

She blinked at him. "My lord, I don't understand . . . you said . . . what?"

He didn't blame her for the confusion in her amber eyes and the way her hand trembled as she placed her wine on the table beside her.

She couldn't imagine that the man who had bullied and derided her could now profess faith in what he had emphatically denied.

He reiterated, "I believe you. You are a princess. You can be a fraud with your creams and your unguents and not be a fraud about being royal. I don't know all the circumstances that brought you to this place, but everything about you shouts nobility. You *are* a princess." His mouth twisted in self-derision, and he paced away, melting into the shadows of the library. "And I don't give a damn, because I still desire you."

Clarice wanted to spin, to dance, to shout her glee to the sky. After so many years of exile and coldness, to have anyone else say they believed her would make her skeptical about their motives. But to have this man, hardened and cynical, say he gave credence to her claim . . . she could scarcely believe her own reaction. She knew he didn't lie. This man didn't have to stoop to such chicanery to achieve his goal. Why would he? He had already obtained her cooperation in his masquerade.

He had already possessed her. Now he gave her the greatest gift he could give her. He gave her his trust.

Gliding across the faded carpet, she went to him and put her hands on his shoulders. "I desire you too."

His eyes were inscrutable. His body felt hot beneath her grip. Slowly he lifted his hands and grasped her wrists. "So?"

Her chest rose and fell in quick, silent breaths. "So . . . my lord, if you want me, I'll have you. For now. Until your charade is over and it's time for me to leave." She twined their fingers together. Lifting one of his hands to her mouth, she kissed it, then bit one knuckle.

He jumped as if she'd hurt him, and his eyes blazed with sparkling sapphire warning. Cupping her chin in his hand, he lowered his head. With his mouth hovering above hers, his warm breath caressing her face, he whispered, "Since you're giving yourself to me, could you call me by my name?"

"Robert." She tasted the syllables and found them, and the intimacy they implied, sweet. "Robert."

He brushed his lips to hers. Greedily she welcomed his tongue as it slipped inside her mouth, wanting to experience the harmony he gave her when they melded and sang the song of passion. No two people had ever kissed as they did, with this glorious sliding and tasting, the tenderness and the violence. She wrapped her arms around his shoulders and held his head in place, demanding everything he could give her, each thrust of his tongue, each heated breath.

Then he drew back. Turned his head. "Listen. The carriages are at the front door. The gentlemen have started to arrive." His gaze came back to hers, but as abruptly as if it had never been, the passion was gone. Instead, his eyes calculated and weighed her. "I must explain exactly what I require of you in this masquerade. Are you ready?"

Ready? Yes, she was ready. But he wasn't speaking of that, and she didn't care. Right now she would do as he wished for no more reason than that he wished it. Yet she wouldn't confess that to him. She might be infatuated with his lovemaking, but she knew his ruthlessness all too well, and she wouldn't give him leave to walk on her. In a steady voice, one that didn't betray the traces of want that lingered in her, she said, "Tell me exactly what you wish of me, and I'll tell you if I can do it."

"I have faith in you, my princess." His lips moved, his voice was deep and low and made promises he did not speak. "And when you're done, I'll ensure that Blaize is completely yours, forever."

She was thinking of more than a horse when she echoed, "Forever."

Nineteen

Ye don't find cream in a ditch.
—THE OLD MEN OF FREYA CRAGS

Colonel Ogley had waited his whole life for this. To arrive in triumph at MacKenzie Manor. To revel in the flattering glances of the ladies, the admiring comments of the gentlemen. To have Brenda, his wide-eyed, wealthy wife, clinging to his arm.

To savor the well-hidden chagrin of the earl of Hepburn.

Oh, Hepburn said all that was proper. He welcomed Ogley into the grand foyer of

MacKenzie Manor with every appearance of gratification.

But Ogley knew the truth. Hepburn hated him. Ogley had made sure of it during their years together on the Peninsula and in all the days after. Ogley had made sure that the snot-nosed lordling who had been given to him as a subordinate officer had grown into a bitter, disillusioned man. In fact, the only goal Ogley had failed to achieve was Hepburn's painful death.

But actually, having Hepburn live to host this celebratory ball was proving even more satisfying. Moreover, having him see Waldemar, Hepburn's own former aide, standing straight and still behind Ogley gave him a feeling of power unmatched by any act of war or brutal massacre. There was nothing Hepburn had that Ogley had not taken. Well, except his title, and Ogley expected to receive a barony soon enough. How sweet it was to know Hepburn hated his guts, yet was forced to pretend respect.

"Colonel Ogley, Mrs. Ogley, we're so privileged to host a ball in your honor." Lady Millicent, who looked somewhat like Ogley's own wife, hurried forward to greet them. "I read your book, Colonel Ogley, and I'm in awe of your exploits on the Peninsula. I hope that if you're not too tired from your journey, you'll join us in the drawing room this evening and tell us of your heroism."

The guests gathered around produced a spattering of applause.

"Yes!" Brenda clutched his arm. "Please, Oscar, you know how I love to hear you speak."

Ogley patted his wife's hand and smiled benignly at Lady Millicent. "Isn't Mrs. Ogley wonderful? She's heard the stories countless times on our victorious tour of England, yet still she urges me to tell them once more."

"Oh, Oscar." Brenda blushed with delight. "How could I not love to hear the tales you tell? To know you willingly rode into such danger, time after time—why, it's almost like a fairy tale."

Ogley stiffened, but Hepburn said nothing. He looked not even faintly sardonic. It was as if he had forgotten the truth, and that Ogley did not believe. The arrogant bastard never forgot anything, and that was the one reason Ogley had tried so hard to get him killed. That he hadn't succeeded spoke the world of Hepburn's luck—and skill.

But, really, what could Hepburn do *now*?

If he tried to tell the truth, no one would believe him. He'd be perceived as a petty glory-seeker. His jealousy would add luster to Ogley's fame. Ogley smiled in self-congratulation. He had trapped Hepburn in a hell tailored specifically for his outdated sense of honor, and Ogley reveled in Hepburn's misery.

"Colonel Ogley, Princess Clarice asked to meet you." Hepburn stepped forward, a woman of uncommon beauty on his arm. "Your Highness, this is the colonel whose heroics you've admired in the pages of his book. Princess Clarice, Colonel Ogley and his wife, Lady Brenda."

"Please," Brenda said, "I prefer to be called simply Mrs. Ogley."

"I understand, Mrs. Ogley." Princess Clarice's oddly colored amber eyes were admiring as she gazed on Colonel Ogley. "What an honor to be the wife of such a hero!"

"So I believe." Brenda didn't have the sense to worry about the pretty princess or Ogley's reaction to her. Brenda believed only the best of him, including that he remained loyal to his wedding vows.

It was not his intention to enlighten her.

But he smiled seductively at the princess.

"Of course I'll be speaking of my exploits this evening in the drawing room. To do so will be my greatest pleasure." He didn't know where Princess Clarice was from and he didn't care. She was a fine piece of woman flesh, and he would gladly share the source of his heroism with her.

She looked startled at his brash admiration, as if he had misunderstood her interest in him. Which he hadn't; he'd been an officer long enough to recognize the glow a female exuded when she wanted a man.

His gaze shifted to Hepburn, who frowned and watched them. Better yet if Hepburn had an interest in her. Taking Princess Clarice from Hepburn would be the final cannon blast in a battle that had begun as soon as Ogley had heard Hepburn would be placed in his regiment, and such a disappointment would blow Hepburn all the way to hell.

"Colonel Ogley, Mrs. Ogley, if you'll come this way." Lady Millicent interrupted before he could do more to secure his case with the princess.

Which, as long as Brenda stood there, was a good thing. But no doubt Princess Clarice would make herself available later.

As Lady Millicent led them up the stairs,

Ogley waved to the crowd of nobles and servants gathered below. God, he loved being a hero. He gave a special wave to Princess Clarice and smiled as Hepburn's gaze narrowed in suspicion.

Then Ogley turned his attention to Lady Millicent, who said, "We've put you in the master's chambers, and anything you wish, anything at all, you have only to ask."

Taking his wife's hand, Ogley patted it softly. "You're so weak and tender. The trip has exhausted you. Let me order you a tray so you can lie down before the evening's festivities."

"Really, Oscar, I feel fine. To be with you on this victory tour doesn't weary me." Brenda touched his cheek. "It invigorates me."

He allowed a weighty frown to slip over his features. "Please indulge me. You know how I worry about you." He lowered his voice so Lady Millicent couldn't hear. "Especially since you could possibly be in a delicate condition . . ."

He almost felt guilty about the expression of pain on his wife's face. She had avowed her intention to give him the gift of a son, not realizing that he took precautions to ensure no children came from their union.

She was the daughter of a wealthy, influential baron. Her father had issued Ogley an annual allowance. Her father's money was the reason Ogley had been able to buy a prestigious command. And all of that because Brenda worshipped him. Ogley intended that nothing should take his place in her life. Not even his own child.

Bowing her head, Brenda murmured, "Yes, dear, of course I'll do as you wish."

As the footman opened the door to the master's chambers, Ogley asked, "Lady Millicent, would you make sure my wife has a tray in our room so that she can join us later in the evening?"

"Of course!" Lady Millicent turned to Brenda in a flurry of concern. "Have you the headache? Could I send up a tincture too?"

While the ladies chatted, Ogley gazed at the magnificence of the MacKenzie master suite. He recognized wealth when he saw it. The large sitting room could be described only as magnificent, with chairs grouped around the fireplace, a writing desk stocked with paper, pens, and ink, a carpet so old the colors were faded yet so posh it still looked superb, and drapes of royal purple and gold. The carved table was adorned with an embroidered velvet runner and gold salver for calling cards. There Waldemar, dressed in a servant's livery, unloaded Ogley's war mementos from the bag he carried with him everywhere.

The door opened into the bedchamber, and inside Brenda's maid stood beside the gilded bed, turning down the covers. The bed stood on a dais, as if the laird of the MacKenzies were some petty monarch worthy of worship. The royal purple and gold was echoed in the bedcurtains and the coverlet, and Ogley reflected bitterly that Hepburn must feel like a king when he slept there.

But Hepburn had given up the bedchamber to honor Ogley, and that made Ogley smile. Did Hepburn fear Ogley? Did he think to bribe him? Did little Lord Hepburn imagine that if he flattered Ogley that Ogley would forget Hepburn's insults and play fair?

There was nothing fair about that night in London fourteen years earlier when a young, drunk Lord Hepburn had challenged the newly commissioned Ogley to a sword-fight—and won. And laughed.

Ogley hated being laughed at. He had been the third in a poor, noble family of six rough-and-tumble sons, and it seemed he had always been the one who fell out of the tree or flipped off the sled or hid under the table and got caught. He had been the scapegoat for all his brothers, and he had hated it, retaliating by sneaking around and getting them in trouble. They in turn hated him. When he turned twenty and his father bought him the commission, it was the best thing that ever happened to him. He loved the army. Loved the uniforms, loved the formality and the chance to command lesser men who had no choice but to obey. He didn't care if none of his fellow officers liked him. He was dashing and handsome, the ladies liked him, and he saw opportunity there.

Then Hepburn's victory had made Ogley the butt of every jest by every officer in the army. Worse, Hepburn compounded his transgression by appearing the next day— and apologizing. The worthless blackguard apologized for being intoxicated and unforgivably rude, and that apology underscored one thing—that Ogley had been beaten in swordplay by a seventeen-year-old so drunk, he could scarcely stagger.

It wasn't until Ogley had married Brenda and bought a new commission, a better commission, that the mockery had eased.

Oh, some still whispered behind his back, but none of the lesser officers dared say anything, and when a superior officer had teased him . . . well, Ogley had learned how to get revenge on his brothers. Teaching a mere officer a lesson was nothing. A mere hiring of thugs to teach the officer better manners.

Of course, Ogley had been sent to the Peninsula in retaliation, but for a man of his talents, even that wasn't so bad. He was out from under Brenda's adoring, smothering gaze, and in the wreck left behind by the struggle between the French and English on Spanish and Portuguese soil, there were opportunities for profit.

Best of all, the elder earl of Hepburn had grown tired of his son's frivolous ways. To put an end to Hepburn's rowdiness, he'd bought Hepburn a commission. A commission that had sent Hepburn right into Ogley's regiment.

Even now Ogley chuckled in remembrance. How delightful it had been to give the lad the most recalcitrant of men from the dregs of the prisons to tame, then demand that he lead them into missions from which they would never return. Hepburn always led them out . . . some of them. Their numbers

dwindled as they were killed, but Ogley volunteered his regiment for another mission,
and another, taking care that no one in command should know it was Hepburn who succeeded while everyone else failed. In the
isolation of the Peninsula, it was an easy
thing for a man with intelligence and time to
write up the exploits as his own and send the
manuscript away to be published. By the
time Ogley resigned his commission, he had
returned to England as a hero.

His gaze lingered on Waldemar.

And no one dared tell the truth, certainly
not Hepburn. Not as long as Ogley held
Waldemar in his power. Ogley would have to
be a fool to let Waldemar go—and Ogley
prided himself on his cleverness.

Brenda slid her hand in his. "Isn't the master's suite marvelous?"

"It is indeed." Satisfaction spread like oil
through his gut, and he smiled at Lady Millicent. "I thank you, Lady Millicent, for placing
us here."

Lady Millicent fluttered like any spinster
given a compliment. "It was my brother who
insisted."

"I hate to think he's given up his room for
us," Brenda protested.

"No, please, don't distress yourself." Just like Hepburn, Lady Millicent spoke with that faint Scottish accent that betrayed inferiority. "My brother doesn't sleep here. Since his return from the Peninsula, he has preferred to stay in a cottage on the estate."

"That makes me feel better." Brenda beamed.

Sometimes her kindheartedness gave Ogley a bellyache.

"Doesn't it you, Oscar?" she asked.

No. He wanted to displace Hepburn. Putting his hand under her arm, Ogley held too firmly. As Brenda squirmed beside him, he said, "Lady Millicent, I beg your pardon, but my wife really does need to rest."

"Of course, I'll make sure I send up a tray." With a brisk curtsy Lady Millicent left the room.

"That was abrupt." Brenda tugged at his bruising fingers.

But decisively he led her into the bedchamber. He helped her onto the mattress. He kissed her forehead. To her maid he said, "Make sure she rests." Leaving the room, he shut the door behind him.

Waldemar was supervising the arrival of their trunks. "Put the bags there by the door, lad. Ah, lassie"—he pinched the maid on the cheek—"t' see a pretty lass such as yerself does me 'eart good."

The footman grinned and the maid giggled. Everyone liked Waldemar, with his sandy-blond hair and his handsome countenance. His good-humored blue eyes glinted from beneath blond eyelashes and brows, and freckles marched across his nose. He looked like the picture of honesty and sincerity—as long as one didn't notice his long, thief's fingers and swift, catlike walk.

Waldemar had been dragged out of the mud of prison and given a choice between fighting for Mother England—or death. He'd taken the voyage to the Peninsula, of course, but once there, he'd tried to escape. Tried to avoid his duty. Been insolent and cocky. Nothing Ogley had done—not the thrashings, not the isolation, not even the branding—had changed him.

Then Hepburn came along, dashing, high-spirited, noble Hepburn, and Waldemar had chosen to follow him . . . into hell.

At least Ogley had done his best to ensure Hepburn was in hell every minute of every day, and he'd been successful. He counted that as one of his proudest achievements.

Now Ogley cleared his throat.

The maid stopped giggling. The footman sidled out the door. Waldemar straightened to a military posture. His smile disappeared. His mouth snapped shut.

"So how did it feel"—Ogley picked up his verbal dagger—"to see your old commander once again?"

"Passing fair, sir." Waldemar marched to the table and placed copies of Ogley's book into a basket to be transported down to the drawing room later.

"He appears to have suffered no ill effects from his time on the Peninsula." Ogley rubbed the gilding on the picture frame and considered whether he should buy some portraits to hang in his bedchamber.

"None whatsoever, sir." Waldemar laid out Ogley's belt and saber, his field decorations and his epaulets.

"Except for that scar on his forehead. It didn't heal well. Did you notice?" Ogley poured himself a glass of brandy and pretended to be embarrassed by his lapse of memory. "But how silly of me. His scar matches the scars on your arms, the ones you got while rescuing him from that fire. *How* did that happen?"

Waldemar didn't move. Didn't lift his gaze. "I don't remember, sir."

Slowly and with great relish Ogley slid in the blade. "You'll have to read it in my book."

Waldemar said nothing. Nothing. He was as mute and expressionless as a dummy.

Ogley chuckled. "I do believe that at last you've become everything a commander could want in an aide."

In a flat tone Waldemar said, "Yes, sir."

In truth Ogley had at last seen clear signs that he had at last broken the man Hepburn called unbreakable. There was an emptiness in Waldemar's eyes, a lack of expression on his low-class, tenement face. He had grown almost boring, but Ogley would never give him up. Never. Waldemar was his for life. Ogley had won where Hepburn could not. He intended to flaunt his victory beneath Hepburn's hooked and insufferable nose.

"I imagine you miss Hepburn and all the grand adventures the two of you had together," Ogley taunted.

Waldemar paused for a painful, telling moment. "I don't remember any adventures, sir. I believe you were the one who experienced adventures."

Strolling across to the window, Ogley

swirled the pungent liquor in the glass. "Yes. Yes, and don't you forget it. I'm the one who broke into the French armory and stole their ammunition. I'm the one who rescued Hepburn from the French prison after his foolish spy attempt. I'm the one who—" He broke off abruptly.

A shapely woman walked across the broad expanse of lawn below. Her glossy black hair had been pulled back into a chignon, and in it she wore a comb with a mantilla draped artfully around her face. He couldn't see her features through the lace, but the way she walked—hands folded before her, pacing across the grass as if no emergency on earth could make her break into a run—reminded him of Carmen. It was that stately, sensual stride that had first attracted him to her, and this woman wore a scarlet gown in the same shade and style Carmen had so favored.

He blinked. But it couldn't be Carmen. He'd left her behind without a backward glance when he'd returned to England and his wife. There was no way Carmen could have followed him here to a village in Scotland.

Seeing Hepburn must have brought forth memories better discarded.

Then the woman turned her head and stared.

"Christ Jesus!" Ogley jumped so hard, he slopped the brandy onto his clean starched shirt.

It was her. It was Carmen.

"Sir, is there something wrong?" Waldemar asked.

Ogley leaped away from the window. "Yes. You can explain *that!*" He gestured violently.

Keeping a wary eye cocked on Ogley, Waldemar walked to the window and looked out.

"Well?" Ogley snapped.

Waldemar cringed as if he feared Ogley would strike him. "I . . . don't see anything, sir."

Ogley shoved Waldemar away and stared outside.

It was true. She was gone.

Twenty

Only those who row the boat make waves.
—THE OLD MEN OF FREYA CRAGS

In the shadows of the trees Robert threw a brown cloak over Clarice and held her still. At the upstairs window he could see Ogley and Waldemar staring down at the lawn. Ogley slammed open the window, stuck his head out, and looked about wildly.

Quietly Waldemar surveyed the scene. Robert knew the moment he spotted them. They looked at each other. The two men nodded at each other in subdued satisfaction. Then, while Ogley yelled, Waldemar shut the window.

Waldemar had learned the skill of observation during his years as a housebreaker, and it was he who had taught Robert to look beyond the obvious. For all Ogley's sly skills, he'd never learned that, and that was why, around the campfires, he was so often the butt of jokes.

Of course, it hadn't mattered. He got his revenge in a million petty ways and one very big one. He always sent Robert out on the most dangerous missions, and now he held Robert's best friend in eternal servitude. The situation was not to be borne, and Robert intended to end it here and now.

Keeping his arm around Clarice and the cape over her head, Robert said, "Walk with me. You can put yourself back together in my cottage."

Obediently she followed him, and when the door shut behind them, she tossed off the cloak.

It was odd to see her standing there, familiar in her stance and her regal attitude, yet a stranger in her looks. Working from a miniature portrait of Senora Menendez, Clarice had made her features resemble Carmen's to a frightening degree. Somehow she had darkened and lined her eyes, giving them an almond shape. Her mouth was redder, lusher, colored in the pucker of a kiss. She had created hollows under her cheekbones, and her chin looked broader. With the black wig and mantilla, and the addition of the scarlet gown, Robert thought—hoped— Clarice could pass for Carmen at close range if Ogley didn't examine her too carefully.

They had waited in the trees, Clarice enveloped in the brown cloak. Knowing Ogley as he did, Robert was sure the colonel would want to look over the estate and gloat that he held the lord of the manor in his power. Ogley had done just that. When he had looked out the window, Robert had said, "Now," and Clarice had taken her stroll.

When Ogley had leaped away, Robert called her back and she ran to him. She still didn't know why she was doing this, but she no longer asked. Thank the Lord, for Robert didn't want to tell her. He didn't dare take the chance that she would refuse to hoodwink the man she believed to be a hero.

Tomorrow they would tighten the thumb-screws with another appearance, and with Clarice's help and the grace of God, by this time two days hence Waldemar would be on a ship in Edinburgh harbor.

With Clarice's help and the grace of God . . .

She stood watching Robert with eyes that saw too much. "Could I ask you a question?"

Inevitable, he supposed. "Of course."

"You were in Colonel Ogley's command. What did you think of him?"

He lifted his eyebrows. That was not the question he had anticipated. "Why do you ask that?"

"He's not what I expected. I thought he would be a man out of the normal, a great man occupied with great things. Instead, he's . . . he made me uncomfortable. He leered at me." She searched for the words as if she feared she wasn't making herself clear. "In front of his wife."

Hepburn nodded slowly.

Which seemed to tell her all she needed to know. "So he isn't the hero we all want to worship."

"Worship him if you like." Taking her by the waist, Hepburn pulled her close, wanting her heat to warm him. "But love me."

Although she yielded, her body pliant against his, still she asked, "It's Colonel

Ogley for whom I'm performing this charade, isn't it?"

She was too acute. "Why do you say that?"

"Because I looked up to see who was gazing at me from the house."

Aghast at her daring, he asked, "You looked?"

"Yes, I looked. Don't worry so." She placed her hand against his cheek. "I have a mirror. I know I was successful in making myself look like *her*. I fooled him, didn't I?"

Yes. Ogley's behavior had made it clear that he did think he'd seen Carmen. Robert nodded, enjoying the caress of her hand against his skin, the stroke of her thumb against his lips. "You fooled him. I always knew you would."

"So the game begins." Freeing herself, she walked into the bedchamber and shut the door behind her.

He looked at the cottage that had seen so much of his misery on his return. The two rooms had been used thirty years before for the overflow guests who came to his mother's parties. The living room and bedroom were of generous proportions, and were handsomely furnished and decorated, if a little old-fashioned. He had been comfortable living here alone, and now, with the advent of Colonel Ogley, Robert was able to use his isolation to good advantage.

When the door to the bedchamber opened, the Princess Clarice he recognized stepped out with her pink day dress loose on her shoulders. Coming to him, she turned her back. "Will you finish buttoning me?"

The buttons at the top of the gown gaped open, showing him a smooth expanse of golden skin, the ridge of her spine, and the cool column of her neck. He didn't want to button her; he wanted to unbutton her, to take right now what she'd promised him. *If you want me, I'll have you,* she had said. Then she'd added, *For now.*

He wanted that act of joining with her even before he had done his duty. The woman was a peril to him and his intentions.

On the other hand, the base of her neck, with its tendrils of wispy curls, tempted him, and what was the harm in one kiss?

Clarice felt the touch of his lips against her skin and closed her eyes on a wave of bliss and triumph. With a little twisting and turning she could have fastened her own buttons, but she needed the reassurance that she was more to Robert than a mannequin and a charlatan. She needed to know that she attracted him as he attracted her. And she wanted his kiss . . . all of his kisses.

He moved close against her, his body heating hers. His mouth opened against her skin, and he tasted her as if she were cream and he were a cat. His lips slid down her spine, lingering on each vertebra, sending chills down to her toes. She swayed with the onset of passion and wondered how this man had so quickly accustomed her to his touch. She was like an instrument who, until she met Robert, had played discordant music. Now, as his fingers glided across her bare skin, she could play a symphony and each note would vibrate in perfect tune. But for him. Only for him.

Stepping back, he cleared his throat and brusquely fastened her buttons. With his hands on her arms he walked her toward a chair, turned her, and pushed her into the seat. She stared up at him, not comprehending his briskness as he backed away.

Suddenly, without warning of any kind, she saw a blur of movement. A big man with sandy hair, dressed in a servant's livery, leaped from the open window toward Robert, catching him around the waist. They went tumbling across the floor, and before her astonished eyes Robert tossed his attacker over his head. The attacker landed flat on his back, then with a "Ha!" he sprang to his feet and jumped at Robert. He was younger and bigger than Robert, but Robert rolled, catching him on the head with a close-fisted blow that made a sound like a muffled gong. As if it were nothing, the fellow shook it off and kept coming. The struggle was intense and silent, the two men punching and tossing each other with a careless disregard for anything but victory.

Clarice shook with anxiety. It was just like yesterday. Would this end in blood, gore, and death too? She pulled her feet up, stood on the chair to stay out of the way . . . to jump on Robert's attacker if necessary.

She could think of nothing but Robert's mad fury about the MacGees, and the man stalking through the night. This must be him; he must have decided to attack at last. But Robert in a rage was formidable, and she actually feared for his attacker. Robert would kill him.

Then, to her astonishment, in a move so swift she didn't see the details, the attacker rolled Robert onto his face and sat on Robert's back, Robert's arm twisted behind him. In an accent thick with cockney the fellow said, "Ah, lad, that was no fight. Ye've grown weak in yer old age!"

"My shoulder," Robert moaned. "You've dislocated my shoulder."

Jumping to the floor, Clarice picked up a vase and held it high over the attacker's head, ready to bring it down and take him out.

But the man let Robert go at once. "'Ey, man, I didn't mean t'—"

Robert rolled, caught him under the knees, and before Clarice could blink, Robert was on top, sitting on the attacker's back and saying, "Old age and treachery will always win over youth and compassion." He cranked his attacker's arm up so high, Clarice winced. "Surrender," he demanded.

His attacker grunted, the muscles in his neck corded, his head lifted to ease the pain. "Ye silly fool, o' course I surrender."

Robert let him go at once.

The fellow rolled over and faced Robert. They stared at each other. Clarice held her breath, waiting for the recriminations to begin.

But both men started laughing. They were *laughing.*

The attacker had a smile so bright, he could start the birds singing. "Ye tricky bastard, I thought I 'ad killed ye." Looking up, he saw Clarice posed with the vase still in her hands. "Ye've got a good woman there, Robert, she's ready t' defend ye with yer precious crockery."

Still laughing, Robert looked up at Clarice. Their eyes locked for a long while. His smile faded, and she could see nothing but him, tall and dark and so full of laughter and rage and sorrow, she could feel each emotion as it coursed through his veins.

Inexplicably her eyes teared. She had thought he was in danger. Her heart thumped, her fingers trembled—and the fight had been nothing but a wrestling match between two friends.

She'd been afraid for him.

She lowered the vase.

She'd been a fool.

Dusting his hands, Robert stood and helped the fellow to his feet. With a formality at odds with his rumpled appearance he said, "Princess Clarice, this is the most worthless man in Christendom, Cornelius Gunther Halstead Waldemar the Fourth, formerly of London, formerly of Newgate Prison, formerly of the Peninsula, and my good friend." He laughed. "My very good friend."

Somehow Clarice wasn't surprised to hear Waldemar had spent time in Newgate.

As Waldemar bowed low, Robert continued. "Waldemar, this is Princess Clarice of Beaumontagne, second in line to the throne and the lady who'll free you ere the week is out."

And Robert was very free with personal information. She frowned at him in disapproval.

Taking the vase, Waldemar kissed her fingers. "I appreciate yer efforts, Yer Highness, especially since it's little liking I 'ave workin' fer 'Is Nibs. But when the little colonel saw ye all dolled up like Senora Carmen Menendez, he was so scared, I scarcely kept from snorting out loud."

"Did he recognize her?" Robert asked urgently.

"Recognize 'er?" Waldemar rocked back on his heels and grinned. "Aye, that 'e did. Almost expired right there on yer fancy rug. Thought 'e'd seen Carmen fer sure, and 'e didn't like it one bit."

"He thought it was Carmen even when she turned her head and looked at him?" Robert demanded.

"Robert, don't worry." Waldemar still grinned. "'Is complexion was *green*."

Robert looked at her. "You did it. You duped him."

"From a distance," she said. "We shall see how I do closer up."

"A woman wi' courage. I like that. Yer 'Ighness, if ye ever decide t' get shed o' this idle fellow, this 'Epburn, I beg ye remember, I'm the man fer ye." Looking sideways at Robert, Waldemar added, "I've got better ancestors."

"All of whom you've made up." In a display of jealousy she knew to be fallacious, Robert took her fingers away from Waldemar's. "She'll never want anyone but me."

Which Clarice feared was true, but she didn't need Robert telling everyone. Pointedly she removed her hand from Robert's and held it with the other, close to her waist. "I don't understand. Waldemar, why did you attack him?"

With an elegant flourish Waldemar escorted her to her chair and seated her. "'E needs t' keep on 'is toes. Livin' 'ere in 'is 'ome, being at one wi' the birds and the flowers, makes a man soft. And our friend Robert can't afford t' be soft. Not wi' the ol' pillager in the 'ouse."

For the first time, the laughter between the men stopped, and they stared grimly at each other.

"Colonel Ogley, you mean," Clarice said. "Isn't this dangerous?"

"No," Robert said.

"Aye," Waldemar said at the same time. Turning on Robert, he argued, "Don't lie t' the lass! She needs t' know the truth about 'im."

"Ignorance is not bliss," she argued.

Robert inclined his head in reluctant agreement. "Colonel Ogley is not very bright."

"But 'e's sneaky, and 'e's underhanded, and 'e smells trouble miles away."

Robert hitched his trousers at the knee and perched on the edge of a table. "He's selfish right to the bone, and he thinks I'm doing what he would do in my place. He thinks I've brought him here to declare the truth so the world knows who the true Hero of the Peninsula is . . . when in fact I don't give a damn."

Wiggling his eyebrows at Clarice, Waldemar waggled his thumb at Robert and mouthed, "The 'ero."

Clarice nodded and mouthed, "So I comprehended." Aloud she said, "I think I deserve to know. What are we attempting to achieve? What is my role? Who am I playing?"

Robert didn't stop Waldemar when Waldemar plunged into explanation. "Ye've done a fine job o' being the woman called Carmen Menendez, a lady o' Spain who 'ad fallen on 'ard times. Ogley wanted a woman t' warm 'is bed, so 'e told 'er 'e was unmarried, promised t' bring 'er t' England when he returned and marry 'er there. O' course, when it came time t' leave, 'e abandoned 'er wi'out a backward glance. 'E's got a wife. She worships 'im, and 'e's damned careful not t' upset her."

"Because she has the money," Clarice guessed.

Waldemar pressed his finger flat on his nose. "Ye're a smart one, fer a princess."

Oddly she didn't feel insulted. Rather, she considered herself to be accepted by this man Robert called his friend. "So I'm playing the part of Colonel Ogley's used and abandoned mistress to force him to . . . do what?"

"To do what he promised." Robert's mouth was grim.

"I don't blame ye," Waldemar said. "Ye know that."

"I was stupid," Robert answered. "I believed he would keep his word."

Waldemar challenged Robert with his stance and his words. "If this doesn't work, I'm goin' anyway."

Robert said, "It will work. I swear it will."

Frustrated with their talk that told her nothing, Clarice demanded, "What did Colonel Ogley *do?*"

Robert sat very still, a dark shadow in the room. "Ogley promised that if Waldemar went on a last mission with me, and we survived, he would release Waldemar from the army with a commendation for bravery."

Waldemar poured them all glasses of port, and when he gave Clarice hers, he confessed in a low voice, "Robert's pop 'ad died, and Robert 'ad already bought 'imself out o' 'is commission. 'E didn't have t' go on the mission. 'E did it fer me."

Robert watched them. "Dammit, Waldemar, we're in the same room. I can hear you talking."

"Despite 'is advanced age, 'e's not deaf yet," Waldemar added still in an undertone. Then he took up the story in a louder tone. "We survived, barely, and o' course, Colonel

Cockscum laughed in Robert's face when 'e asked fer me freedom. Told 'im that promises made t' one such as I were no promises at all, and told 'im 'e done 'im a favor by teaching 'im about 'ow t' treat a servant—dangle a carrot at the end o' a stick and when 'is servant reached fer the carrot, use the stick on 'im."

The story made Clarice sick. She faltered. "I liked thinking there was a hero in this world."

"There is," Waldemar said. "Only a few, and I've met them all."

"You're one of them," Robert said.

Waldemar ignored Robert, shrugging at Clarice. "It's just not Ogley."

"Colonel Ogley, that was wonderful!" Lady Millicent led the applause at the end of the presentation. "You speak so vividly, I feel as if I were there during your heroism in the French prison. Won't you please tell us who it is you rescued?"

Ogley looked around the drawing room at the well-dressed aristocratic guests. Brenda was there, beaming her pride. Princess Clarice was there too, dressed in a fetching off-the-shoulder evening gown of pale green velvet. Smiling wryly, Ogley shook hands with the gentlemen. "I cannot. That wouldn't be the act of a gentleman, would it, to tell the truth about a fellow officer's rash act?"

The crowd murmured their approval while Ogley kept a respectful distance from the ladies, even the lush and ready Miss Trumbull, who smiled at him with such sultry invitation. With Brenda sticking so close to his side, he didn't dare show interest.

Besides, the skin between his shoulder blades itched as if he had a gun aimed at him. His eyes darted around the drawing room, searching, searching . . .

Carmen couldn't be here. It was impossible. How would she get here? Why would she come?

Well . . . revenge for ruining her reputation, of course, but what would she hope to gain? And as to how she got here—would Hepburn have brought her?

Ogley paled at the thought. Of course. Hepburn. On the Peninsula, Ogley had claimed Hepburn's life and made it his own. How much Hepburn must hate seeing Ogley get the adulation that Hepburn deserved! Even now Hepburn watched with an ironic smile while Ogley was treated with a respect he had previously only dreamed of having.

Ogley pushed through the crowd, determined to confront Hepburn right then. But Hepburn was speaking to his butler and signaling to Lady Millicent, who nodded.

It was time for dinner, a very formal dinner meant to honor Ogley and Ogley alone. He couldn't get to Hepburn now.

Was Hepburn dodging him . . . ?

No, he was performing the duties of a host who wished his guests to be comfortable. He couldn't have fetched Carmen from Spain to Scotland. It was too absurd to think he would go to all that trouble.

That afternoon, had Ogley been dreaming? Waldemar had claimed to see no one on the lawn, and when Ogley had looked again, she was gone.

They didn't think they could drive him crazy, did they?

He ran a finger around his suddenly tight collar.

"Won't you walk this way, Colonel and Mrs. Ogley? Dinner is served." Lady Millicent led the group into the dining room. The long table bore shining white linen, sparkling silver, and bouquets of flowers. "Please, Colonel Ogley, we beg that you take the place of honor."

Usually, in all the celebrations that had

been given for him, he enjoyed the compliments more than anything. Now he didn't wish to sit at the head of the table with his hostess, Lady Millicent, on his right hand, and Princess Clarice on his left. He didn't even care that Princess Clarice's bosom rose in fine, curved mounds from the neckline of her gown, and when she moved, they jiggled in a most enticing way. As he looked down the table at Hepburn, Ogley felt like the old Greek Damocles, who had sat in the king's chair only to notice that a sword dangled over his head attached by a hair.

The sword would drop. The only question was when . . . and would Ogley be fast enough to dodge the fatal blow?

Twenty-one

Life is too short to dance with an ugly man.
—THE OLD MEN OF FREYA CRAGS

All the drapes in Robert's bedchamber were open, allowing the waning moonlight to flood the room with its unearthly white. As Clarice stepped in, it was surprisingly bright. She could see the shapes and details very well, yet the pale illumination bleached the colors from the carpet, from the duvet and the bed-curtains. It turned the dark wood furniture and the doors into square blocks of black and the pictures into faded imitations of reality.

And on the bed she could see Robert's outline, leaning against the pillows as he waited for her.

He could see her too, she knew. She still wore the light green velvet gown Lady Millicent had had made over for her. The fine material hung in perfect folds around her, fitting like a dream. This evening, during the long hours of waiting and socializing, she had stroked the velvet, taking delight in its luxurious texture. Robert had watched her, his gaze hooded and distant, yet she had known that every moment he wanted her.

Now she smiled, a small, secret smile of triumph. Yes, she was being foolish, leaving her bedchamber and making her way to him. Yes, heartbreak would undoubtedly follow. But someday, when she was back in Beaumontagne performing the role for which she'd been bred, she would have the memory of this night, and whatever nights were to come.

Rising from the bed, he paced toward her, a large, graceful, shadowy figure of a male. He wore trousers, but his feet made no noise on the hardwood floor; he was barefoot.

When he stopped a few inches away from her, her heart leaped into her throat. She wasn't afraid of him; she no longer believed him mad, and she understood his insistence on his charade. But now he stood so close, she had to tilt her head to look up at him. He was very tall. He was very strong. He fought brutally. More important, last night he had taken her in a flurry of desperation and need. He hadn't meant to, but he had hurt her with his size. And tonight she had come to him again.

But she was not helpless. She was a princess, born to rule, and tonight . . . tonight she would discover the potency of her authority. Tonight she would take charge.

"I feared you might change your mind."

His shirt was open at the throat, and in the deep V of his neckline she could see the dark froth of hair that covered his flesh. "I gave my word."

"And a princess never fails to keep her word." He sounded as he had sounded when she first met him: neutral, mildly interested in her reply—and implacable.

She breathed in the scent of him, the scent she had come to know so well, and her pulse leaped. Hepburn had marked her with his passion—*would* mark her with his passion—but she would mark him too. "I do my best."

The silence stretched between them, a silence not of discomfort but of questions.

"Is that why you're here?" His voice was a rumble in the darkness. "To keep your word?"

He was so absurd, she wanted to laugh at him. She didn't; he wouldn't like it, he wouldn't understand. But she could tease him, and she did. "Robert, have you ever looked in a mirror? Larissa declared you the Catch of the Season for more reasons than your title and your wealth. The way you walk, that cutting blue gaze, that dark air of smoky opulence . . . you have a way about you that makes a woman look twice and want to follow you wherever you go."

In the darkness his eyes glinted with black sparks. "Some women manage to resist my charms very well. I seem to remember that when you first met me in Freya Crags, you couldn't wait to get away."

"Because I knew this is where I would end up." Cupping one hand over the jut of his shoulder, she rubbed away the tension beneath the skin. "Wanting you with all my body and soul. Offering myself for the time we have . . . what woman wants to find herself reduced to begging? But here I am."

His voice warmed. "I haven't heard you beg."

"Please," she said. "Please."

At last he stirred from his immobility. Swinging her into his arms, he strode toward his bed.

He placed her across the sheets and followed her down, pressing her weight into the mattress. She delighted in the heavy sensation, in the scent of him settling about her, in the determination of his grip. He kissed her, a slow, deep, thorough penetration that gave her time to adjust, to enjoy the savor of his essence, and deep inside her body delight began its shift to the desperate, clawing passion he so easily roused in her.

She nipped at his lower lip.

Lifting his head, he groaned.

She thrust her hands into his hair. The strands slipped through her fingers, black silk of the richest texture. She pulled him back down and soothed the small wound with her tongue. Opening his lips over hers, he devoured her as his hips moved against hers. It was too much, overwhelming her senses, yet not enough. She wanted more of him, more of his taste, his weight, his strength—until it was over. Until she was gone.

The sweet and wicked poignancy bit deep into her soul, and in a sudden savage motion she put her hands on his shoulders and pushed him onto his back. He resisted for a surprised moment, then yielded, sprawling onto the mattress, his arms and legs splayed wide.

He was a feast to all her senses, tall, broad, hard . . . she trailed her fingers up his thigh and found the length of him beneath his trousers. The heat of his arousal burned like a brand, and she wanted that brand deep within her. Sliding her body along his, she eased her hands inside his open shirt and spread it wide. The muscles of his chest rippled and flexed as he fought to remain still. The rough hair along his breastbone curled into her palms, the simple pleasure almost more than she could bear. "Sit up," she commanded. When he obeyed, she stripped the shirt from his shoulders and flung it away.

In the stark moonlight he was as glorious as any of the statues in her palace. The shadows of his muscles played over his pale skin, luring her onward, enticing her to see if all of him matched the marble perfection of those immortalized Renaissance noblemen. Yet before she could reach for the button on his trousers, he caught her hands and pressed them flat against his stomach. He moved her palms over the ripples of his abdomen and onto his chest. There she resisted him, taking a moment to find his nipples in the nest of hair and stroke them with her fingertips.

He made a rough sound of desire. His eyes half closed as she leaned forward and replaced one hand with her mouth. With her tongue she circled his nipple. It hardened and stabbed at her, and she experienced an identical reaction as her own nipples swelled and peaked. It was as if whatever she did to him echoed in herself. Whatever he did to her echoed in him. And each echo magnified like some magical connection between them.

Lifting her head, she smiled into his face.

He looked grim and cruel and impatient, but he didn't scare her. He would never hurt her; she knew it in her bones.

He placed her hands on his wide shoulders, opening her body to him. His gaze probed hers, then slid downward over her breasts, her waist, her hips, to her calves sprawled hoydenishly from beneath her skirt. Her first instinct was to cover her legs. Her second, and best, was to revel in the heat of his obsession. Slowly she stretched and flexed. Her hem inched up toward her thighs. Her bodice drooped over her bosom. She tossed her hair back over her shoulders, deliberately displaying the pale length of her neck.

"You torment me." His voice was low and intense. "Every moment since we met has been a long, slow tease where I imagined your body stretched under mine, atop of mine, beside mine, while I took you in every way possible."

His words made yearning curl through her loins. Her blood moved through her veins, slow and strong, beating with the rhythm of the ancient carnal dance. "You took me once. Will tonight be different?"

His hands, as he reached for her, were broad and strong, long-fingered and capable. "Oh, yes. So different. Tonight there'll be no pain, just unending pleasure." His fingers stroked the hollow of her throat, slid along her collarbones, and outlined her silhouette down to her waist. Then in a slow sweep upward he cupped her breasts.

The sensation of pleasure and surprise was so strong, she had to close her eyes to control herself. Yet that didn't help. In the total darkness she felt more acutely the caress of his thumbs circling her nipples, imitating that motion she'd used on him. And if he put his mouth there . . . the sweetness of anticipation pierced her and she waited, breathless for his next move.

Instead, he leaned closer, sliding his arms around her, and his fingers moved to open the buttons at the back of her dress. He was so close to her, she felt his breath on her face, and the heat of his body warmed her, but he made no move to kiss her or hold her close. He just slowly, deliberately, slid the buttons loose, one by one.

Her lids felt heavy as she opened them. He was there, his head tilted down toward her, and he watched her with an expression of challenge. He wanted her to recognize each step she took on this long journey from almost innocent to experienced lover. Lifting her chin, she smiled at him, eased her hand down, and tucked her fingers into his waistband. "Did you think I would change my mind?"

The gown grew looser as he freed ever more buttons. "I have heard that princesses are notoriously flighty."

"Not this princess. Not . . . not for a long, long time." Not since she had realized there was no one to care for Amy except . . . her.

She had dedicated her life to caring for Amy. Now she would have these moments for herself.

Gathering her sleeves in his hands, he slipped the gown off her shoulders, taking her chemise, too, in the smooth motion. The material caught on her nipples, then slipped down to her waist. She found herself holding her breath. Would he find her beautiful? Other men, crude and obvious, ogled her breasts through her clothing. She cared nothing for their opinions. Robert was her lover. She cared everything for his.

He didn't know of her anxiety. She took care to show no expression. Yet he whispered, "Beautiful. Your body is beautiful." Leaning down, he pressed a kiss on the upper slope of her left breast.

A pang of desperate desire shot through

her, and she pulled her arms free of the sleeves. "You aren't like other men."

He lifted his gaze to hers. Enigmatically he asked, "Other men?"

"The women talk to me. They gossip, they giggle, sometimes they tell me their deepest secrets, and one and all they say that their men are fast and uncaring. But you . . . you're too slow." Taking his hand, she pressed it to her breast. "I'm dying of want, and you are a turtle."

He smiled, his white teeth gleaming in the moonlight. "In the end you'll thank me, my princess." He rotated his hand as he pressed a kiss on her other breast. "My darling."

She didn't know what to believe, she knew only that deep within her, desire writhed with a life of its own. Every inch of her skin longed to rest against him. She wanted his hands on her hips. She wanted to seduce him, to kiss his lips and thrust her tongue into his mouth and taste him again.

So she placed her hands on his jaw and held him still as she found his mouth with hers. Warm and smooth, his lips held her enthralled for endless moments while she explored the contours, and when he responded with a like pressure, she gave a murmur of enticement. His mouth opened under hers, following her lead as if *she* were the master of seduction. She tasted him with her lips, her teeth, her tongue, enjoying the now-familiar flavor of his passion. With deliberate inducement she cupped his shoulder blades and pressed her breasts against his chest.

She hoped to stir his passion to haste. Instead, she discovered that the touch of this man's skin against hers aroused in her overwhelming tenderness and frantic passion. Imperiously she opened the buttons on his trousers and put her hand inside.

He filled her palm. The softest skin covered the rigid shaft, like velvet over steel, and she stroked down its length to the base, then back up to the rounded head. She hadn't realized that a man would be so large. So *insistent,* and she swallowed, trying to moisten her suddenly dry mouth. To take him inside of herself . . . what had seemed eminently desirable a few moments before now seemed impossible.

In a hoarse whisper she said, "If I were given to qualms, I would have them now."

"I pray you do not," he whispered back. "For I will die if I don't take you tonight, and I know you, my princess. You take your responsibilities seriously. You'd suffer to know that I died of love for you."

"Would you really?" She stroked him again, and that secret thrill once more ran like sparkling champagne along her veins. "Die for me?"

"If you don't take me soon, I'll expire before your eyes."

Silliness, of course, to think that this strong, experienced man cared so much for her. Yet the words pleased her. "Then we should rid ourselves of these clothes so I may save your life."

"God, yes." He lifted her out of the crush of her gown.

She tugged at his trousers and under-drawers until he was revealed to her. She caught only a glimpse of his erection before he tumbled her onto her back. The move surprised her, and with a soft laugh she wrestled with him for dominance. As if her strength were greater than his, he slowly gave way.

Absurd fancy, but she liked to know he felt comfortable with her in charge. When at last he sprawled on his back, she leaned against his chest, held his arms above his head, and smiled into his face. "Do you surrender?"

"I do." He didn't return her smile.

Slowly her laughter faded. He was there, beneath her, naked from head to toe, and she . . . except for her stockings, she was naked too. The scent of him rose to her nostrils, heady and rich, like a sun-ripened burgundy or carefully tended leather.

"What will you do with me now?" he asked.

"Just what I want." He was magnificent, the embodiment of all that was male and perfect in this world.

She stroked him, seeking the ripple of his arm muscles and the contours of his chest. She enjoyed the resulting assurance that in a fight he would triumph. He was a warrior. He would always keep safe anything dear to him—and just then she felt dear to him.

She slid down, and his belly tempted her. She kissed him, first one side, then the other, on the narrow concavity above his hipbones. The skin there was smooth and hairless, but just below, hair grew in abundance, and thrusting out of that, his manhood.

She should be shy. She hadn't seen it last night, had only felt its jagged thrust. And she had never before seen one on a living, breathing man, and this . . . this looked nothing like the occasionally draped statues in the palace. This was a shaft, pale, long, and thick, erect and fascinating.

As she trailed one finger down his span, she marveled at its heat. It stirred at her touch, and the sudden harsh rasp of Robert's breath broke her concentration and returned a margin of sense to her mind. "Robert," she whispered. "I don't think we can do this."

His fingers tucked a wisp of hair behind her ear. "Because you're a princess and I'm a mere lord?"

"No. Because surely our sizes don't match."

He rumbled. She thought it was a laugh, but he choked it off. "We matched last night. We will match again. I promise." He smiled, that kind of knowing smile that reminded her of how ruthlessly he had forced her cooperation in this masquerade.

A cold shiver drenched down her spine, and she started to back away.

Then he stroked his hands across her breasts, and the gust of need made her forget about his smile and her sanity.

As he caressed her, his hands provided

the flame and passion that heated her skin. She'd sensed this the first time she'd seen him—that he knew how to drive a woman to the edge with skill and a deep inner blaze of passion hidden deep within him. That he could make her blood sing in her veins.

His body glistened as the moon shone on each ripple of muscle and bone, and abruptly she remembered—she was in charge. While he caressed her arms, warming them with his touch, she rubbed his chest, his shoulders, his belly. Their hands twined and crossed, giving and receiving pleasure in a slow sensual dance. Again he stroked her breasts, cupping them, lifting them, circling the nipples with his thumbs. He looked into her face as he caressed her, a small smile on his lips as if he knew, and gauged, his effect on her.

He didn't know. No one knew *her,* knew the events that had formed her. He said he believed she was a princess, and this man, tough and cynical, wouldn't bother to lie. But perhaps he thought her royal blood made her soft and weak, when in fact the opposite was true. Perhaps he thought she would lose her nerve, let him take the lead, or even try to back out completely.

But no. She was bold and strong, and she acted on her valor. Firmly, gently, she rubbed her palms in small circles down his hips. She allowed her gaze to slither down his body, a smile on her own lips. Taking a sustaining breath, she clasped him in her hands and stroked his length . . . and he groaned deep in his chest. He reached his arms wide and clutched the sheets, and in a burst of exuberance she realized she held him helpless.

Sliding her leg over his hips, she sat atop him as if he were her throne. She marveled at his shape: the broad shoulders, tapering to a narrow waist, and the thrust of his hipbones against his skin. She trailed her finger down the hair on his breastbone, down through where it narrowed on his belly, and into the nest of curly thatch on his groin.

He watched her with narrowed eyes as his hips rolled beneath her. "Ah, princess, from here I can see eternity."

"And I feel . . ." She wanted to say something equally eloquent, something romantic, but truth to tell, what she felt was his shaft, long and hot, stretched between her legs. Her weight rested on it, and she sensed its caged power. For now it was quiescent, but she didn't imagine it would be content to remain so. Soon it—and Robert—would make demands, and her task was to take charge and lead it where and when she wished. Her task was like taming the tiger—it surely could be done, but she would always know the tiger was unpredictable and wild. Yet for the short time they would be together, she would hold the whip hand. That was, after all, why she believed she could survive this encounter without harm.

She moved on him, testing her own endurance, her own resolve.

His eyes were half closed as he watched her. "I want you as I've never wanted anything before."

She pressed her palms against his stomach for balance. She liked this: sitting atop him, the sheets crumpled beneath her knees, moonlight and the freshening breeze streaming through the open windows. The encounter gave her a sense of freedom she'd never experienced. This night would have no repercussions. This night was a time set apart from reality, and she refused to consider how it would affect the fate of her dynastic marriage or whether it would alter the stream of history. In fact, she refused to wonder what her grandmother would say.

Yet obedience to duty was a hard habit to break, and for one moment, she hesitated.

Then he smoothed his hands down her sides, over her hips and down her thighs, and she forgot duty. He rubbed her with the flat of his palms as if the mere touch of her skin gave *him* pleasure—and heaven knew it gave *her* pleasure. She stretched like a cat and moaned as the gentle sensation gave way to a deeper feeling, one of need and heat and drive.

His hands roamed down her belly into the inner sanctuary of her femininity. She caught her breath as his two fingers gathered her nether lips and squeezed them gently. Her eyes fluttered shut; all thought of duty fled her mind and pleasure flooded in to replace it. One of his fingers roamed more intimately, opening her to his touch, and she gave a hum of delight.

"You like that." His husky voice sounded deep and sure.

"Oh, yes. Oh, yes." That finger found her nub and rubbed in a circle around it. Around and around until she wanted to shriek for him to touch her. She felt swollen with need, and her hips moved without volition now, giving the ultimatums her female body demanded.

And he obeyed. His finger pressed and rubbed directly on her, and she . . . she arched above him as the shock tore through her body. She no longer knew where she was, who she was; she was nothing more than a being composed of joy and desire.

As her climax faded, her determination strengthened. She was a princess. She was on top. *She was in charge.*

Shoving Robert's hands aside, she took his shaft in her fingers and ran her fingers over the head, slick with a single pale drop of semen and the evidence of her own satisfaction. Lifting herself, she carefully placed him at the entrance to her body and, sitting up straight, she eased herself down. His thickness opened her wider than before; her tissues stretched to accommodate him, and she groaned as the fullness seemed more than she could stand.

Then he groaned too, and she grew strong on a sense of triumph. And desire was always there, urging her to take more chances. This was what she had come for. To fulfill the promise of bliss once more.

He held her hips, guiding her slowly downward.

Rebelling against his direction, she took

charge of the rhythm, forcing Robert to go along with her. She reveled in the power of having a dynamic man between her legs, in riding him through the long hours of darkness until the sweat glistened on his brow and he writhed beneath her in a desperate submission. She wanted to stretch out the sensations, and she did, swirling her hips as she rose and fell, moving quickly, then slowly, teasing him with the feather of her fingers down his breastbone. She loved the look of him as he let her take him. The moonlight striped his skin, caressing him as she did. His eyes glinted, and his mouth curved in a half-smile as he watched her. He seemed to know without words that she wished to dominate him. Would dominate him.

In the places where they touched, their skin burned. Sitting above him, she watched him through half-closed eyes, a small sliver of her mind taking pleasure in the comeliness of his countenance, the strength of his body. The other part of her brain was consumed with sensation. Her knees pushed against the mattress, lifting her over him again and again. Inside her, his penis filled her in grand surges. He touched the deepest part of her, setting sparks like fireworks through her womb, through her soul, into her heart.

Now something greater than them both took over and commanded that she move more quickly, demand pleasure more rudely, gasp and moan in the grip of a need so reckless, it clouded her mind and drove her to desperation. Beneath her, Robert's hips rose and fell. He groaned in the agony of need she brought forth from him. This was what she wanted. This was what she loved. This knowing that *she* had taken *him.* She pressed her hands against Robert's belly, sitting up straight, moving on him and knowing that soon, climax would take her. The other climaxes would be forgotten in the heat of this one, this special one that she had brought forth with her strength and her control.

She whimpered as deep within her the spasms started. She moved with an eager violence, demanding satisfaction, and more satisfaction. Below her, his groans escalated as he drove hard, his penis hot within her. He held her thighs in his palms, lifting her, shoving her, filling her. Their movements grew more frantic, yet he thrust and she took at the same rate, with the same need. Her heart thundered in her chest. Her breath rasped in her throat. She leaned over him, her hands on the mattress beside his head, wanting to be close to his warmth, to hear his gasps and be one with his orgasm. In the moonlight his features were outlines of ecstasy, while within her his shaft jerked, giving proof of his compulsion. Triumphant, she rode him all the way through his satisfaction until he collapsed beneath her.

Then she crumpled too, her head resting on his chest, hearing the subsiding thunder of his heart.

The connection between them seemed almost mystical: his body, jutting, intruding, taking; her body, soft, yielding, accepting. Together they formed one being.

He didn't dominate her with his sexuality. She wasn't in thrall to the enticement of his body. It was a mutual enjoyment they brought each other, and she commanded as much authority as he did.

She fell asleep on that comforting thought.

Twenty-two

A princess never betrays her true emotions, or lowers herself to familiarity with those of lesser rank.
—THE DOWAGER QUEEN OF BEAUMONTAGNE

She woke to find Robert over the top of her. His shoulders blocked the slanted moonlight. Clarice could see nothing of his expression. She only knew that he weighed heavily on her, that she was stretched beneath him like a virgin sacrifice on an altar. That his mouth was on her nipple, sucking so strongly that she dug her heels into the mattress to keep from writhing in absolute, abject submission. Her body ached with need, as if he had been touching her, tasting her as she slept.

That frightened her, to think he had been there in her dreams.

Breathlessly she asked, "What are you doing?" And when he didn't answer, she tried to bring her arms down from over her head—to find them anchored there, held by his hands on her wrists.

"Robert. Let me go." She tried to struggle.

And he laughed. Laughed against her breast. Then he nipped it, the scrape of his teeth almost painful against the swollen tissue.

Between her legs she throbbed with need.

With need? How was that possible? The sun promised to light the sky soon; she'd been asleep only a few hours, and she'd fallen asleep satiated. Now she wanted again. Wanted him between her legs, thrusting, feeding this hunger that left her hollow and empty.

This was mad. She was mad.

More insistently she tried to struggle, but her fight was greater than his. She was fighting the darkness and her sleepiness and her own desire, which thrummed in her ears and made her lids heavy.

What had happened? When had the balance of power changed? Or had it always been this way? Had he been in charge? Had he been indulging her?

He kissed her face, pressing his lips over her eyelids, her cheeks, her mouth. He lingered nowhere, and lost in delight, her head followed him, wanting more of his touch. His damp tongue probed the depths of her ear, the dampness and the rush of his breath sending a thrill down her spine.

Muttering now, she asked again, "What are you doing?"

In a voice as deep and rough as night itself, he said, "I'm going to show you pleasure such as you've never experienced. I'm going to be under your skin and in your mind." He shoved the covers aside, baring her skin to the cool early morning air. Sitting on top of her, he leaned close to her, pressed his hard, hot erection into her belly, and whispered, "Tomorrow night and every night, you're going to come back to me, not because you want to, but because you have to."

She flinched as if he had hit her. She

twisted beneath him. "Tomorrow night. I'll come back tomorrow night if I want to. But every night? I can't stay here. I can't be here. You can't make me."

On a harsh chuckle he kissed her. He kissed her without his usual finesse, with the rough lustiness of a warrior set free from the captivity of civilization. His tongue invaded her mouth, moving in and out without subtlety, dominating her. And when she had yielded, struggling no longer, straining to match her body to his, he lifted his head and whispered, "Oh, my darling. You don't know what I can do."

He scared her with his wild talk and his ferocious kisses, and she whimpered like a child. He pushed her toward some revelation she didn't want, some need she couldn't bear, and when he was done, she didn't know who she would be.

He didn't give her time to think. His mouth came down to her breasts, licking the tender skin on the underside, sucking lightly on each nipple. His breath cooled the warm moisture he left behind, his mouth tasting her with a thoroughness that stole her breath away. Her nipples beaded harder than ever before. It was almost painful, definitely impetuous—and desperate. She wanted her hands free, not to fight him, but to claw at him, to demand more.

Yet he didn't care about her demands. He was doing as he wished, and he wished to kiss down her breastbone to her bellybutton, to probe the depths with his tongue in a slow, masterful imitation of intercourse. She found herself moaning in the delight of what he was doing, and moaning in anticipation of what was to come. Her legs shifted on the sheets, restless and seeking. She ran the arch of her foot over his back, urging him closer when she should have been kicking him away.

Dawn was lightening the sky now, and she closed her eyes. Somehow, that made this more of a dream, less of a reality, and that was good. That meant that someday, when she lived in her cold marble palace, she could pretend this had never happened. That there had never been a time when she had been nothing but a fragile feminine shell of desire. That there had never been a man who forced her toward unwilling climax and everlasting passion.

Everlasting. Oh, God, what an awful word. She would forget . . . wouldn't she? This wouldn't haunt her forever . . . would it?

Robert freed her hands.

She didn't even notice, for he caressed her sides, taking joy in the curves beneath her arms, of her waist, of her hips. His hands slid between her legs, opening them wide, and his palms stroked the insides of her thighs almost to the thatch of hair. She held her breath, waiting for his touch.

But nothing happened. Nothing. And he commanded, "Look at me."

Reluctantly she opened her eyes and saw at once he had known what she was doing, pretending like a child who couldn't face the truth.

"Look at me." With one finger he traced the outline of her femininity.

The tender contact was almost more than she could bear. She wanted to shout at him to hurry, to go deep, harder . . . oh, God, to *hurry*.

His gaze locked with hers, and he smiled at her, a smile that mocked her flimsy control. He could tame her at any moment, and he knew his power, and she knew it as well.

The silence was profound as his other fingers joined the first, brushing at her hair, then sliding down to open her to the air, and to his touch. He handled her with a surety that sent her fingers groping at the sheets, trying to find an anchor in a world that tilted and threatened to shift out from beneath her. He circled her opening, sank his thumb a little way inside. "Nice," he said in that voice as intoxicating as brandy and just as heady. "Hot. Wet. So wet. Do you want me inside of you, darling?"

"Yes." It was too late to worry about her pride. Not when her muscles lapped at him, trying to pull him deeper.

"Not yet. You'll have to wait."

"How long?" How long could he torment her?

"You're so new." He paid no attention to what she wanted, to what her body demanded. His thumb slipped out of her. His fingers found her nub and caressed it, fondled it. "You don't know that intercourse takes the edge off for a man."

Without her volition her hips rocked, making the motions of intercourse. She could barely form the question. "What do you mean? I thought I felt—"

"This?" He shifted, placing himself between her legs. His erection nudged at her opening. He smiled into her face. "No mistake. I'm so hard I could burst with it. I want you, but I've wanted you since the first moment I saw you."

"Then . . . do it for me. . . ." She tried to reach for him, to place him at her opening and bring him inside her.

But he caught her wrists. "No. Not yet. Not until I can't wait anymore." He moved his hips so the tip of him slid along her damp, smooth skin, inciting riots of sensation within her flesh. As if the strength of his arousal caught him unaware, his eyes half closed. "There's a richness to the feel of your flesh, like living silk, and I'll never get enough of it. Of you."

She almost sobbed as she strained toward him, toward mating. "Robert."

Before she could say more, he kissed her again, one of those savage, warrior kisses that ravished her senses, took her breath, created a creature that was his and his alone.

When he lifted his mouth, he chuckled. "You're good, and you don't even know what you're doing. Open your eyes."

She hadn't realized she had closed them. She struggled, raised her lids, found his face right against hers.

"Watch me," he commanded.

He moved down her body. She thought he would kiss her breasts, then her belly. But no. No, he had a darker purpose in mind, and when she realized it, she cried out and struggled.

He placed one large hand on her rib cage to keep her in place.

She tried to close her legs.

He was between them. He nudged her knees up so that her feet rested flat on the sheets.

She writhed, not knowing if she feared him or wanted him. Both, she supposed. Neither. Laboriously she worked her elbows beneath her, sat up, looked down at him, and whispered, "Please."

"Please what?" His mouth nuzzled the crease between her legs. "Please taste me? I intend to."

His tongue separated her nether lips, then caressed the soft, pale, moist inner skin. It felt . . . good. So good. She shouldn't like it. She should be embarrassed. But voluptuous exhilaration overwhelmed everything else. His tongue licked her, a long, slow motion that went from one end to the other. Over and over again he licked as if seeking some-thing—and with each repetition she trem-bled, her arms threatening to give way beneath her. Exposed to the air and to his caress, her skin grew more and more sensitive. When at last his mouth closed around her already swollen nub and sucked gently, Clarice collapsed against the pillows in a climax that drove all thought from her mind.

It was too much. Too much. Her lungs burned, her blood turned to molten fire. Her skin ached where it rested on the sheets, as if every contact was too much to bear. "Stop," she said. "Please stop."

Robert wanted to laugh at her plea. Stop? No, indeed. He didn't want to. Not yet. Not until he'd thoroughly taught her the lesson he wanted her to learn. He entered her with his tongue, lapping inside her, tasting the sweetness of her climax and driving her on to another one. She moaned, a low, insistent sound that could never be mistaken for anything except what it was—a woman in the throes of undeniable passion. He listened, his eyes not yet open, with the satisfaction of hearing that song from Clarice. From his princess.

And at last, the need—for it was need—became too much for him to bear. Rising over her, he waited until the last crest had swept her, and she reclined, panting, on the sheets. He waited until she noticed he was above her, then reluctantly opened her eyes. Emphatically, ruthlessly, he said, "You wanted power over me. That's fine. You have it. But remember—I have the same power over you."

Her eyes opened wide, as if she were surprised that he had probed her mind as well as her body.

Then, in a single sweep he pierced her, plunging to the hilt. This time he controlled her in every way. His body pressed her into the mattress. His hands and mouth forced erotic sensation on her. His cock probed her depths, and she could do nothing to stop him.

Climax struck her immediately, a warm, wet inner explosion that rolled on and on.

He didn't come. He could wait . . . barely. Just this one time. To make his point.

He paused long enough for her to catch her breath before driving into her again.

She was swollen from their previous encounter, but more than that she was overly sensitive because he had caressed her breasts, ministered to her with his mouth, thrust his tongue inside her passage.

Her craving had never stopped, and she was out of control.

She came again and again, the muscles inside her milking him until he was in a frenzy equal to hers.

He loved her excitement. He exulted in her excess. He whispered in her ear, "More. Give it to me. All of yourself. You can't hold back."

And she couldn't. She trembled. She screamed. Tears rolled down her cheeks, yet still she held him, her legs and her arms wrapped tightly around him to keep him close. He led her, setting the pace, their bodies rising and falling in the tides of passion, their blood rushing in their veins, the breath hurrying from the lungs.

At last, at long last, he couldn't wait anymore. His balls drew up, fiercely demanding release, and with a shout he gave himself over, filling her with his seed.

There had never been a woman like Clarice. She was light to his darkness, and as he sank over her, pressing her into the bed, enforcing his possession in one last act, he wondered—what would he do when it came time for her to leave him? Would he let her go? Or would he keep her . . . by any means possible?

*   *   *

"Come on, darling, you have to go back to your bedchamber." Robert urged Clarice to her feet and tossed her gown over her head.

He buttoned it while she swayed, her knees ready to buckle, so worn out with hedonistic delight she could scarcely stand. Outside, the sun had risen over the summits of the hills to touch the tops of the trees. "It's light," she muttered. "I hope no one sees me." Because after last night, there could be no doubt what she'd been doing. Catching a glimpse of herself in the mirror, she saw a woman with swollen lips, with hair impossibly tangled, with a glow that could be described only as carnal. Or perhaps embarrassed, for she had done things she had never imagined were possible, and reveled in them, and with . . . with him. With Robert.

His gaze met hers in the mirror, and the way he looked at her made her want to squirm. With shyness. Or perhaps with desire. Which surely was impossible. She was sore between the legs. She couldn't accept his possession again. Yet her body clamored for him as if it hadn't a bit of sense, and right now she wondered if it had. For if Robert pointed to the bed again, she would climb in and give herself to him without a thought to her pride or her control.

"When you get to your bedchamber, I want you to have a tray brought up to you. Then you should sleep."

"I don't think I could." For as tired as she was, a jittery excitement held her in its grasp. The exhilaration of flaunting her upbringing, she supposed. Of taking a lover.

But her lover said, "You must. You want to be fresh tonight, to charm Colonel Ogley, then be alert enough to change your gown in a rush, to disguise your face, and make it look like Carmen's, and when you see Colonel Ogley, to play the scene as his dramatics demand it be played."

"I know. You're right."

"Waldemar is depending on you. Justice itself is depending on you. And I . . . I have every faith in you." The tips of his fingers tenderly brushed her neck. "I've never met a woman as clever or as talented or as beautiful. I want to take care of you for the rest of your life."

Oh, God. She loved him.

Well, of course she did. There was never a doubt she loved him. The emotion she felt for him had pulled her, almost unresisting, into this situation fraught with peril and deception. She didn't truly know Robert, but she burned for him, and that was dangerous. So dangerous.

And she loved him, and that was the most dangerous of all.

"I'll do as you wish. I'll sleep as long as I can, and be at leisure for the rest of the day."

"Good, for I kept you awake long after you should have been asleep."

Color flooded her face. She had been more than awake. She had been overwhelmed.

In that deep voice that turned her blood to honey, he said, "Now we'll go back. I'll make sure no one sees us."

"Sees us?" Alarmed, she tried to twist around and face him. "You can't take me back. If someone saw you with me, that would be disaster."

Looking deep into her eyes, he asked, "Do you really think I would let you face the perils of returning across the lawn and through the corridors on your own? After all that has passed between us?"

No. No, certainly not. He hadn't ruthlessly enforced his will on her, marked her with his passion, for another man to see. He would escort her to her bedchamber, and with his skill, no one would see them.

Pray God no one would see them.

As he went to get the all-enveloping brown cape, she tried to comb her hair with her trembling fingers, and tried to stop herself from asking the question that clamored to be asked. But as he wrapped her up and pulled her close, she couldn't stop herself. "Why did you do that to me? Last night? Why did you take me like . . . like some Viking marauder on a raid?"

Tilting her chin up with his finger, he gazed into her eyes and gave the one answer she never wanted to hear. Echoing the words she had given him on the floor of his study, he said, "Because you needed me. Because *you* needed me."

Larissa's mouth twisted into her most scornful sneer. She knew it, for she practiced that sneer in the mirror for best effect. That grimace successfully undermined other debutantes when they imagined themselves in the role of society belle, and put amorous, unsuitable, *poor* young men in their places. Right now, as Larissa watched Lord Hepburn stroll across the lawn, Princess Clarice wrapped in his cape and tucked under his arm, the sneer felt utterly natural.

Princess Clarice. That bitch. No wonder she had had the nerve to refuse Larissa. She was sleeping with His Lordship. Rolling around on his sheets like a strumpet in heat, taking money for her abilities, no doubt. Well. Larissa would save this information until the proper moment, and somehow she would make her royal hoity-toity highness pay for her insolence.

Oh, yes. Princess Clarice would pay.

Twenty-three

Love is like the ague.
The more afraid ye are, the more likely
ye'll suffer it.
—THE OLD MEN OF FREYA CRAGS

Clarice couldn't sleep. She wanted to. She knew she was exhausted physically and mentally. She knew she needed to be alert tonight. But unbidden, doubts and an inexplicable exhilaration ran through her mind.

Not so inexplicable, really. She smiled at the fat cherubs who decorated the ceiling of her bedchamber. She was in love. For the first time in her life, she was madly, deeply, truly in love.

And with Robert MacKenzie, the earl of Hepburn! Of all the unsuitable men!

Unsuitable. Oh, yes. That was where the doubts came in. She could almost hear Grandmamma. *Of all the unsuitable men! What were you thinking, Clarice Jayne Marie Nicole? A mere earl? You are a princess, and not just any princess, but a princess of Beaumontagne!*

Wincing, Clarice flipped her pillow, found a cool place to rest her cheek, and tried to ignore the echo of Grandmamma's autocratic, stiffly correct voice.

Which brought her back to Robert. Her body was sore, but it was a good sore, as if she'd spent a day of absolute freedom riding Blaize through the meadows and over the hills.

She chuckled. Robert would not appreciate the comparison. But she loved him, and when she thought of him—his deep voice, his blue eyes fringed with sinfully long, dark lashes, his smooth, black hair—a thrill rocked her body unlike any other she'd ever experienced. She couldn't stop smiling. It was shameful. She was shameful.

It *was* shameful, because yesterday Amy had come to her to talk and Clarice had abandoned her to go to Robert. Family came first. Clarice knew that. Grandmamma had pounded that into her head. And Amy . . . Amy needed her. Oh, Amy wasn't happy with her right now, but Clarice knew the truth. Amy was a bewildered child looking for direction.

Clarice chewed her lower lip. Amy had pointed out that Clarice was younger than Amy when Clarice had taken responsibility for her baby sister, but Clarice had had to grow up quickly. She wanted to protect Amy from the shocks of such an abrupt transition into adulthood, and she would. As soon as this ball was over, she would go to Freya Crags and make everything right with Amy.

She wondered if Robert would let Amy live in MacKenzie Manor. He didn't know that Clarice had a sister, but he showed a great sense of responsibility for his own family, and for Waldemar too.

Clarice wiggled under the covers as a vision of Robert floated through her mind. He was everything a woman would want.

Handsome, conscientious, and a lover such as she had never imagined. Thank heavens, for if she had she would have searched for such a man the world over.

But she knew he didn't suspect the truth about Amy. Perhaps that secret would displease him, especially when he realized Amy had been planted in the village to help sell the royal secret creams.

Clarice sat up as she considered that. He might not appreciate such a well-thought-out scam even though he planned just such a scam for tonight. Men had an illogical way of thinking that anything was acceptable for honor but not to feed a starving family.

And Robert hadn't mentioned that she should stay longer than tonight. In fact, yesterday she'd been the one to state she would make love with him *until your charade is over and it's time for me to leave*. Mayhap he believed her.

Her eyes widened, and she tossed the covers aside. Maybe he didn't want a princess, especially not a princess who had lain with him, to live with him and contaminate his own younger sister's morals. She would feel the same way in his position.

She took her gown from the chair where

her maid had placed it, flung it on over her chemise, and fastened all the buttons up the back. She was certainly capable of performing such a small task for herself; she'd done without a maid for most of her life. Donning her slippers, she combed her hair and wondered what to do, then headed downstairs to the one woman who would allay her fears. To Lady Millicent.

She found Millicent in the center of the ballroom crowded with bustling servants, clad in her oldest gown, directing Norval in a brisk voice. "Put them in front of each mirror and use only the finest beeswax candles."

"Aye, Lady Millicent." The footman staggered away with an armload of polished silver candelabras.

The lad couldn't bow; he was too weighted down, yet Clarice watched him and thought he should have at least tried.

"I want the flowers placed in heavy vases that can't be tipped over," Millicent instructed the head gardener. "Tonight I won't have water splattered on the waxed floor."

He tugged at his forelock. "Aye, mistress, 'twas just what I planned anyway."

Clarice didn't like his attitude. The gardener was an elderly man, probably an old retainer, and he treated Millicent like a child.

Millicent ignored his insolence. Waving the butler forward, she said, "Lord Hepburn has asked that champagne circulate at all times, and that Colonel Ogley's glass, especially, be kept full. Are your servers ready for the challenge?"

"Of course, m'lady." The butler sniffed. "As if I would ever allow the Hero of the Peninsula to drink his glass dry!"

"For if you did," Millicent said crisply, "I would be vexed, and you'd be traveling on the first coach back to London."

The butler sputtered with the same indignation he might have if his small dog had nipped at his heels. The chatter in the ballroom faltered. The servants exchanged wary glances with each other.

Clarice, too, stood amazed. She had never seen Millicent assert her authority. Perhaps it had never before happened. But apparently, when everything depended on the outcome of an evening, Millicent would make her wishes known and in no uncertain manner.

Drawing herself up, she stared icily, her gaze touching each and every one of the servants. "I am depending on all of you, and I will take it most unhappily if anything, anything at all, happens to mar this ball. Do you understand?"

"Aye, m'lady." The chorus of voices was soft and uncertain, and most of the servants bowed or curtsied.

Millicent turned her gimlet gaze on the butler, standing stiff and affronted.

In a soft voice she said, "Do you wish to board the coach *before* the ball?"

Lowering his chin in defeat, he gave a short, jerky bow. "I will personally oversee everything, m'lady, and it will be perfect."

"Very good." Millicent smiled with chilly satisfaction.

And Clarice felt foolish wishing for a moment of Millicent's time *now*.

But Millicent caught sight of Clarice, and her smile blossomed. "Princess Clarice, how good to see you." She swept a hand around at the ballroom. "What do you think?"

The walls were a glorious gold, and the pillars that ran along each side of the long, wide room were expertly painted to resemble black marble. The tall vases were truly black marble, and the gardener's assistants were arranging sprays of pinkish-red stock and white oxeye daisies. Millicent had placed gilt-framed mirrors on the wall between every pillar, and Norval was setting the candelabras in front of each mirror, so that when the candles were lit, the ballroom would glow with a thousand flickering lights.

"It's beautiful," Clarice told her, "and will be more beautiful tonight."

Millicent nodded in satisfaction. "I'm very pleased with the effects. Very pleased." Her gaze snapped back to Clarice, and she indicated a small table covered with papers. "Your arrival couldn't have been timed more perfectly. I'm ready to sit down, although, I confess, I must remain here to supervise the chaos. Shall I ring for tea?"

Seeing her chance to help, Clarice relaxed. "You rest and let me do it." Snapping her fingers, she brought the servants back to attention. "Your mistress needs tea and refreshments. Bring two cups, please, she has invited me to partake." She watched with satisfaction as the butler, in his turn, snapped his fingers at one of the maids and one of the footmen, and they took off at a run. Sinking down in the chair placed for her convenience, Clarice asked, "Do you have a moment for me and my silly curiosity?"

"For you? Of a certainty, I do." Millicent waved the hovering servants away. "What it is you wish to know?"

Now that Clarice faced Robert's sister, she didn't know what to say. *Does your brother love me?* No. Oh, no. So she prevaricated. "I've never been the real hostess for a party. Do you look forward to it with anticipation?"

Millicent looked taken aback. "Anticipation? Most definitely not. It's a strain from the first guest to the last dance."

"But you take pleasure in other balls, the balls you don't host, no doubt."

Millicent stacked her papers. "No, I don't enjoy them either. I'm afraid all social occasions are a strain to me." She held up one hand. "I know. You think I should enjoy myself as you do. But you're beautiful."

Now, this Clarice knew how to put right. "Not really. I'm too short, mostly in the limbs." She extended her leg to show Millicent. "My skin is tanned from the sun, and there's not a thing I can do about it, because I must travel from town to town. My ears stick out like open carriage doors, which is why you'll always see my hair pulled tight over them and pinned at the back. But no one notices my deficiencies, for I don't give them a chance."

The servants brought in the tea. Millicent poured two cups, put cream and sugar in both, and passed one to Clarice. After one nervous sip she put her cup down. "Your Highness, what do you mean?"

"Whenever I walk into a party, I remind myself that I'm a princess, and I pretend I'm the hostess, so it's up to me to make everyone comfortable. I introduce people to each other and find something about each person on which I can compliment them—that's not always easy." Clarice winked at Millicent. "I take a moment to talk to the dowagers. They're invariably the funniest people in the room, and I get more enjoyment than I provide. By the time I've done all that, everyone's happy and they think I'm beautiful."

In a timid voice Millicent protested, "But I'm not a princess."

"You're the hostess," Clarice returned promptly.

"Yes. Yes." Millicent ran her hand down the faded material of her skirt and looked thoughtful.

Taking a fortifying breath, Clarice said,

"But I didn't seek you out to bore you with the details of my beauty." She chuckled so Millicent would know she was joking.

"Oh!" Millicent focused on Clarice. "Yes, what can I do for you?"

"I was wondering if your brother has ever had a—" She gulped her tea, then gasped as she burned her tongue. "That is, I was wondering if His Lordship . . . if there's been talk of—"

"A betrothal?" Millicent guessed.

"Yes! Of a certainty! A betrothal." A little more cautiously, Clarice sipped the tea to moisten her dry mouth. In a rush she said, "I thought perhaps I should look over the debutantes and see who would suit him," and cringed because Millicent would surely call her on such an absurd lie.

She was in love with Robert, and apparently love and stupidity went hand in hand.

But Millicent didn't blink. "I don't think so, but thank you for asking. Robert has never been serious about any young lady, but he's very determined. He'll choose his own bride, and if I know my brother, he'll choose her based on her kindness and liveliness, and not for such silly reasons as her dowry or whether we know her family."

"Good. That's good. I mean"—heavens, Clarice felt foolish—"he seems so . . . alone."

"Aye. I've worried about him, especially since his return from the war, but in the last few days he seems better. Not so grim, and alive in a way I had feared I'd never see again." Millicent extended a plate. "Biscuit?"

"No, I thank you." Last night's tiredness had caught up with Clarice, and suddenly she couldn't keep her eyes open. "I must go take a nap before the ball."

"Of course you should." Millicent's mouth curled into a smile as she watched Clarice wander away, dazed and exhausted. Would Robert choose his own bride? Millicent thought so. She also thought she had considerably contributed to the outcome.

The ballroom looked well arranged. It was time for the footmen to change into their formal livery, for the maids to go help the guests dress for the ball, and for Cook to get down to the serious business of making dinner. But first—standing, Millicent clapped her hands. "Go get your tea—and remember, tonight the MacKenzies are depending on you, all of you. Now make haste!"

The servants dropped whatever they were doing and did as she instructed.

Millicent smiled after them. Between the servants and Princess Clarice, she thought tonight would go very smoothly. She would be much more relaxed than she had ever been at a ball, even if she didn't dare to pretend to be a princess.

Robert spoke behind her. "Millicent, can you help me?"

She jumped. Swiftly she turned, her hand on her chest.

He was dressed in the casual garb of a country gentleman: brown tweed and black boots. His gaze was steady and his eyes serious.

"But of course. I'll do whatever you require." And marvel at the fact he had asked her at all. Glancing around at the empty ballroom, she said, "Let's go into my sitting room." She led him into the small east-facing chamber.

He indicated she should sit on the sofa, and when she had, he seated himself beside her. A silence fell, and not a comfortable silence. It seemed, for all that they were brother and sister, as if they didn't know what to say to each other.

What would a princess do? A princess would offer her assistance. For no one else would Millicent have been so bold, but now she asked, "Robert, please, what is it? I wish to help you."

He stood and looked down at her, his blue eyes sharply observant, as if he had never seen her before.

She had been too audacious. "That is, if you wish me to."

"Yes. You do, don't you?" He reached for her hand, then, as if he didn't quite dare touch her, he pulled back.

In a rush of boldness she caught his fingers and held them in hers. "I always want to help you."

He looked at their joined hands helplessly, as if he didn't know what he was supposed to do now. Clearing his throat, he said, "You do help me. All the time. You take care of the house and you cared for MacKenzie Manor after Father died." Robert laughed bitterly. "More important, you raised Prudence after I left, and I'm not fool enough to think Father did anything to assist you."

Millicent had learned never to complain—no one cared about an old maid's ordeals. "It wasn't so difficult."

Robert paid no attention to her falsehood. "What an awful man Father was."

The two of them sat facing forward, not

looking at each other, both remembering the man who had so constantly made their lives miserable. Their father had been a martinet, an ex-officer who came into the title after a series of mishaps left him the heir. He was ill prepared for the responsibilities of wealth and privilege, yet he'd been well aware of his duty to the MacKenzie family. He'd married their mother, a gentlewoman of no fortune, and done his duty so often, she'd suffered through six pregnancies. She'd died in birthing Prudence, and Millicent had wept bitterly, for Mother had been the only person standing between the children and their father. Of course, Father had found Millicent's tears a weakness and her shyness an annoyance.

"How did you survive the years alone with him?" Robert asked.

His frankness made her uncomfortable. "I shouldn't complain. After all, he was my father, and I'm supposed to honor him."

"You're his daughter, which meant he should have had a care for you. For all of us. Instead, he used us as his whipping posts."

She was shocked that Robert at last said what they'd always thought. At the same time, it freed her to show the compassion she'd always felt but curbed out of respect for Robert's pride. "He never whipped Prue or me. He took the rod only to you. I'm sorry I couldn't stop him."

"He whipped you too. Unmercifully and without ceasing. He beat you with words, and I was sorry that *I* couldn't stop *him* too."

"I know. I do know."

When Robert had left, sold to the army like a conscript rather than the nobleman's son he was, only Millicent's memory of her mother gave her the courage to stand between Prudence and their father. For the most part, she'd been successful, deflecting Father's malice away from Prudence and onto herself.

Prudence didn't know. Dear girl. Every miserable moment had been worth it, for Prudence was as innocent and vivacious as Millicent had never been. Prudence would be a debutante. She would dance, she would flirt, she would marry and have children. She would be everything that Millicent had ever dreamed of being, and that made Millicent's sacrifice worthwhile.

"I'm sorry I abandoned you to Father," Robert said. "I worried about you."

"I worried about you too, all the time you were gone, but truth to tell, I hoped things on the Peninsula would be better for you." She sounded stupid, and she hastened to explain herself. "I beg you believe me—I don't think war is easy. But I hoped when you got away from Father and among other jolly young men, you might occasionally have fun of a manly sort."

For the first time, Robert looked at ease. Leaning back, he studied her. "Fun of a manly sort, heh? What might that be?"

He was teasing her, she realized. He was teasing her! It was almost like old times when their father had gone visiting and they were alone and happy. "You know." She waved her other hand. "Drinking, cards . . . women."

Robert barked a laugh. "There was some of that, Millicent. I promise, there was some of that."

She studied his face anxiously. "But most of it was difficult."

He dismissed his travails with a shrug of one shoulder. "What I wanted to say was— Millicent, I'm grateful for all that you've done for me. You've done more for me, for Prudence, and for the estate than a hundred women, and you've done it all without complaining when you should have been heartily complaining." He looked into her eyes. "I thank you, and I want you to know how much I admire you. You are the dearest sister any man has ever had the good luck to possess, and I thank God for you every night. Especially now, with all the work you've had to do to bring this ball to fruition."

Millicent didn't know what to reply. No one had ever expressed their admiration of her before. She didn't expect it. But she liked it.

He continued. "I'm back to take care of things. I know I've not done a good job so far, but I promise in the future I'll do better. For tonight . . . I beg you, take the time to enjoy the fruits of your labor."

"What do you mean?"

"Dance, drink, dine, and gossip," he said. "Isn't that what ladies like to do at balls?"

"I don't know," she said frostily.

"I've said the wrong thing. My apologies." He stood and bowed. "I shouldn't have bothered you."

She hadn't meant to chase him away. Not when he looked as if he labored under some distress. "Robert, sit down. You can ask me anything, you know. I'll do my best for you."

With a show of reluctance, he perched on the edge of the sofa. "You could do me a favor."

"Anything," she reiterated.

"Lord Tardew is a friend of mine. Well, you remember Corey. He visited here often enough."

"Yes, I remember." How could she forget?

"He'll be here tonight."

"I know." Princess Clarice. Had she been talking to Robert about Millicent? But she wouldn't have been cruel. She wasn't like that. And Robert wouldn't try deviously to push them together. He knew very well that Millicent couldn't appeal to a man like Corey.

But Robert didn't seem to know any such thing. He lowered his voice. "I haven't told you everything about my reasons for wanting this ball."

Dazed, she shook her head. "Haven't you?"

"And I won't. Trust me, it's better if you don't know the details. But I'll not have time to slap Corey's shoulder and be his friend as I have in the past, and I don't want him wondering why." Robert gazed at her in appeal. "I know it's another duty on your already duty-filled plate, but would you dance and flirt with him and distract him? I know you can."

Her heart twisted. Did Robert know about her infatuation with Corey? Was he mocking her?

But no, he appeared to be serious.

"I can't flirt." She hated to admit the truth. She liked hearing Robert flatter her with things that weren't true. "I don't know how."

Robert chuckled. "You don't have to flirt. Just smile at him and act interested. He's a shallow fellow. He'll believe you infatuated and court you most assiduously."

"There are other lasses whom he'll find more to his taste."

"None as attractive as you, Millicent. I heard him say you've got a grand figure. Dress to show it off. You've got the most beautiful smile in the world. Lavish it on him. Plus, you have a reputation as being impervious to flirtation. Yes, I promise, when he realizes he will conquer a citadel no one else has touched, he'll be after you at once." Robert squeezed her hand. "Do you mind dreadfully, dear sister? For if you do, I'll try to find another way to distract him, although none will be as effective."

"No! No, I'm glad to assist you as I can." Millicent took deep breaths, for it seemed she had suddenly ascended a mountain where the air was thin.

"Good." Robert clapped his hands to his knees and stood up. "I admire your boldness and your initiative more and more, and I have every faith in you. I'll go now, but remember—keep him distracted all evening!"

"I will." In a daze Millicent watched Robert stride from the room.

Then he returned. "I hope you don't mind, but I ordered a gown from Mistress Dubb, made to your specifications. She's clever about fashions, and she told me she'd take care of the matter. If you don't like the gown, though, don't fret yourself. All of your gowns are admirable when they're on you."

He left again, leaving her with her hands limp in her lap. He admired her? Her boldness and initiative? He had noticed what she'd done while he was gone? He noticed what she did to run the house? He *appreciated* her? She could scarcely comprehend these new developments.

All this time she had thought herself almost invisible, and as time went on, she grew more and more invisible until it almost seemed that everyone looked through her.

But Robert had said differently, and for some reason, hearing one voice declare his admiration made all the difference in the world.

Standing, she walked, stiff-legged, toward her bedchamber.

Moreover, Robert had given her a mission. To flirt . . . with Lord Tardew. With dear, beautiful, noble Corey MacGown. And Robert had made it sound like an important matter.

She opened the door to her bedchamber, staggered inside, and went to her dressing table. There, placed among the silver-backed brushes and staid clips, were jars such as Princess Clarice sold. And a curling iron. And on the bed, a gorgeous gown of the most provocative cherry-red.

Millicent knew it was provocative, because her eyes popped when she saw it.

"Ma'am?" Her maid hurried forward. "His Lordship said I was to help you dress and coif, and if you need help you're to call Princess Clarice."

At the offer Millicent's spine stiffened. "No. I know what to do. Now I have only to do it."

Twenty-four

A princess always utilizes her handker-chief and checks her buttons before entering the ballroom.
—THE DOWAGER QUEEN OF BEAUMONTAGNE

Millicent had never had people look at her as they did now. With confusion and disbelief. When Colonel Ogley and Mrs. Ogley entered the room on a polite round of applause, the colonel himself saw her and did an inelegant double take.

But keeping Princess Clarice's advice in mind, Millicent walked into the ballroom with a smile fixed on her lips. She glided rather than walked, the thin satin of the cherry-red skirt swishing around her legs, and she wondered if the gentlemen could tell she had left off her petticoat.

Seeing the scandalized look on Mr. Trumbull's hangdog face, she realized they could.

The newly cut fringe brushed at her forehead in a maddening manner, like midges swarming against her skin. She barely refrained from swatting at it, but she kept her hands in a graceful arc at her sides as she crossed the hardwood floor. The ballroom was as beautiful as she had hoped, and as they looked around, Lady Mercer, Lady Lorraine, and Mrs. Symlen smiled. The debutantes were wide-eyed and awe-stricken, and even Lady Blackston nodded a sour approval.

Millicent instructed the leader of the orchestra to start the music, then turned back to the beautifully dressed crowd on the ballroom floor and smiled graciously. She damned well would be confident if it killed her.

And she found she enjoyed the glazed, openmouthed stare young Larissa gave her—especially since Larissa sported a fiery red and pustulous spot right between her eyes.

With all the enthusiasm of a puppy Prudence bounced up and sputtered, "You wouldn't let me dampen my skirts, and you look like *that*?"

Millicent's confidence took a fast dive. "Do I look ridiculous?"

"You look dazzling, not at all like yourself, but you're wearing a breathtaking red gown and I'm wearing"—Prudence plucked discontentedly at her blue skirt—"this boring old thing."

"You look lovely, and absolutely appropriate for someone of your age."

"I don't want to look appropriate. I want to look stunning too."

"When you're my age, you can wear a cherry-red gown." Lowering her voice, Millicent distracted Prudence the best way she knew how. "In the meantime, did you see Larissa's spot?"

Prudence put her head close to Millicent's. "Yes, isn't it awful? All the rest of us girls don't have spots because we used the royal secret creams. That'll teach Larissa to listen to her mother. And have you seen Princess Clarice? Isn't she a stunner?"

Millicent looked around. At the edge of the ballroom Princess Clarice stood clad in a gown of glowing silver satin with touches of dark blue braid at the shoulders and a dark blue ribbon tied beneath her breasts. She wore her golden curling hair twisted back in a stern style that gave her face a grave distinction, and a peacock feather bobbed above her head. "She looks beautiful, as usual," Millicent said.

Robert walked in, offered his arm to Princess Clarice, and started with her in a circuit around the room.

Prudence gave a soundless whistle. "Older Brother looks handsome too. Larissa's right. He *is* the Catch of the Season—and with that spot, she hasn't got a chance."

Millicent found herself tittering along with her sister.

"Maybe Princess Clarice can win him," Prudence speculated.

Millicent clasped her hands before her. "Maybe so." With a squeeze to Prudence's hand she said, "Behave, and have fun."

As she moved off, Prudence called with a giggle, "Which one? I can't do both."

Millicent heartily prayed for Robert's engagement every night, for Princess Clarice had changed him even more than Millicent had dared hope. Robert was himself again, suave and social, no longer a man whose life-less eyes made her want to cry.

That was Millicent's doing. She had urged Princess Clarice to come and stay with them. She had pushed them together as often as possible. She had done everything in her power to create an atmosphere conducive to romance, and she was proud of herself. The knowledge that she could do one thing right gave her the courage to trust her voice, and she began to speak to people. "Lady Mercer, how elegant you look. Are those the famous pearls I've heard so much about?"

Lady Mercer cackled as only an old lady could. "Damn, young lady, I never thought to see the day, but you've done it. You've really done it, and to hell with your father, heh?"

Before Millicent could think of an answer, Lady Mercer pinched her cheek hard and used her cane to thump away toward the matrons' corner.

Smile, Millicent thought. *Smile and go on to the next guest.*

Mr. Gaskell intercepted her next. He was no more than Prudence's age but of good family with a large fortune, and his choice of bride had already been an object of much speculation among the debutantes. Right now his large brown eyes were fixed on her in a manner she'd never seen before. It almost looked like adoration. He bowed stiffly, his chin never dipping into his stiff collar, and in a nervous voice he asked, "May I beg the next quadrille?"

"From . . . me? Well . . . yes, of course, I'd be delighted." And guilty, for she knew very well the debutantes would be furious with her. But this was rather agreeable.

He bowed again and backed away, his gazed fixed not on her face but on her breasts. Good heavens, they hadn't grown overnight, had they? And more to the point, the dress wasn't cut that low, was it? She was tempted to look but managed to refrain.

In a fluster she decided she should go check with Cook to make sure the dinner was proceeding and would be ready at midnight. And on the way she could go and tuck a fichu into her neckline. But when she turned, she almost buried her nose in a high starched white collar and a perfectly tied cravat.

The earl of Tardew, Corey MacGown, stood before her. Tall, golden, blue-eyed, he had a perfect figure perfectly set off by his perfectly cut green breeches and a perfectly designed green-and-blue-striped jacket. As she slowly lifted her eyes to his, she realized he was staring at her as if he had never seen her before.

Her smile faltered. Her lips trembled. Then she heard a titter off to the side and knew they were being watched—not kindly either. Her chin came up. Her smile blossomed. In a composed voice she said, "Corey, how good to see you again. Oh, dear, I beg your pardon, I should call you Lord Tardew, but we've been friends for so long, I forgot."

"Friends?" he said stupidly. "Do I know you?"

His ignorance shocked her. Had he truly never observed her better than that? "Lady Millicent MacKenzie, at your service." She dipped into a curtsy. "*Now* do you remember?"

"Lady Millicent!" He placed his hand flat on his chest. "No, you were . . . that is, I scarcely recognized . . . that is, you look lovely tonight."

"I thank you." Robert had asked her to keep Corey busy, so although she wanted nothing so much as to lift her skirts and run into the safety of the kitchens, she put her hand on his arm and went to work on his sense of competition. "Will you do me a favor?"

"Anything!"

"Will you dance with Prue?" She smiled coyly and realized this thing called flirting was getting easier. "I have all these silly boys asking me to dance, and she's going to be angry if no one asks her."

Corey's large blue eyes narrowed as an idea struck him. An idea she had put into his head. "I have a better plan. Why don't I dance every dance with you, thus making it impossible for the lads to ask you? Then they'll have to ask Prue."

"How very clever you are, Corey." Millicent smiled up at him and distantly noted how easily she had manipulated him. "But you know that's impossible. If I dance every dance with you, that would be tantamount to declaring our betrothal."

"Perhaps that's not such a bad idea," Corey said.

He was suggesting a betrothal? He wanted to marry her? This was her dream! Why wasn't she fainting into his arms?

And the sensible part of Millicent—which was the largest part of Millicent—answered, *Because he didn't even recognize you ten minutes ago.* How she hated sensibility. It had such a way of tromping on one's illusions! Her breathing was remarkably calm as she fluttered her eyelashes. "I think it is."

"Lady Millicent." Lord Aldwinkle interrupted them with a bow. "I would love to escort you into dinner."

Corey shouldered him aside. "You're too late. I already asked her."

"You didn't!" Millicent wasn't going to have him think he could have her for the asking.

"I was going to," Corey declared.

Mr. Mallett joined them. "We all know where good intentions lead you, eh, Lord Tardew."

The gathering crowd chuckled while Corey knit his brow. "Where?"

Everyone treated him as if he were a wit, and he laughed along with them, but Millicent had the dreadful feeling that he didn't understand the jest. And if that were true, if Corey wasn't intelligent . . . what with her illusions shattering and the strain of being the center of attention, it was going to be a very long night.

"Look at that." Clarice watched Millicent while Robert watched Clarice. "She's the newest belle. I do adore my transformations, especially when they succeed so exceptionally."

Robert steered Clarice through the crowd,

making sure everyone saw her and took note of the shimmering silver gown, the peacock feather, the golden hair. "You're very beautiful yourself."

She slanted a sideways glance at him, one that made him remember last night in a manner so explicit, he wondered in a moment of alarm if he would have to excuse himself until the physical result had subsided. Tersely he instructed, "Smile."

"I know how to do this," she answered in an undertone. "Trust me."

Trust her? He did. Inexplicably he trusted her. And he wanted her. God, how he wanted her. Wanted to pick her up, take her away from this ballroom where the gentlemen leered after her in reckless longing. Take her away from the danger she faced—the danger he had created for her.

Lord Plumbley stopped her and begged her for a dance, and Robert watched as she shook her head regretfully. "I fear I sprained my ankle riding today, and I can't dance at all. But I can sit and allow you to bring me punch." She smiled winsomely.

Lord Plumbley trembled with eagerness.

Robert wanted to thump him in his silly, quivering chin. Instead, with a curt nod he moved Clarice along. In an undertone he said, "He hasn't a ha'pence that isn't spoken for by the moneylenders."

"Unfortunate man." Clarice sounded compassionate, which was not what Robert had intended at all. "I shall have to see if I can find him an heiress. I mean . . . if I remain in Scotland for a while."

Before Robert could reply, she tugged at his arm. "You're moving too quickly. We need to stroll along as if we haven't a care in the world."

She was right, of course, but he was torn between his worry for her and his need to free Waldemar. Everything was going according to plan, and she was so calm and smiling, she might not have understood that the whole weight of his charade rested on her. Yet she did understand, and her confidence made him proud and made him swear she had possessed his soul. Without her he feared he would slip back into the darkness that had been his prison for so long. When this was over he would do what was necessary to convince her that she must remain at MacKenzie Manor. She *had* to stay with him.

Mrs. Birkbeck stopped them and asked to be introduced to the princess, and when he had obliged, he stood back and watched Clarice charm her and Mrs. Symlen, then Lady White. In an undertone she spoke to Lady Lorraine—last minute advice, he supposed.

When Clarice rejoined him and they had moved away from the little group and into a space bare of guests, she asked quietly, "There is something I have wondered—why didn't you just tell me the reasons why you wanted me to perform this masquerade? They're noble reasons, and I'm proud to do my part in freeing Waldemar. Why the secrecy?"

He joined his gloved hands behind his back to keep from touching her as they walked. He looked bored, as if he were making everyday conversation, and he kept his voice low when he answered. "You were like everyone else. You had heard of Ogley's heroism. You wanted to believe it. And why not? Those feats he wrote about really happened. Would you have believed it was Waldemar, a criminal sentenced to hang, rather than Ogley, who performed them? And would you have believed me when I said Waldemar deserved to be given his freedom and a commendation that would allow him to go wherever he wished and be whatever he wanted?"

"Probably not," she admitted.

He looked around at the warm, crowded ballroom. At the clump of gentlemen around a decked-out Millicent, at the couples dancing the country dances, at the servants circling with glasses of champagne. "We've done our duty. Everyone here has seen you."

"Everyone except Colonel and Mrs. Ogley." Clarice turned her smooth, calm face to him. "There's no avoiding them, Robert. I must speak to him directly. If this charade is to work, he must have no doubt that I'm here in the ballroom."

Ogley would believe the princess wished to admire him. Ogley watched Clarice as if he had only to reach out and take her, and Robert had seen him act on his baser impulses before. Tragedy followed.

But not this time.

"Very well." Touching the middle of Clarice's back, Robert guided her toward the crowd around the colonel and Mrs. Ogley. Clarice moved closer to him as if for protection. Looking at her smiling profile, Robert knew he would do anything to protect her.

Waldemar had volunteered to make sure

that Colonel Ogley did nothing to harm Clarice in her disguise as Carmen. After meeting her, Waldemar had begged to be allowed to escape without the necessary papers. But both Robert and Waldemar knew that if he did so, he could never return to England without taking the chance of being caught and prosecuted as a deserter— and hanged.

For all of his criminal background, Robert had come to know Waldemar as one of the greatest men he'd ever met, and he wanted Waldemar to have the honors due to him, to have a chance at a peaceful life or an adventurous life or even an honest life, if he wished it. Now, with every step, with every moment, they all moved closer to the denouement. Robert and Waldemar, Ogley and Clarice. They would be actors in the play Robert had written, and God help them all if they failed to convince Ogley that Senora Carmen Menendez had truly followed him from Spain armed with a thirst for vengeance and the tools to extract it.

"Mrs. Ogley, how lovely you look tonight." Robert bowed to the thin, flat-chested, plain woman clinging to Ogley's arm.

"Thank you, my lord. What a magnificent

ball you've given in honor of Oscar." Mrs. Ogley's wide eyes glowed.

"It's a privilege to pay tribute to such a hero." Robert stopped one of the circling footmen. "Your glass is almost empty, Colonel Ogley. Have another."

"Thank you." Ogley grinned into Robert's face as if relishing Robert's disdain.

"I understand there'll be fireworks later," Mrs. Ogley said.

"So there will," Robert replied.

"Lord Hepburn says that nothing is too great to celebrate Colonel Ogley's heroism." Clarice lavished admiration from her amber eyes on Ogley.

With heavy gallantry Colonel Ogley said, "Then perhaps you'll do this hero the honor of performing the next quadrille with me."

"I shouldn't." Clarice dithered when Robert knew damned good and well she should refuse. "I twisted my ankle today, but . . . this is the only opportunity I shall ever have of dancing with a hero. Yes, Colonel Ogley, I will be delighted to dance with you."

Robert made an aborted move to stop them. She was right. If Ogley danced with her, that would reinforce his belief, when he confronted Carmen, that Clarice was in the ballroom. But he didn't want Ogley to touch her, not even her hand.

Ogley knew it, too, and cast a triumphant glance at Robert as he led her onto the floor to join the set that was forming.

The fawning crowd that surrounded the hero moved away to watch.

Mrs. Ogley said, "What a lovely couple they make."

With a start Robert realized he should ask her to dance—and he hadn't danced since his return from the Peninsula.

But before he could, Mrs. Ogley said, "Oscar loves to dance, and I'm dreadful at it. I can't remember the moves, and I have no sense of rhythm. He shows great patience with me, but I'm hopeless."

"I must confess, I'm hopeless also." Furthermore, Robert wanted to stay right there and keep an eye on Ogley. Ogley, who made Clarice uncomfortable with his lascivious interest.

But after a moment Robert realized a good host would be making conversation. If only he remembered how. Looking sideways at Mrs. Ogley, he saw her examining him with open curiosity.

"You don't look like a spoiled young lord," she pronounced.

"Don't I?" She was frank, franker than he had expected.

"Not at all, and that was what Oscar called you. Was he jealous?" When Robert didn't answer right away, she continued. "Because I know he gets his little megrims about people, and I think you're one of them. His manservant, Waldemar, is another."

"Oh?" Robert wondered if Ogley had suggested she find out what she could from him . . . but no. Ogley would never trust a woman with such a mission. So what was her objective?

"When we get done with this victory tour and retire to our country estates, I'm going to urge Oscar to get a new manservant."

Jolted, Robert asked, "Really? Why?" They were retiring to their country estates? He wondered if Ogley knew about that.

Choosing her words with care, she said, "Not everyone realizes it, but Oscar can be petty, and I would rather he didn't have the chance to be so."

She was smarter than Robert had realized, wiser about her husband, and he didn't suppose it was mere coincidence that she confessed these things to him. She knew more than she let on—to him, and most definitely to Ogley. "What will happen to Waldemar?"

"I don't care. I think if ill treated, he could be dangerous, so I suppose Ogley will have him sent to another regiment. Oh, dear!" She stared wide-eyed at the dance floor. "Princess Clarice is hurt."

"Oh!" Robert clearly heard Clarice's exclamation. "Oh, I'm so sorry, Colonel Ogley, but I can't continue."

The lines of the country dance faltered as she limped away on Ogley's arm, then reformed with new vigor amid a wave of sympathetic murmurs.

"Dear, dear." Mrs. Ogley hurried forward, Robert at her side, and met Ogley and Clarice as they exited the dance floor. "Your Highness, can I help you?"

"I feel so foolish, making a scene." Clarice leaned heavily on Ogley's arm and limped as if she were in pain. "Could I prevail upon you to take me to a quiet alcove where I could recover in solitude?"

Robert recognized a cue when he heard one. "This way, Your Highness. In the window seat you'll be able to put your ankle up, pull the curtains, yet peek out and watch the dancing if you wish."

"That's grand." Clarice smiled at him, her lush lower lip quivering bravely. "Thank you so much, my lord."

"I'll get you some punch." He turned away before he gave in to the inappropriate desire to laugh.

How did she do that? Take a moment fraught with tension and transform it into a reason for merriment. And how did she make him want her when his whole being should be concentrated on making this operation run smoothly? He didn't understand himself anymore, and he was almost grateful to the people who stopped him to question him about Princess Clarice's well-being. They distracted and annoyed him enough so that by the time he returned with the punch and some biscuits, he could effectively place the plate in Clarice's hands with crisp disinterest.

She accepted it and waved him and the hovering Mrs. Ogley away. "Go on and enjoy yourselves. I'll be fine here by myself for a while. Later I'll slip away to beg a cold compress for my ankle."

Colonel Ogley stood outside the alcove,

looking eager to get away from any hint of injury and back to the adulation he enjoyed so much, and when Mrs. Ogley tucked her hand in his arm, he led her away without a backward glance.

Robert fussed with the curtain for a moment, closing it almost all the way. "Well done," he said. "Are you ready for the next act?"

Clarice took an audible breath, and when she answered, her voice was low, husky, and tinged with a strong Spanish accent. "I am ready, my lord. I will not fail you."

Twenty-five

Pretty is as pretty does, but ugly goes right t' the bone.
—THE OLD MEN OF FREYA CRAGS

If Ogley hadn't been watching Hepburn, he wouldn't have seen Waldemar sneak into the ballroom, sidle up to his old commander, and speak with an animation Ogley thought he had beaten out of his lowborn aide. This looked ominous, especially when Hepburn nodded abruptly and left the party with Waldemar at his side.

Ogley hadn't forgotten the sighting of Carmen, and he didn't really believe he was having delusions. She was there. For some reason the bitch was there and Hepburn knew about it. Ogley should have suspected this. Hepburn was jealous, wanting the honors Ogley had taken as his own, so he and Waldemar were planning something.

Well. They couldn't put one over on Oscar Ogley. He would stop them before they had a chance to bring their scheme to fruition.

And if it wasn't her, if the occasional twinge of guilt led him to see Carmen where she wasn't . . . then undoubtedly they were up to a different kind of conspiracy. An intelligent man like himself could always profit from other men's mischief.

Brenda broke into his musing. "Oscar, you have a most peculiar smile on your face."

"Yes. Thank you. It is nice, isn't it?" He wasn't making sense, and carefully he placed his champagne glass on a tray. Perhaps he shouldn't have indulged in quite so much of the excellent beverage. "If you'll excuse me, I shall go and get some air."

Tugging at her gloves, she said, "I'll go with you."

"No!" he snapped. As she drew back, he softened his tone. "I mean, you can't come where I'm going, Brenda."

"Ah." She nodded wisely. "I hope you feel better when you return."

He wanted to correct her, but sometimes when Brenda looked at him, it was as if she saw more deeply into his soul than he wished.

So with a bow he escaped from the ballroom, arriving in the doorway in time to see Hepburn and Waldemar whisk around a corner toward the darkened center of the house. He followed their voices through the winding corridors, remaining back far enough that they were oblivious to his presence.

After all, they were not the only expert trackers here.

They ended up in Robert's candlelit study, and luckily for Ogley, that coarse imbecile Waldemar didn't quite shut the door behind them.

Their voices grew louder, but they weren't speaking to each other. They were speaking to someone else, someone who they were trying to bully.

Oh, this was very interesting. Ogley shifted closer.

Then he recognized a voice he hadn't heard for over a year. A voice he had hoped never to hear again.

Warm and womanly. Husky with the

smoke of thin Spanish cigars. Heavily accented. *Carmen's voice.* "You tell me I cannot come to the ball, yet what reason have I to stay apart?"

In revulsion Ogley staggered back against the wall. He put his hand to his chest above his rapidly beating heart.

She blathered on. "I will go and speak to her, to his skinny, pale wife, and tell her what he has done to me."

As Ogley sneaked along the corridor until he could peek into the half-opened doorway, he tried to reassure himself. *She won't do it.* Then, remembering how she had looked, so sick and wild with grief, when he had told her he was returning to England and cared not a whit what happened to her or their child, he changed that to—*They won't let her do it.* But Hepburn and Waldemar despised him. Trying desperately to get his breath, he let his hand stray to the dagger he kept on him for just such an occasion as this. *I'll stop her.*

It was her. She stood there in her azure strumpet gown, her black hair dressed in its familiar chignon, the inevitable lace mantilla draping her bare shoulders and partially swathing her face. The light was low, but he saw her pace in that patient, steady walk toward the desk where Hepburn stood, and Ogley wanted to run into the room, dagger lifted, and slash her to ribbons before she could destroy his life. Only one thing—no, two—kept him from it. Neither Waldemar nor Hepburn would allow him to bestow justice as it should be rendered.

"He left me with nothing. I am noble, but my family, they will have nothing to do with me because of my disgrace." Ogley heard a thump as Carmen pounded her chest with her fist. Melodramatic as always.

Damn her.

He wiped a trickle of sweat off his forehead and tried to think. He had to *think*.

So it was true. Hepburn, that troublemaker, had brought her here.

"What will his skinny, pale wife say when I tell her how I wandered the countryside, my baby in my arms? His baby." Carmen's voice vibrated with passion.

And Ogley wanted to spit in disdain. Ridiculous, silly exaggeration, and so he would tell Brenda.

But he couldn't fool himself. If Carmen actually managed to get her claws into Brenda . . . if she told her of their liaison, worse, of their child, he would be served with separation papers and left out in the cold to starve. Brenda adored him, but he never made the mistake of thinking she would put up with such a betrayal.

And she was a woman. She might take Carmen's side, say that if he was going to roger some dirty foreigner, he should have provided for her later. As if he should pay for services when he no longer received them!

Carmen's voice continued on and on, driving stakes into his head. "My little Anna has no papa. The other children make fun of her, they call her a bastard."

Brenda wanted his child. If she found out he had abandoned a daughter . . . his armpits grew so wet they stained his uniform.

Carmen's voice lowered to a sad croon. "And sometimes my baby cries from hunger."

Ogley couldn't stand it anymore. All those damned histrionics. Ridiculous, absurd melodrama. Slamming through the door, he pointed his finger at the three shocked faces turned to him. "You can't do this to me. I won't let you."

Carmen started toward him, hand raised, but Waldemar caught her arm. She turned on him like the virago she was, but Hepburn said, "Senorita, no! I will handle this."

Flipping out her fan, she held it in front of her face and flapped it in a fury while her amber eyes flashed with . . . how odd. Ogley had thought her eyes were a deep brown. But hell! What did the color of one woman's eyes, more or less, matter in the end? With a shrug that rudely dismissed her, he turned to Hepburn. Hepburn was the puppet master here. Only Hepburn mattered.

Hepburn gestured to Waldemar, who kept a hard grip on Carmen's arm and hustled her toward the door. Ogley stepped back, but her skirts brushed against his legs. A wave of perfume made of fresh flowers and sweet spices washed over him, and she hissed *"Bastardo"* in a venomous tone.

He swung after her, staring as Waldemar pushed her down the corridor, then turned back to Hepburn. "I demand to see Carmen alone."

"No. Oh, no." Hepburn laughed lightly, scornfully. "What are you going to do, kill her?"

And because the thought had crossed his mind, Ogley flushed an ugly red.

"No," Hepburn said, "I promised her that you're not going to see her alone and intimidate her. She wants to knock you off your pedestal with all these people watching, and I can't think of one reason why I shouldn't let her."

Ogley could feel the spit gathering at the corners of his lips and drying. "My wife."

"Will be shocked and stunned to hear that you kept a mistress, I'm sure."

"She'll understand." Ogley didn't convince even himself. And what if Carmen betrayed the truth about the real Hero of the Peninsula? It was bad enough to think of all the people who had gathered to honor him turning away. But for Brenda, who admired him, it would be a shock from which she would never recover. A shock from which his marriage would never recover. A shock from which his pocketbook . . . it didn't bear thinking of!

"Mrs. Ogley will be more appalled and stunned to discover you ruined a young lady of good family." Hepburn hammered his words home. "That you lied to Carmen about being married, that you abandoned her with nothing for her efforts but an illegitimate child."

"It was only a daughter." Worthless things, daughters.

Hepburn tapped the edge of his desk. "You haven't given your wife a child, have you?"

Ogley swiped at the edges of his mouth, trying to make himself look suave and debonair when in fact he was desperate. Perhaps an appeal would help, man to man. "I would have left Carmen a stipend, but I don't hold the purse strings in the family. Every year I have to go to Brenda's father for an allowance. Surely you see I couldn't afford to pay Carmen."

Hepburn, that rich, noble swine, did not relent. "You could have given her the earnings off that book you published."

Ogley was trapped. Trapped by nothing more important than a little pussy taken because he wanted it. Taken what was rightfully his.

He went berserk with frustration. He slammed his fist into the wall, then cradled it under his arm as he paced in a froth of temper.

Hepburn stood immobile as if Ogley's fury impressed him not at all.

"Don't lie to me, Hepburn." Ogley pointed at him. "You set this up. You planned this ball especially with the view to ruin me."

Hepburn didn't deny it. The swine. The crazy, ungrateful swine.

Ogley raged toward him. "You envy me

because I took your heroism and your exploits as my own."

"I don't give a damn whether anyone knows who really detonated the French ammunition depot. But I have something in common with Carmen."

Spitefully Ogley said, "Yes, I screwed you both."

Hepburn didn't flinch. "Worse than that. You lied to me. You made a promise that you didn't keep."

For a moment Ogley didn't know what Hepburn was talking about. Then he remembered, and the light dawned. In an incredulous tone he said, "This is about Waldemar? You want me to release Waldemar?"

Hepburn inclined his head once, a gracious, righteous movement that made Ogley want to shoot him. "No. I don't want you to release him. You're going to give him everything you promised. A commendation for bravery in battle, and his freedom in perpetuity."

"He's a thief. A damned beggar off the streets. A bastard who doesn't even know who his parents are." Ogley could scarcely credit such stupidity for a man of Hepburn's background. "He's nothing! You're an earl. Why do you even care?"

"Why ask now? You never did understand." And Hepburn looked aristocratic now, his nose wrinkling as if Ogley stank. He sneered at Ogley as if he knew something about decency that had escaped Ogley's attention.

"He saved your life. That's what you've been prattling about, isn't it? Didn't you save Waldemar's life? Eh? So you're even. He saved your life." Ogley snorted. "You're his superior. That's what he was supposed to do."

"Perhaps." Robert's gaze lingered on Ogley in a manner that conveyed Ogley's fate if he'd ever put himself in danger. "But I place a great value my life nevertheless."

"You price it too high. Not even your father cared about you. Do you know what he wrote to me when you came into my regiment?" Hepburn didn't show a sign of interest, but Ogley knew better. "He said you were his heir. He said you were worthless, that he'd bought you a commission to straighten you out, and that I was to do it using whatever means were necessary. He didn't care what I did to you. He didn't care if you died." The spittle formed at the corners of Ogley's mouth again, but he no longer cared. "You embarrassed him."

"Yes, I know. He thought I was worthless.

He was wrong." Opening his desk, Hepburn pulled forth a paper covered over with writing. "Here it is. Waldemar's commendation and release from the army."

Hepburn really couldn't be bothered that his father had abandoned him to suffering and death, and that made Ogley all the angrier. Ogley's own family didn't believe him when he said he was the Hero of the Peninsula, and they had the proof in a leatherbound book. Their indifference made him furious, and Hepburn didn't care? Damn him to hell. Would Hepburn always be one step ahead?

Coolly Hepburn continued. "All you have to do is sign Waldemar's release and put your seal on it, and I'll pay Carmen what she needs to support herself and your daughter. I'll make sure Carmen never bothers you again—and you'll never have to beg your wife for support."

"How do I know Carmen won't return for me?" Ogley asked, savage with disappointment.

"Because I keep my word and I'll make sure she does too."

That was the truth. The ruthless blackguard believed in honor and loyalty, and he always kept his word. With a vicious curse

Ogley pulled up a chair. Hepburn placed the inkwell at Ogley's elbow, pushed a pen into his hand. The pen trembled as Ogley dipped it into the ink, then stared at the inkwell and wondered what would happen if he knocked it over on the paper.

As if Hepburn read his mind, he informed him, "I have another agreement written up."

So with a vicious slash Ogley signed *Colonel Oscar Ogley* across the bottom of the commendation and discharge.

Hepburn splashed red wax beside his name.

Ogley pressed his ring into the wax.

Hepburn took the paper, folded it, and locked it in a drawer. And they were done.

Standing, Ogley leaned over the desk toward Hepburn and with malevolent purpose said, "I'll get even with you for this. Somehow I'll make you pay for this humiliation."

Hepburn was unimpressed. "I believe that's my line, spoken when I left Waldemar behind with you on the Peninsula. I was insane with rage then. Tonight has gone a long way toward soothing that rage." Hepburn leaned forward, pressed his face close to Ogley's, and focused a venal intent on him that made Ogley draw back. "But we're known for going insane, we MacKenzies, when we're in a fury."

With a shock Ogley saw the blue fire in Hepburn's eyes. His eyes burned like the flames of hell, threatening Ogley with death and devastation.

"If I were you," Hepburn said, "I would call it even with the MacKenzies."

Ogley jerked back, horrified to see, for the first time, the real Hepburn. Hepburn *was* a madman, and Ogley was lucky to get away with his life.

A sound like cannon fire made him jump, and a shower of colored sparks rained down outside the window.

As calmly as if his ferocity had never been, Hepburn said, "The fireworks are starting. They're in your honor, Ogley. Go out and accept your accolades. After all, that hero's pedestal is already shaky under your feet. With a little push the marble could crumble around you." In a tone that sounded like kind advice he added, "Too many people know the truth. Be careful what you do. Be very, very careful."

Twenty-six

No good happens after midnight.
—THE DOWAGER QUEEN OF BEAUMONTAGNE

Ogley stood apart from everyone else on the terrace. He listened to the thin, high whistle as the fireworks climbed high in the sky, watched the showers of red and gold sparks that exploded before his eyes, heard the boom a moment later. He kept his straining fists shoved into the pockets of his jacket and a grimace on his face. Maybe it would pass for a smile, maybe not, but he didn't bloody well care.

He had watched Hepburn and Waldemar

gallop down the drive, Waldemar hooting his triumph at the moon, and now Ogley was done pretending to be a good fellow. He had been outmaneuvered by the man he'd hated more than anyone in his whole life, and he wanted to beat someone, to make someone suffer. He couldn't play the loving husband to Brenda. He couldn't pretend to be a hero to the crowd of admirers who stood a little distance away.

What infuriated him more than anything was that Hepburn didn't care that Ogley had usurped his deeds and his bravery. For Hepburn what he'd done in the war was nothing more than what should be done, and Ogley was welcome to take credit for all of it. Hepburn wanted nothing more than Waldemar's freedom. He had gotten his way, and at the same time he'd managed to make Ogley feel small and insignificant. Damn the noble swine of an earl. Damn him all to hell!

"You saw them too, didn't you?"

"What?" At the sound of a woman's voice beside him, he turned and looked. One of the debutantes had joined him in his isolation. What was her name? He squinted as he tried to remember.

Then a boom shook the air, green sparks

lit up the sky, and he clearly perceived her thin features. Ah, yes. Miss Trumbull. Miss Larissa Trumbull.

"I saw you follow them." Her voice was thin and nasal and filled with spite. "Princess Clarice left first, sneaking out of the ballroom. Then Lord Hepburn followed her. They thought they were fooling me, but they weren't. I know what they were doing. I saw them after they'd spent last night together."

"What?" He felt foolish repeating the same word, but he felt that Miss Trumbull was showing him the way, shedding light on what had previously been hidden. "Hepburn and Princess Clarice are lovers?"

"I thought you knew. I thought that was why you followed them."

No, I followed Hepburn so I could be humiliated and coerced. Of course Ogley didn't say that. But he wondered what he could do with this information that Miss Trumbull had so freely given him, how he could use it to get a little of his revenge back.

And then get the hell out of MacKenzie Manor before Hepburn came after him. "Princess Clarice is rather lowering herself by rutting with a mere earl, isn't she?"

Miss Trumbull laughed bitterly. "She's not

really a princess. She's nothing but a peddler selling cosmetics and creams to all these silly ladies who—"

Ogley grabbed her arm and twisted it. *"What?"*

"Ouch! Ouch, you're hurting me." She squealed loud enough to attract attention.

He dropped her arm and muttered an apology, then said, "But you have to tell me what you mean."

"Princess Clarice sells creams and unguents . . . and *cosmetics* to color the cheeks and make your eyes look more exotic. I wager every lady tonight was wearing her royal secret color emulsion to make herself look better. Everyone except me." Self-consciously Miss Trumbull touched the spot in the middle of her forehead.

Carmen's eyes. Her eyes weren't the right color. "Can the princess disguise herself, make herself look like someone else?"

"She never said, but I think she could. I think she could do all kinds of deceptive things." Maliciously Miss Trumbull added, "She's just a strumpet masquerading as royalty, and you know what I think? *I* think—"

He strode away in the middle of her discourse.

Carmen hadn't smelled right. Carmen reeked of cigars, thick and rich with the scent of tobacco. That woman in Hepburn's study smelled of fresh flowers and sweet spices.

When he'd danced with Princess Clarice, he'd reveled in her light perfume . . . and that's what *Carmen* had smelled like when she brushed past him in Hepburn's study.

Of course. Carmen wasn't there. That woman hadn't been Carmen, she'd been Princess Clarice in disguise. Hepburn had made a fool of Ogley and he was laughing right now. Bursting with laughter, slapping Waldemar on the back with laughter, laughing until his eyes ran with tears.

But—Ogley headed across the terrace toward Princess Clarice—Hepburn wouldn't be laughing tomorrow when he returned. No indeed. Because Hepburn was an honorable man, and he wouldn't want his compatriot, his lover, hurt.

No! Ogley changed course and headed toward the stables. No, better than that. Ogley had seen that look in Hepburn's eyes. Hepburn adored his phony princess, and somehow Ogley was going to destroy her. Really, it couldn't be too hard, could it? She was a peddler. A false princess. A liar and an actress. There had to be people who wanted her dead.

All Ogley had to do was find them.

Dawn was trying to break through the gathering clouds as Robert and Waldemar staggered toward the ship. The ship that would carry Waldemar from Edinburgh to London.

"I can't believe ye did it." Waldemar's accent was thicker than coney stew. "I can't believe ye finally bested the ol' cocksucker."

"Someone had to bring him down." Hepburn was so tired and happy, he almost felt intoxicated. It was as if a great weight had been lifted from his shoulders, and at last he was free. "In the end it wasn't that hard to outwit him. Rather like fighting an unarmed man."

The two men fell on each other's necks and howled with laughter.

"Ah, ye've got a way wi' words, ye do." Waldemar took a deep breath. "We couldn't have done it wi'out the princess, and I never got a chance t' thank 'er."

"I'll tell her." The dock thumped hollowly beneath Robert's boots. He couldn't wait to tell her . . . everything. He imagined talking to her, their heads on the pillows, their bodies exhausted from making love.

"Tell 'er more than that. Tell 'er ye love 'er."

"What?" Hepburn peered blearily at his friend. "What are you talking about?"

"Ye love 'er, man. Didn't ye know?" Waldemar rumpled Hepburn's hair. "Ye're the brains in this operation, and ye didn't recognize yer own pitiful state?"

"Huh." Hepburn let the meaning sink into his brain. He loved her?

Nonsense. It hadn't been love that had sent him into her arms.

True, she had been a virgin, and he always made it his custom to avoid virgins.

Yet after that fight he hadn't had a choice. He'd made an instinctive, desperate lunge for her. He been desperate for her. For Clarice. Only for Clarice.

Then the next night—my God, he'd made love like a man with something to prove. "I love her?"

Waldemar laughed. "Any fool can see it."

That second night he had had something to prove, for she'd made him angry when she mounted and rode him as if he were Blaize, that damned stallion she controlled with the power of her honeyed voice and the strength of her thighs.

Robert grinned. Although that was an apt

description of him. A stallion who had caught the scent of his mare. He had thought of nothing but impressing the memory of that night on her so that she would never look at another man without seeing him.

"I do love her." He tasted the amazement the words brought him.

"Plain as the nose on me face."

"I love her."

"I'm starting t' think ye're telling the wrong person, ol' champ." They stood at the foot of the gangplank. The freshening wind tugged at all the vessels in the harbor and blew Waldemar's hair into a cloud around his sharply intelligent face. "What are ye going t' do about it?"

"I don't know. I didn't realize it before."

"If ye're interested in me opinion—"

"I am."

"I'd go t' an inn and get a good day's sleep."

Robert's soaring heart sank. "I can't do that. She might leave. I left instructions that she be detained if she tries to go, but she is more intelligent than any woman I've ever met. I fear to be away for long. I fear she might slip away."

Waldemar laughed rudely. "Nay, she won't leave ye."

"How do you know?"

"I could say that she'll wait fer 'er reward fer successfully pulling the wool over Ogley's eyes, but the truth is—she's fond o' ye."

"You'd better be right." Still, Robert shook his head. "Ogley's leaving today, and I must make sure he goes."

Waldemar's eyes gleamed with glee. "Don't worry about the colonel. 'E thinks ye're like 'im. 'E thinks everybody's as low and despicable as 'e is. I've been his valet and his whipping boy long enough t' assure ye—by now 'e's convinced 'imself ye're going t' change yer mind and tell 'is poor wife the truth about who did all that heroics on the Peninsula. 'E's got another ball t' go t', and 'e's a coward. 'E specializes in running. 'E's hoping ye're going t' forfeit the pleasure of 'umiliating 'im more. Out o' sight, out o' mind, 'e's thinking."

"Are you positive?" Robert demanded.

"Positive," Waldemar answered. "Do ye want t' see Princess Clarice before ye've had a chance t' clean up?"

Robert looked down at himself. He smelled like sweat from the hard ride, but— "I want to see Clarice *now.*"

"Ah, me dear friend." Waldemar slung his

arm over Robert's shoulders. "'Ye shouldn't propose marriage t' the girl in yer state."

"Propose marriage." Robert took a long breath. "Of course. I shall propose marriage." Marriage! Four days earlier he would have said marriage was the furthest thing from his mind. Now the idea dominated him. "But, Waldemar, it's not that easy. She won't have me. She's a princess."

"Princess, 'ell. She's a woman. I've seen the look on 'er face. She adores ye." Waldemar ruffled Hepburn's hair again. "Women do, ye know. Must be that way ye have about ye o' keeping 'em up all night 'umpin'. Where ye get yer stamina, I'll never know."

"Oatmeal," Hepburn told him.

Waldemar pointed his finger at Hepburn's nose. "Ye're lying. Tell me ye're lying."

"All Scotsmen eat oatmeal, and all of us can make love all night." At Waldemar's palpable disgust, Hepburn fought to ward off his grin.

"Might be worth it," Waldemar muttered. Then aloud he said, "Besides, a bird in the 'and is worth two in the bush."

That caught Hepburn off guard. "What do you mean by that?"

"I mean, better a wealthy, handsome earl that she's caught than a prince she might have." The captain yelled a warning, and Waldemar waved a hand. "I've got t' go, and I don't know 'ow t' say it, except just—thank ye. Thank ye always and forever." He caught Hepburn in a rough hug, then released him and ran up the gangplank. As the crew pulled it up, he leaned over the rail and yelled, "Remember! A real princess from the fairy tales will follow 'er true love, not some pansy-breeched prince she's never met wi' pretty-girl hair and a fancy lisp! Princess Clarice is yers fer the taking. Ask 'er! Ye'll see!"

Twenty-seven

God sends us adversity as a moral tonic.
—THE DOWAGER QUEEN OF BEAUMONTAGNE

Clarice woke to a sense of urgency she hadn't experienced since . . . well, never. That was because she had never before been derelict in her duty to Amy. She tried to argue with herself as she dressed in her familiar black-and-red riding costume. It had been only three days. Amy couldn't get into trouble in that amount of time.

But Amy had come to MacKenzie Manor wanting to talk about something, something she must have thought was urgent, and Clarice had paid her little attention. And Amy was barely seventeen. A mere adolescent. She *could* get in trouble in three days, horrible trouble, and Clarice needed to go and check up on her.

And on the villagers. She'd promised to play checkers with the old gentlemen at the alehouse, and to help the ladies in the village with their complexions. Once she had ascertained that Amy was all right, she would do those things. A princess never broke her word—and lately Clarice hadn't been acting like a princess. She'd been acting like a woman in love.

She stopped combing her hair and pressed her palm to her forehead. What had she been thinking?

Grandmamma would say it wasn't so much what she'd been thinking as what she'd been thinking with.

And Clarice had to stop it. Stop it now. She was in love. In love with a Scottish earl. In love, without a future, without a home, without anything but this fierce adoration for a man who . . . who guarded his mind so carefully, she didn't know what he thought. About her, about them, about anything.

She had gotten herself into a dreadful predicament, and she didn't know how to get herself out. But she did know the right things to do, and the first was to see to Amy.

The ladies and gentlemen who had attended the ball until the wee hours of the morning were barely stirring when, at noon, Clarice sneaked out of the house and down to the stables. Blaize welcomed her with an eager whinny, and before long she was galloping toward Freya Crags, a belated panic stirring her blood.

The Scottish sun had shown its favor for the MacKenzies for the last four days, shining brightly on their ball and all its mechanisms. Now it was gone, hidden behind a clabbering of gray clouds that bespoke an incoming storm. The wind whipped the veil on her hat and slapped at her cheeks, obstructing her journey as it changed direction and pushed the horse from one side to the other.

Freya Crags seemed quiet when she cantered across the bridge, not at all as it had the first time she rode into town. Yet she felt a pang of longing. This was where she had met Robert for the first time. She had feared him then. Feared his attraction. Feared his darkness. Now she missed him, wished that he would hurry back from Edinburgh to answer the questions that plagued her.

Did he love her, or was she nothing more than a passing fancy?

The Freya Crags market was gone. A few men stood in a huddle and gossiped. A woman carried buckets of water hung from a yoke around her neck. The old fellows, wrapped in shawls, huddled out of the wind in front of the alehouse and waved a hearty welcome. She waved back and threw them a kiss but headed toward Mistress Dubb's shop. Yet they called her, and after a moment of hesitation she indicated she would come and speak to them. She knew that before ten minutes had passed, Amy would hear that she was in the village, and perhaps Amy might like the warning.

The princess is in town, Mistress Dubb would report.

Would Amy rush out to meet Clarice? Or would she sulk in a dark corner of the shop and wait for Clarice to approach her?

Poor Amy. And poor Clarice, who didn't know how to make everything right. She didn't think there was a way.

She walked Blaize to the stables and

delivered him, with a payment of coin, to be placed in a warm stall and given a rubdown.

Then she strolled to the alehouse, smiling at the five old men because they deserved her full attention.

They stood as she approached, and bowed. "Hamish MacQueen. Henry MacCulloch. Gilbert Wilson. Tomas MacTavish. Benneit MacTavish," she recited.

"Yer Highness, ye remember our names!" Henry said in astonishment. He always spoke too loudly. She remembered that from the first time they'd met.

"But of course." She caught Gilbert as he bowed and once again almost toppled over. "I make it a point to remember the names of all the handsome gentlemen I meet."

They beamed.

"Did ye come fer yer game o' checkers?" Tomas asked.

Helping Tomas into his seat, she said, "I don't think I should. I'm distracted today, and I fear I would play badly."

Tomas rubbed his papery hands together. "All the better."

She laughed aloud and shook her finger at him. "A terrible man, you are." She liked the sounds of their voices: gravelly with age and warm with the Scottish accent. She thought that Robert would sound like them someday, and she wondered if she would be there to hear it.

"Ye're looking sad, Yer Highness." Hamish fumbled with the sleeve on his amputated arm. "What's wrong?"

The pins had come loose, and she could see he was embarrassed by his disarray. Looking into his eyes, speaking calmly and directly, she said, "Mr. MacQueen, your sleeve has come undone. Might I help you put it back together?" She didn't wait. She took the loose pins and threaded them through the material to close the gap. "If you'll bring me your shirts, I'll sew buttons and buttonholes at the ends of your sleeves. Then you won't have to fool with these wretched pins."

"A princess shouldn't ha'e t' sew my buttons," Hamish sputtered.

She didn't ask him who would. For all she knew, he might have outlived his entire family. Instead, she said, "I like to sew, and I like you. That makes my work doubly blessed."

"Eh?" Henry cupped his ear and turned to Benneit.

Benneit shouted, "She says she's going t' sew Hamish's shirts."

Henry pounced. "So, Yer Highness, ye're going t' stay at MacKenzie Manor?"

She tried to think of what to say. Would Robert ask her to stay? In the end she did nothing more than shake her head. "I don't know."

The old men exchanged speaking glances.

She would have liked to know what they were speaking about.

With an assumption of ease she seated herself on the stool before the checkerboard. "I would like to order us all an ale. Where's the owner of the alehouse?"

Tomas chortled and rocked back in his chair so far, she thought she was going to have to catch him again.

"She found herself unexpectedly busy." Gilbert put his finger over his lips to mime silence.

By that she assumed the old men were being discreet.

But before she could press them for the gossip, Hamish advised, "Yer Highness, strong wind blowing from the east."

"What?" She turned and found herself staring at Mistress Dubb, making her way across the square from her seamstress shop.

Clarice's heart leaped with delight. Amy wanted to see her.

But that was foolish. Mistress Dubb wouldn't run Amy's errands.

Mistress Dubb reached Clarice and creaked into a curtsy. "Yer Highness, what a pleasure t' have ye here in Freya Crags once again. Have ye come t' give this auld face a treat?"

"I have," Clarice assured her. "But first I was hoping to speak to Miss Rosabel."

Mistress Dubb puffed like a teakettle. "That awful thing. I don't want t' talk aboot her."

Clarice half rose in alarm. "Why?" *What had Amy done now?*

Mistress Dubb pulled a long face. "She left me in the lurch wi' half a dozen orders and na way t' fill them, that's why."

A surge of panic brought Clarice all the way to her feet. "What do you mean, she left? She couldn't have left."

"I tell ye, she's gone," Mistress Dubb said.

"Where? When?" Clarice demanded fiercely.

The old men were nodding.

"Yesterday, but she left wi'oot a word t' me,

so I dunna know anything else." With a beefy hand Mistress Dubb pushed Clarice back onto the stool. "Dunna blame yerself."

Clarice gaped at her and feeling weak, sat without a whimper.

"Dunna go thinkin' that because ye made her pretty she decided she could go out in the world and find herself a man."

"Oh." Clarice's breath exploded from her in a rush. "You're speaking of *that*. No, I never thought—"

"Although it's true, is na it?" Mistress Dubb lectured without ceasing. Lectured without understanding. "Pretty girls always find the men. When I was young, I found them—or, rather, they found me. That's what I was hoping ye could do fer me, was make me pretty again—"

Clarice couldn't bear the sound of that voice anymore. She cut her off with an abrupt, "Did *anyone* see what direction she was going?"

"Nay." From her bosom Mistress Dubb pulled a paper sealed with a blob of wax and handed it to Clarice. "But maybe 'tis in this letter she left fer ye."

The seal had been tampered with, although not broken. Clarice raised her disbelieving gaze to Mistress Dubb, and her eyes must have held some royal power, for the guilty seamstress muttered as she scuttled away, "Dropped it. I'll leave ye here t' read it."

Dread in her heart, Clarice weighed the letter in her hand.

Henry gestured kindly. "Go on. Read yer letter."

Breaking the seal, Clarice perused Amy's beautiful handwriting:

Dear, best, kind Clarice,

I told you I did not want to be a princess anymore. I know you did not believe me, but it is true. I hate waiting for my life to start and knowing that I'm ill suited for that life. Why? Because I've been free to wander the countryside, to speak to normal people, to see the worth of work.

I am not willing to live the kind of life we've been leading. So I am going away to somewhere where no one knows me, where I can learn who I really am and what I am capable of.

Do not worry. I know, you believe that you must. But search your mind. Be fair. You know I'm capable of caring for myself. I always go into town before you. I always find a situation of steady work in a respectable shop. I promise you, I will be cautious and intelligent, for I have learned from a brilliant teacher— you, dear Clarice.

I beg you, please do not try to find me. I promise that as soon as I am settled, I will put an advertisement in the papers and assure you of my well-being, and I have faith we will see each other again.

If you truly wish it, may you find your way back to Beaumontagne, marry a prince, and live happily ever after. I know you think I know nothing because I am your younger sister—

"I don't think that," Clarice protested, but with a sinking heart, she knew it was true.

—but if you ask me, you are too vibrant to suffer such a fate, so think well before you return.

Until then, I hope you stumble on whatever it is you truly seek. Farewell, dear sister, farewell.

Lovingly, your sister forever,
Amy Rosabel

In an effectual disarray Clarice crumpled the paper, trying to get a breath, trying to understand what had happened. "Amy," she whispered. "Amy." Her baby sister. Out in the world by herself, searching for something that didn't exist. An identity beyond princess . . . there was no such thing. Amy couldn't pretend to be one of the common crowd. Why would she even want to be like . . . like Mistress Dubb, or these old gentlemen? They worked so hard for so little, and were tied to a village or a city and a family or . . . well, all right, princesses were tied to a country too, and bound by endless ceremony. They had their husbands chosen for them and were judged solely by their abilities to breed sons. Clarice had tried to convince Amy being a princess was all wonderful, although she had known in her heart that it wasn't.

But royalty was their duty—and their fate.

Henry broke into her musings. "Miss Rosabel, yer sister, isna she?"

Dumbfounded, Clarice stared at the old man. "Did she tell you that?"

"Nay. The little lass kept t' herself mostly," Gilbert said.

Gently Henry said, "But when ye get t' be as auld as we are, ye ha'e naught t' do but observe the people around ye, and ye get guid at it."

"Womanish talent," Benneit grumped.

Henry ignored him. "So we noticed that ye and she ha'e similar ways aboot ye, and when ye talk and she talks, sometimes there's the faintest hint o' a faraway land in yer voices."

Clarice couldn't see the sense in lying. The old men weren't going to snitch on her. "She *is* my sister. She's a princess too." She held out the crumpled remains of the letter. "And she's gone. If she would have waited, we would have gone back to Beaumontagne and everything would have been very well."

"But if ye didna go back t' yer kingdom, ye could do whatever ye liked." Gilbert leaned forward. "Ye could be a spinster and live in a cottage."

Amy wanted to do that, or so she had said. For the rest of her life she wanted to design clothes, beautiful clothes for the wealthy women to wear.

Henry added, "Or ye could wed a wealthy man and be verra happy fer the rest o' yer days."

"A wealthy, titled man." Hamish waved his single hand. "Say . . . an earl."

Subtle they weren't, and an idea sprang to

life in Clarice's mind. It wasn't Amy she thought of, but herself. If she, Clarice, weren't a princess, what would she want to do? To know that no country depended on her existence. To choose her husband based on something besides his pedigree. To be just Clarice, with no title weighing her down . . . inevitably her thoughts went to Robert. If she weren't a princess . . . if he weren't a Scottish earl . . .

"Ye know, a princess should be free t' follow her heart." Hamish coaxed her along, trying to make her see things his way.

"A princess owes it t' the rest o' us t' ha'e a happy ending," Benneit said.

"Womanish," Henry mocked him.

"Shut yer maw," Benneit said. "Can't ye see she's thinking aboot it?"

She loved Robert so much. Because of that love, she had done one selfish thing. She had given in to the need she sensed in him and lain with him, and when she did, he had filled a need in her she hadn't known existed. They were each illustrious people on their own, but together they were remarkable. They were happy. They were whole.

Catching sight of the letter in her hand,

she smoothed out the wrinkled sheets and a few hot tears trickled down her cheeks.

Yet how could she think of herself *now*?

The old men gathered around and awkwardly patted her back. "There, there," they said. And, "It's fer the best."

Maybe they were right. Maybe it was for the best. Amy didn't want to be found. If Clarice went after her, Amy would resist returning, and Clarice couldn't force her. Didn't even want to force her. She wanted Amy to have what Amy wished, and if that included her freedom, then Clarice had to stand before Grandmamma's throne and, for her sister, lie like a trooper.

Of course, because Amy had her freedom, and because they didn't know where Sorcha was, Clarice would have to do *her* duty. She would go back to Beaumontagne. She would marry whoever was chosen for her. She would breed sons who would inherit the throne.

She couldn't live for Robert or with Robert, so for Amy's sake Clarice would ride away from Robert MacKenzie and never look back. If, fifty years from now, she still cried into her pillow at night, well, that was the burden a princess carried.

Sniffing, she straightened her shoulders. "All right. I've come to a decision."

Clearly delighted, Henry said, "I knew ye'd see things our way!"

From across the bridge she heard shouting.

Gilbert studied her. "I dunna know that she's seeing things our way."

"She has t' see love is more important than anything else," Tomas argued.

The yelling grew louder.

Clarice paid little attention. "There are different kinds of love. One is a love of duty and of honor. Hepburn knows that love. So do I."

Now the yelling made her stop to look. It penetrated even Henry's hearing, bringing his head around. It wasn't a pleasant sound, this shouting. It was discordant, containing a current of fury that caused Clarice to rise.

Shuffling their feet, the old men strained their eyes to see across the bridge—where, stomping in the lead, came that bully Clarice had met the first day she came to Freya Crags. The man who'd made fun of her, bet her ten pounds she couldn't make Amy pretty, then sneaked away before she could make him pay. What was his name?

Hamish spit on the ground, a crude and

scornful statement. "We've got trooble. It's little Billie MacBain."

Billie waved his fists, his face screwed into a wild triumph. Behind him marched soldiers. English soldiers. And striding beside Billie MacBain . . . dear Lord!

Clarice staggered backward.

Beside Billie MacBain marched Magistrate Fairfoot, the man from whom she'd stolen Blaize. Tall, distinguished-looking, he carried the weight of his office on him and had a twist of cruelty to his mouth.

"English knaves," Henry bellowed, but this time there was so much shouting, no one heard him except for his friends and Clarice.

"They're hunting me." Clarice shouldn't panic. She'd been in worse straits. "It's me they want."

The old men didn't look shocked or ask her what she'd done wrong. Benneit said, "Then we'd best get ye oot o' here before they can get their filthy hands on yer royal person."

Some of the villagers, women mostly, trailed after the English. The soldiers carried muskets over their shoulders, and they glanced about as if they would love to fire on the crowd.

"Oot the back o' the alehouse." Hamish urged Clarice toward the dim interior. "There's an alleyway behind the shop."

Her heart thundered in her chest. This was what she feared. This was her nightmare.

Gilbert said, "Don't worry, Yer Highness. We'll point them in the wrong direction."

She looked again at the oncoming troop. She swallowed. She nodded. "Thank you." She ran for the inside of the alehouse, calling back, "Thank you!"

As she freed the latch, she was already planning how to get to Blaize. She wouldn't be able to saddle him, but she could use the mounting block and ride him bareback. They'd take the paths across the countryside, ride toward MacKenzie Manor. . . .

Her lungs hurt as if she'd already run for miles.

No. No, she couldn't go back to MacKenzie Manor. Fairfoot would hunt her down there, denounce her as a criminal, and tell the ladies they had been defrauded. They'd be willing to hang her themselves.

Robert wasn't there to save her.

Besides, she couldn't go running to Robert. Not now. Not ever.

Poking her head out the door, she checked

the alley. It was empty. The soldiers hadn't planned ahead. They hadn't covered her escape.

Quietly she closed the door behind her. The wind whistled through the alley, tearing at her hair, chilling her bones. Clutching the lapels of her jacket, she kept her head down and hurried to the corner.

With any luck she'd be gone before Magistrate Fairfoot realized she wasn't in the shop. Before he got his filthy hands on her, used her as an example to all the women in his district, and raped and hanged her.

Her heart thumped in her chest. She could make it. With each step she became more sure. She was going to make it.

She turned the corner.

And ran right into Colonel Ogley's arms.

Twenty-eight

He who lies down with dogs shall rise with fleas.
—THE OLD MEN OF FREYA CRAGS

The next morning, as Robert approached MacKenzie Manor, he reflected with satisfaction on a ring in his saddlebag. He didn't know if its beauty was enough to entice Clarice to marry him, especially after the way he'd treated her in bed . . . well, he had enjoyed *that*. In fact, he'd never been so close to heaven.

In all honesty, he couldn't say he was

sorry. Not when he thought of how wonderfully she'd tasted, or the way she'd moved under him, and the warm clasp of her body around his cock, like a living glove holding him, stroking him . . .

The gravel of the drive crunched under Helios's hooves. The trees dripped big splashes of rain on him while protecting him from the steady drizzle. Robert caught sight of MacKenzie Manor, and hoped that the ring's glittering stones would keep Clarice's attention long enough for him to plead his case. How odd to feel so uncertain about someone he hadn't known existed a week earlier! But somehow she'd insinuated herself into his heart.

The house loomed before him now, and he urged Helios faster.

It appeared Waldemar was right. Robert did love her. Loved her more than he'd ever loved anything or anyone.

As he dismounted at the front steps of MacKenzie Manor, Millicent flung open the door and rushed toward him. As soon as his feet touched the ground, she grabbed him by the shirtfront and demanded, "Where have you been?"

He didn't suppose there was any use lying to her anymore, so he said, "In Edinburgh, seeing Waldemar off."

"Leaving me to try and protect Princess Clarice! A bad choice, Robert, a bad choice indeed."

At once he knew. Something had gone wrong. Ogley. In a fury so deep and instantaneous he could scarcely speak, he said, "Tell me."

"She's been arrested!"

He looked up at the wide double doors and saw Prudence standing there, looking forlorn and confused.

Millicent continued. "Colonel Ogley found this magistrate from Gilmichael—"

Robert didn't wait to hear another word. Handing Helios over to Pepperday, the waiting hostler, he said, "Saddle the fastest horse in the stable." Helios had had a hard ride from Edinburgh. He couldn't make it all the way to the border.

"M'lord, we have Blaize."

Robert turned his sharp gaze on the hostler. "The magistrate didn't take him?"

"The princess left him in the stable in Freya Crags. The stableman sent me a message," Pepperday said. "I went and got the stallion immediately."

Hepburn acknowledged the important information while absorbing and interpreting the rest. "Then saddle Blaize."

Pepperday ran toward the stables, calling back, "Aye, m'lord. Anyone who rides like Her Highness doesn't deserve t' hang on an English gibbet."

Grabbing his saddlebags, Robert raced for his room with Millicent and Prudence on his heels. He'd done this a hundred times before. Left on a mission at a moment's notice. He knew what to do.

Once there, he emptied the saddlebags and loaded them with supplies. A knife. A good, strong coil of rope.

His hands were shaking. He was sweating.

Another knife. A pistol. Another knife. His lockpick kit.

"Robert." Prudence's voice trembled. "Why do you need so many knives?"

He glanced up, surprised to see his sisters in the room. "I'm good with knives."

"I thought you were good with your fists," Millicent said.

"That too." He wished Waldemar were still

with him. To free someone from prison was a two-man task. But Robert would have to do it on his own, or die trying. And death wasn't acceptable, for if he died, Clarice would hang. Looking around, he asked, "Are there any fireworks left?"

"Yes." Millicent went to the door and ordered they be brought to the stables.

"Why?" Prudence asked.

Robert glanced up at his little sister. Her face was white. She bit her lips, and her eyes were too large in her frightened face. "Fireworks might come in handy." Swiftly he brushed his knuckles across her cheek. "Don't worry."

Prudence turned with a sob and ran from the room.

The ring.

As an afterthought he thrust it into the bottom of the saddlebag. He would give the ring to Clarice tonight, after he had rescued her—for he would rescue her. He wasn't sure of her answer, but a lass who just been rescued would be most grateful to her rescuer. Not that he wanted gratitude from Clarice. He wanted—would have—love. But gratitude might weight the scales a bit.

"You *can* get her out," Millicent demanded rather than asked.

"Yes." Flinging the saddlebags over his shoulder, he headed down the stairs toward the stables.

Millicent followed. "You did all those heroic deeds for which Colonel Ogley took credit. Isn't that correct?"

"Maybe."

"So you can rescue her. Isn't that correct?"

"Perhaps." What did he know about the fortress at Gilmichael? "It depends where they're holding her. I'll be playing with a fixed deck of cards, and they'll be holding the trump."

In a voice that made the servants jump, Millicent demanded, "Can one of the men go with you? Can I go and help?"

Touched by the offer, he said, "No, dear. No. No one here can help with this. It's likely to be dirty and painful, and—" For the first time since he'd swung out of the saddle, he looked at Millicent, really looked at her, and realized she hadn't gone back to her previous plain appearance. She was as beautiful as she had been the night of the ball. "Is Corey smitten?"

"Yes." She sounded truculent. "I suppose he is."

"Why? What has he done?"

She kept up with Hepburn's long strides without complaint. "He won't leave. He says he's here to give me support in my hour of need." Her eyes sparkled with a dangerous light. "How spending time chasing me around trying to get me to listen to hunting stories is support, I will never know."

As they approached the bustling stables, a tiny ray of amusement pierced Robert's grimness.

She continued. "Corey's nothing but a big, dumb . . . foxhunter."

Apparently Corey had fallen from grace with a vengeance. "Yes, dear sister, that's all he's ever been."

She waited while Robert asked if Blaize was being saddled, then she said, "I thought . . ."

"You thought that Corey's pretty face hid some depths? None at all. He's vain and he's selfish, he's none too bright, and he's used to every woman falling at his feet." Robert plunged into the depths of the stable. "But in Corey's defense, he hasn't a mean bone in his body, and if he's telling you his hunting stories, that means he's miserably in love with you."

"Well, I am not in love with him," she said crisply.

Pepperday was dealing with Blaize's hostility at being saddled by a man other than Robert.

Accepting the fireworks from one of the stable lads, Robert placed them in his saddlebags while he asked Millicent, "Is Corey going to offer for you?"

"I suppose. I don't want to marry him. At least, not now."

Robert couldn't wait for Pepperday to manage Blaize any longer, and shouldered him out of the way. "What *do* you want to do?" He tightened the cinch on the saddle.

"I think I want to go with Prudence to Edinburgh." Millicent handed him the bridle. "I want to enjoy her Season, and see what other men are out there."

As he placed the bit in Blaize's mouth, Robert wondered—had Millicent changed? Or had she always been like this but hadn't known how to become her real self? Flinging the saddlebags over Blaize's back, he asked, "Marry someone you like better than Corey, then?"

"I've got my own fortune. Perhaps I will never marry." She kissed his cheek. "I can't believe you're still here. Go and fetch Princess Clarice. That magistrate is a blackguard, and after this no one will ever consider Ogley a hero. I'll make sure of it."

Swinging himself into the saddle, Robert urged Blaize into a gallop.

He heard his sister call, "Bring Clarice home!"

Clarice sat wide-eyed in Gilmichael Fortress in a cell in the dark on an iron bed with her knees tucked up to her chest, and wondered if rats ate princesses.

Probably. Unfortunately.

More unfortunately she was getting sleepy, for in the day and a half since she'd been taken, she hadn't had a lot of rest.

She'd survived a wretched ride out of Freya Crags on a broken-down horse Colonel Ogley had procured, may he rot in hell, with the rain beating down and the wind whipping her hair around her face. Her hands had been tied before her, as if a dangerous criminal like her could escape the escort of an English troop of ten armed men.

They—she, the men, Colonel Ogley, and Magistrate Fairfoot—had spent the night at an inn in the small town of Stoor barely across the English border. They seemed to hope that the border kept them safe from Hepburn's wrath.

Fools.

That night Colonel Ogley had been deep into his role as a high-minded army colonel, a hero, and the man who had discovered the truth about the phony princess and was bringing her to justice. He obtained a room for her in the inn, locked her in, and kept the key. She couldn't escape, yet neither could Magistrate Fairfoot get in, and the way he watched her, the way he touched her, made her sick with fear.

The next day Colonel Ogley had left. Left to meet his wife so they could return to his victory tour of the ballrooms and country homes of the ton. She'd never thought she'd be sorry to see the back end of Colonel Ogley, but when she looked into Magistrate Fairfoot's gloating eyes, she wanted to call Ogley back and beg for mercy.

Mercy from the man she'd made a fool of? She, more than most women, understood the delicacy of a man's self-esteem. But that's what desperation did for a lass. Made her stupid.

After that it had been a short ride to Gilmichael and a long walk from the watery sunshine of the out-of-doors into the depths of the fortress. Magistrate Fairfoot took care to point out the gibbet with its noose swinging in the breeze.

She ignored him.

Daylight showed only too clearly the aging gray stones, the bars, and the leering guards. The sunshine was also, well, illumination. It even made her cell on the upper level of the dungeons—reserved for criminal dignitaries, Fairfoot told her—less unpleasant. At least she could see the cell as she walked into it. Damp stone walls. Damp stone floor. A small, high window. An iron bedstead strung with ropes and covered by a mildewed mattress. A chamber pot. A pail of water. Not so bad for a prison, really.

Best of all, Fairfoot ordered the men to cut her bonds, shove her inside, and leave her alone. She was happier than any prisoner had ever been, and all because he walked away. He was gone.

But after she checked the small dimensions of her cell, looked up at the window, judged it impossible to reach, and sat down on the rope bed, she realized there were no other prisoners. She couldn't hear the movements of the guards at the other end of that long, long corridor. Her prison was utterly, totally silent. That unnerved her, gave her time to think of how it would feel to hang by her neck, choking, oh, God . . . but she couldn't dwell on that. Not when the hours passed and no one came with food. When she finally yelled, no one responded. No one could hear her. She was alone.

When it clouded up again, the cell grew dim. When the sun set, it was pitch dark, so black a darkness, it pressed on her eyeballs and she had to touch them to see if they were open.

But she could hear—the scuttling of beetles, the chirping of rats. The clatter of her teeth. She was cold. She was scared. She was sleepy. She didn't have a blanket. Thank heavens Amy had left when she did.

At least Amy had escaped this fate.

If only Robert were here.

Clarice wanted Robert, and she didn't know where he was.

Had he come back from Edinburgh and

found her gone? Did he think she had run away from the passion they shared? Did he think she was a coward to go without a farewell?

But what an absurd notion. Robert knew everything that went on in the village. The old men would tell him, and he would mount his horse and come to rescue her.

Wouldn't he? He'd slept with her. She'd done what he asked and played his charade to perfection. He wouldn't abandon her here . . . would he?

But he had never said he loved her. He had never asked her to be his wife. He had never even indicated an interest in taking her as his mistress, a solution that had crossed her mind as reasonable for a princess who loved a man she couldn't marry.

She had discarded that solution as unworthy, but even now it lingered in her head. And lingered. And lingered.

Her head. It was nodding onto her knees. She'd drifted off to sleep.

What had roused her?

The scuttling and the chirping had stopped. And far away, down the long, long corridor, she heard the clang of a barred door. Without thought she found herself on her feet. They prickled as the blood rushed back into her limbs, and her shaking stopped as a flush of hope heated her chilled body.

Was it Robert?

The tiniest bit of candlelight shone along the corridor, and she risked the rats and the insects to run to the door. She pressed her face to the bars, trying to catch a little more of that light. She wanted to bathe in the light, absorb the light, save it to fill the darkness. It grew, flickering across the walls, a single candle carried by a single man.

She stumbled backward.

Carried by Magistrate Fairfoot, his distinguished, craggy face made horrible by his smile.

The trembling started again, harder. She was cold. She was hungry. She didn't have a single defense of any kind. She was ten inches shorter and weighed seven stone less than he did. And he had come to rape her.

This was the kind of abuse Fairfoot enjoyed. The kind where he had all the advantages. The kind where he got to torture someone smaller and weaker.

But an illumination greater than the sun at noonday rose and shone inside her. Robert

MacKenzie would come for her. Of course he would. It didn't matter if he loved her, wanted to marry her, wanted to make her his mistress, or if he had decided he had had enough of bedding her. She had been a guest in his home, and she had been abducted from his village by a pair of despicable villains. He wouldn't stand for that.

Moreover, he had promised her his masquerade would go well, and Colonel Ogley had made him a liar. If there was one thing she knew, one thing she could trust in this unstable world of vain ladies and cruel magistrates, it was that the earl of Hepburn was a man of honor—and his honor demanded that he come for her.

The key rasped in the lock. The door swung open.

She stiffened her spine.

When Fairfoot stepped through the door, she smiled at him. Smiled scornfully and used the only weapon she had left. In a slow, amused drawl, she said, "When Lord Hepburn gets here, he's going to cut you into little chunks of rooster meat. And I'm going to watch."

Twenty-nine

*The world's going t' hell in a handcart,
so ye might as well enjoy the ride.*
—THE OLD MEN OF FREYA CRAGS

Robert walked across the drawbridge over the dry moat, pulled his pry bar out of his saddlebags, and pounded on the sturdy and locked oak doors.

While he waited for an answer, he looked up at the tall, menacing bulk of Gilmichael Fortress and wondered how in the hell he was going to get Clarice out of there. Especially at night, and especially when he hadn't been able to glean one bloody bit of interesting information out of his foray around the fortress. Fact of the matter was, it had been built four hundred years earlier to protect the English border from the Scottish marauders, and it looked like every other English fortress. Large. Impenetrable. Inescapable.

But Gilmichael wasn't a big town. Surely not many prisoners shuddered in their fortress, and surely not many guards watched over them. A few men should be easy overcome and Clarice easy to find, and with God's grace Robert and Clarice would be well on their way before that damned magistrate had been notified of their escape.

Of course, Robert would have to come back and take care of him—Robert flexed his knuckles—but that was a pleasure that would have to wait until he had Clarice tucked up tight at MacKenzie Manor. And if Fairfoot had hurt her, he would die in the most painful and humiliating ways Robert could devise—and Robert could devise quite a few.

He pounded again. The wood muffled the sound, but someone had to be manning the gatehouse.

If Waldemar were here, he would at this moment be climbing a rope up the side of the fortress and moving like a shadow through the corridors, finding the prisoner, freeing her, and providing backup for Robert if necessary. Breaking into a prison was always better as a two-man job, but there was no choice tonight. Waldemar was safely on his way to London. And getting him there made this mission look like a breeze.

But Robert must miss him more than he realized, because for a second he thought he saw a man dangling from a rope on the outside of the fortress wall. He started to jump back, to take a closer look, when the tiny, barred guard window was opened and a deep voice snarled, "What do ye want at this 'our in the night? Don't ye know the curfew?"

In a tone of absolute disdain Robert snapped, "I don't care about your silly curfew. Don't you know who I am?"

"Nay." The guard sounded a little more cautious. The light inside the guardhouse shone around his shaggy head, and Robert could see a behemoth of unusual size and breadth.

Robert got in his bluff immediately. "I'm Colonel Ogley. You have heard of me."

"Nay." The guard drew the word out.

"I'm the Hero of the Peninsula. I performed great feats of daring. I won medals. I saved hundreds of English lives. I captured that prisoner you received today."

Behemoth scratched his head. "Nay. Magistrate Fairfoot did."

That liar. "Do you know Magistrate Fairfoot?"

"Aye, I work fer 'im."

"Then you know the truth."

Behemoth worked through that, then nodded slowly. "Aye. So ye captured that lass. So?"

"I want to see her. Now."

"Ye and everybody else."

A flame of irritation roared to life in Robert's mind. "What do you mean?"

"Magistrate Fairfoot is wi' her right now."

Black rage blinded Robert for a moment. *Damn Fairfoot to hell! He was going to pay.* But Robert got himself under control. He allowed only an edge of irritation in his tone. "He started without me? By God, I'll have his balls for this. How long ago did he go in?"

Behemoth scratched his stubbled cheek. "Since the last strike of the hour."

Pounding on the oak with his pry bar, Robert pretended it was Fairfoot's head. "Open this door. Immediately!"

Robert's authority got through to Behemoth this time, because the little window slammed shut, and after a few minutes the big door creaked open.

"That's better," Robert snapped as he marched in, straightening his coat and hoping Behemoth didn't demand to look through the saddlebags. "Now, lead me to the prisoner."

"I can't leave me post, Colonel Ogley." Behemoth closed and locked the doors behind them.

Robert sighed an exaggerated sigh. "Is there no one in this place who can escort me?"

"Um." Behemoth scratched his whiskery chin. "If ye go straight across to the keep, there'll be more guards. They'll take ye."

No matter how much Robert wished, he couldn't race across the lawn. Behemoth would be watching him, and perhaps the guards in the keep. So he nodded majestically and marched across the open area, finding an odd delight in imitating Ogley's military affectations. A slim revenge, but that was all to be had right now.

The door to the keep was locked, and he pulled out his pry bar and again used it to knock.

The guard who answered this time was neatly groomed, older, and by his bearing a professional soldier who had been mustered out.

In a word, suspicious.

Robert burned to get inside, to get to Clarice before Fairfoot had his way with her, but he also knew how to play the game of soldier. He did it now with a stiffly erect posture and an expressionless face. "I am Colonel Ogley. I have come on Magistrate Fairfoot's invitation to deal with the prisoner."

"What prisoner would that be?" the guard asked.

"I'm not a fool, and I don't mistake you for one. The only prisoner you've received today. The woman who claims to be a princess. Let me enter *at once*."

To Robert's delight, the guard stepped back to let him in. "Aye, sir, but Magistrate Fairfoot didn't mention ye would be coming."

Another guard stood close by, a flintlock musket held in his arms.

The first guard continued. "So we'll 'ave t' check with 'im first. Usually, 'e likes t' do these things alone."

Robert allowed a chilly smile to crease his lips. "Usually, he doesn't have me to contend with, does he? But I understand. You have to do your duty."

The guard nodded and relaxed, recognizing in Robert a soldier who comprehended the fine points of protocol.

"What's your name?" Robert asked.

"I'm Ranald."

"Well, Ranald, I'll just follow you to the cell where she's being held."

"I can't allow ye do that, but ye can go wi' me t' the gate."

"That will do." That would more than do. Once he knew where Clarice was incarcerated, he'd dispatch this fellow and the other guards, take out Magistrate Fairfoot, and he and Clarice would be on their way. A simple plan, working simply well.

They climbed stairs up, then they climbed stairs down. And down. She wasn't on the lowest level of the dungeons, but Robert's gut burned at the thought of Clarice, with her delicate skin and her wonderful scent, at the mercy of every sort of vermin. At the mercy of Magistrate Fairfoot.

Deliberately he stepped on Ranald's heels, and when Ranald turned back in a huff, Robert snapped, "Double-time. I'm in a hurry, man!"

Ranald marched briskly.

They reached a central room, half buried in the castle. There, three guards stood or sat in various attitudes of attention and discomfort. One of them held a musket. The other two were empty-handed, but Robert didn't make the mistake of thinking them unarmed. For a paltry town on the border, the men in Gilmichael Fortress were remarkably alert and well prepared, and Robert speculated that Magistrate Fairfoot was so completely despised that he feared the citizens might take it into their mind to dispatch him.

Going to the guard with the musket, Ranald spoke in a low voice.

Robert clearly heard the answer. "Are ye mad? It's worth more than me life is worth than t' go down there and interrupt 'im now. You know what 'e likes t' do t' the ladies when 'e gets 'em in there. 'Ang around, ye'll 'ear the screaming start soon."

While he was speaking, Robert let his saddlebags slide to the floor. Leaning down, he cast a smile at the men, assessing their positions, and casually rummaged in the contents.

Before the guard had finished his chilling speech, Robert had a knife in each of his hands. He sent one winging toward the biggest threat in the room: the man with the musket. He threw the other at Ranald, catching him in the throat.

Both fell. The musket clattered on the stone floor. And while Robert pulled another knife from his sleeve and prepared to launch it at one of the two remaining guards, he was brought up short by the sight of a pistol held in Ranald's hand.

Robert's luck had run out.

Ranald was bleeding from his throat. He was wheezing. But Robert could see his own death foreshadowed in the military man's gaze.

Robert couldn't die. Clarice needed him. As he dove to the side, a musket blast rocked the room.

When he looked again, Ranald was dead, his head shattered by shot. Another of the guards had a knife in him—and Robert hadn't fired the weapon or thrown the knife.

In a smooth motion he kept rolling, came to his feet, and turned to the doorway.

A man, a stranger, stood there. Tall, razor-thin, with dark hair and bottomless dark eyes. He wore black, and he'd wiped dirt across his face. He had broken into Gilmichael Fortress, and he moved like someone who knew what he was doing. He had taken the sort of action Waldemar would have—and Robert was ready to kill him.

The stranger discarded the smoking musket but held a pistol in his hand pointed at the remaining guard. In a cool tone, with an accent that sounded very much like Clarice's, he said, "Tie him up, will you? I'll get the keys. We haven't got a lot of time."

It appeared he was on Robert's side.

Unknown allies made Robert uneasy. They always had an agenda of their own. Pulling the rope from his saddlebags, Robert said, "Thanks, but who the hell are you?"

"Don't you recognize me?"

Robert flashed him another glance—and did. "You were sneaking around before the ball. You're the man I hunted—and couldn't find."

"What the hell was that?" Magistrate Fairfoot dropped his fist but retained his hold on Clarice's throat. "If those imbeciles accidentally shot off a musket, I'll have their nuts to roast."

She saw stars, but she managed to croak, "I told you so. It's Lord Hepburn."

Fairfoot's grip tightened until she thought he would crush her windpipe, and he glared, his eye sockets dark holes in his shadowed face. Then he let her go as swiftly as he'd grabbed her.

She sucked in air, one harsh breath after another, trying to fill her oxygen-starved lungs.

She had been afraid he would rape her. Death before dishonor, Grandmamma would say. But in her long and regal life, Grandmamma had never been choked and punched, had never had to realize that she loved a man and anything, any humiliation, any hurt, was worth living to see him again.

For Fairfoot hadn't appreciated Clarice's razor-sharp comments about his cowardice and his impotency, nor had he liked her assurances that Robert would come for her and snap his twiggy little neck. It was the last insult that had driven him to attack, and if that shot hadn't sounded . . .

Staggering, she sank onto the bed and stared hopefully at the bars.

Was it Robert? Had he arrived in time?

Fairfoot was more than a little concerned now. He stood at the door. Peered down the corridor.

As her breath rasped in her throat, she

tried to think of what to do now. How to help—herself and Robert. Should she attack Fairfoot from behind?

Her gaze dropped to his belt. Could she take his keys and get out of there? She glanced around. She did have weapons of a sort. A bucket of water. A chamber pot. The candle, burning hot and bright.

Then Fairfoot turned around, and she realized it was too late. He held a dagger, fourteen inches long and shining with a sharp edge and a glittering tip. He pointed it at her. "If it *is* your aristocratic lover, he's going to have to get through you to take me."

She massaged her bruised throat, stared at the point of the dagger, her mind blank with misery. She didn't want to be a human shield. Not if she had to protect Fairfoot.

Then, behind him, she saw rather than heard a movement, the merest whisper of motion. Was it Robert? Was it rescue?

Distraction. She needed to create a distraction. The best she could do was croak, "Did I say you were a coward? It's good to be right."

"Not a coward, darling. Smart enough to want to live and make you sorry." Fairfoot flicked the blade at her. "Get up. Come here."

Keeping an eye on the corridor, she slowly

stood, pretending to be more injured than she was, trying to get enough air in her lungs to make her move. She sidled closer to Fairfoot, closer than she ever wanted to be again.

As she got within arm's reach, she said, "This isn't going to work. Lord Hepburn is going to kill you no matter how you try to hide." And as Fairfoot made a swipe for her, she dove for the candle, knocking it over, plunging the cell into total blackness.

"You stupid bitch," Fairfoot roared, and she heard the clatter of keys as he tried to locate her. The steel of his blade struck the stones of the walls, the metal of the bucket.

She kicked the chamber pot toward him. By his shriek, she knew she had scored a bull's-eye. Crawling under the bed, she rolled into a little ball on her side. She prayed Robert was coming now, before Fairfoot located her, because she shivered with teeth-chattering fear. She was, she discovered, as big a coward as Fairfoot.

Fairfoot thrashed about, making a sweep of the cell. He cursed her with all his crude vocabulary. He was coming closer. And closer.

Above the noise of his footsteps and the sound of his voice, Clarice heard a thin, high whistle. She'd heard it before. Lifting her head, she strained to identify it—

Boom!

The explosion deafened her. The flash blinded her. She smelled the acrid odor of gunpowder. Sparks of red and gold shot everywhere, burning thin trails before her dazzled eyes.

Fireworks. Fireworks like she'd seen at Robert's ball. Fireworks for celebration.

Fireworks for freedom.

Without another thought she rolled out from under the bed and launched herself through the sparks and flame at the screaming Fairfoot. A bone-jarring tackle to his knees brought him down. He went over like a tall oak, cracking his head on the bedstead.

He lay without moving.

Cautiously she sneaked up on him.

Still he didn't move.

Snatching the key off his belt, she made for the doorway. The sparks were still flying when she stuck the key in the lock.

Down the corridor she could hear the pounding of feet. Above the roaring in her ears she had only one thought. It had better be Robert. After all this, it had better be him.

And it was. He was holding a torch, and never had she loved the sight of him more.

As she stumbled out of the cell, he wrapped his arm around her. "Are you hurt?" He ran his hand over her hair, over her body. "Did you catch a spark? Are you burned? On fire?"

"No!"

"Where's Fairfoot?" He waved the torch in the cell. "Dammit! Did you kill him yourself?"

"Knocked him out." She slammed the iron bars shut and locked them. "Let's go!"

"You could have left him for me." Grabbing her arm, he ran with her toward the light at the far distant doorway.

"I was under the bed. It protected me." She found that despite her recent strangulation, she could breathe well enough to run. Distantly she reflected that panic was a splendid encouragement.

When they reached the guard station, she found the room in shambles with three corpses, a trussed guard—and a man, a stranger, dressed all in black and waiting for them.

She didn't like his face. It was too thin, almost aesthetic in its severity, and it reminded her of someone. Someone who made her very wary.

She would have backed away, but Robert flung his saddlebags over his shoulder and said, "Let's go, then."

And the stranger joined the escape.

As they ran up and down stairs and through the grim corridors, Robert pulled a knife from his sleeve. The stranger did the same, and both men handled their blades with the ease of experience. Robert stopped her just before they reached the last room. Pushing her against the wall, he commanded, "Stay here."

The stranger rushed inside. Robert followed. And when fighting finished, she cautiously poked her head inside.

A guard rested on the floor while the stranger tied his arms behind his back.

Then they resumed their rush, out onto the lawn and into the blessed fresh night air. She had a stitch in her side, but she still ran. Nothing could keep her here at Gilmichael Fortress, so close to Magistrate Fairfoot and his damned gibbet.

As they approached the outer guardhouse, they slowed. Robert held up his hand for silence, and the two men again indicated she should wait while they cleared the guardhouse.

She was content to let them. Her throat hurt, she didn't know if she would ever get enough air, and various bruises were starting to make themselves known, including a painful one on her cheekbone made by Fairfoot's fist. With a wry sense of humor she reflected that she must be feeling better, for she didn't relish looking in the mirror tomorrow. Vanity was once again rearing its head.

But she did relish going home with Robert.

Her gaze rested on him as he sneaked up on the gatehouse. Nodding at the stranger, he freed the latch and the two men charged in. She heard a thumping, a single shout, then silence.

Robert came to the door and gestured her in, and she went gladly. He had saved her. Nothing in her life could compare to this moment. For too long she'd had to get herself and Amy out of scrapes. Now Robert had rescued her as if she were a delicate princess, and she was enchanted with her role. And with him.

Inside the gatehouse the stranger was removing a cudgel from one unconscious

guard. One very large, very dirty, very unconscious guard.

With a sigh of relief she walked into
Robert's arms.

He held her so tightly, their flesh seemed
to meld into one being. He rubbed his cheek
on the top of her head. She snuggled into his
chest, listening to and relishing the beat of
his heart. The musky scent of him enveloped
her, and she wanted to stay there, in his
arms, forever.

But the stranger noisily cleared his throat.

Robert lifted his head, and as if the
stranger had spoken, he said, "He's right.
We need to get as far away from here as
possible. When the guards struggle out of
their bonds and let Fairfoot out of that cell,
there's going to be hell to pay."

"I know." She reluctantly drew away. "I know."

The stranger was watching them calmly,
his face an inscrutable mask, and again
something about him caught her attention
and made her eye him warily. She knew him.
She would swear she knew him. In the light
of the gatehouse the conviction grew in her,
and some compulsion dragged her toward
him. Stepping in front of him, she demanded,
"Where have I seen you before?"

"Three nights ago, on my estate, sneaking through the trees," Robert said.

"No." She shook her head, and a knot twisted in her stomach. "That's not all."

"No, that's not all." The stranger's deep, dark eyes scorched her. "Remember, Clarice. Think back . . . to that day your sister Sorcha was given the title of Crown Princess and betrothed to—"

"To you." She whispered because she couldn't bear to speak aloud. "You're Rainger. You're the prince of Richarte."

Thirty

It is just as easy to love a prince as a pauper.
—THE DOWAGER QUEEN OF BEAUMONTAGNE

Too late. Robert stared at Clarice, at her prince, and thought, *Too late.*

He'd waited too long to tell her that he loved her. Now her prince was here, ready to sweep her away to Beaumontagne, and she would go because—

"No," he said. "No, listen!"

Prince Rainger turned his head as if hearing something from the depths of the keep.

"We've got to get out of this fortress." He offered his arm to Clarice.

Presumptuous bastard. On her other side, Robert offered his. She looked between them both, then laid her hand on Robert's arm.

The prince stepped back, not vanquished, but waiting.

"Can you run some more?" Robert asked her.

"To get out of here, I could run all the way back to—" She stopped.

Back to MacKenzie Manor? Say it. Back to MacKenzie Manor.

But she didn't. Instead, she amended it to "Yes, I can run."

He supported her as they raced out the door. He didn't have to. She was holding up well. But he wanted to touch her, to assure himself she was still his.

He'd waited too long to lay his claim.

While Robert and Clarice ran, Prince Rainger slammed the door to the gatehouse with a solid *thunk*.

About halfway up the wooded hill opposite the fortress, Clarice began to gasp. She hadn't recovered from her ordeal, poor lass, and Robert pulled her to a halt. They were out of sight of the gatehouse, and somehow he didn't expect to see Magistrate Fairfoot coming out. Not yet.

The prince didn't join them. Perhaps he was sensitive to atmosphere. Or perhaps he knew how much Robert hated the price he was exacting for his assistance.

Or perhaps he was waiting for Clarice to tell Robert it was over so he could take her away now. Immediately.

But it wasn't over. Not until Robert had had his say. "Clarice." In the intermittent moonlight he could see dirt on her face. But when he tried to wipe it off, she pulled back and winced. He understood: He added another good trouncing to Fairfoot's already bulging account. "What did that cockscum do to you?"

Her smile was lopsided. "Not nearly as much as he wished to. Nothing . . . nothing . . . he didn't hurt me. Not the way you think."

Robert had to embrace her again, in relief for her and relief for him—if Fairfoot had raped her, Robert would have gone to prison for the murder of an English magistrate. Holding her, he breathed deep of her beloved scent and treasured her as his most valuable possession.

Too late.

She didn't let him hold her for too long. Not for nearly long enough. Easing herself free, she assured him, "Truly. Fairfoot is rather sensitive when someone insinuates he hasn't the resources to satisfy a woman."

Shocked and appalled, Robert said, "You didn't tell him that. Not when you were alone in the cell with him!"

Lifting her chin, she replied, "Yes, I did. That was when he hit me, and I have to tell you—it was almost worth it to see him blush. I think I may be more right than I realized."

She filled Robert with pride at her courage, and fear for her well-being. He could keep her safe, but . . . he glanced at the prince, who stood far enough away to give them privacy. The prince who was not, as Waldemar had said, blessed with pretty-girl hair and a fancy lisp. This prince was tough and determined, and he appealed to the one thing against which Robert had no weapon—Clarice's sense of duty.

Too late.

Robert plunged his hand into his saddle-bags, all the way to the bottom, where the little wooden box rested. "Clarice, listen to me."

"No."

"I bought you a ring." He brought it out, fumbled with the lid. "In Edinburgh. I want you to marry me."

She closed her eyes, turned her head away. "No. Don't."

"I *beg* you to marry me." He couldn't believe she wouldn't listen. He was the earl of Hepburn. He was the true hero of the Peninsula, and she knew it.

He was hers.

The moon floated in and out of the clouds. The light filtered through the leaves, showing him her anguish, her sorrow.

He was hers. Together they had defeated Colonel Ogley, freed Waldemar, been more than they ever could be apart. Didn't she know that? How could she not know that?

"Look." He opened the box. "The amber is the color of your eyes. The sapphires are the color of mine. The gold is what holds us together. Beautiful gold. Look." He held it out, but he was doing this all wrong, for she didn't look at the ring.

Instead, she looked at him. "Do you know who I am?"

"My lover. My wife."

She covered his lips with her hand. "Don't say it."

He kissed her palm. He moved it aside. And added softly, "My dearest and only love."

She took a quivering breath. "I'm a princess. I didn't ask to be, but I was born a princess. I've spent the last few years of my life waiting to go back to Beaumontagne and *be* a princess. Nothing ever got in the way of that dream . . . until you."

"Then being with me is the right thing to do."

"No. No, it's not. Amy—my sister Amy, Miss Amy Rosabel—has run away. She doesn't want to be a princess, and I am too fond and protective of her. I want her to be what she wants, not what some accident of birth made her." Clarice swallowed. She dusted her fingers across her eyes. "But don't you see? That leaves me to do the dutiful thing."

Savagely he commanded, "Stop saying duty."

She corrected herself. "The honorable thing."

"Stop saying honor."

She glared into his eyes. "I will when you do."

She had a way of silencing him.

More gently she said, "You and I have things in common. Values in common. That's why we've dealt well together. That's why I . . ." She struggled to speak. Laid her hand on his cheek. A silver tear trickled down her face. "I love you." She covered the ring, and his hand, with hers. "I love you."

He couldn't answer. His heart, the heart he had thought was dead, broke.

The soft sound of a horse's whinny slipped through the air. Clarice's head jerked around. "Blaize." Without knowing his location, she walked to the place where Robert had tethered Blaize.

"Oh, my pretty lad." Threading her fingers through the horse's mane, she dropped her head into his neck. "Blaize, my beautiful boy. You're here."

As Robert watched her hug the horse she loved, he felt a hitch in his breath. She was saying good-bye. To the horse. To him.

And he couldn't fight her. She thought she was doing the right thing, and he suspected, he feared, that she was right. Carefully he put the lid over the ring, and over his dreams.

"You brought him," she said. "You rode him to my rescue."

Pocketing the ring, Robert walked to

Blaize, to Clarice, and quietly reassured them both. "He wouldn't be left behind."

"I *did* steal him, you know." Her face tightened. "He's Magistrate Fairfoot's horse, and I can't take him with me."

"I brought Blaize from MacKenzie Manor, and he'll return with me. When I get done with Fairfoot, he'll beg to sell me Blaize, and any other horse in his stable." Robert wanted to comfort Clarice, but he didn't have the right to touch her. Not anymore. Instead, he rubbed Blaize's coat and stared at her, trying to soak in enough Clarice to last for the rest of his life. "Blaize will have a good life."

"Thank you, Robert." Her thank-you echoed softly through the woods.

He cleared his throat, trying to say the right thing. "You—Princess Clarice, you have a good life too."

She lifted her head. "And you, Robert."

Was she jesting? He shook his head.

"Yes." She was princess enough to put a royal imperative in her tone. "You have a good life. Promise me."

He didn't want to promise that. He wanted to howl at the moon. He wanted curse at fate. He didn't want to taste his food, smell the roses, mind his clothing, dance as if he heard the music. But she wasn't going to let him get away with sulking. Somehow, he knew she would get her way.

Which she did with a single word. *"Promise,"* she insisted. "It's the one thing you can do to make me happy."

He capitulated. "I promise."

The prince called, "Your Highness, we need to leave."

How Robert hated the sound of that deep, accented voice. It was the voice of a nightmare made human.

"Right away," she called back. She stared at Robert. Lifted a hand toward his cheek. Pulled it back. Turned and walked to the place where the prince stood waiting with two horses.

The blackguard had come prepared.

Robert watched Clarice, the love of his life, ride away with the man she would marry, and he did nothing. Absolutely nothing, except wave a hand to her when she turned around for one last look.

He couldn't believe it. He was letting her go. Just like that. Because she'd used words like *honor* and *duty.* And because, well, he couldn't force her to marry him against her will. For one single mad moment he'd considered it.

Unfortunately the minister didn't exist who would call a forced union a legal marriage. And even if one did, she would still say *honor* and *duty* until Robert relented and allowed her to go.

So he watched Clarice ride away and wished he could do something. Something like smash his fist into the wall or get drunk or beat someone up. Something that would relieve some of this terrible clawing frustration in his gut.

From Gilmichael Fortress, he heard a gigantic *bang.* The doors swung wide, and three men stood there, carrying torches and short iron clubs.

Fairfoot, looking rumpled and furious, and his thugs.

Robert smiled. He rolled up his sleeves. He stalked back up the hill.

His frustration wouldn't have to wait long for relief at all.

Thirty-one

In the end, a princess must do her duty.
—THE DOWAGER QUEEN OF BEAUMONTAGNE

The summer sun was dipping toward the west when Robert walked across the village square to the alehouse and squinted down at the checkerboard. "Look at the dust on this board," he said. "Is everybody in this village afraid to challenge you five hearty men?"

"I dunna know why." Old Henry MacCulloch widened his eyes innocently. "We ne'er cheat."

"Do you not?" Robert asked. "I've heard differently."

"Ye canna believe everything ye hear, m'lord," Benneit MacTavish answered.

"Fearsome, you five men are." Seating himself on a stool before the board, Robert rubbed his hands. "So—who do I beat first?"

The old men hooted in unison.

"Think ye're right clever, do ye?" Hamish MacQueen creaked to his feet. "I'm the man t' take ye doon."

"First," Benneit MacTavish added. "Ye're the man who'll take him doon *first.*"

Robert waited while Hamish settled himself across the board.

"I'll be takin' me turn before ye, o' course," Hamish said. "Ye'll be feelin' pity on an auld soldier wi' only one hand."

"I'm a busy man." Robert shoved a black chip out. "I don't have time for pity."

The other old men hooted again and pulled their chairs closer to watch the action.

As if in an aside, Benneit's brother, Tomas, said, "M'lord, we chased Billie MacBain oot o' Freya Crags."

"Now, Tomas, ye know that's na true," Benneit chided. "After his folly in turning Princess Clarice over t' that colonel and that English magistrate, we *encouraged* him t' leave toon."

"Encouraged him?" Robert suffered a pang at the mention of Clarice, yet he almost welcomed the pain. In the three weeks since she'd walked out of his life, he'd come to yearn to hear her name, to speak to someone who knew her. The truth was, he would rather miss her than never to have known her.

"When ye live as long as we ha'e, ye hear things aboot a man." Henry's wrinkled mouth twisted as if he tasted something nasty. "Things he'd dunna like t' have noised aboot, if ye know what we mean. And so we pointed that oot t' Billie."

"I see." Robert kept his gaze glued to the board as Hamish moved a red piece. "I'm glad to hear you helped him see the right thing to do. I fear I would have been rough on him had I found him."

"It gets worse for Billie." Gilbert Wilson made a *tsk*. "We hear he was drinking in a tavern at Edinburgh when the king's sailors did a bit o' conscripting. It seems Billie has gone t' sea."

Benneit nodded peacefully and folded his hands over his small belly. "Wi' his disposition, the fresh air will do the lad guid."

"Eh?" Henry cupped his ear and leaned toward Tomas.

"He said," Tomas shouted, "that the fresh air would do Billie guid."

Henry nodded. "Na doubt, na doubt."

"Got a few bruises there, lad." Tomas pointed at Robert's face. "Been fighting, ye ha'e."

Robert gingerly touched the mark left when his face had smashed Magistrate Fairfoot's fist. "This is nothing. You should have seen the other fellow."

"Did ye trounce him guid?" Gilbert Wilson asked.

Robert thought back on the carnage of that night. "Fairfoot'll be no good to any woman ever again. Neither will his friends." And Robert felt a great deal of satisfaction knowing that—that the guards who supported Fairfoot and Fairfoot himself would long remember the name of Hepburn, and never, by God, ever imagine they could come onto his lands, into his village, and seize something which was his.

But Clarice was his no longer.

Hughina stepped out of the alehouse, four dripping mugs in her grasp. "M'lord." She distributed the ale to the old men. "I didn't know ye were here. I'll get ye an ale." She patted Gilbert on the shoulder. "Aye, I'm getting yers too, Mr. Wilson." With a smile and a nod she disappeared into the dimness of her shop.

Robert stared after her in surprise. "What happened to her?"

Henry MacCulloch whispered, "We thought Brody Browngirdle from over on the River Raleigh would mayhap cheer her, so when he came int' town, we told him Hughina gave out free ale t' travelers."

Wonderment colored Robert's voice. "Why, you old charlatans. You didn't."

"Sure, and we did," Hamish said.

"What I could have done on the Peninsula with a regiment like you five," Robert said admiringly. "So your plan worked."

"By the time they got it straightened out, they were talking fit t' kill." Henry pulled a long face. "O' course, he never got his free ale."

Hamish cackled. "Nay, it's na ale he's getting."

Setting down his chip, Robert laughed aloud. When he got done, he noticed the silence and looked around at the old men. They were staring at him as if they didn't recognize him. He held out his hands, palms up, and spread his fingers. "What?"

In a carefully neutral tone Henry said, "So I suppose it's true."

"What's true?" Robert asked.

Henry exchanged glances with the others. "We thought ye were fond o' the princess, but there's some in the village who say ye sent her away because she catered t' the sin of vanity."

"Because she peddled creams and potions, do you mean?" If it had been anyone but these men questioning him, Robert would have snapped off their heads. As it was, he said gently, "Is it a sin to make people happy? Because that's what she did. She gave a whole company of scared debutantes confidence in themselves, and that's a gift that few can top." Millicent, too, had changed, although he suspected it wasn't her appearance that gave her such confidence. No, it seemed that all she had needed was someone to express confidence in her—and he had. He wouldn't have done it, though, if Clarice hadn't torn the hide off him, so she could be given credit for Millicent's transformation also.

At the same time, his people had learned a valuable lesson about following the lead of someone from outside Freya Crags. A few of the men and women had come to him on his return and fervently begged his pardon for their part in capturing Princess Clarice. And that was as it should be. He wouldn't persecute them. Neither would he forget.

Stepping out of the shop, Hughina handed Gilbert his ale, then with a glance at the serious faces, she scuttled back inside.

Gilbert took a long drink. "Yet the princess is gone, and ye're happier than ye've been fer a long time."

"I love her." Robert looked around at the old men, pinning each one with his gaze. "And she left me. Did you know that? She left me to return to her country. She's going to marry a prince."

Tomas sputtered. "I though better o' her. What did she think she could find in some foreign country that was better than in Freya Crags?"

"She's in fer a sad surprise if she thinks some sissy prince is better than the earl o' Hepburn," Benneit said indignantly.

"She didn't do it because she wanted a prince. She wanted to stay here with me, but she has to do her duty. It was a matter of honor." Robert said the words easily, without bitterness. After all, he had made her a promise.

"Eh?" Henry cupped his ear and turned to Gilbert.

Leaning forward, Robert shouted, "I said, it was a matter of honor."

"Ye are taking it well," Henry shouted back. "We thought ye'd be as ye were when ye came back from the war."

Robert looked around the square. Life in Freya Crags proceeded just as it always had. The women came to the well for water. The children played in the puddles left by the rain, the old men rocked in the sun . . . nothing had changed, and he took comfort in the continuity. "But then she wouldn't have taught me anything, would she? Then there'd be no sign of her passing, no sign at all." He made a move on the checkerboard.

Tomas sighed and intoned, "Sometimes life smells like a cabbage rose, sometimes it stinks like cooked cabbage."

"A man's got na right t' complain as long as he's got thirty-two teeth and the sense God gave him," Gilbert added.

Henry grinned, showing the gaps in his own teeth. "Which between the five of us, is aboot what we've got."

The five old men started laughing, and laughed so hard, Benneit wheezed.

Robert slapped him gently on the back to start him breathing again, and heard a commotion across the square. Heads were turning, voices were rising. He couldn't quite see what was happening, and the events of the last months had made him wary. Standing, he squinted toward the bridge where everyone was pointing.

And saw, on a small white mare, a woman dressed in a black-and-red riding costume. Her hair was blond and loose about her shoulders, her mouth was smiling, her amber eyes were searching . . . and when her gaze found him, her smile exploded into pure joy.

Clarice. It was Clarice. He stood with his hands hanging at his sides, the sun on his face, an odd ringing in his ears. He couldn't believe it. He thought that by now she would be across the Channel. He had tried not to worry about the French troops. Prince Rainger had proved to be a capable man, and if he failed, Clarice was remarkable at surviving and prospering. So everything would be all right on her journey through Spain toward Beaumontagne.

But she wasn't in Spain or Beaumontagne. Faintly he heard the old men babbling behind him, and it sounded as if they were saying, "Praise God. Praise God."

She was here, in Freya Crags, her body lush and desirable, her complexion a little more golden, her pleasure palpable.

And Robert MacKenzie, the officer who had done all the things that a hero must do: developed stratagems for attack, performed rescues from the most guarded of English fortresses, detonated the French ammunition depot and did it on a moment's notice— he could think of nothing to say, nothing to do as the woman he loved rode across the square toward him, her gaze fixed on him as if he were the lodestar.

The crowd followed her, growing larger, and the faces were wary and interested and eager.

When she was close, she stopped her horse and said, "Sir, I'm a peddler. I sell things."

"Sell things?" he repeated, not comprehending why she would say such a thing here, now, when there was so much more to say.

She just grinned down at him.

With a jolt his stunned mind started working. He drew himself into military posture, took an officious tone, and said, "I'm afraid you'll have to get permission from the lord of Freya Crags before you can sell things here."

"Oh, dear." She put her gloved finger to her cheek. "I hear he's quite the frightening chap. Do you think he'll let me?"

"It depends on what you're selling."

"Happiness. I'm selling happiness."

"In that case"—he put up his hands and she slid down into them—"I'm buying."

Epilogue

In the end, love conquers all.
            —THE OLD MEN OF FREYA CRAGS

He was back from Edinburgh.

Clarice leaned back in a chair with her feet on an ottoman and her eyes closed, and smiled as she recognized Robert's footsteps. In the two years of their marriage, she had come to know his sound, his scent, his touch. She reveled in everything about him, even his passionate madness, for he strictly controlled that madness, and he reserved it for her. All for her.

Kissing her gently, he rubbed her swollen belly.

"Um." Opening her eyes, she put her hand over his and feasted her eyes on his countenance. On the strong bones of his face, the silky black hair, the treasures of his blue eyes.

He was still dressed in his traveling clothes, his boots scuffed from the hard ride, his saddlebags over his shoulder. "Are you awake, then?" he asked softly.

"I was sitting here feeling him kick. He's a fine, healthy lad."

Robert teased her with a smile. "*He* could be a daughter. It's not as if the babe's mother and both of her aunts are docile and domestic."

She pushed herself into a more upright position. "I'm almost mooing, I'm so domestic."

"A man would have to be a fool to answer that." Before she could retort that all men were fools, he dropped the saddlebags and scooped her out of the chair.

He seated himself with her in his lap. It was his favorite position, even with the added weight of the child pressing him down.

"How is Millicent?" Clarice asked.

"She's very well, the belle of Edinburgh

and a leader of the bluestockings. She sends her love and told me to do this." He kissed her cheek.

"She's a dear." Clarice looped her arms around his neck. "And Prudence?"

"She and young Aiden are having their first fight."

"About what?"

"I don't know."

"Is it serious?"

"I don't know that either. I got out of there as quickly as possible."

Clarice sighed. Men never paid attention to the important things. "That's probably what they were fighting about," she said darkly.

Robert cast her a confused glance, then from his saddlebags withdrew a letter stamped with the royal seal of Beaumontagne. "Here's your note from Grandmamma."

Ah, Grandmamma. On that day two years earlier when Clarice had stood on the dock in London and stared at the ship that would take her across the Channel, she had thought of Grandmamma. She had thought about Amy finding her own way in the world, and about Sorcha, lost. She had turned to look at Prince Rainger, and found him looking at her with an odd twist to his mouth.

"I find," he had said, "I'm not much interested in marrying a woman who is already in love with another man."

She had been startled. "Have I been sulking?" She had thought she'd admirably hidden her misery.

"You've been tragically brave." He held up his hand when she would have objected. "Perhaps I should say—tragically cheerful. You're everything a princess who has been crossed in love should be."

"I thank you." During their journey she had discovered she rather liked Rainger. He'd grown up to be a reliable man, a man as good with his wit as he was with his fists, and she had tried to tell herself that marriage to him wouldn't be so dreadful.

Then she thought of Robert, and every night she did as she was afraid she would do. She cried into her pillow.

Rainger continued. "You know, you have two sisters I have yet to find, and your grandmamma, a terrifying woman, is too disagreeable to die. I fully expect she'll live forever. And the truth is, she won't let me marry any of her granddaughters until I've found all of you. So you, Clarice, would be sitting in the palace, waiting, while I rounded up Amy and Sorcha."

She began to see what he was saying, and her hopeful heart tripped and hurried. "I see."

"So if you were to go back to Scotland and marry your earl of Hepburn, Beaumontagne would not be harmed."

She swallowed. She wanted to do the right thing, but what was that? "What if you don't find my sisters?"

He bent his dark gaze on her. "I will."

He would too. That was why Clarice had told him that Amy had hared off to the north of Scotland, when in fact Amy hated the cold and would go south. Rainger needed to concentrate his search on Sorcha.

Now, as Clarice sat in Robert's lap, she held Grandmamma's letter and sighed. "Every month, month after month. Do you think she will ever cease demanding my return?"

"If the news of an impending birth didn't stop her, I don't know what will." Rubbing her back, he eased her discomfort while she moaned in appreciation. "We'll go to Beaumontagne when the baby's old enough. Tell her that next time you write." He wrapped his arms around Clarice and held her close.

As always, when he embraced her, she knew she had found her home. He kissed her so that she knew he had missed her. With such passion that she remembered why they were lovers. As if they'd been separated forever.

In a way they had. They had given each other up. They had thought they would never see each other again.

Now she lived at MacKenzie Manor, and even with her worry about Amy and Sorcha and Grandmamma's endless nagging, never had Clarice been so happy.

But when he drew back, she could see he had serious news. "Don't be alarmed." He drew the Edinburgh newspaper out of his bags. "But it's Amy."

She snatched the paper from him. "Is she ill?" As Amy had promised, there had been bulletins in the newspapers, sometimes as frequently as once a month, sometimes only four times a year. She had assured Clarice she was healthy and happy, but she never revealed where she was. "Or is it Godfrey? Did he find her? Has he hurt her?" For Godfrey's role in scattering Beaumontagne's princesses had been revealed, yet despite

Grandmamma's attempts, the perfidious messenger hadn't yet been captured.

Now Robert looked grim and at the same time tried to reassure Clarice. "Amy's fine. Or, rather, she was. The advertisement is dated three months ago."

"Three months ago?" Clarice's hands shook too much for her to read. "Why three months ago?"

"I suppose it took time to get here, and I doubt they felt any compulsion to publish it promptly. Here." He pointed at a small box with only a few lines inside.

"Quick." She thrust it at him. "What does she say?"

Taking the paper, he recited, *"Clarice, have kidnapped a marquess and am holding him for ransom. Need advice. Come as soon as possible. Amy."*